# DEATH FROM THE SHADOWS

SPACE ASSASSINS 4

SCOTT BARON

Copyright © 2020 by Scott Baron

All rights reserved.

Print Edition ISBN 978-1-945996-39-9

No part of this book may be reproduced in any form or by any electronic or mechanical means, including information storage and retrieval systems, without written permission from the author, except for the use of brief quotations in a book review.

*"Victorious warriors win first and then go to war, while defeated warriors go to war first and then seek to win."*

*— Sun Tzu*

# CHAPTER ONE

It was an incredibly short period of time, but the tales of slaughter and carnage at the hands of a strange visla, one of whom none had ever even heard of, were spreading slowly through the conquered systems.

Rebellions were quashed with his iron fist, and entire planets fell to the mysterious man with the Council of Twenty's forces behind him.

Thousands had perished at his hands, and those who had been fortunate enough to find themselves spared had been subjugated or forced into slavery. After the hostilities ceased, a small contingent of Council forces would remain, their presence an enduring threat of what would befall the citizenry if they rose up once more.

And then, without word or warning, he would depart, off to the next unfortunate world that had drawn his attention.

Word of the man had reached Visla Tordahl well before the Council force appeared in orbit above his world, and he had taken ample precautions against such an incursion.

For many years the Council of Twenty had coveted his

realm, and it seemed the day had finally come where they were going to make an attempt at it. But he was not giving up his world without a fight.

Additional forces had been called in to defend against the mighty new caster, and Visla Tordahl had spent considerable time pouring his power into the konuses and slaaps worn by those newly enlisted men. They were wielding considerable magic, and it would not be an easy conquest for this mysterious visla and his Council troops.

The Council ships, however, remained in orbit, sending in a contingent of Tslavar mercenaries instead. The first wave of attackers to crash upon the shores of Tordahl's defenses would not be the Council's finest, but, rather, paid goons whose lives were of little consequence.

The large sum of coin expended in their slaughter would ultimately be worthwhile if the world fell. And the men of action who so willingly joined the fray were promised sizable pillage in the pursuit of this world. It was enough to drive them headlong into the blistering defense, against their own best interests.

The first wave made it to the ground, but at the cost of nearly all of their ships, and a hefty portion of their men. Nevertheless, the deep-green Tslavar forces emerged from the broken craft with bloodlust in their eyes, charging into the fray with near reckless abandon.

The attacking visla's plan, it seemed, was to force the local reinforcements to expend much of their combined power on the violent pawns thrown onto the playing field. And it was working. Spells were flying thick and heavy between the opposing forces, and many fell on both sides.

Visla Tordahl's stronghold soon fell under attack as well, as the Council craft that had been holding back swooped in and launched a barrage of fierce magic, pounding the defenses, forcing them to not only defend themselves, but to also reveal their key casters' positions in the process.

With that, they were more easily targeted, and the attacks upon them refined. It was a clever ploy, Tordahl had to admit, but he was fully powered and ready. From what he could see of the attackers, it looked as if his men would push back this force.

Yes, there were a large number of mercenaries on the move, and they were pressuring his ground forces fiercely, but the Council had appeared to have only sent a limited contingent of actual Council craft. It was an unusual strategy, and one that would fail, the visla was pleased to note.

Slowly, his forces drove the attackers back.

"Advance. Destroy the attackers, and show no mercy!" Visla Tordahl commanded over his skree.

The troop leaders on the ground received the message and commenced their push, driving the mercenary forces into a hasty retreat. Magic was expended without reserve, and the barrage was brutal in its intensity. There was no way the Tslavar mercenaries could hope to fight against such a display.

A lone ship streaked down to the front lines from above, the magical defensive spells thrown at it dissipating as if they were no more than tissue paper.

"Increase the intensity!" Visla Tordahl commanded his casters, an unsettled feeling growing in his gut.

The ship continued on its path, unharmed and unfettered, until it landed just in front of the retreating forces. The craft's hatch opened, and a tall man wearing a high-collared coat stepped forth and strode onto the battlefield. Tordahl's troops immediately recognized the new arrival as the principal threat facing them and redirected all of their efforts against him.

The man was obviously a visla, and an incredibly powerful one at that. In fact, he was so strong that his magic was actually visibly crackling off his body in waves. At the sight of him, Visla

Tordahl felt that sinking feeling in his gut solidify into a solid lump of fear.

He was a powerful man, but *this*? This was something he had never encountered before. For the first time in his life, he was not the strongest caster on the planet. Not by a long shot.

"I am Visla Jinnik," the invader bellowed out, his voice amplified by a projecting spell that carried it all the way to Tordahl's stronghold. "Surrender now and you will be spared. This is your one chance. Do not waste this opportunity."

The newcomer continued walking toward the front lines, the defensive spells parting for him and the attacks still being cast bouncing off his own shielding spells. He stopped, surveying the hundreds of men and women casting against him with all of their might. It seemed they were not giving up so easily.

Visla Jinnik shook his head and sighed.

"So be it."

He raised his hands and uttered the words to a particularly potent spell, the unleashed magic blasting out in a fierce wave. Tordahl recognized the spell immediately and threw up his defenses just in time to protect himself.

His casters and men attempted to do the same, but the vast majority were either not strong enough, not quick enough, or both.

The men closest to the origin of the spell burst into a fine mist. The magic blasted through them like a wave knocking down a child's sandcastle as if it were an afterthought. But the power continued, spreading out as it went, laying waste to those too weak to defend themselves before shifting to a stunning spell.

It was a particularly horrible piece of magic. One that the very few who even knew how to cast it refused to utilize. Only the most violent, and most powerful, would even think to. And only the absolute strongest even could. But this man, this Visla

Jinnik, was wielding it with his full power, and to devastating effect.

Visla Tordahl felt the power buffet his defensive spell. As soon as it had passed, he replied in kind, casting the strongest spells he knew in rapid succession, the deadly magic flying true toward the invader.

Jinnik was forced to focus more of his power on defending himself. He actually smiled at that. It was good to see someone standing up for their world. Defending it against the Council no matter the cost. He respected the man for it, even as he returned the attack, his magic flying straight for the visla now that he had revealed his position.

Tordahl desperately cast his strongest defensive spells, throwing up a powerful shield of magic around himself. It held for a moment, allowing him an instant to marvel at the sheer power of the man taking his life. Then his magic failed, and the spells flew true, dropping him to the stone floor of his stronghold parapet, dead.

Word of the visla's fall spread immediately through the forces, and all who still survived surrendered at once. Without the visla supporting them, there was simply no way they had any hope against these attackers.

And this Jinnik, whoever he was, was so powerful, and so brutally deadly, that they knew their choices had been reduced to dropping their weapons or death.

The Tslavar forces surged forward, collecting the dropped arms of the fallen. Most were drained of magic to the point of being little more than paperweights, but they were taken all the same. Then the men and women were separated by perceived value.

Many would be sent back to their homes to work the land—to keep the realm thriving. But a great many would face a different fate. Those were pulled from the others and forced to kneel while one of the Council lackeys secured gleaming golden control collars around their necks, the magical restraints sealing into a seamless band as the captives entered their new life of slavery.

The Ootaki and Drooks who had been in Tordahl's possession were rounded up and taken to the Council ships, the spoils of the conflict, now a part of the invader's power supply.

And like that, another world fell to this unusual visla and his Council forces. It was a pattern that repeated on many worlds, though not all of them were rebellions in need of quashing. Some were outright conquests, as Tordahl's land had been. An asset grab.

Visla Jinnik was an unknown. A man who had apparently never been a part of the Council of Twenty's machinations in the past. But suddenly, out of the blue, he was now a most powerful tool of the Council, and one to be feared and reckoned with.

Jinnik surveyed the dead and enslaved of yet another world and sighed. He then turned and walked back to his ship to take his leave of this place. People cowered in fear as he passed, wary of the man who had enslaved them all.

Little did they know, he, too, was wearing a thick control collar, hidden underneath his high-collared coat. He was as much a slave as they now were, and with his young son held captive, he had no choice but to do as he was told.

And that meant carrying out these horrible acts, all in the Council's name. But if it meant saving his boy, he would conquer endless worlds if he had to.

"You did quite a number on that one," the Council emmik running the operation said as he locked Jinnik back in his cell.

"Too many dead," Jinnik replied with an exhausted sigh. "When will this end?"

"Sooner than you expected," the emmik replied with a curious chuckle.

The ship lifted off and departed the system, and after that, reports of this Visla Jinnik's actions across the galaxy suddenly fell silent.

The man who had slashed and burned his way across a good many worlds, it seemed, had abruptly vanished. And no one knew why, or where he had gone. But the fear of him remained, and that lingering dread would last a long, long time.

## CHAPTER TWO

The vendor stalls of Sorlak were something of a marvel for those unfamiliar with the more colorful marketplaces in the Delvian systems. The loose network of inhabited planets encompassed in those realms were chock-full of artisans, craftsmen, and all manner of agriculture.

As a result, the marketplaces on each of the habitable worlds were bustling places of commerce, and shoppers and traders from far and wide frequented them on a regular basis.

Of those worlds, Sorlak was the most civilized. A quiet planet, for the most part, with its distance from the pulsing, yellow sun at the center of the system putting it firmly in the comfortable zone of perfect temperatures year-round. It was not an Eden, but definitely a pleasant place to be.

That was not to say there was no violence or crime, but the Council more or less stayed away, and the outlaw and mercenary types found it more suited their needs to simply shop on those worlds than cause drama. But no world, even the most civilized, was entirely free of that element. Those sorts just tended to stay hidden more.

Naturally, when the pair of deadly Wampeh Ghalian

assassins strode through town, they immediately clocked the most unsavory of the lot with an ease that came from years of practice. For one of their profession, ignoring a potential threat, no matter how minor, could prove fatal.

Hozark walked at the front, leading young Happizano, the son of the powerful Visla Jinnik. He had rescued the boy not once, but twice from kidnappers, the first of which had taken the boy to coerce his father into doing the Council of Twenty's dirty work for them, drawing from his great magic stores at their bidding.

The second time the boy had brought upon himself after stealing one of the shuttle craft belonging to Hozark's pilot friend, Uzabud, in an attempt to find his way home on his own. Unfortunately, the youngster not only lacked the requisite skills to manage that sort of a voyage, but he was also unfamiliar with even the most basic of captain's skills.

Like how to identify threats in the void of space. Threats like pirates, for example.

Happizano had been captured by a band of Outlander pirates and taken as a slave, ready to be sold off to Visla Ravik, though that was later revealed to only be a front.

The *true* puppet master behind it all was Visla Maktan. One of the Council of Twenty. And for whatever reason, he was amassing power however he could.

That included young Happizano, and not just for the power his father held, but because the youth appeared to share his father's gift. Ultimately, Hozark and his friends had rescued the boy from the pirates as well as the Council.

And the Council had brought out a deadly asset. Hozark's former lover, Samara, whom he fought aboard the stormed pirate craft before being blasted out into space and damn near dying in the process.

But they had survived, and since then, Hozark had been

saddled with the youngster while they sought out his father in order to return his son to his side.

Hap, for all he had been through, seemed in good spirits. It had been a few weeks since he had escaped the kidnappers' clutches, and he had rebounded as only a ten-year-old could. Of course, a bit of additional attention had to be paid to keep his spirits up.

"Young Jinnik," Hozark said, handing the boy some coin. "We have spent much time in transit, and you have handled yourself quite well. Why don't you go purchase yourself a treat?"

"Really?"

"Yes."

"Thanks, Hozark," Hap replied, then trotted off into the sea of potential customers milling about the stalls.

Demelza had been walking behind the pair, her sharp assassin eyes making sure there was no trouble lurking around the corner. But this was Sorlak, and trouble never materialized. Nevertheless, the stout woman was ready for action if need be.

Uzabud and his copilot, Laskar, were off galivanting elsewhere in the marketplace, eating, carousing, and acquiring baubles they had no use for, no doubt, along with the best alcohols they could procure.

Bud had once been a space pirate, after all, and some habits died hard.

Henni, the angry, violet-haired young woman they had rescued several worlds back, was resting up aboard the ship after eating far too many Horakin berries. She would be fine, eventually, but for the moment she did not want to stray too far from a restroom.

Happizano headed straight for the sweets vendors farther along the winding stalls in a rush. He was like a kid in a candy shop, and while these were outdoor vendors and not actual storefronts, the analogy held true.

"And two of those sticky buns," he said, completing his

purchase with still a bit of coin to spare for perhaps one more treat before they lifted back off into the utter boredom of space.

It was not the greatest environment for a ten-year-old to pass his days and weeks, but necessity was necessity. He was a target, after all. A third kidnapping simply was not an option.

"Hey!" he blurted as a couple of larger boys bumped into him in passing.

"Watch where you're going," the nearest one said, then headed off with his friend.

Hap felt something was odd about the two, and a moment later he realized what it was. His pocket was now lighter the few coins that had been there just a moment ago.

"Hey! Come back here!" he shouted.

The older boys took off running, and young Happizano chased after them as fast as his legs would carry him. They weaved around carts, then diverted abruptly into a long alleyway. Hap plunged in headfirst in pursuit, the echoes of his footfalls ringing off the hard walls.

He rounded the next corner to find the larger of the two boys standing there waiting for him.

"I'll take those," the boy said, his hand extended.

"You can buy your own. Oh wait, that was *my* coin you stole," Hap said, holding his bag of sweets tight in his grip.

"Give me the bag."

"No." He turned to leave, but the other boy had stepped behind him and was blocking his way. And he was moving closer.

"He said hand over the bag."

"They're mine," Hap protested.

He didn't even see the first punch coming, nor the second or third. In a quick flurry of blows, the two larger boys had driven him to the ground. The nearest bent down and snatched up the bag of sweets.

"Ya shoulda just given 'em to us," he said, laughing as he walked away, eating poor Hap's sticky buns.

Happizano slowly pushed himself up to his feet and brushed off the dirt. His nose was bleeding, but only slightly, and his cheek had been scraped by one of the boys' fists.

Little did the boy know that Hozark had been standing nearby, invisible beneath his shimmer cloak, watching the whole thing unfold. The youth had shown courage, chasing the larger boys, and he had even stood up to them when the tables turned. But he was not familiar with the ways of the rough back alleys found on every world.

Happizano had been raised in the privileged confines of a powerful visla's estate, and these sort of things were utterly foreign to him. It was a painful lesson he had just allowed to occur, but Hozark knew it had to unfold without his intervention. The boy had to learn, and the best way to do that was firsthand.

The Wampeh assassin silently slipped out of the alleyway as Hap wiped the dirt from his palms and clothing and walked back to meet the others.

"What happened to you?" Demelza asked when she saw the telltale signs of a fight on his face.

"Nothing. Can we go, please?"

Hozark gave Demelza a look. "A good idea. Head back to the ship. I shall follow shortly."

## CHAPTER THREE

The two bullies casually wove their way through the familiar maze of stalls and shops, saying their hellos to the familiar faces of the vendors as they passed. They stopped at a small stand selling a variety of beverages, their containers chilled by a little touch of magic.

"Two cups of Arambis juice," the smaller of the pair said as they strode up to the stand.

"You have coin?" the woman asked with a wary look.

"Of course we do," he replied, slapping payment down on the counter.

She seemed almost surprised, but she was certainly not going to turn down their payment.

"All right. Two Arambis, coming right up," she said, pouring a pair of tall cups, then pulling power from her konus, quietly reciting the chilling spell she used dozens of times a day.

The containers frosted on the inside, the contents cooling immediately. The spell was only a very minor one, but it would effectively keep the beverage cool long enough to be consumed at a pleasant temperature.

"Thanks," the boy said as he grabbed the two drinks and headed off with his friend.

The two sipped at them as they walked, content in their day's haul. It had been good fortune to find not only a rich kid, but one who coughed up food as well as coin. Not a bad day at all.

They took a small walkway toward their favorite hang-out spot. It was rather secluded, which made it the perfect place for them to safely dig through their haul.

Over time, they had dragged a few items into the area to provide some creature comforts, and that included the pair of crates they took seats on, using a third as a small table. They spread out the coin and goods they'd stolen that day, young Hap's the most recent addition.

The two bullies sorted the items and added up the coin they had pickpocketed from not just Hap. A good haul for so early in the day, indeed. They laughed at their good fortunes and tucked into their stolen goods.

The bag of fresh pastries were the first to be opened, and the stolen goodies were still warm from the ovens.

"I'm glad he got these from Yanna's stall," the larger of the two said as he snatched up one of the treats and took a big bite. "She's got the best sticky buns."

"Yeah. And the kid bought two of 'em," his friend replied through a full mouth.

"Easiest score we've had in a while too. What a pathetic piece that one was. He didn't even *try* to fight back. I mean, who just gives up that easy?"

"Well, he did try to *talk* tough," the other boy said with a laugh. "I guess he's used to Daddy taking care of problems for hi--"

The boy's words were abruptly cut off when he and his friend suddenly found themselves hoisted off the ground by powerful, invisible hands and slammed up against the wall, their feet left dangling.

Hozark shook his head slightly as he uttered the spell controlling his shimmer cloak, making him visible once more. The two youths looked properly confused and terrified.

As was his intent.

The pale assassin stared hard at the boys a long moment, and under his gaze they stopped squirming. His grip was like iron, and there was simply no way they could break free. At best, they might just anger the strange man further than he already appeared.

Finally, the mysterious assailant spoke.

"You robbed my friend," he said in a low growl.

The boys were scared, no doubt. They were used to perhaps getting a beating from time to time if they were caught picking pockets, but this was something different. Something *serious*, and far more terrifying.

Hozark stared silently again, intimidating the boys with his unblinking gaze. He was actually rather enjoying teaching these two a lesson, and he had no intention of causing them any harm. They were just children, after all, and it was his firm belief that all children deserved the opportunity to learn and grow.

But he would not let them know that.

It was how he had become one of the deadliest assassins in the galaxy, after all. Taken as a young boy and given a new chance. Shown a world he never knew existed. And, eventually, even made into a full brother in the order. A Wampeh Ghalian. And he had thrived ever since.

These two, however, did not possess the requisite innate talents for that sort of a future, but, perhaps, he could at least steer them to reconsider their ways.

"We don't know who you're talking about," the larger of the two said in a desperate attempt.

"Oh, I'm sure you do."

"Really, sir, we don't. You've made a mistake. We didn't rob anyone."

Hozark was not amused by their reluctance to admit their guilt. They were scared, yes, but apparently used to getting away with their little capers with minimal consequences. This would not do.

He was reluctant to waste magic on these two, but a little display suddenly felt well worth the expenditure. Hozark drew power from his konus and quietly uttered a spell, the magic firmly pinning the boys to the wall. He released them and stepped back, the two remaining suspended in the air. It was a most unusual spell, and one few knew how to cast.

*That* seemed to make an impression, but for good measure, he decided to go all the way with these two. Hozark pulled out a pair of wicked blades from their hidden sheaths and pressed them against each boy's soft belly.

"Shall I open you up and reclaim the pastry you stole from him? Will that refresh your memory?"

"Oh, *that* boy. Uh, yes, of course. We remember him. It was just a lark, though. We didn't mean anything by it."

"You *beat* him. A boy half your size. And after you had already taken his coin."

"How do you know that?" the boy asked, at a loss.

They had been alone in the alley when they'd robbed him, and there was no way the kid had run home to tell on them in the short time since they'd left him lying on the ground.

"I have my ways," Hozark said, smiling wide and sliding his fangs down into place.

"A Gh-Ghalian!" the smaller boy said, his pants suddenly becoming quite damp as his bladder released in fear.

The larger of the two managed to keep control of his bowels, but only just. Regardless, the look of abject terror in their eyes told Hozark the lesson had sunk in.

"You would do well to remember that you never know who it is you are robbing," he said. "And the next person may not be so forgiving as I."

Hozark sheathed his knives and walked to the pile of coin on the table. He surveyed the boys' meager quantity and recovered the exact amount he had given Hap earlier that day. He then took a few additional from the small stack.

"Restitution for your act," he said, pocketing the coin, but leaving the boys the rest of their haul.

Hozark was not going to steal from children. That was dishonorable and distasteful. And Lord knew he had picked plenty of pockets in his time. He turned and walked several paces, then faced the boys once more, pausing a long moment, just to give them that last bit of reinforcing fear.

"*Uzmanti orkus*," he said, releasing the spell.

The boys dropped to the ground and fell to their knees. He hadn't been holding them terribly high, but the fear he had instilled in them had left their legs far too weak to stand. For the moment at least.

He then turned and vanished into his shimmer cloak, disappearing before their eyes. It was a fun trick, and one he would never do in front of a true adversary. But for these children, the effect would serve to reinforce the fear that they could be watched at any time, anywhere.

"Ah, you are looking better, young Jinnik," Hozark said a short while later as he casually strolled into the ship's galley.

"A successful outing?" Demelza asked, looking at him with knowing eyes.

"Indeed," he replied, placing a bag in front of the boy. "I believe these are yours."

Hap looked in the bag. Indeed, it was full of sticky buns and treats, though he could have sworn he hadn't purchased quite so many.

"Thanks, Hozark," he said, his eyes slightly averted. "Sorry I didn't say anything."

"Do not be sorry. You have never had to deal with a situation such as that before. There is no shame in admitting you do not know something. It is how we learn and grow."

"But it was pathetic," the boy said. "They just took everything, and there was nothing I could do about it."

"Yes, but, again, you simply were not prepared for this sort of a situation. Your father has always protected you. And while that is an admirable thing, it does not serve you well in times when you are on your own. You need to be able to defend yourself, for there will not always be another to protect you."

"But what am I supposed to do?"

He looked at Demelza and gave her a little nod.

"I have an idea," she said. "Would you like us to teach you?"

Hap perked up a bit. "You're going to teach me to be a Ghalian?"

She grinned. "No, nothing of the sort, I am afraid. But we can teach you how to handle yourself should you find you have landed in a difficult situation in the future. Would you like that?"

"That'd be great," he said, his mood lifting.

"But be forewarned," Hozark said. "Training of this nature is not easy, and it will require much effort on your part. But if you truly apply yourself, I feel you could very well become a formidable adversary, in time. Yet you shall not begin as such. You may fail at times. In fact, you *will*, and often at first. But that is how we all started out. There is no easy path here, but the end is worth the effort. Can you commit to this?"

Hap nodded his head. "I can," he replied. "I'll be ready. First thing tomorrow."

Hozark chuckled. "Oh, young Jinnik. We start today."

## CHAPTER FOUR

"Again," Demelza said.

Happizano reacted by bending into a forward roll, whacking his head and shoulder on the thin training mat she had laid out on the compartment's floor. It was a courtesy for the youth. Ghalian assassins never used mats for training. The pain of mistakes was a great motivator, and the footing tended to be a bit different than in real combat.

But Hap was just a boy, and not a Wampeh Ghalian aspirant. And he was starting from scratch with nary a minute of combat training in him. And growing up in a luxurious estate tower as he had, he lacked even the most rudimentary skills many of his peers possessed after a childhood of falling down and getting up again.

It was painful. Painful and boring. But Hap did as Demelza said and executed a rather crude forward roll for the umpteenth time.

"Better," she said. "Now backward."

He did as she asked, rolling as she had shown him, his head pushing to one side, allowing his body to curl backward over his rounded shoulders.

"Forward."

He rolled forward again, this time over the opposite shoulder. He had found that he favored his right side more than his left. Something Demelza had told him was quite common.

"Most have a favored side," she said. "It is a weakness you can learn to take advantage of, in time."

"What's your favored side?" he asked her.

"Wampeh Ghalian train to be entirely ambidextrous in combat."

"Ambi what?"

"Ambidextrous. It means we use our left and right side interchangeably. We have no favored side. It makes it far easier to not only deal with opponents who favor either left or right, but it also makes it more difficult for them to counter our attacks. Shifting stances is not something most train in, and it is a weakness we exploit."

"Then I want to be ambidostris."

"*Ambidextrous*," she corrected. "And it is my hope to eventually help you attain that goal. But first, you must learn the most basic of skills. And that is how to fall without hurting yourself. A great many fights wind up on the ground, and it is quite often that impact that causes more damage than the event causing it."

"But you don't fall."

"Not much, anymore. But that is because of years of training. And rest assured, Hap, I still wind up on the ground at times. We all do. And not always from combat. In fact, once, I was thrown from a spooked Malooki that came up short and sent me flying over its head."

"A Malooki? Weren't you hurt?"

"That is where this training came in handy. It was muscle memory. Instinctive. As I flew through the air, my body knew what to do. And that was a variant of what you are practicing right now. Rolling out of a fall to allow your body to spread the load of the impact and lessen its force, all while redirecting it to your benefit, bringing you back to your feet once more. I shall demonstrate."

Demelza took a few steps back, then lunged forward, executing a diving front roll. It was nothing for her, but for the boy it seemed a most impressive feat of physical prowess. She then ran to the wall, jumped high, her legs bending and absorbing the impact then pushing her backward into a diving roll the other way.

"That's so cool!"

"Yes. And useful in combat. To be able to use any abrupt shift in your physical positioning to your advantage. But today, we focus on the most important and basic principle. Keeping your body from harm. But you've been training well. Let us give you a break from that for a moment and work on a bit of body positioning."

Hozark strolled into the chamber to watch the boy's progress. Demelza was a fine teacher, and if she ever wished to have that title officially, he would be certain to put in a good word for her with the other four of the masters of the order. She had most definitely earned it and proven her worth on more than one occasion.

As she had young Hap practice standing in a slightly lowered stance, learning to find his center and control his balance, Hozark found himself reminiscing about his own initiation at roughly that same age. He had been taken from his world by a strange man and transported to an even stranger facility. One full of Wampeh. Wampeh just like him.

They all possessed the same gift he did, to varying degrees. The ability to suck the power from another by drinking their blood. It was something of a revelation to him. But that came later. First was a rather difficult bit of training. Training that started quite a bit more brutally than young Happizano was receiving.

"How is he coming along, Demelza?" he asked as he studied the boy's stance.

His legs seemed to be shaking a bit from the effort. Good. It would make him stronger. And that would serve him well should the time ever come when he needed to use such skills.

"He shows promise," she replied as she pushed on the boy's shoulders and hips, urging his body to feel how to respond to the shifts in position. "Despite lacking any prior training, he does seem to have a knack for the basics."

"Excellent."

"When will you show me how to fight?" the boy asked.

"Soon enough, young Jinnik. But remember, you are not like us. Violence is not your path. In addition, recognize that no matter what your mind may wish, you are still a boy. Do not attempt to achieve more than your growing body can accomplish."

"But Henni is small, and she can fight."

"Yes, but she is also older, stronger, and far more experienced," he replied, omitting the additional fact that the young woman was also a bit unhinged at times. "Remember this lesson, Hap. Rule number one. Run when you can. A wise man knows when *not* to fight. Protect yourself and avoid conflict unless you have no choice."

"But you have a choice," the boy said.

"Yes. But that is the path of the Wampeh Ghalian. That life is not for you," he said. "These lessons will help you identify a situation and avoid it, if possible. For example, today, two larger boys attacked you. And while you were attempting to stand up for yourself, you were distracted by one while the other struck you."

"How did you know that? I didn't tell you that."

"I am a Wampeh Ghalian, young Jinnik. I think by now you have learned that I see more than most," Hozark said. "Now, let us discuss that particular situation."

The boy shifted on his feet, standing up taller.

"I did not say to relax from your stance," Demelza chided.

"Sorry," he said, lowering his hips again, though his legs were getting quite sore.

Hozark nodded approvingly. "Good. You listen well. Now, heed this lesson. When you are faced with multiple opponents, as you were today, immediately observe their interactions and determine which of them is the leader."

"How?"

"They will be the one directing the other's actions, though often quite subtly. Many times the follower will not even realize they are doing so. But the one who takes the lead is who should be of interest."

"Okay. I think it was the bigger one," Hap said.

"Indeed," Hozark said with a smile. "You see? You *were* paying attention. You have a sharp mind, Happizano, and we shall hone it further. Now, in the instance such as this, where you have identified the leader, if it becomes apparent that violence is imminent, you must aggressively take the leader down. Do so violently, and as quickly as you can so as to shock the others by your actions."

"But then they'll just beat me up."

"Not necessarily. Their lackeys will, more often than not, give up the fight if their leader is no longer egging them on. It is a pack mentality that a great many fall into without realizing. However, if they do not back off, you will at least have made them hesitate, and that is often enough for you to enact rule number one and make your escape."

"Okay, I guess. But they were so much bigger than me."

"Size is of no matter if you strike in the right place. I return to your own comment about Henni. She is a small woman, but she causes great damage with her attacks. And do you know how?"

"Because she has knives?"

Hozark stifled a chuckle. "No, though those do help, of course. But when unarmed, she attacks the weak spots. The throat," he said, tapping beneath the boy's chin. "The eyes. The knees. The groin. All are weak points on most races. Naturally, many types do not possess the same basic physiology, but the principle holds true. Find the weakness and exploit it with the least effort possible. Does this make sense?"

"Yeah, I guess."

"There is one thing I would like to add," Demelza said. "If it is a situation where you believe you will likely be confronted by these individuals again, break a bone if you can, even if just a finger."

"Why? Won't that make them come at me even harder next time?"

"If they do, it is because they would have anyway, but a broken bone often makes even an angry defeated opponent and their friends think twice about a second attack. And if not, their hesitation in memory of the prior injury will buy you time and space."

Hozark nodded his approval.

"Hey, whatcha doin'?" Henni asked as she popped into the compartment.

"We are working on some basic training for Happizano to teach him to defend himself," Demelza replied.

"Ooh, cool. Can I play?"

The two Wampeh glanced at one another, clearly thinking the same thing. Henni was a much smaller person, and actually a better practice partner for the boy to start with. Additionally, a bit of formal training time, even if a step backward from her usual skills, might prove grounding for the overly excitable young woman.

"I think that would be a wonderful idea, Henni. Thank you," Demelza replied.

In no time, their Ghalian teacher had the pair working on

several basic, but extremely effective combatives. Nothing excessive, as Hap was building his foundation, but their teacher knew from her own experiences that practicing stances and rolls would bore anyone to tears if not broken up with a bit of fighting.

Henni was actually doing quite well, her normally boundless energy reserved as she took the lessons to heart and actually learned a few tips that would make her an even more efficient fighter.

Hap, however, seemed a bit confused by the new movements. They weren't clicking. It simply wasn't instinctive for him. Not yet, anyway. They needed a way to help his mind wrap around the concepts, and Hozark had an unconventional, but likely functional, idea.

Bud poked his head in the door at the sound of the combatives being drilled over and over by the pair.

"Oh, fun," he said. "You guys wanna learn some really dirty pirate tricks?"

Hozark patted his friend on the shoulder. "I believe we shall save those for a later time, my friend," he said. "But I do have a little something in mind that you might enjoy."

## CHAPTER FIVE

"I have to admit, even for you, this is an unusual idea," Bud said as he flew in low orbit after exiting their jump just above their destination world.

Hozark reclined in his seat. "We could use a bit of respite, and this will provide us an excellent opportunity to not only acquire provisions and a fresh-cooked meal, but will also, almost certainly, allow young Happizano to observe much of what we have been teaching him firsthand."

"I can't argue that," Bud said. "Faranzial is definitely the place for that."

"It is at that."

"So, shall I take us in?"

"Indeed."

"Okay, then. Down we go," Bud said as he began their descent from orbit.

Faranzial was a trading world, but one that had something of a rough reputation. It wasn't necessarily a dangerous world, but it did have quite a reputation for violence. An unusual reputation, at that.

It seemed to be by some unspoken agreement that lethal force was almost never employed there. Fights broke out frequently, and people let off steam, but that was typically as far as it went. The result was entire sections of neighborhoods that sometimes devolved into street brawls, the combatants usually making up after and buying one another drinks. A city-wide fight club of sorts.

Bud set them down in the main landing zone. It was a spacious area that allowed for plenty of room between the parked craft. A beneficial layout that allowed the more inebriated pilots to fly––ill-advised as it was––without crashing into other vessels.

"Now, stay between us, young Jinnik," Hozark said as they exited the ship.

He took the lead, with Hap behind him and Demelza bookending the boy. The others filed out and sealed up the ship, then fell in behind them as they moved into the rowdy streets of the main city's central area.

They could have walked the entire way, but Hozark decided it was best to acquire a ride on one of the floating conveyances frequenting the area. Hap was here to learn, but it might be a bit much for the boy if they thrust him into the full chaos of the city immediately. Better to ease him into it slowly after they'd had a chance to eat, drink, and relax a bit.

The driver took them to one of the better establishments in town, and, importantly, one that had an open seating area in front, facing a large plaza. It was dinner and a show, essentially, as, more often than not, brawls would break out with almost predictable regularity.

"Now what, Hozark?" Hap asked.

"Now, young Jinnik, we shall partake in a nice, relaxing meal."

"But I thought you said this was a training stop."

"It is. I want you to pay attention to the goings-on in the

plaza. Watch the men and women as they interact. Gauge who is the true threat and who is no more than a yapping mouth."

"Oh, you looking for Laskar?" Bud asked, pointing to his copilot.

"Ha-ha. Very funny."

"You're the one with the mouth," Bud shot back. "Anyway, speaking of mouths, let's get our meal. I'm hungry enough to eat a Malooki."

"You, I am not sure about, but I feel our little friend here might just be capable," Hozark joked, nodding to Henni.

The small woman had already begun tearing into the fresh bread that had just been placed on their table with gusto. It really was something, the way she put away such quantities, but with her boundless energy, it was not as if she didn't put it to good use.

Their meal came quickly, and it was an impressive spread. A big pot of stew, some roasted vegetables and tubers, a flatbread seasoned with some sort of cheese and oil, and a noodle-like substance that grew underneath the giant leaves of the local oceanic kelp.

Hozark knew this world and its offerings well and had taken the liberty of ordering for them all. They would be eating in the manner often called "family style." In this place, however, it was more apt to be called marauder team-style, or pirate crew-style. In any case, the food was fresh, hot, and plentiful.

"Oh, this stew is incredible," Henni said between mouthfuls. "What's in it?"

"Best you don't ask that sort of thing around here," Bud said. "Just enjoy and don't think about it."

Henni paused, looked at the bowl in front of her, then shrugged and kept eating. They were well into their second course when the first signs of a brewing fight appeared.

"There," Hozark said, pointing at a man pacing back and forth at the far end of the plaza. "Do you see him, young Jinnik?"

"The angry-looking guy?"

"Precisely. Good eyes. That will serve you well. Always note a person's physical attitude. As you observed, that man seems agitated. Not just his pacing, but also his posturing. Now, do you see where he is glancing? The object of his ire?"

"His what?"

"Ire. His anger."

"Oh, uh, it looks like it's that orange-haired woman over by the fountain," the boy replied. "The tall one."

Indeed, he was shooting hate daggers from his eyes at her, but it was not the look of a lover scorned. This was something else.

"Watch closely," Hozark said. "See where the first blow comes from. Learn to predict the violence before it commences."

Hap leaned forward, staring intently. "But my father always says a man should never strike a woman."

"And in genteel society, that may hold true. But I think you might be surprised what women are capable of."

No sooner had Hozark made the comment than the agitated man decided to confront the woman. Their words could not be made out from the distance and across the din of the plaza as he strode toward her, but it was clear this would not end well.

"Should we help her?" Hap asked.

"Oh, Hap, I do not think she will need our help," Demelza said with a knowing grin.

The woman didn't hesitate. As soon as the man drew close, she leapt into action, landing a flurry of fierce blows to his face and abdomen before kicking him square in the chest, sending him sliding backwards.

The man wiped the blood from his lip then rushed her, throwing wide, looping punches that came nowhere near connecting. The woman was fast, bobbing and weaving around his attempts, her fists and elbows pummeling him with every opening his attack provided.

"Do you see his hips?" Demelza asked. "What we practiced earlier?"

"He's off-balance," Hap realized. "And he's throwing with his arms but not his body."

Hozark and Demelza shared a pleased look. It was starting to click. The boy had paid attention, and he was proving quite a quick study. But observations were one thing. They also needed to teach him how to act. To react. How to protect himself. But this was a good start.

The woman began toying with the man. He was clearly outclassed, and the fight was all but guaranteed to end quickly. Hozark and Demelza saw the two men approaching from the woman's rear, as did Bud and Laskar. Henni noted it as well.

"Hey, that's not fair," she said, taking umbrage at the woman about to be blindsided.

"True. But fights are not fair. The goal is to win, and that is not always according to some archaic rules system. In the real world, fighting dirty is a perfectly acceptable option," Hozark said.

Henni, however, had suffered a great many injustices in her time as a slave, and later, as a pickpocket on the street, and she was not about to let a woman be beaten in an unfair fight. She leapt to her feet, ready to join the fray, when both Hozark and Demelza grabbed her and sat her back down.

"What are you doing? I can help her!"

"She does not need your help," Demelza said with a knowing grin.

"But she's outnumbered."

"Is she, though?"

The newcomer assailants were almost upon the woman, positioning themselves to strike from behind, when three seemingly unaffiliated observers suddenly blindsided them with a quick attack, choking them into submission and hauling their unconscious bodies out of the way of the fighting pair.

"How did you know?" Henni asked.

"Never assume you only have one opponent," Hozark replied. "Everyone is a potential threat, and you must assess them all. Those three, while watching the fight, were also constantly scanning the crowd. Not something you do if you are a casual bystander enjoying a brawl."

Henni cocked her head slightly. "Huh," was all she said.

"Hey, look! It's the punch you showed me!" Hap said, tugging on Demelza's arm.

The woman had thrown a very basic straight punch right into the man's stomach, doubling him over from the force. She had thrown with her hips, not her arms, and the force behind it was far greater for it. Just as the boy had learned only a few hours prior.

The fight ended shortly thereafter when the man caught a blow to the corner of his jaw, snapping his head to the side and knocking him unconscious. Rather than continuing to beat on the man, as might happen in some other, more dangerous places, the woman merely spat on her fallen opponent and went about her business.

"That was so cool!" Hap said.

"Not exactly the best display of technique," Demelza noted, "but nevertheless, a good, real-world demonstration to help the concepts you have been learning make better sense. I hope that was the case."

"Totally. And that was so cool!"

She chuckled. "Yes, so you have said. And now, what do you think? Shall we order dessert?"

## CHAPTER SIX

The remainder of the meal had been spent discussing what Hap had observed in the little skirmish. Fortunately, it seemed that with a hot meal in his belly, the boy's mood had taken a turn for the better.

It was still difficult for him at times, being separated from his father, and though they were doing all they could to return him to his lone surviving parent, finding Visla Jinnik once he'd left his home to carry out his servitude to the Council had proven a very difficult task. Even for the Ghalian spy network.

But at least Hap had finally settled into a semblance of a normal life with his unlikely guardians. He made no more attempts to steal a ship and fly himself home. Not after the dangerous situation there was better explained to him. And now that he was learning interesting new things from his protectors, he had something to focus on besides his rather depressing situation.

He would get home eventually. But no one knew how long that would be. And though none of them had ever planned on caring for a young boy, the group had come together admirably to make his stay with them as bearable as possible.

"I'm just sorry you didn't get to see a *real* fight, kid," Bud said. "That was over too quick, and it was more of a beatdown than an actual fight."

"I don't know. It was pretty cool," Hap said.

"I'm with Bud on this. Not enough fighting," Henni chimed in.

"Well, you cannot have mayhem *every* time," Demelza said. "Now, what do you say we head back to the ship. It has been a long day, and I am sure our young friend here would benefit from a good night's sleep."

"I feel fine," the boy protested.

"As you will, *today*. But *tomorrow* the soreness will set in. Trust me on this. When you first begin a new physical endeavor such as this, your body will experience certain effects from the unfamiliar stresses."

"Yeah, it's true," Bud said. "Trust her on this one, Hap. I learned that lesson the hard way on more than one occasion."

"Okay, I guess."

"Then it is settled," Demelza said. "We return to the ship. Enough excitement for today."

Hozark called over the serving man and settled their bill with a large stack of coin from his pocket. Once that last detail was handled, the group headed out, crossing the open plaza for one of the adjacent pathways.

"I think a walk would do us some good after all of that food," Bud said. "Whaddya say, Hozark?"

The Wampeh thought on it a moment. "I do not see why not. But young Happizano shall walk between Demelza and myself."

The two Wampeh took their positions, and Bud and Henni wandered out front while Laskar took up the rear. They weren't expecting any trouble. It was simply a precautionary formation done more out of habit than any fear of danger.

Funny enough, this was actually one of those rare occasions where danger *was* about to rear its ugly head.

Seven rather burly men appeared out of the nearby doorways where they had been standing in wait after seeing Hozark pull a tidy sum from his pocket as he paid for their meal. An easy target. Just three men to their seven. The others in their group were only two women and a kid.

"You there. Pale guy. Give us your coin," one of the smaller men said.

"There. Do you see what we can learn from something as simple as that statement?" Hozark asked the boy, ignoring the man.

"That he's the leader of the group?"

"Exactly. And what do we do when we know who the leader is?"

Hap looked at the seven large men and hesitated. "Uh, we take them out?"

"Precisely. Now, in this situation, however, things are a bit more fluid, and we must adjust accordingly."

"Hey, pretty boy. I said give me your coin!" the man repeated.

"Just a moment. I am teaching the boy an important lesson."

That was not a reply the man was expecting. "You telling me to hold on? Who the hell do you think you are?"

It was obviously about to devolve from a verbal to a physical conflict, that much was clear. Bud and Henni were still in front of the group, and both turned to look at Hozark. He gave them a little nod, and smiles bloomed on each of their faces.

The green light.

Bud shifted his gaze to the youngster. "Now pay attention, Hap. There'll be a quiz on this later."

Henni just shook her head with a sigh, but a little grin was creeping onto her lips. "So, we gonna do this?"

"Oh yeah. But remember, no killing."

"You suck all of the fun out of things," she griped.

"Will you two ridiculous little––" the nearest would-be

mugger started to say before a swift kick to the groin from Henni's diminutive boot buckled him forward. Bent over as he was, his jaw was in perfect position for her flying knee to the face.

She didn't wait for the others to react but launched straight into a frenzied attack. Bud followed close behind, and moments later, a frenetic brawl filled the pathway.

Bud and Henni played off of each other seamlessly, one lining up a dazed opponent for the other to finish off. It was a tag-team violent ballet, and the duo were exceptional in their choreography.

Just a minute later, the last two of the muggers were all that remained. It looked as though it would all be over quickly, but Bud noticed that one of them was holding a skree in his hand.

The bastard had called for backup.

Running footsteps echoed out against the walls as a dozen more men spilled into the crowded space.

"Uh, guys? A little help here?" Bud called out to his friends.

Hozark rolled his neck slightly. "Demelza, watch the boy, please."

The master assassin then calmly strode into the fight. Where Bud and Henni were a bit impulsive, fighting in bursts of adrenaline, Hozark was the very picture of smooth and calm. He moved quickly through his opponents, using this happenstance as an impromptu opportunity for a teaching experience.

He flowed from one attacker to the next, masterful in his efficiency of motion.

"See how he uses so little energy while effecting the most damage?" Demelza asked the boy. "Even larger opponents fall easily when the right force is applied to the right place. And note his footwork. See how he positions his hips to deliver the maximum energy behind his blows?"

Hozark was moving as slow as he dared, to afford the boy a

chance to better see his technique. Normally he would have laid out all of them in half the time, if that, but today was different. And, he found, it was actually somewhat pleasant, slowing down and enjoying the process.

Of course, the men on the receiving end of that process were not so thrilled.

Henni and Bud, though still amped up from the fight, nevertheless stopped to watch the Ghalian master at work. It wasn't something they saw often, a Wampeh Ghalian doing his thing in full view. Or *mostly* doing his thing. No one was dying today, after all, and they knew he was holding back considerably.

"Damn, he's really good," Laskar marveled as he watched the pale killer move.

"He is one of the best," Demelza replied.

Hozark was careful not to damage the men too greatly. They were, after all, only after his coin, not his life. In short order, the newcomers had joined their slumbering friends on the ground, and no one would be skreeing for additional backup.

"Well, that was refreshing," Hozark said with a satisfied look. "Unexpected, but a good lesson for the boy, I think. Nothing quite like a real-world demonstration to help the lessons sink in."

"Yeah. And we got a really good meal in the process," Henni said. "But do you think we could maybe stop and grab a little something on the way back to the ship?"

"You just ate," Bud marveled.

"Well, yeah. But fighting's hungry work."

Bud looked at his friends. "Always about food, this one," he said with a laugh. "She's so small. Where does it all go? I swear, it's like you've got a little black hole in there somewhere."

"What? I get hungry," she retorted.

"Fair enough," Demelza said. "And now, back to the ship."

They began walking, stepping over the slumbering attackers. Henni tugged at Hozark's sleeve, looking up at him with those galactic eyes.

"Yes, Henni," he said. "We can pick up a little snack on the way."

## CHAPTER SEVEN

It was an odd and almost directionless bit of existence, searching for Happizano's father across the systems, but to no avail. Normally, the Ghalian network of spies and informants were famously competent, but in this instance, all leads kept turning up nothing.

There were still other options, naturally. But those were favors typically saved for a *very* rainy day. In this instance, however, it appeared there was little else to do but call one in.

"We need to stop at Drambal," Hozark informed his pilot friend while the others were relaxing in their quarters.

It was a rare bit of alone time for the two men who had previously spent quite a lot of solitary time together on the missions they partnered on every so often.

Since they had been abruptly thrown together for a longer duration than usual after the surprising reappearance of Hozark's old--and formerly deceased--flame, Samara, they also had constantly been in the presence of others. Bud's ship was now housing far more than its usual crew of two. But it was not all bad.

Laskar was a useful addition. Cocky and annoying, but a

talented copilot. Demelza, likewise, was highly skilled as an assassin and a valuable member of their team. Henni? She was a stray, but one with great potential.

And then there was the boy. A child Hozark had been saddled with when he rescued him from the Council of Twenty, only to find the man who hired him to do so was now under their yoke. And missing, it seemed.

And they were doing their damnedest to find him.

"Drambal? Uh, okay. But why?" Bud asked. "That's not exactly a hub of culture and excitement. Or anything, for that matter."

"There is one there I would speak with regarding our young guest's father. If he is still residing on Drambal, he may be able to help in our task. I am growing disconcerted at the difficulty we are having in locating Happizano's father."

"And you think you might know someone who can find him? Someone outside of your usual network?"

"I am loath to approach him for something of this nature, but yes, I believe so."

Bud pondered a minute, then nodded. "I guess Drambal it is," he finally said. "I'll have Laskar plot us a course." He paused. "Uh, are we telling the others why we're going there? Seems it might make them a bit uneasy if they knew your spy network was having such a hard time. Well, everyone but Demelza, that is."

"I think not, on this particular occasion, and for precisely the reason you mention. I particularly do not wish to alarm the boy any more than he already is. He seems to be adjusting to this transient life better by the day."

"He's adapting, for sure. But the kid misses his dad."

"I am well aware. Hopefully, this stop will help us locate him at last. I certainly wish it, for his sake."

"Me too," Bud said. "Hey, I'm gonna send a long-range skree while we're there and see if one of my old pirate buddies can put out some feelers in our own network. It's nothing like yours, obviously, but you never know when you might get a lucky hit. Someone, somewhere, might have seen or heard something, after all."

Hozark nodded. "Any help is appreciated at this point, my friend. For both ours, as well as young Happizano's sake."

---

Drambal was a rather bland world. And on that utterly unremarkable planet, Uzabud guided them to a rather unremarkable city, inhabited by unremarkable people. It was the cultural equivalent of the color beige, or the taste of water. There, but not.

"I have an errand to run," Hozark said to the curious crew when they set down. "This should not take me terribly long, so please, enjoy the marketplace, but do not stray too far. I should think we will be aloft again quite shortly."

Before he could be assailed with questions, he stepped off the ship and strode off at a brisk pace through the throngs of ordinary people.

"What's that all about?" Laskar asked.

"Beats me," Bud lied. "I think he needed to recharge his konus."

"Here? I can't believe there are any power users of substance on this world," Laskar said.

"Hey, it's just a guess. He could be off chatting with some other Ghalian for all I know. Right, Demelza?"

"It is possible," she replied. "I have found that where Master Hozark is involved, it is typically best not to question his motives. He is one of the Five, and that is more than enough to satisfy my curiosity."

"Well put," Bud agreed. "So, in the meantime, let's hit the marketplace. Henni, how about you and Demelza take Hap and maybe find some baked goods."

Though Henni did not like being made to play nursemaid, the promise of food at the end of the task was enough to motivate her compliance. Demelza, naturally, was already planning on shadowing the boy after his recent incident.

"All right. I'm gonna see about finding a long-range skree to use. Ours is still busted, and it's been a little while since I checked in with Lalaynia. Might be that her boys have rustled up some juicy intel for us from the pirate network."

"I'll join you," Laskar volunteered.

"Nah, it'll just be a simple call. Go have some fun and meet us back here."

Laskar hesitated. "Uh, okay, I guess."

"Cool. I'll see you all in a bit," Bud said, then headed out into the city to make his call.

"Well, then. I guess we're off to find food," Henni said with a grin. "Come on, Hap."

The boy and the two women headed out, leaving Laskar to fend for himself. For all of his talk, however, he seemed rather put out at being left on his own. Out of the loop, in a way. But he trudged out of the ship to go see what he might find in the small, unremarkable marketplace.


Hozark had made good time through the winding paths leading to the humble façade of the animal trader's holding pens and auction block. Once inside the plain building, the boring air of the city dissolved as the shrieks and bellows of myriad beasts filled the air.

Apparently, a fairly powerful spell had been muting them from the outside world. Of course, Hozark was well aware of that, as he had been the one to acquire that bit of magic for the man in charge. Orkin was his name. A stout fellow with a ridge of tiny horn-like protrusions running across his forehead and back down his neck.

His skin was a reddish gray and tough like a rhino's hide. Six stumpy fingers graced each of his powerful hands, which were attached to likewise burly arms. The man was formidable, and despite his relatively short height, he was clearly not one to be trifled with.

A Zomoki was acting up in its pen, shrieking and spitting its magical flames as Hozark walked closer. Orkin had a sturdy control collar on the beast, but as it was a juvenile, he was loath to force it into submission with magic. Instead, he was attempting to earn its trust. Or, at least, gain some modicum of control without having to shock the poor thing.

Flames shot out, harmlessly hitting the floor, but then the animal turned its head toward the newcomer and prepared for a full spray.

"*Actazi noh*," the man said, triggering the safeguard spell on the control collar.

The Zomoki's flames trickled from its mouth as the painful spell did its job, stopping it from attempting its attack.

"Lotta nerve, Hozark," the man said. "You know better than to interrupt a man when he's working with a beast such as this."

"Indeed, I do, Orkin. But I am afraid I am in need of your assistance."

At this the man's orange-rimmed eyes seemed to flicker with interest. "You're calling it in?"

"Apparently, I must," the Wampeh replied.

"So, we're even after this?"

"We will be even," Hozark said.

Orkin's smile grew wide, and he clapped his visitor on the shoulder. "Why didn't you say so? Come, let's have a drink!"

He ushered the Wampeh into his nearby office and shut the door, sealing it with another muting spell. Another spell Hozark had taught him, in fact. None would be eavesdropping today.

"So, old friend, what is this momentous event that calls in your marker? You need someone killed?"

"You know I would do that myself."

"Right. Right. Maybe you want dirt on the Council's latest attack plans? You know I have ears in all places."

"Yes, I do. And, admittedly, the Council's plans are of great concern to myself and the order, but that is not exactly why I have come to you."

"Not *exactly*?"

"No. I am searching for *one* man."

"Seems like something your people could handle just fine," Orkin replied. "What's so special about this man?"

"We are in possession of his son. Kidnapped to force him to do the Council's bidding. Once they are reunited, he will be freed of his servitude, and the boy will be safe with his father. But all word of him has ceased, and the boy is without his parent."

Orkin's smile faded. "You know I was an orphan."

"I do."

"You know how I feel about violence toward children."

"I do as well."

Orkin sighed. "Then you know I'll help you regardless of my debt. Who's this man you're looking for. If he's under Council control, I'll know where to find him."

"His name is Jinnik. *Visla* Jinnik."

Orkin's eyes widened slightly. "So, *that's* why he's doing it?" he mused.

"You know of him?"

"Oh, that I do."

"And doing what, exactly?"

"I'm sure your spies have told you that several worlds have fallen to Council control of late. And at the hands of a brutally powerful visla, no less. One who came out of nowhere. Unknown before all of this. A man going by the name of Jinnik."

"He's the father of the boy in my care. The man who tasked me to rescue him."

"An unusual contract for you, is it not, Master Hozark?"

"Very. But let us just say that one to whom *I* owed a debt called it in."

Orkin nodded. "Well, this Jinnik, he's been laying waste to entire rebellions in recent weeks. Thousands killed and as many enslaved in the process."

"We have heard much the same," Hozark noted.

"Then you also know that he's gone missing."

"Which is why I have come to you. More than any, you have deep ties within the Council. Some might say deeper than our most loyal Ghalian spies, even."

"Oh, you know I'm just a simple beast trader these days," he replied with a gleam in his eye.

"*Of course* you are," Hozark said with a wry grin. "But one who is undoubtedly still in contact with at least some of his old resources."

"Perhaps. But I can tell you this for certain. This Visla Jinnik is gone. None have seen him in recent days. And odder than that, it appears his actions were not carried out at the full Council's request."

"Oh?" Hozark said, genuinely surprised.

"No."

"At whose behest, then?"

"Names have been hard to come by, but Visla Ravik has been mentioned in passing."

"Not shocking. We believe he is involved with another in the Council. A power grab, though we cannot discern precisely what end they are trying to achieve."

"You mean Maktan, don't you?" Orkin asked.

"Indeed," Hozark said with a little grin. "You *are* still tied in, I see."

Orkin quietly mused the situation a moment. "There has been nothing concrete tying Visla Maktan to these events, yet his name has reached the ears of too many of my people to be coincidence. Despite how he may outwardly appear, it is my belief that the man may very well be behind this particular scheme."

"The Ghalian are of this belief as well," Hozark said.

"So, are you going to, uh, *rectify* the situation?" Orkin asked with an arched brow.

"We shall see how this all plays out."

"Well, word is, he was involved in the torture and experimentation on a lot of power users of various types," the man said, fixing his gaze on Hozark. "Including a Ghalian."

Hozark was in complete control of his emotions, as always, but the mention of poor Aargun and what had been done to him nevertheless caused the tiniest of twitches in his jaw.

Orkin, ever observant, noted it and nodded. "I thought as much. I will continue to search for answers on your behalf, Hozark. And should I find any, I will relay them to the order to pass to you, wherever you may be."

"Thank you, old friend."

"Don't thank me yet. If rumors are true, this could be a far bigger mess than you want to handle."

"And yet, here I am."

Orkin nodded. "Good luck, my friend. You'll need it."

## CHAPTER EIGHT

Hozark took an uncharacteristically lengthy walk back to the ship. His meeting had not produced the results he had hoped for, and he found himself needing to process the situation. Walking often provided him a sort of moving meditation, and on this world, devoid of threats as it was, he could actually even allow himself to enjoy it a little.

He looped around the small greenbelt that separated two quarters of the city near Orkin's place. The sounds of the small stream's water gently babbling was a much-appreciated bit of white noise adding to the calming effect.

Ravik being involved was a given, and it seemed Maktan's role was more than just conjecture at this point. And he was almost certainly the one behind the experiments. The ones that had left one of the order's top students a cripple.

Maktan would pay for that, in time. But they had more pressing matters at hand. A young boy in need of his father, for starters.

Hozark completed his meandering circuit of the park space and headed back to the ship. The others would likely be finished with their excursion by now. Much as they all enjoyed exploring the marketplaces on different worlds, Drambal's offerings were rather slim.

He knew his assumption was correct when he heard the voices of his crewmates coming from the galley when he entered the ship. All were back, it seemed, and having a rather lively conversation.

"Hey, you want some sweet tea cakes?" Henni asked as he strode into the galley.

"Oh, so *now* you share?" Bud griped.

"You have your own stuff," she shot back. "But Hozark didn't get any. It's only fair."

"Thank you, Henni," Hozark said, politely accepting one of the small pastries.

"So, did you have any luck with whatever it was you were doing?" Laskar asked.

"Yes and no. I reached out to an old associate who still has some contacts with eyes and ears in places the order's spies do not regularly frequent."

"Did he know where my dad is?" Hap asked.

"I am sorry, young Jinnik, but he did not."

"So, it's more of what we've been hearing all along," Bud said. "Looks like the guy's always on the move and tough to pin down."

"Indeed. And word of his actions seem to be corroborated."

"What's he doing?" Laskar asked.

"Just your usual stuff. You know, conquering worlds. Crushing rebellions rising up against the Council of Twenty. Killing a bunch and enslaving more," Bud interjected.

Demelza glanced at Hap, then flashed Bud a look.

"What?" he asked. "The kid's going to know sooner or later. Better to hear it from friends. But anyway, I reached out to my old buddies, like I said, and asked them to put some feelers out. See if they might be able to pick up some information from the whisper network."

"You think that'll work?" Henni asked.

"Well, they said to stop off at Urgus in a day or two and they'd relay what they found, if anything. Can't hurt to try, right?"

"That's a bit of a trek, though," Laskar noted. "You sure they'll be able to get something?"

"You got anything better to do?"

"Valid point," the copilot said with a chuckle. "Okay, if no one has any objections, then, I'll plot us a course for Urgus. Hozark, you cool with that?"

The Wampeh nodded once. "At this point, any potential leads are worth investigating."

"All right, then," he said. "Hey, and while we were in town, I did reach out to some old friends as well, just in case. I figured you never know when maybe someone might have seen or heard something. Maybe we'll get lucky."

Hozark nodded. "Thank you, Laskar. Every bit of help in this is appreciated."

Hap's spirits were clearly lowered by the news of not only his father's continued disappearance, but now also by knowing what he had been doing all this time.

"Why would he help the Council?" the boy asked. "He can't stand them. He's always going on about how they stick their noses into other people's business where they don't belong."

Demelza slid closer to the boy. "You see, Hap, your father is a very powerful visla. And right now, he does not know that you are safe with us. As a result, he is doing all of those things they ask of him because he believes *they* will keep you safe. Rest assured, he is not some monster out to conquer worlds. He is a caring father who is worried about his son more than anything, and he is doing whatever he must to ensure your safe return."

It wasn't exactly a pep talk, but, despite his young age, Hap understood how his father's powers sometimes made people act around him. Always wanting favors and the like. So this, in its own strange way, actually made sense.

"Hey, I'll tell ya what," Bud said, hopping up to his feet. "Why don't you come with me to the command center, and I'll show you how to *properly* use a Drookonus? Would you like that?"

Hap seemed to perk up a bit, albeit slightly.

"I guess that'd be nice. My dad used to show me stuff when we'd take trips, but he always had his staff doing the flying."

"Well, it's time to learn," Bud replied. "It's a useful skill to know. But you've gotta promise me you won't go running off again. Deal?"

"Deal."

"Great. And I have an idea. Maybe, if you are really, really careful, I'll even let you take the ship up out of the atmosphere from here. What do you say?"

"You want to let him take off in a crowded city?" Laskar asked.

"Everyone is pretty well spaced out. There's plenty of room. And I'll be there with him. Besides, we already know he can launch," Bud said with a chuckle, referring to Hap's recent adventure stealing one of the smaller shuttle craft and heading off into space.

Of course, he was then captured by pirates and nearly sold off to the Council of Twenty, but that part of the story was nowhere near as fun to tell.

"What about how to jump? Will you teach me that too?" the boy asked their copilot.

"That's a bit more complicated," Laskar replied. "You'll need to wait to learn that bit. For now, just focus on regular old flying."

"Come on, Hap. Let's take her airborne," Bud said, leading the way to the command center.

"Thanks, Bud. This'll be fun."

"My pleasure, Hap. Hopefully we'll find your dad soon. Then you can have him teach you all the really cool stuff a visla knows. But for now, it's flight lesson time."

The pair stepped into command a few moments later and settled into their seats.

"You ready?"

"Ready."

"Okay, show me how you activate the Drookonus."

Hap cast the spell without hesitation. It wasn't the most perfect casting Bud had ever witnessed, but it was far better than he'd anticipated. The boy had potential, he had to admit.

"Nicely done," he said. "All right, now. Let's take her up and head out of the atmosphere."

Hap carefully cast once more, and the ship pivoted, then, with only a few jerks, it made its way up into the black.

## CHAPTER NINE

The smell of acrid smoke hung in the dimly lit air, and the sharp tang of molten metal wafted across the spacious chamber, imbuing everything within it with a lingering stink.

Crates were stacked against the far wall. Not many, but their contents were steadily growing as the green-and-black-skinned metalsmiths churned out more konuses and slaaps from their forges.

They were a particularly nasty race, one with a penchant for strife and violence, but they did know how to craft weapons. And their metalsmithing was undeniably of a high quality.

They had worked in the secret facility for some time now, but unlike previous months, they were now producing their wares at a greatly increased rate, and with good reason. The metal workers had been idle for far too long awaiting a new magic source to power their weapons, but, at long last, one had finally been delivered.

The control-collared man had been so incredibly strong when he first arrived. Scary strong. Power actually crackled off his skin in waves when his anger flared. It was unlike anything any of them had ever seen before.

How he had come to be in their possession, filling their magical weapons with his power one after another, was something of a mystery to the workers. But they were not about to look a gift Malooki in the mouth, and they made quick time putting his power to use.

Visla Jinnik had killed for the Council. Crushed their enemies. Enslaved them. But this? This was something different. To be creating such a cache of weapons, there was something far more afoot than was being let on.

On top of that, these weaponsmiths were not the usual Council of Twenty laborers. These were off-book thugs for hire. Someone on the Council was in charge, that much was clear, but it was a well-kept secret. Who, and why, for that matter, was a mystery.

Visla Jinnik had been angry when they first brought him to this place. And that anger produced a sizable outflowing of power the weaponsmiths were able to harness into a batch of freshly forged konuses. The metal had not even fully cooled when they directed his carelessly spilled magic into them with their arcane spells.

It had been an incredibly visceral tug Jinnik felt when they harnessed that power. As if a part of him was being pulled free from the inside. Of course, he had powered devices in the past, as did pretty much all power users, but this was different. This felt like a violation.

"Thank you for that," the Tslavar guard overseeing the workers said. "Makes their work easier."

"Is this what you would have of me now?" he asked. "Pouring my power into weapons for the Council?"

"Not my place to ask," the man replied. "Nor is it yours. It's just for us to do as we're told."

"I am a *visla*," he reminded the man.

"And yet you wear a control collar. Trust me, it will be far easier on you if you just go with the plan and do as you're told."

"And that would be charging these konuses?"

"For now, yes."

"It is distasteful, creating weapons."

"From what I hear, you've got no problem laying waste to entire populations if need be."

"That was different."

The Tslavar guard snickered. "Sure, keep telling yourself that. So long as you do what's expected of you, you can believe whatever you want."

It had gone on like that for a while. Jinnik restrained, reluctantly powering batch after batch of new weapons. The drain was significant, and while his magic replenished itself during his rest periods in his cell, he was nevertheless in a state of perpetually reduced strength.

When he had first arrived, he even thought he might hope to break the powerful control collar restraining him. His magic had sufficiently recovered during the long flight to their new location that it might have been possible.

But they had his boy, and his compliance was the one thing keeping the child safe. So he did as he was told, pouring his energy into the hot metal as the new konuses came from the forges.

It only took a few days before he began to feel his power diminish to the point he was unable to recover fully before his next session with the metalsmiths. And that, he realized, was by design. Even if he wanted to break free, he was now simply unable to. The Council was using him, draining him for their own terrible goals.

But after all he had done, all the death and slavery at his hands, he had finally had enough.

When the Tslavar guard brought him from his cell to power up a new batch of weapons, Visla Jinnik was slow in moving. When he was directed to charge the newest devices, he did so, but at a fraction of his potential.

"Oy. You hard of hearing?" the guard asked.

"Why all of this?" he asked. "What does the Council have planned that requires so much bloodshed? For what purpose do they mean to use my power against innocents?"

The guard looked at him askew with a sneer. "None of that's for you to worry about. Not if you want to see your boy again."

Jinnik abruptly stopped charging the devices. Despite his weakened state, a faint crackle of power rippled across his skin, but just for a moment.

"Prove to me my son is alive."

"You'll best be stoppin' this foolishness and gettin' back to work," the guard replied.

"Prove my son is alive," he said, his firm gaze as cold as ice.

The Tslavar uttered the words activating his collar's shock spell. Jinnik winced at the pain and fell to his knees, gasping for breath when the jolting pain finally ceased.

"Now, back to work," the Tslavar said.

Jinnik slowly rose back to his feet, then took a deep breath and stood tall.

"Prove to me my son is alive."

The guard shook his head. Then he cast and dropped the visla to the ground again. Jinnik looked up at him with watering eyes and pushed himself back to his feet.

"You can torture me all you want."

"Don't tempt me."

"*But* I will make it unbearably difficult for you," Jinnik added. "And what will happen then, hmm? You will fall behind schedule, no doubt. And I have a feeling you would not want to upset your employer, now, would you?"

The guard hesitated, the stun spell on the tip of his tongue. Jinnik saw and knew his ploy had worked. There was fear in the man's eyes at the thought of displeasing his superiors, whoever they may be. He didn't know who was running this show, but whoever it was, this man obviously feared him, and significantly at that.

Gears were spinning in the Tslavar's head as he struggled to find a way to compel the suddenly recalcitrant visla to comply. Ultimately, he realized there was simply no other choice.

"You will keep working," he said. "And we will provide you with your proof. But it will take time. Your boy is not close."

Jinnik's hard gaze softened slightly. "You will prove he is all right?"

"We will. But you've gotta do your work in the meantime. Do we have an arrangement?"

The visla slowly nodded. "Very well. I will continue, for now, but at a somewhat slower pace. You will be able to massage your progress results to meet your employer's expectations. For now. But that will only work for so long. Consider that your motivation to be timely in your efforts. Provide proof that my son is safe, or you fall behind schedule."

"I'll see to it," the guard said. "Now, keep your end of the bargain and get to work."

Jinnik walked to the work area and slowly pushed his power into the orange-hot konuses as they were presented to him one by one. The guard left him to his labors and hurried to his private office space, where a long-range skree was kept in case of emergency.

This, he thought, if anything, constituted one, as he reached out to his distant contacts to report in. This could become a problem of epic proportions.

## CHAPTER TEN

Bud seemed a little bit anxious as they made the jumps to Urgus. Hozark supposed he had a good reason to be. He hadn't seen Lalaynia and his other pirate friends since the utter clusterfuck of a Council blockade at Drommus.

They had survived, he knew full well, and had given the Council ships and their mercenary lackeys one hell of a good fight before driving them off, but the price had been steep. A lot of good men and women died that day, and no matter if it had been for a just cause, it would be difficult to look their friends in the eye.

Of course, the pirates willingly took that sort of risk as a part of the job. A hazard of their lifestyle. But that occasion was no simple raid and pillage operation. It was all because the Council had come looking for a fight. They had come for Happizano and were willing to engage any who might stand in their way.

Unfortunately for them, that was an entire fleet of pirates ready and willing to fight to the death to protect their own. And they'd done so with great vigor.

"We almost there?" Hap asked as Laskar plotted in their next jump.

"Kid, are you really doing the 'are we there yet' thing?" the copilot asked.

"It's just, we've been jumping for a while now."

Bud leaned over from his captain's chair. "Because we're taking the safe route, is all," he said. "There's been a lot of unusual stuff going on lately, and we're just being a little extra cautious this time around."

"Yeah. Last time we met up with these guys, we wound up in a Council crossfire," Laskar added.

"To be fair, that was almost certainly the doing of Captain Darvin when he reached out to inquire about what to do with the boy," Demelza noted. "Regardless, it is agreed. A modicum of safety in our approach makes quite a good deal of sense."

"So, that was just a really long way of saying we're not there yet," Hap grumbled. "Fine. I'm gonna go get a snack."

He marched out of command, leaving the amused trio to their own devices.

"The kid's like Henni. Non-stop eating," Bud said.

"Yes, but *he* is growing," Demelza noted.

"True. Henni's got no excuse other than a metabolism that burns like a frickin' sun. I swear, since she's been aboard, she's put away more food than I thought possible for someone her size."

Demelza grinned. "Perhaps. But she most certainly does have the energy to burn it off."

"True," Bud replied. "Now, as for the kid's question, what do we have left, Laskar? Two more jumps?"

The copilot checked his star charts. "Yep. One more after this and we'll be in the right system."

"Perfect. Plot us for a long approach in. I want to give them plenty of time to see us coming after what happened on Drommus."

"You got it," Laskar said, tweaking their jump course ever so slightly.

. . .

Urgus was just a gleaming blue-green orb in the distance when they exited their jump into its system. The warm, yellow sun at its center cast a relaxing, cheerful glow upon the world, keeping it temperate and pleasant most of the year round.

It was a moderately lush planet, though one not possessing much in the way of industry or agriculture. A rather simple world and one that only possessed a handful of cities large enough to be worth visiting.

"Seems like a pretty boring place," Laskar mused as they drew closer. "Not much going on there at all."

"More importantly, no Council ships anywhere near," Bud said. "I'll take us down. They'll be expecting us."

"Down where? I don't see any pirate ships down there."

"Trust me," the pilot said with a grin, then began the descent through the atmosphere.

The city was ahead, a rather drab and squat settlement that spread out wide rather than climbing high. No sense in using good magic to support tall structures when there was so much land around on which to build. But Uzabud was veering away from it, heading toward a group of small lakes nearby.

"Uh, Bud?" Laskar said.

"What is it?"

"The city's over there."

"Uh-huh."

"And we're going the wrong way."

Bud flashed an amused grin. "Trust me."

He flew down low, close along the shoreline of the smallest of the bodies of water.

"Bud?" Laskar said uncomfortably as they dropped toward the surface.

"Jeez, what?"

"We don't have the magic to fly underwater."

"I told you, *relax*. I've got this."

Hozark walked into the command chamber to observe their approach. "Ah, a marvelous-looking world. They are well aware of our arrival, I assume?"

"Yeah, they know we're here."

"Who? There's no one here, and you're about to splash us down in the middle of a damn lake!"

"Ye of little faith," the pilot said, then dipped them right toward the water.

The surface shimmered and splashed as they passed through the thin layer of magically suspended water and pushed beyond the force spell beneath it. A moment later, they found themselves inside a vast underground landing chamber.

"Holy shit," Laskar gasped. "A hidden dock."

"Told ya not to worry," Bud chuckled.

Henni came bounding in to join them, Hap in tow. "Wow! Look at all those ships!"

She was not exaggerating. The secret hideout was chock-full of pirate ships. And there were other vessels there. A fair number of smugglers and other ne'er-do-wells had taken up refuge there as well. An underground community of men and women of adventure and mischief, and utterly hidden beneath the surface of the seemingly boring world.

Just as they wanted it to be.

Bud steered them toward the empty berth waiting for them beside Lalaynia's massive pirate craft and set down. There were a good amount of his former crewmates milling about, waiting to greet their friend.

"Bud! Good to see you made it in one piece!" said a jovial man with a golden sheen to his skin and a full head of deep-blue dreadlocked hair.

"Askus! Glad you kept all of your limbs intact," Bud shot back, warmly embracing the man.

"That was some hairy shit back at Drommus. I don't know

what you did to piss off the Council, but damn, if that wasn't a good fight."

"We weren't looking for one, though," Bud replied. "Where's the captain?"

"Right behind you, Bud," Lalaynia said, the tall woman striding right through the parting crowd. "You're looking well."

"You too, Cap. Glad you didn't take too much hurt in all that mess."

"We got a fair share of booty from the Council ships we disabled. More than enough to make it worth our while. Plus, the Council just earned themselves a very high spot on the pirate shit list for pulling that little stunt. Attacking at Drommus? They know better."

"And they've been reminded. Most violently," Askus added.

Lalaynia chuckled. "Come on. The other captains are waiting for us."

The group fell in behind her as she led the way. "Good to see the rest of your crew are well. And this must be the kid we all heard so much about."

"His name is Happizano," Hozark said. "And he is very thankful for your assistance in his recovery."

"Pleased to meet you, Happizano," she said. "Glad you are with us."

"Me too," the boy said. "And you can call me Hap, if you want."

"Very well, Hap. Welcome to Urgus."

"Thanks," he replied. "Hey, can I ask you a question?"

"Of course," the Valkyrie-like pirate replied with a grin.

"Do you guys have anything to eat?"

# CHAPTER ELEVEN

The walk through the hidden pirate bay was uneventful, for the most part. Bud was met with friendly smiles and greetings of good cheer, though one or two people did appear to hold a grudge of some sort. And for a moment, it even looked like they might be foolish enough to try to start something.

A little smile from Hozark, his fangs clearly visible, was more than enough to give them second thoughts.

The men and women in the underground hideaway were out in force, enjoying themselves during their bit of shore leave. Of course, there was a thriving gambling, drinking, and sexing industry in this den of iniquity. But there were other things to do as well. And one of them caught Henni's eye as they passed.

A makeshift arena had been set up, no more than fifteen feet across. Within it, two shirtless men were having at it with bare fists. One was a beast of a man, his defined musculature partly obscured by his incredible amount of dark maroon body hair.

The other was a far leaner fellow with close-cropped silver stubble on his head. His own variety of hair was closer to wire, they noted, and every time he would get close enough to headbutt his opponent, new pinpricks of blood would well up on the larger man.

The two circled one another like a pair of very different apex predators deciding who was going to be king of the hill. Both were men of violence and action, and neither was going to back down one inch. Tough and confident, the both of them, just as pirates should be.

Fists and elbows flew as the men clashed once more, the sound of the impacts a series of resounding, heavy thuds that could be heard over the roar of the crowd.

"That's awesome!" Henni gushed as she veered toward the violent display.

"Hey, not now. We're expected," Bud said, pulling her along by a fistful of her clothing.

"But it looks like so much fun," she said.

A pair of female pirates warming up on the periphery caught her attention. Her eyes sparkled as she looked up at Bud. He already knew where she was going with this.

"Yes, you can try it out if you like. But no knives. And only after we meet with the others, okay? We're supposed to be joining them for a little meal."

"But I'm not hungry," Henni said, clearly eager for her chance to jump into the fray.

"You're not hungry? When are you ever not hungry?"

Lalaynia had been listening to the exchange with great amusement. She'd seen the girl fight on Drommus and had been quite impressed with both her aggression as well as her prowess. Sure, her skills needed a little refinement––a lot, if you were being honest about it––but what she lacked in formal training, the deceptively small woman more than made up for in gumption.

"Oh, let her play, Bud," she said. "It's not like anyone will mind if your friend doesn't join us for this confab."

Henni's eyes positively lit up at the pirate captain's words. She spun and looked at Bud with an eager gaze.

"Oh, all right. Go have fun. But remember, no stabbing, and no killing. This is recreational fighting, ya dig?"

"Okay!" she replied with a giddy chirp and was gone in a flash.

"You know we're gonna have to clean up after her, right?" Laskar said quietly.

"Yeah, most likely," Bud replied.

The group rounded a corner and came upon a large tent erected beside a rather battle-scarred ship. From within, the smell of roasted meats, grilled vegetables, and slow-cooked soups wafted out to greet them.

Lalaynia smiled at her guests. "We had enough of a heads-up that you were coming to allow us to put together a little feast, of sorts. I hope you enjoy it."

They entered the tent, where six other captains were awaiting them. They rose to greet them with warm welcoming hugs and hearty claps on the back.

"Oh, that was quite a good show at Drommus," a stout man with a dense, black beard said. "Haven't had that much fun since we raided the vineyards at Mirafar, eh, Parmus?"

"That's for sure," the other captain replied with a jovial laugh, the small tentacles dangling from his jaw wiggling as he did. "And it reminded the Council very clearly why they do not meddle with Drommus. Honestly, it's amazing they even tried."

"I am afraid that was our fault, in a way," Hozark said.

"You're the Wampeh behind all this?"

"Yes. My name is Hozark, of the Wampeh Ghalian."

"Oh, we know who you are. Something of a legend, if I do say so myself. A pleasure to meet you, Hozark."

"Likewise."

"And we know about the boy here being targeted by the

Council. Believe you me, there are some things we all find distasteful, and abusing children is one of them."

"In any case, your assistance was greatly appreciated," the Wampeh replied.

"Any friend of Lalaynia's is a friend of ours. And besides, we got some pretty good salvage out of it. The Council ships had some choice goodies on board, and what we were able to scrape from Darvin's wreck wasn't bad. For an Outlander, that is."

"Agreed," Lalaynia said. "Now, come. Let's eat while we talk, shall we? I know I for one am famished."

Bud looked over the spread appreciatively as he took his seat. "Oh, Henni's gonna be sad she missed this."

"We can pack up a container for her," Lalaynia said. "Now, we have much to discuss. You requested information on the boy's father. All of us have reached out to our networks to see what we might uncover for you in this regard. I have to tell you, the information we have heard back is not good."

"You're talking about the mass slaughter and enslavement, right?"

"Yes, Bud. It seems Jinnik is making something of a name for himself, tearing across the galaxy as he is."

"Under duress," Hozark noted. "He does what he does to protect his son."

"I understand that," she replied. "But that doesn't do anything to put the men and women affected by his actions at ease. Thousands enslaved. Far more under Council control."

"All of which would have been avoidable if we merely knew where Jinnik was to reunite him with his son. Once that is no longer being held over his head, he will no longer be under the Council's sway," Hozark said.

"And we are looking for him. But it appears as though he has straight up vanished without a trace. For one as notorious as he has become in so short a time, that's no simple trick."

Demelza piled her plate with food and took a seat beside

Hozark. "And this is why we must do all we can to locate him before he is forced to act again," she said.

Lalaynia began helping herself to the feast as well. "To that end, our people are working as hard as they are able. If he's out there, we'll find him."

The group ate and discussed the various rumors that had been floating around regarding the visla. It looked as though he had indeed made quite an impact on some peripheral Council affairs. But these were not main Council issues, and it seemed his actions were not driven by the main body itself.

Someone, or someones, within the Council were making moves, and they all had theories.

The discussion was lively, and the pirate captains each had their own particular flavor to bring to the conversation, but as they were in a tent, the sounds from the outside occasionally filtered in. By the time they had finished their meal, the roar of a crowd going wild was plain to hear.

"What in the worlds is that?" Bud asked.

Lalaynia grinned, knowingly. "Likely the fights. My guess is your friend is making quite a show of it."

"Oh, boy. We'd better check on her before she gets herself into some serious trouble."

"Can I come?" Hap asked. "I wanna see!"

"Oh, all right. Come on," Lalaynia said.

"I shall accompany you," Demelza said, rising to join them.

The three walked quickly toward the sounds of cheering spectators.

"Sounds like quite a lively bunch," Bud noted.

"More than usual, I'd wager," Lalaynia said as they reached the edge of the crowd. "Make a hole," she said, pushing through the group of spectators.

What they saw when they reached the fighting ring was shocking. Henni was there, of course, sweaty and grinning from ear to ear. But the pirate in the ring with her was not a woman.

Judging by the bruised and beaten female contenders on the sidelines, she'd already worked her way through all of them. Now she had moved on to taking on the men. And she was actually making a good showing of it.

The man she was fighting was significantly larger than she was, but her blows were landing with notable force.

Demelza nudged Hap. "Do you see? She is using the techniques I taught you."

Henni threw punches, driving with her hips and trying to punch *through* the much bigger man. The impacts were startlingly crisp, and the man was actually flinching from the tiny woman's bombardment.

The crowd was going wild every time she landed a solid shot, and again every time the man missed an opportunity. It was clearly getting to him, being shown up by a woman, and a small one at that. In a rush, he forewent the typical choice of attacking with feet or hands, opting instead to tackle the small woman in a rush, pinning her to the ground.

She fought like a dervish as the man's weight pressed down on her. He was attempting to get in position to deliver a winning blow, but she was so quick and slippery that he couldn't quite get in place. Henni, for her part, was now fighting on a purely visceral level, it seemed.

"We need to stop this," Bud said, seeing how she was moving, the panicked way she had begun to fight as she was pinned under the man's bulk. "She's not okay with this."

"I agree," Lalaynia said.

They were about to step in and stop the fight when Henni let loose a shrill cry and drove both of her fists into the man atop her abdomen. He was blasted clear, flying back a good fifteen feet before hitting the ground with a pained thud.

The crowd abruptly went silent.

Slowly, Henni climbed to her feet and dusted herself off, her eyes sparkling more than usual, and dangerously at that. She noted the abrupt silence and looked at the crowd, suddenly self-conscious. They were staring.

She had just performed a most unusual bit of magic. And she was not wearing a konus.

"Uh," she said, looking at her hands, confused and embarrassed. Then she turned and ran off.

Lalaynia looked at Bud with a curious stare. "So, what exactly is the deal with your friend, again, Bud?" she asked.

Bud just stood there, mouth slightly agape as he marveled at what he'd just seen. "I really don't know," he said. "I honestly don't."

## CHAPTER TWELVE

It took only a brief search to find where Henni had gone after she raced off following her unusual display of magic. She could have gone anywhere, but, Demelza reasoned, given her previous experiences on the streets, and the relatively comfortable existence she had come to know since joining her new friends, her room on their ship was her most likely destination.

Henni hadn't wanted to talk. Not at first, anyway. But once she had showered off the sweat and blood from the fights, she began feeling a bit more open to discussion. She was still a bit skittish, though, so her friends decided to wait until she had eaten something.

After the display she'd put on, the young woman was utterly famished, and she absolutely powered through the sizable container of food the others had set aside for her with gusto.

While she ate, Demelza pulled Hozark aside to speak with him privately.

"She used power, Master Hozark. And she did so without even realizing she was doing so."

"The trigger?"

"A panic of sorts. She was pinned down."

"Given her experiences on the rather rough streets of Groll, I can only imagine what memories that must have brought forth."

"Yes," Demelza said. "She undoubtedly endured much, both as a slave, and later living in squalor on the streets, as she did. But now she is well-fed and healthy, and her energy has returned."

"And her power, it seems. It appears our initial assessment of her was correct, then. She *does* possess a degree of magic within her. But, apparently, with absolutely no connection to it, or control over it."

"What should we tell the others? Happizano and Bud both witnessed the event. Only yourself and Laskar were not present."

Hozark pondered a moment. "I think we play this off as just a fluke reaction. We all know there is some sort of power within her. Let us not make her overly concerned about it until we are in a position to properly assess her true skills."

"We downplay it as a minor bit of magic that happened to spill out. Laskar possesses a modicum of power, so I'm sure he'll understand the occasional uncontrolled burst," Demelza mused.

"Exactly. And once we are back with Corann, we shall see about discovering more about our unusual friend's true background. And her true potential."

The two Wampeh rejoined the others at their table. Hap was busy regaling them with tales of Henni's display while the woman ate.

"It was so cool! She was all, 'Bam!' hitting the guy, then she punched him, just like Demelza showed us."

"It was just a fight, nothing more," Henni said through her full mouth.

"Yeah, let's just let her eat," Bud said, noting the look in her eyes.

"But what about the magic? It was awesome! Like, my dad sometimes does that, where stuff just happens, you know?"

"It was simply an unusual surge of power that had been building within Henni since she joined us," Hozark said. "All of the nutrition from the food she has been putting away allowed her system to generate a bit of magic, is all."

"Really? You think that's all it was?" Hap asked, a bit disappointed.

"I would wager on it, young Jinnik," Hozark said, flashing a little look to Demelza.

"Happizano?"

"Yeah, Demelza?"

"I was thinking. Perhaps, now that you have seen some more of these techniques in action, might you be up to practicing a bit?"

Hap perked right up. "Will Henni come too?"

Demelza turned to the little woman. "Well? Would you care to join us?"

Henni stopped eating for a moment. "I don't know. I don't want to hurt anyone."

"Do not fear. I am sure that was a fluke occurrence. And the act of slow and conscious practice might even help you regain your center."

The violet-haired woman thought on it a long moment as she chewed another mouthful. "I guess," she finally said. "But lemme finish this first."

"Of course."

In short order, Henni polished off the entire contents of the container, plus a few items from the ship's stores for good measure, then headed off to join Demelza and Hap in their makeshift training compartment.

"Quite a day," Bud said. "I'm just sorry we're not any closer to figuring out where the kid's father is."

Laskar shifted in his seat. "Well, I didn't want to say anything until I was able to confirm it, but I reached out to a few friends from the old days."

"When did you have time?" Hozark asked.

"When Bud tracked down that long-range skree to call Lalaynia."

Bud eyed him curiously. "You did?"

"Yeah. When you were finished, I made a quick call. Anyway, I got a hold of a long-range skree when we were heading back to the ship after Henni's fight, and reached out to a them again to see what they'd heard. I figured, with everyone else on the lookout, it couldn't hurt to have my guys looking too."

"And?" Bud asked.

"And it may be nothing, but one of them said there were some rumors of Visla Jinnik being holed up in a Council holding area just outside of Flammis. You know the place, right? The capital city on Lordzal."

Hozark pondered what he had been told. "Interesting the Ghalian spies did not hear of this first. That is a commonly frequented world."

"Hey, sometimes these things happen. Right place, right time," Laskar said.

Hozark mused the intel report. "Interesting."

"Seriously," Bud agreed. "I'll have Lalaynia check with her network. She can skree them straightaway. If there's chatter there, they'll pick it up in no time."

"And I will reach out to the Ghalian spies as well," Hozark said, rising to head for his ship. "I will return shortly."

"No skree?" Laskar asked.

"We do not use them unless absolutely necessary," he replied. "Do not worry, there is a spy nest relatively nearby. We should have an answer from them by morning."

With that, Hozark headed out, taking his shimmer ship and jumping away to make the face-to-face contact that his kind preferred. Lordzal was not too far away, and the spy network could make their inquiries and get him results in no time.

Bud checked with Lalaynia, but her pirate network had only

heard the slightest of chatter about *someone* being held in the Council facility on Lordzal. Still, it was looking as though the facility was in use.

Hozark returned the following morning before Hap had risen. He was becoming a bit of a deep sleeper following Demelza's training sessions. Something most would be, considering her demanding regimen.

"I have news," he told the others. "The Ghalian spies do not have hard proof, but there are indeed whispers of Visla Jinnik being held on Lordzal."

"That's great news! I'll set a course," Laskar said.

"Not so fast," Hozark said. "We must not get the boy's hopes up. He has gone through a lot, and this could very well prove to be no more than a rumor. We will keep him close, in case this proves to be an accurate report, but until it is confirmed, we shall tell him we are simply surveying another planet."

"Seems like a reasonable precaution," Bud said. "So what do we do?"

"We land and make it seem as though we are just another vessel stopping over to shop the marketplaces and acquire provisions. While you and the others do so, Demelza and I shall make our survey of the facility in which the visla is allegedly being held."

"Sounds like a plan. So, when do we start?" Bud asked.

"We start now."

"Oh. Shit. Uh, come on, Laskar, let's get that course plotted and get a move-on."

"Right behind you," his copilot said.

Just a few hours later they arrived at the relatively tranquil world and descended to the landing zone within the city. Hozark and Demelza were first off the ship, invisible under cover of their shimmer cloaks. The others stepped off a moment later and headed toward the commerce area to do a bit of innocuous shopping.

As the others casually browsed the stalls in the marketplace, the two Wampeh made quick time to the outskirts of the city. As had been reported, there was a definite Tslavar presence at the Council facility. It wasn't much to look at as far as buildings went. Just a simple agricultural center for storage and shipping. But, as the assassins knew all too well, looks could be deceiving.

"This appears to be the facility," Hozark said from beneath his shimmer cloak. "Let us proceed."

Quietly, without a trace, the two Ghalian killers made their way closer. If things went as they hoped, young Happizano would soon be reunited with his father. But first, they had to get inside. And things were never as easy as they seemed.

## CHAPTER THIRTEEN

Bud thought their part of the plan was by far the most pleasant. While the two assassins were skulking around, possibly encountering Tslavars, booby traps, and all other manner of nasty things, he and the other members of the shopping entourage were actually having quite a nice afternoon.

It was pleasant out, with just a light breeze and warm skies. The smells of the different vendors' stalls and carts wafted through the air, lending the whole affair a rather festive and homey feel.

Laskar found himself quite taken with the colognes one of the stalls had on display. The natural aromas of the local flora had been enhanced and intensified by a rather novel application of botanical magic.

"Really, Laskar?" Bud chided. "You think you're a society fella all of a sudden?"

"You don't have to be wealthy to like to smell good," he replied. "Maybe you should try it sometime."

"I smell *wonderful*, my friend."

"Sure thing, Bud," Laskar said with a laugh. "Sure thing."

Hap was also having a fantastic time perusing all of the wares to be found on this novel planet. Hozark had given him some coin before he and Demelza had headed out on their errand so he could pick up a thing or two as a treat.

He was vacillating between some pastry and perhaps a few faintly magical toys when a young boy not much older than himself approached the group carrying a large tray hung around his neck with a strap. There was an assortment of glistening, red balls, no larger than a tangerine, lining the tray.

"Mora drops?" he asked, offering his wares.

"What are they?" Hap asked, having never seen the unusual sweet before.

"Oh, you're not from around here."

"No, we're just stopping off to look around a bit," Hap said.

"Well, here. Try one for free. It's a local specialty."

"Really?"

"Sure," the boy said with a warm smile.

"Thanks," Hap said, picking up one of the balls and taking a bite.

A powdery puff escaped his mouth as the flavors were magically engaged once the protective candy shell had been broken. Hap's eyes went wide as the taste shifted and evolved on his tongue.

"These are amazing!"

"Thanks. Everyone around here loves them. They're a traditional after-school snack. You want more of them?"

"Yeah, definitely. How much are they?"

The adults watched with silent amusement as the two juveniles negotiated a price for a fairly large box of the unusual treat.

"Thanks again!" Hap said as the boy moved on to continue selling his wares.

"My pleasure. Enjoy!" he replied.

Bud watched the youngster make his way through the crowd, a smile on his face as he greeted everyone in his path.

"Man, there are some really nice people in this place," he said. "It's a welcome change from what we've been up against lately."

The others nodded. It had been a bit of a tough road of late, and a little common courtesy really went a long way for the weary travelers.

"So, whatcha got there, Hap?" Laskar asked Hap.

"Really good candy. You want to try one?"

"I'd love to. Thanks."

Laskar plucked one of the balls from the container and studied it a moment, then took a bite of the sweet. His eyes went wide, and he had pretty much the same reaction that Hap had.

"Guys, you've *gotta* try these."

Henni and Bud looked at one another and shrugged. No one had to twist their arms when it came to food, that was for sure.

"Oh, wow. We need to find that kid and buy up the rest of these," Bud said. "They're are amazing."

"A local specialty," Hap said with a grin as he popped the rest of his in his mouth.

Henni enjoyed the sweet as well, though a clothing vendor's goods had just caught her eye. She made a quick detour across the stalls to better examine the colorful attire, the others following behind.

"You should try it on," Bud said. "That'd actually look good on you."

"I don't know," she hesitated, judging the garment. "Excuse me," she asked the vendor. "Does this come with sheaths for these?" she asked, flashing her daggers.

"Jeez, Henni, please. Don't go waving those things around," Bud said.

"What? I was just asking a relevant question."

"Yeah, while waving your knives around."

The vendor looked at her with a slightly amused grin. "Yes, dear, I can add sheaths to it, no problem."

"Really?"

"Of course. I make all of the alterations myself, right here."

"That's fantastic. But how long would it be before they'd be ready?"

"Come back in a half hour. It'll be done by then."

Whatever hesitation Henni may have been experiencing disappeared in an instant. She dug in her pocket and paid the woman up front with a broad grin.

"See ya in a half hour!"

Bud fell in beside her as she flitted off among the other stalls nearby.

"You don't have any coin," he said in a hushed voice.

"Not before we landed. I do now," she replied.

"Henni, you can't pickpocket here."

"Says who?"

"Says me. And Hozark, for that matter," Bud said with a frustrated sigh. "Look, you can still pickpocket, just don't do it anywhere we have to stay incognito, okay? We can't afford to have a big commotion when we're supposed to go unnoticed."

"Don't be so boring, Bud," she shot back.

"Boring?"

"Yes. Boring."

"You're calling me boring."

"Yep."

"I'm a pirate, Henni. We are most definitely *not* boring."

"Uh-huh," she said with a sarcastic grin, then headed off to join Hap at a nearby pen full of small, fluffy creatures the likes of which he'd never seen before.

"Ooh, look at them. They're so cute!" she gushed, leaning in and scratching the nearest one behind the ears.

Laskar elbowed Bud and shared an amused look with his

friend. "That is one strange girl," he said. "Like, I'm talking legit mad, that one."

"You're telling me?" he replied. "I mean, knives one minute, then fluffy critters the next. The woman is a total dichotomy."

"And she's living on our ship."

"I know," Bud groaned exaggeratedly. "Heavens help us."

## CHAPTER FOURTEEN

While a group of apparently innocuous visitors were shopping in the marketplace, picking up knicknacks and sweet and savory treats, a pair of pale assassins were silently making their way around the perimeter of the Council agricultural facility at the outskirts of town.

It seemed normal enough. A simple, industrial structure with no overt mercenary presence. But upon closer inspection from within their shimmer cloaks, the two Wampeh Ghalian noted a few inconsistencies with the building's alleged use.

For one, the footprint seemed a bit large for the purpose it was intended for. As if a slightly smaller structure had been built atop something somewhat larger. And on top of that, several of the workers appeared to be sporting weaponry within their work attire.

Not exactly normal for simple agriculture workers. And especially telling, given the alleged true nature of the building.

Communicating in hushed whispers, Hozark and Demelza made a circuit of the entire building. Front and rear entrances seemed to be the main ingress and egress points, but several access points dotted the facility all the way around. It was, for all intents and purposes, a fully functional and completely normal agricultural facility.

But the best hiding places were often in plain sight. Something the assassins knew all too well.

Hozark quickly scouted a small granary adjacent the main building.

"It will suffice," he whispered to the seemingly empty air where Demelza was waiting for him.

The two slipped inside the granary and removed their shimmer cloaks. Immediately, they applied the special Ghalian spells to alter their appearances, making them appear just like the other workers who were milling about the area.

Each grabbed a few sacks of grain and hefted them to their shoulders. It seemed floating conveyances were in short supply, and they had noticed many workers carrying their loads by hand. Not the most efficient method, but a magic-conserving one, no doubt.

The two disguised Ghalian fell in a little bit behind another worker carrying a load and slipped into the facility in his wake, passing the secret guards easily in the process. The security was fair, but nowhere near the levels they would expect for a facility holding a powerful visla against his will.

But not all was as it seemed, and if Hozark's hunch about the facility was correct, this entire operation was simply a cover, quite literally, for the real Council affairs taking place below their feet.

They walked to the depository area and unloaded their burdens, stacking their bags neatly with the others. They then casually changed direction, moving toward a more central part of the facility.

"Do you sense them?" Hozark asked.

"Yes. Very faint from here, though," Demelza replied. "But there is warding nearby."

"Indeed. And we know what that means."

The duo split up, doing the infiltration thing they knew so well as they blended in with the other workers as if they had always belonged there. It was what made the Wampeh Ghalian such effective assassins. They were not only exceptional killers, they were masters of infiltration and disguise.

And very, very patient. A great many of their most difficult assassinations required levels of patience that would drive most hired killers mad.

Hozark was the one who found the warded door, hidden on a central wall that appeared to back up to another storage room. But the wall was thicker than it should have been, and that meant just one thing. It was hiding something in that secret space.

He and Demelza quickly formulated a plan. There was a bit too much foot traffic in the area to simply disarm the wards and open the door at their leisure. They would need a distraction.

Demelza nodded toward a particularly high stack of sacks of grain across the chamber. It wasn't terribly precarious, at least not under normal circumstances, but with a little carefully applied magic, the seemingly stable structure could be made to tumble.

"Ready?" she asked as Hozark prepared his disabling spells for their assault on the hidden door.

"Ready," he replied.

Demelza turned back to the sacks of grain and watched the flow of men and women in the facility. When the traffic was at its densest, she quietly cast, her spell pushing the stack with subtle force. An abrupt jerk would have caused suspicion, but a slow fall would just seem to be another bit of bad luck.

"Look out!" a woman shouted as the tall stack began to pick up momentum as it fell.

Everyone scattered, diving out of the way of the tumbling mass. Hozark took full advantage of their preoccupation and began casting his well-practiced disarming spells. In just a few moments, he had the door unlocked and the spells negated.

Meanwhile, grain had come crashing to the ground, the sacks bursting open, sending their contents flying in all directions like an edible snowstorm. The workers were beside themselves, not knowing exactly what to do.

There was a mad scramble to attempt to contain the spillage to just a small area, and all hands jumped to action to help. It was that confusion that allowed the two newcomers to slip through the secret door, vanishing from sight in an instant.

Inside the hidden space, both Ghalian had their weapons and spells at the ready the moment they passed through the door. They were uncloaked, and so long as they were visible, it would be far easier for an adversary to attack them.

But there was nothing but silence in the air.

Hozark nodded to the staircase at their feet and began slowly descending, his footsteps not making a sound. Demelza took up the rear, but neither foresaw any following in their wake.

Down they went until they were fairly deep beneath the diversionary structure above. The staircase curved slightly, and Hozark slowed his stride until he finally stepped out into the empty space. He stood upright, his body relaxing slightly.

"Empty," he said.

The two looked around the vacated chamber. It was a larger facility, originally designed for holding, torturing, and extracting information by any means necessary. A Council of Twenty black site. One of the rumored hidden facilities they had heard of over the years.

Many had been found and destroyed, typically in a way that made it seem like an accident, but they always knew that many others survived. And now they had discovered one.

"There are traces of power here," Hozark said, reaching out with his finely honed senses. "But there is nothing fresh."

Demelza walked over to one of the restraint tables and examined the thick straps that had held countless victims in place, saving the tormentors' magic for things other than binding. They noted they had been thoroughly cleaned, as had the entire apparatus. When this place had been shuttered, it was not in a hurry.

"It seems we have been led to a dead end," she said.

Hozark paced the chamber, then began surveying the empty cells and rooms connecting to it. All were vacant, and had been for some time, but this place was still stocked with the basic tools of a Council black site.

"Yes, a dead end, but a good lead, all the same," he said. "The Council may yet return to utilize it one day. We shall notify the order of this place's existence and keep an eye on it for future activity. Who knows? This may not be an entirely wasted stop after all."

The two Ghalian assassins made a final sweep of the space, then ascended the stairs back to the upper level. Hozark peeked out the hidden door. The workers were still busy cleaning up the mess Demelza had made, and it looked like they would be for some time.

They quietly stepped back out onto the work floor and made their way to the exit, heading back to meet their friends and report what they had found.

Demelza was glad they had not told Hap of the possibility his father was here. The letdown would have been great for the boy. At least he had enjoyed a nice outing on a relatively safe world, and for the poor child, that was something the poor child could really use about now.

## CHAPTER FIFTEEN

The ship sat quietly in the landing area, innocuous and unremarkable. The two passengers who walked up to the craft and stepped aboard didn't draw any scrutiny. Why would they? Just another pair of normal people on a normal day.

No one knew they were the two deadliest people on the planet.

"Hey, how'd it go?" Bud asked as Hozark and Demelza walked into the command center.

"An interesting outing," Hozark replied, quickly scanning the room. "Where is young Happizano?"

"He said he wasn't feeling too good. I think he overdid it on sweets. But you've gotta try these things he picked up. What were they called, Laskar?"

"Sorra drops, I think."

"No, they're called *Mora* drops," Henni corrected. "Pretty tasty, actually."

"Yeah, for real. But there's a lesson about moderation here," Bud added. "I think the poor kid got carried away."

"The folly of youth," Demelza said with a soft chuckle.

"Yeah," Bud said. "Can't say I haven't been known to overindulge from time to time myself."

"We know all too well, Bud," Demelza noted.

"Ha-ha. So, anyway, Hap's in his room and we can talk. What'd you guys find out there? Is his dad here?"

"There is indeed a Council facility hidden at the outskirts of the city," Hozark informed them. "An agricultural facility of fair size."

"And it's a fake?" Bud asked.

"No, it is a legitimate operation. But what is interesting is what it is built on top of. There is a larger structure under the one visible from the surface. Demelza and I infiltrated the building and gained access to it."

"A secret storehouse?" Laskar asked.

"Not exactly that," Hozark replied. "We found its true nature when we reconnoitered the hidden level."

"So, wait. There's a secret area?" Bud said. "That sounds like exactly the kind of place they'd be hiding Visla Jinnik. Was he down there?"

"Unfortunately, no. Though the facility was definitely a Council black site, and it was still fairly well stocked for that purpose, but there were no signs of recent occupation. The traces of power were very, very faint, and very, very old. Whatever they had been doing there, this place was abandoned long ago, and not in a hurry. It was shuttered for business with some care."

"Shit, I'm sorry, Hozark. My guys really thought it was a good lead," Laskar said.

"There is no need to apologize. While we may have come up empty on the search for Visla Jinnik, this was nevertheless a useful discovery. This facility is one of the Council black sites that have been sought out and destroyed over the years. It will be added to the order's books and monitored from now on. You did well."

"Thanks. I still feel bad for the kid, though. I really hoped we'd find his father here. It's gotta be tough on him."

"Yes, it is a disappointment. But it is good we did not inform him of the possibility of his father being here. The letdown would have been great."

Henni leaned over Laskar's shoulder, staring at the star charts he had before him.

"Hey! Do you mind?"

"Nope, not at all," she replied.

Bud chuckled. "Well, we might as well get back to it. We were just prepping a course out in case we'd need to lift off. I guess there's no reason to stay now."

"You were preparing for flight, and Hap decided to skip his lesson?" Hozark noted.

"Yeah. He really must be feeling pretty crappy," Bud said. "He usually loves this stuff. And he's actually been picking it up pretty quickly."

"So have I," Henni interjected, leaning farther over Laskar's shoulder.

"Yes, we know. You're a flying and navigating savant," the copilot said. "Now, would you mind getting off of my shoulder?"

The violet-haired woman relented with a huff. "Fine. I saw enough anyway."

"To plot a course? Not likely," Laskar said, dismissively.

"Would you two quit it? Just prep for flight. We'll head out in a few minutes."

Hozark turned to Demelza. "It really is unlike Hap to miss his flying lesson. He must truly feel ill. Let us check on the boy. Perhaps we can help ease his discomfort."

Demelza nodded and followed him into the corridor. The walk to Hap's quarters was very short, and they were there in just a few moments. What they saw when they entered was not a boy who had overindulged in sweets, however. There was something else going on.

Happizano was lying on his bed curled up in a ball, his pale-violet skin somewhat ashen in color. Heat could be felt radiating off of him as they drew close. A fever, but not of natural origins.

"This is not a mere stomachache," Hozark said, quickly kneeling beside the boy and resting his hand on the youth's head. "Happizano, can you hear me?"

Hap opened his eyes with an uncomfortable squint.

"Hozark, I don't feel too good."

"I can see that, young Jinnik, and I am going to help. Can you describe the sensation to me?"

"It's like my stomach and head and everything are knotted up. And I feel really, really tired."

Hozark reached out with his senses, drawing power from his konus as he studied the ailing boy.

"Anything else? Any strange smells, sounds, or tastes?"

"Yeah. I can't get this sweet taste out of my mouth. It's like there's a piece of candy stuck there, and I can't wash it out. But I haven't eaten anything in a while, and I drank a bunch of water when we got back."

Hozark looked at Demelza with a very concerned look. "Apply a series of blocking spells at once. The Araganus variants."

"The Araganus spells?"

"Yes," Hozark said, his eyes speaking what he did not wish to say aloud in front of the child.

"I shall begin at once," she replied, sliding her heaviest konus onto her wrist and casting the powerful spells.

Hozark rushed back to the command center.

"The sweets. Did you all eat them?" he asked.

"Yeah. They're really good. Hap left the rest in the galley if you want to—" Bud said as Hozark took off down the corridor. "Hey! What's up?" he called out, then hurried after his friend.

Hozark found the container still on the dining table and began immediately scanning its contents with careful magical probing. His spells were specialized, tools of the Wampeh Ghalian known to but a few outside the order. As master killers, they also had to be able to identify dangerous magic not of their own origin. And it looked as though that was what he was now dealing with.

"What are you doing?" Laskar asked as he and the others rushed into the galley.

"These sweets have been poisoned."

"How can you tell?" Laskar asked.

"A Ghalian trick," he replied.

"Wait. The candy is poisoned?" Henni asked.

"I am certain of it."

The young woman's eyes went wide, and she rushed to the waste disposal bin to try to make herself vomit.

"But we *all* ate them," Laskar said. "And *we* don't have any symptoms of anything."

"Henni, you may stop your attempts at regurgitation," Hozark called out to the girl. "This is a very specialized compound, only found on one particular Council-controlled world. And it only affects those who have not yet matured to adulthood. You are fine."

"How do you know all of that?" Laskar asked.

"Again, a little-known secret of my order," he replied.

"But Hap?" Bud asked.

"He is a juvenile. As such, he is now suffering from the compound's full effects. A rare, wasting magic that will likely get worse." He studied the near-empty box. "How many of these did he ingest?"

"Four or five, I think."

"Then it was a sizable dose. These symptoms will most certainly compound over time."

"What do we do?" Henni asked, eyeing the uneaten sweets as if they were death in a box.

"We return to the city to try to figure out how this happened. Who knew to target him like this," Hozark said. "Come. We go immediately."

# CHAPTER SIXTEEN

The walk through the city was one filled with confusion and chaos. The streets were full of panicked parents and ailing children, all trying to find out what had happened.

"Look at them all," Henni said, horrified at just how many kids had apparently fallen ill.

As with any unknown contagion, people were eyeing one another with distrust, unsure if their friends and neighbors might be a disease vector, spreading the illness to their own household. It led to a fast-spreading air of uncertainty and near-aggressive caution among the populace.

Yet those with affected children were simultaneously putting their own safety behind that of their offspring as they searched desperately for help, unaware that they were all perfectly safe from the seemingly instantaneous contagion that had exploded among the city's kids.

Some of the children had apparently fallen ill away from home and were sitting on the ground or up against buildings, rocking slowly in their misery.

One of the unfortunate youths was the cheerful young boy

whom they had interacted with earlier that day. Bud did a double-take as he noticed him from a distance.

"Hey, that's the kid who sold us those poisoned Mora drops!"

The group spun to look where he was pointing.

"Let's grab him and bring him to the ship. We can torture him in private and find out who did this," Laskar said with surprising venom in his voice.

Hozark placed his hand on the copilot's shoulder and looked deep into his eyes. "The child appears to be quite ill as well, Laskar. Undoubtedly an unfortunate victim of this affair. And even if he were not, these are *children* we are speaking of. One must show mercy for the young who do not know any better."

"But he poisoned Hap."

"Yes, but he was also almost certainly being used as an unwitting tool in this affair. And, judging by his condition, he is most certainly suffering the same fate as young Happizano is."

It was true, the boy's color was not good, and he was visibly ill, as nearly all of the children they saw were.

"I can't believe someone poisoned the whole city," Henni said. "Who would do such a thing? It's horrible."

"The Council member who took Hap's father, I bet," Laskar said. "That Maktan bastard, no doubt. He's the one behind all of this, right, Hozark?"

"We lack proof at this time, but it would seem likely," the assassin replied. "Only one of the Twenty would have access to this compound. And both the plant and its cure are found in only one place. And that place is securely under Council control."

"So, this is a trap?" Bud asked.

"Not exactly a trap. But definitely a ploy to bring the boy into the grasp of the Council once more. It would seem that an intentional misinformation campaign was waged, and we fell for the lure."

"You mean, it was *my* sources?" Laskar asked.

"I am afraid so," Hozark replied. "Whoever was spreading the story of Visla Jinnik being present on this world did so to a specific group of people. Those they knew would likely relay the information to one of the select few that make up our crew. They've interacted with us before, and I fear true anonymity for you is a thing of the past."

"My gods, I'm so sorry."

"There was no way for you to know they would stoop to this level. Even for the Council of Twenty, abruptly attacking an entire populace of innocents like this, and children, no less, is nearly unheard of. The boy must be exceptionally valuable to them to go to these lengths to recover him."

"You think it's because he has the makings of his father's power?" Bud asked.

"Perhaps. But he is young, yet, and his own nascent powers require nurturing to grow and come into their own. No, I would think more likely than not his father is growing reticent of the acts they are forcing him to do. That is possibly the reason there have been no attacks in recent weeks. And if that is the case, the boy would be much-needed leverage to press him back into action."

Hozark and Demelza both observed the flow of the throngs in the streets, and they each noted something interesting. Interesting and telling. There were a few Council officials moving through the city, stopping and speaking with parents and their children as they took note of the issue unfolding.

But these were not mercenaries, or any military type, for that matter. These were clearly aid workers of some sort, and real ones at that. The assassins were quite skilled at sniffing out disguises and concealed weapons, and these people bore none.

"Do you see them?" Hozark asked the others. "The Council representatives engaging with the populace."

Bud, Henni, and Laskar shifted their attention from the sick kids and panicked parents to the handful of clean-clothed newcomers moving between them. They were speaking to the parents, offering what seemed to be words of comfort and support.

And whatever they were saying, their words seemed to have a very positive effect. Tears shifted from those of panic to hope.

"I shall return in a moment," Hozark said, striding from the group, adopting a look of deep concern instantly, a tiny dose of magic making his eyes appear bloodshot from crying.

"What am I supposed to do? My daughter is dying, and there's nothing I can do to help her!" he said, pulling at his clothes in distracted agony.

One of the Council representatives just happened to be within earshot. Quite convenient, that.

"We are here to help, friend," they said, hurrying over to him. "The Council of Twenty heard of this terrible outbreak, and in their great mercy, they have spared no expense to send help for the children of this world."

"But what can you do? None of the healers have been able to do a thing."

"The Council possesses healers of far greater power and skill than you've ever seen before, and they are setting up an emergency healing center for all of this city's affected youth."

A look of desperate hope flashed across Hozark's tear-streaked face. "Really? You think you can help?"

"We *know* we can. I've been told our healers are familiar with this illness and are acquiring the cure as we speak. It should arrive here by morning. Bring your child, and the Council will do all in their power to restore her to full health."

"You can do this? Really? But we are not rich people."

"This service is being provided to your people free of charge. It will not cost you a single coin."

"You would do this for us?"

"The Council is generous and merciful. Now, if you will excuse me, I must spread the word to the others so we can get this epidemic under control and return your children to you as soon as possible. Remember, come to the treatment center tomorrow morning, and all will be made right."

"Thank you!" Hozark gushed. "Thank you so much!"

The Council representative smiled warmly and hurried along to continue their task. Hozark turned and made his way back to his friends, his face back to normal by the time he reached them, though a slight hint of the bloodshot spell lingered for a moment before finally dissipating entirely.

"What did you learn?" Demelza asked.

"This Maktan fellow is clever. *Very* clever," he replied. "The Council is positioning themselves to be the heroes in this situation."

"But they caused it," Henni said.

"Yes. But the people do not know this. And there is no way they would. In fact, if not for the fact that the Ghalian just happened to know of this particularly rare compound, we would not have been any the wiser, either. And that is likely what they were counting on."

"How so?"

"If we were desperate to cure young Happizano, and lacking alternatives, we would have no choice but to bring him to their healers."

"They have healers here already?" Laskar asked.

"Tomorrow morning they shall arrive, and with the cure, no less. This timing, of course, is all to allow the panic to increase overnight, as well as let the desperation and hope set in."

"What do you mean?"

"Nagus, the Council world where the cure grows, is but a few jumps from here. The cure could be here in hours, not a full day. But this is a manufactured situation, and it serves their purposes to delay in hopes that desperation will force us to make a mistake."

"If we were even here, that is," Demelza noted. "All of this in mere hope of snaring Happizano in this ploy. It is a great expenditure for just one child."

"Indeed. But we are forewarned," Hozark replied. "And forearmed. We shall not be taking Happizano to their facility, but we can utilize their ploy to our own benefit. They do not know we are aware of their machinations, and we can use that to our full advantage."

"You think so?" Laskar asked.

"Yes," Hozark replied. "The Council is bringing the cure to this world. Now we just have to acquire it."

## CHAPTER SEVENTEEN

The cure did not actually need to arrive via ship. In fact, it was already on the ground from the moment the toxin was unleashed, undoubtedly, and the youth-targeting ailment was slow moving enough to not be an actual threat to life for some time.

But the wait until morning was not one of necessity, but rather of pressure.

A night spent with an ailing child was more than enough to spur every parent into action to do anything necessary to cure their offspring of whatever this unknown curse was.

Fortunately for Happizano, his caregivers were not ordinary parentals or sitters prone to knee-jerk reactions and panic. He had Wampeh Ghalian watching over him, and though he was in misery, the assassins attending him were well aware that what he was suffering from was quite intentional in origin.

And they knew they had time.

"Do you see the additional superstructure blended with the craft's hull?" Hozark asked his friends as they walked around the outskirts of the central landing area where the Council's alleged aid craft had settled down.

It was announced that the ship would be used as a temporary recovery and housing facility to help the city's ailing youth. A hermetically sealed vessel to prevent the contagion from spreading beyond those already afflicted.

Of course, the adults were entirely safe, and unless the few unaffected children ate the tainted sweets circulating about the town, mere contact would not harm them in the slightest. But the populace didn't know that.

These were tried and true Council tricks. Using fear and lies to manipulate people into doing what they wanted them to. The Council's stock and trade.

"What?" Laskar asked. "I don't see anything."

"Yeah, it just looks like a Council ship," Bud agreed.

Henni squinted her galaxy eyes, as if she could somehow see what the Wampeh were talking about, though the craft appeared completely normal.

"Don't you guys see it?" she asked. "There's some sort of weird fuzziness around a bunch of parts of their ship. I can't quite make out what it is, but it feels wrong."

Demelza and Hozark both nodded their approval. Henni, it seemed, was slowly learning to trust her innate power after it was abruptly kick-started the other day. It was a minor thing at this point, but the longest race starts with the first step.

"You are correct, Henni," Demelza said. "It appears as though they've applied a dampening field within a false exterior around the more vulnerable portions of the craft. Most would not be able to detect it."

"Where?" Laskar asked, squinting harder.

"I am surprised you are unable to detect anything," Hozark said. "Your power is rather weak, but this should create at least some sort of a reaction with your energy."

Laskar stared at the ship a long moment. "Hang on. I think I see something," he said. "It's really faint, but sort of a blur around the edges at parts."

"Yes, that is part of it," the Wampeh said. "You are getting the hang of it."

"But why? What's it for?"

"Look around the area, Laskar. Study the crowd, the bystanders, the people who seem to be looking a bit too intently at the parents bringing their children for treatment."

"I see a bunch of guards around the ship, but that seems normal if they're worried about people storming them to get their kids help."

"No, not them. While there is a lot of firepower present, the overt Council forces are not of what I speak. Look beyond the uniformed individuals. See what is not intended to be seen."

"Oh, shit," Bud said, his eyes widening slightly. "He's right. You see 'em, Laskar?"

The copilot scanned the area once more but appeared to be coming up blank. Henni elbowed him sharply.

"Jeez, are you blind? There, by the Arambis juice vendor. And over at the cafe, the blue-skinned fella with the eyestalks. And those three chatting on that bench. Plus, the ones walking circles around the perimeter. The ones with blades on their hips."

"A lot of people wear blades, Henni."

"Yeah, but not enchanted ones," she said.

"How can you tell?"

"Can't you? The power leaks out of the sheaths," she replied.

Hozark glanced at Demelza. *This* was something new. It was almost impossible to sense enchanted blades unless they were openly exposed.

"*All* of those?" Laskar asked.

"Yes. Duh."

"Damn, you were right. That's a *lot* of firepower for what's supposed to be a mercy operation," Bud said.

"Yes. A trap of rather impressive magnitude," Hozark agreed.

"And that is not to mention the trio of shimmer-cloaked sentries at the craft's lone open entryway."

"Wait, shimmer cloaks?" Bud asked.

"Yes. Fairly good ones at that. But with all of the commotion, they have been forced to move in unplanned ways, and that makes them detectable. At least, to some of us. It is a trap of many layers, entirely designed to box in young Happizano and any foolish enough to bring him to their grasp."

The group walked as casually as possible, making a loop as if they were not concerned by either the ill children or the Council craft, but as they moved, it was clear there *was* as large Council presence. This wasn't just a hopeful snare. It was a full-fledged trap designed to catch even the most skilled of adversary. One designed especially for them.

The cure was undoubtedly housed inside. That much of the story was true. But beyond that, it was all a carefully designed ruse.

"Damn. What are we supposed to do?" Henni asked. "This is a total shit show."

Hozark scanned the entirety of the area before them, taking in all of the elements in a glance.

"We either try to recover the cure from within, or we have to fly to Nagus to acquire it ourselves."

Bud was looking increasingly uneasy. "But you said it's a Council stronghold planet. Like, crazy protected. And after this, it's sure to be even more so."

"Yes, I am aware. Neither is a good option," Hozark said.

The pilot leaned in close to his assassin friend. "Hey, I want to check something out. Hozark, I'll need your help."

"What is it, Bud?"

"Let's get back to the ship first. I don't feel comfortable talking about it out here."

"Do not worry, there are no shimmer-cloaked individuals in our immediate vicinity."

"Yeah, I know, but this is creeping me out. Let's get back inside, okay?"

"Very well," Hozark said. "The rest of you, please continue your observations. Note the number of children entering, and whether they exit. If so, how long they are being kept within. And see if there are any adults allowed inside with them or if the parents are separated from the youths at the doorway. Bud and I will return shortly."

With that, he and the pilot quickly, yet casually, turned from the scene and made their way back to Bud's mothership.

"Now, what is it, Bud?"

"I had a thought. I mean, if they're going to all of this trouble down here on the surface, then it seems likely they'll be prepared to block any quick escape attempts as well."

"It would seem likely."

"So, can we take your shimmer ship up into orbit? I know the amount of magic required to maintain a shimmer on a ship in space is huge, but *I* still can't detect it even if they do. But *you* can."

"Most of the time," Hozark replied. "But even master Ghalian are not infallible."

"Better than anything I can do on my own, though. And before we even consider stirring up anything down here on the surface, we really need to be absolutely sure we can get out of here in a hurry, if need be. Remember what happened at Drommus. What if they cast a jump-blocking web again?"

"I was actually considering the same possibility," Hozark said. "Come, I shall fly us a distance from the city, then activate my shimmer cloak and take us into space. If there is an additional force in hiding, odds are, we will detect some trace of them."

The two men climbed aboard the Wampeh assassin's craft and lifted off from Bud's mothership, flying slowly and casually away before engaging the cloak and rising into space.

The quantity of Council ships appeared to have increased a bit with the arrival of the alleged cure and convalescence craft on the surface, but upon closer examination it was apparent that these new ships were more than just mercy vessels. They were robust, and seemed to be possessing additional armaments hidden from cursory examination.

More than that, it appeared that Uzabud's concerns were not unfounded.

"There. To the left of the smaller craft on the edge of the formation. Do you see the stars? How they seem to bend?"

Bud looked intently. "Yeah, kinda."

"Shimmer ships. There are several, actually, though most possess the same basic flaw in their shimmer spells."

"Shit, so they're really pulling out all the stops, here. But can they see us too?"

"No. My Ghalian shimmer is far more proficient than theirs. Mind you, what they are employing would indeed fool most, and it is definitely of a higher-level casting than typically seen, but there is more to a shimmer than just the power behind it."

"So what do we do?" Bud asked. "Do we fly to Nagus?"

Hozark considered their options a long moment. "Nagus will be heavily guarded, and there is some urgency to our situation. Happizano ingested a great deal of the compound, and his condition will begin to worsen quickly. I fear we must make at least a preliminary attempt at the cure at hand."

"And if we can't get it?"

"Then we will be in the most unpleasant situation of being forced to make an attempt at the protected crops on Nagus. But for now, we make our stand here. And we need to hurry."

## CHAPTER EIGHTEEN

Hozark descended slowly through the exosphere, ensuring his shimmer-cloaked craft did not generate any detectable heat or water vapor signatures from the temperature shift as it transitioned from space to the atmosphere. Just one more place many less-skilled pilots would have erred in the use of their cloaking magic.

But the master Ghalian was far, far too well-versed to make that rookie mistake.

"We shall take the longer route upon our return," he informed Bud as he set into a long circuit, passing over several other regions on their way back to the others.

They would de-cloak and casually fly back to dock with Bud's mothership, appearing like an average craft to any observing them. The others were sticking close with one another now that the Council was involved, and Demelza would undoubtedly be ensuring that neither Laskar nor Henni did anything foolish enough to jeopardize their plans in the meantime.

It didn't take the two men long to make their way back to the parked ship and land atop it once more, the Wampeh's craft effortlessly sealing against the larger vessel's hull with a few well-practiced spells.

"Where were you guys?" Laskar asked as the pair descended into the ship.

"Yeah, where were you?" Henni asked from his side.

"Jeez, will you please stop shadowing me like that?"

"Demelza said we've all gotta stick together, so I'm sticking together," the violet-haired woman replied, matter-of-factly.

Laskar just sighed. Apparently, she'd taken the Wampeh's directions quite literally, to the copilot's great annoyance.

"We were making a quick loop up top," Bud replied. "Had to check some stuff out."

"Stuff?" Laskar asked.

"Yeah, stuff. You know, like finding out there are not only more Council ships up in orbit, but also some shimmer-cloaked ones to boot."

"A blockade?" Demelza asked.

"Not as of yet. The Council appears to be attempting to seem benign at the moment," Hozark said. "However, we do not know how long that will last."

"Well, shit. So, what now?" Laskar grumbled.

"Now I shall make a more thorough survey of the Council ship so conveniently parked nearby."

"But I thought it was a trap."

"Oh, it is. But perhaps our Council friends have been lax in their preparation. It would not be the first time their overconfidence had left them vulnerable," the master assassin said. "But, first, how is Happizano faring?"

"Not good," Henni said. "He's really sick."

"She is correct in her assessment," Demelza said. "He is slowly getting worse."

"Then time is of the essence. I shall begin at once. Bud, please take Laskar and plot multiple potential jumps from this place. If things go poorly, we may need to depart in something of a hurry."

Hozark then turned and strode from the compartment. Within a minute, he was invisible beneath his shimmer cloak and making quick time toward the Council's trap.

When he was near, the assassin slowed his pace, taking great care to note every single guard and sentry, even those who were cloaked, as he was. There was always the possibility he might miss one, but thus far none seemed to possess the magic and skills to achieve anything near his own proficiency with a shimmer.

The modified ship was a rather large affair. Sizable enough to house a few hundred children, if need be, it seemed. At the same time, it was compact enough to be relatively easy to control the access points and guard any possible weak spots. But there were always cracks in any defense, and Hozark had been at this game a long, long time.

He drew close to the ship and spent a good minute clocking the defenses at the main entrance. It appeared clear, but in addition to the wards on the doorway and the guards standing sentry, there were also cloaked individuals lurking in wait.

It was made to appear difficult, but not impossible. Just the sort of thing a less experienced person might make an attempt at. But Hozark saw it for what it was and moved on.

The other access points were sealed tight and protected by multiple wards and trap spells. The ship was buttoned up tight, it seemed.

It was on his second pass that he found a weak spot in the protective layers. An unused service hatch that seemed to have escaped the attention of the Council plotters who had set this whole plan in motion. Or so it seemed. But as he focused his attentions fully, Hozark caught the faintest whiff of recent magic.

It was not a trap. It was not a ward or alarm. It was the *removal* of those things. Nearly all traces had been scrubbed from the nondescript hatch, but the tiniest fragment remained, and that was more than enough to put the Ghalian on alert.

He spent several minutes reaching out with myriad spells in his arsenal, probing the accessway.

*Very, very well done,* he mused appreciatively as he stepped back from the honeypot entry point. He then spun on his heel and headed straight back to Bud's ship, slipping aboard without any bystanders being any the wiser.

Hozark uncloaked immediately once inside and made his way to command.

"What'd you find?" Bud asked as the Wampeh entered.

"The craft is well guarded. Exceptionally well, in fact. There are ways in, of course, but the whole thing is designed to act as a containment vessel should one be foolish enough to venture inside."

"So, there's no way in without being seen?" Laskar asked.

"There is one way. An unused service access panel."

"Well, that's great news!" Laskar said. "If we can get the kid inside and to the cure, then maybe––"

"No."

"No?"

"It is also a trap," Hozark said.

"But you said it was unused."

"So it was made to appear. But whoever set this up is somewhat knowledgeable in Ghalian ways. It was intentionally difficult, but accessible. Yet, the wards and alarm spells were not in need of bypassing. They had been removed entirely."

"That's a bad thing?"

"When someone has done so intentionally to create an enticing entry point, yes, it is," Hozark replied. "Once inside, we would undoubtedly be noticed, the exits sealed, and the boy captured."

"Can't we make a try for it without him with us?" Bud asked.

"Yes, but that would trigger a full blockade from above. Either way, we are not equipped for this sort of covert action."

"But this is what you guys do, right?" Laskar asked.

"With time, yes. But in a rush such as this, the odds of success are paltry."

A silence fell in the chamber. It seemed they had just had the rug pulled out from under them and were left with the option of bad or worse.

"The kid's getting sicker, Hozark," Bud finally said. "We've gotta do something."

"I am aware, Uzabud. This is a truly cruel trap Maktan has put in place."

"You sure it's him?"

"It seems most likely. Especially given the nature and strength of some of the magic being employed. In any case, we have been left with two terrible options. Either give up the boy to save him, knowing he will be falling back into their hands in the process, or keep him from them and let him die."

"You're kidding, right?" Bud said.

"Sadly, I am not. This is the type of person we are dealing with, Bud. One willing to go to any length to achieve their goal."

An angry look formed on Laskar's face. "That Maktan's an evil bastard," he growled. "We need to take him out, once and for all. Do you think you can do it?"

Hozark pondered his words a brief moment. "The boy is the priority at the moment. We cure him first. *Then* we can worry about Visla Zinna Maktan."

"Agreed," Bud said, sitting up straighter in his seat.

"So, to save Hap, we'll have to give him up," Laskar said. "It seems like the only way. But once they take him, we can follow them when they lift off. They'll cure him immediately, I'm sure, so all we'd have to do is board their ship in flight and do whatever is necessary get the kid back."

It was an audacious plan, and one that might even work under many circumstances. But this was not one such occasion.

"I am afraid that is simply not an option," Hozark replied.

"But it's the only way. Bud's a former pirate, after all. And we've got you and Demelza. You can board their ship and snatch him back once they've administered the antidote."

"Not with the ships in orbit, I am afraid," Hozark said. "They will undoubtedly run one or more diversions to throw off the scent and block any from following while the boy is spirited away. And once they jump, tracking him down would likely be near impossible if Maktan focuses his considerable resources on keeping the boy hidden. We got lucky once, and they were not expecting our intervention. But this time I fear we would not be able to recover him."

Laskar looked at the others, frustration in his eyes. "So what, then? We just let him die?"

Hozark fixed him with his gaze. "No, you misunderstand. We do not let him die. We go to Nagus."

## CHAPTER NINETEEN

Nagus. It was a rather unremarkable planet in a rather unremarkable system that only drew the attention of the Council all those many years ago for one reason. It was home to a variety of endemic plants that somehow converted the rays of the system's pale red sun into their own unique internalized magic.

Some of the flora was quite beñign. Others had developed rather potent curatives. And still others were so toxic that they were quickly destroyed but for a small collection of plants kept in strict quarantine within the vast Council greenhouses.

Of course, once the realization came that they could control *all* of the vegetation on the world that possessed unique properties, the Council grabbed hold of the entire planet with an iron fist, crushing any signs of independent horticulture with great prejudice. They were very quickly the only game in town, and it had remained that way for centuries.

It was in one such massive greenhouse that a particular variety of shrub grew with great vigor. It was unremarkable to look at. Squat, deep green, with glossy, oval leaves and small turquoise flowers that clustered at the ends of fine branches. But for a certain group in desperate need of it, the processed leaves of the shrub were priceless.

Ungall, it was called, though most knew it as spellbalm or blossoming fever break. An odd little plant with healing properties, its inherent magic pulled from the unusual, red sun shining down upon it. It was a bit of an all-around restorative, useful for a great many purposes. Most specifically, it countered the unusual wasting illness brought on by youths foolish enough to ingest the pollen of the Marbus vine.

That plant, too, was under strict control by the Council, the incredibly rare toxic compound only found on one world in all of the known systems. It was so rare, in fact, that aside from a handful of people at the highest ranks of the Council, the very existence of the dangerous vine was unknown to any who had not visited the insides of the greenhouses on Nagus. And the number who had that particular clearance was incredibly small.

In fact, the entire planet was a highly restricted zone, and none but those on Council business were allowed anywhere near it. Every part of the situation reinforced Visla Zinna Maktan's role in the attack on the children in the city of Flammis. Only Council members and their closest lackeys could possibly have carried out the attack.

It was an extremely cruel, yet efficient trap. And under all but the most unusual circumstances, it would have almost certainly succeeded. But Visla Maktan had not accounted for one very unexpected wrinkle in his little plan. Namely, the Wampeh Ghalian's knowledge of not only the toxic compound utilized, but also of the secret world from whence it sprang.

Nevertheless, Nagus was still a Council world, and a stronghold at that. Getting the plant would be difficult––the greenhouses were very secure structures guarded round the clock. But that was just one aspect of the plan, for even something seemingly as simple as just landing there would be a near impossibility.

Uzabud's ship would be blasted from the sky as soon as it broke atmosphere and began its descent, and given the sheer quantity of power users concentrated in one place, and for such a valuable set of assets, it was highly unlikely a shimmer-cloaked craft would be able to land on the surface unnoted.

This posed a rather annoying circumstance for the ill child's caregivers.

"The place is buttoned up tighter than a visla's storage vault," Bud lamented. "The whole damn planet is under constant surveillance."

"Bud's right," Laskar added. "I see the temptation, but let's be real. There's no way we're landing anywhere on that planet, and that means we don't stand a chance of getting the cure."

"But he needs it," Henni said.

"Yeah, we know. But short of walking into that Council trap, I don't see how we're gonna be able to get it for him," Laskar said. "I guess it really is a question of do we hand him over if that's the only way to get him the cure?"

"We do not," Hozark replied.

"But he needs it."

"I am aware. But, as I said previously, we have no option but to travel to Nagus."

"So, what are we supposed to do when we get there?" Bud asked, well aware of the complications Hozark had laid out for him and the others. "We can't just land there and go clip an Ungall shrub, then wave and smile and fly away. They're all locked up and under heavy guard. And, hell, from what you say, we can't even get anywhere near the planet, let alone the greenhouses. So how do we do this? Hap's not doing so good, and we can't afford to dick around while he gets worse."

"Obviously," Hozark replied. "But I have a plan that will get us to the surface without raising suspicion."

"I'd love to hear what that could possibly be," Bud said.

"Oh, my friend. I think you will rather enjoy this one," he replied. "We will be needing to put your skills to use, however."

"Yeah, I know. I'm your pilot. It's a given that you need me to pilot us around."

"While that is a great asset to our cause, that is not what I am speaking of," Hozark replied. "I refer to your other skills."

"Other skills?"

"From your pirating days," the Wampeh replied with a grin. "You see, Bud, I want you to help me steal a Council ship."

The former pirate hesitated as the words sank in. Then the faint beginnings of a smile started to crease his lips.

"Steal a Council ship?"

"Yes. But nothing too big or flashy. We are a small crew, after all, and we wouldn't have use for something terribly large. But a smaller craft, one that passes all scrutiny as it descends through the Council defenses? Oh, that will work just fine."

"We're going to steal a Council ship?" Laskar asked. "Uh, am I the only one who sees a little problem with that?"

"Yep, you're the only one," Henni chirped. "Sounds like a fun plan to me. And besides, we don't have much of a choice."

"We have options," the copilot shot back.

"Not that don't involve immediately surrendering Hap to the Council," she retorted.

Bud was ignoring the two as they sniped at one another. His task was now clear, and he was running through the mental checklist of all the places they might acquire a Council ship of both the size and clearance they needed, but also what additional spells he might need to employ to keep the thing in the air.

That is, unless he could capture one with its own entourage of Drooks. Just a few of them could power the craft with magic to spare, and having live Drooks on board would only further cement their legitimacy.

"Okay," he said. "I've got an idea."

## CHAPTER TWENTY

A craft to commandeer was the order of the day, and Bud set a course to more heavily traveled areas of the adjacent systems to seek out their prey. And oh, what prey it was.

Of course, finding Council ships in Council territory was the easy part. There were literally dozens to choose from, if that was your only goal. Identifying one that could be easily commandeered and put into service in the furtherance of this audacious plan, however, was something else entirely. There were a great many factors in play that affected those plans.

The most obvious issue to be considered was the clear need to avoid the large, battle-ready craft that would undoubtedly prove to be not only impossible to seize with so few people, but would also stand a very real chance of inflicting fatal hurt upon Uzabud's ship if they tried.

Then there was the problem of sheer size. Even a less robustly armed and armored craft would be unwise for them to take over, if for no other reason than they lacked the number of people required to keep a vessel that size in the sky.

So, a smaller ship it had to be. One that was not armed to the teeth. And, most importantly, it had to be a ship of a variety that it would not be noted as missing if it dropped off radar for a few days. One that could come and go without anyone paying it much heed.

"I'm thinking a basic supply ship," Bud said after pondering the issue a bit. "You know the type. Smallish, decent payload size, and most importantly, a common sight in the fleet as they're flitting about and resupplying the larger ships all the damn time."

"This sounds like it would likely be the most logical selection," Demelza agreed. "And a craft of that variety would indeed not be noticed as missing for at least a few days."

"Exactly. The crew is small, and they should be easy enough to put out of commission for the duration of the operation. I mean, for a pair of Ghalian, that is," Bud added.

"So, where do we find one of these supply ships?" Henni asked.

"There are a number of Council-controlled worlds nearby," Hozark said. "However, I feel we must acquire our craft from a location far enough from these systems that the possibility of an unexpected discovery of the missing ship would not put the defenses at Nagus on alert."

"I know just the place," Bud said with a pleased grin. "And we can be there in just a couple of jumps."

Durkus was a busy world. A supply hub utilized by far more spacefaring folk than just the Council. Pirates stopped over there. Mercenaries. Smugglers and traders. It was a melting pot of cultures and professions, and because of that, all tolerated one another, even if they didn't exactly get along. It just made things easier that way.

It also kept you from being placed on anyone's shit list, because if that happened, you'd likely have to fly several systems away to fully resupply, which would be a massive inconvenience.

Convenience. That was Durkus's main appeal. Just about anything you might need could be sourced there, for a price. In this instance, however, it was not goods the Wampeh and his friends were seeking. It was something far more interesting.

Bud took a quick spin around the main docking areas once they landed, talking shop with some of his old pirate acquaintances he happened upon while casually surveying the craft that were currently present.

"Okay, I found us a Council ship sitting off at the landing site just past the textile vendors. Looks like they only arrived recently, so they won't be expected back at wherever it is they're heading for at least a week."

"That should be more than enough time for what we need," Hozark said.

"Yeah. And if it's not, then that means something has gone seriously wrong."

"Which would be bad," Henni said.

"You can say that again."

"Which would be bad."

Bud flashed her a look. "Really?"

"What? You said—"

"I was kidding, Henni. It's just a figure of speech."

"Well, maybe I was kidding too. You consider that?" she shot back.

"You're ridiculous, you know that?"

"You're *both* ridiculous," Laskar grumbled. "So, what do we do now?"

"Now we incapacitate the ship's crew, commandeer their vessel, land on Nagus, infiltrate a Council high-security greenhouse, steal the Ungall shrub, cure Happizano, and make our escape, all without the Council ever knowing we were there," Hozark said.

Laskar groaned. "Gee, you make it sound so easy."

The master assassin smiled. "If we are efficient in our efforts, it should be," he replied. "At least, the early stages. Firstly, we must address the crew. Nothing can happen until they are removed from the equation."

Unlike civilian crews, the Council's workers would be a bit more difficult to waylay. With official Council business on their plate, and severe reprimands in store if they screwed up, the men and women of the supply ship were almost certain to be quite attentive to their tasks.

This meant they would also be far less likely to be easily tripped up by the usual distractions the would-be thieves often used against less vigilant targets.

"There are seven of them," Demelza noted, having clocked the full numbers of the crew as they came and went from their craft. "No more than four are away at any given time."

"Meaning we will have to deal with at least three still aboard when we take the ship," Bud noted. "I hate to admit it, but that's some pretty sound tactics, there."

"Perhaps. But a little subterfuge and we should have no problem taking their craft," Hozark said. "First, we apply a little of the Council's own tactics against them."

"Burn an entire city to make a point?" Bud asked.

"No. We shall do unto them as they did to Happizano. We shall incapacitate their crew with kindness."

"If by kindness, you mean poisoned food," Bud joked.

Hozark grinned. "Precisely. Henni, how do you feel about a temporary role in the food service industry?"

"If it means I get to poison some Council shits, then I'm all for it."

"I thought you might feel that way," the Wampeh said with an amused chuckle. "You will not be killing them, however. These are merely pawns in the Council's larger game, and there is no honor in causing them lasting harm."

"But we can mess them up in the short term, right?"

"Oh, of course."

Henni smiled wide. "Good. Count me in. When do I start?"

"Soon. But first, Demelza and I have one little task to complete. A tiny bit of preparation work. We shall return straightaway."

Hozark and his associate headed out under guise of average travelers to acquire a room for the week. To any observing, they appeared just like any other couple on a layover. And amorous as they seemed, none would think twice of their staying in their room the whole time.

Of course, it would be a slumbering group of Council crew who would actually be inhabiting the chamber. But no one would be the wiser to that fact until well after they'd completed their task. And by then, it wouldn't matter who found out.

As for the trio of crewmembers who would have to be dealt with on the ship itself, after being neutralized, those three would simply have to remain aboard, though hidden in shipping containers for the duration.

Fortunately, the stasis spells they planned to use on them were quite efficient at keeping even the largest of people down for the count, so unless their stolen ship was boarded and searched, and thoroughly at that, they would never be found out.

Henni donned a cute outfit that made her look even less threatening than she usually did and strode off into town to offer free samples of her homemade pastries to those she encountered. One particular batch was set aside for a special group of people, the heavy tranquilizer spells timed to sink in slowly, then lay the recipient out approximately ten minutes later.

Of course, the increasingly groggy victims would be guided from public view by well-meaning bystanders just as their awareness began to wane. Bystanders who just so happened to have an empty room for them to rest in.

By the time they got there, thanks to the careful prompting

and redirection at the hands of the Wampeh and his friends, the spell would have taken full hold, and they would be unable to remember pretty much anything about the period leading up to their luxury incarceration.

Three of the four were happy to sample the free delights the young woman with violet hair was offering, but the fourth politely declined, carrying on about her business, acquiring items to stock her ship with.

"This will require a more *direct* approach," Hozark quietly said to Demelza as he observed the lone holdout make her way through the area.

"I shall handle it," she replied, moving off to shadow the woman.

Demelza quietly cast a painful spell, twisting the woman's nethers in a painful way.

"Oh, are you okay?" she asked when the woman stopped and leaned against a wall.

"Just cramping," she replied. "A bit early, is all."

"Oh, I get them something fierce," Demelza said, holding out a brown, knotted stick pulled from her pocket. "I've got some turkot root, if you want a piece to chew."

Turkot root was a well-known natural pain relief remedy for feminine issues, though it was not as commonly used in this part of the galaxy. And in a situation like this, the innocuous little twig was worth its weight in gold.

"Thank you so much," the woman said, gratefully accepting the offering.

"My pleasure," Demelza replied as the woman began chewing the root. "I'm just glad to help."

The spell embedded in the root was undetectable to all but the strongest of magic users, and even then, only if they knew what to look for. It was almost as effective as the one used in the pastry Henni had so proficiently foisted off on the woman's crewmates, and within just a few minutes the ailing holdout was on her way to joining her crewmates.

"Do you need help?" Demelza said. "I think you should lie down."

"I have work to do."

"You don't look up to doing anything, let alone work," Demelza said. "Look, I have a room quite close by. I have errands to do, but if you want to use it for a little while until you feel better, it would be my pleasure to offer it to you."

The woman hesitated, pondering the offer. Then a new wave of pain washed over her, just as the grogginess began to increase.

"Maybe just for a little bit," she said. "Thank you for being so kind."

"Women have to look out for one another," Demelza said with a warm, sisterly smile that utterly concealed her true intent. "Come on, let's get you horizontal. I'm sure you'll feel a lot better once you lie down."

## CHAPTER TWENTY-ONE

It hadn't exactly been the smoothest execution of a plan the team had ever pulled off, but the end result was all that mattered.

Four Council crewmembers were slumbering in a deep stasis spell in a rented room, none the wiser to what had befallen them. And if the group was successful in commandeering their ship and carrying out their cure-stealing operation, they would have the vessel returned just as they'd found it before the crew had even regained consciousness.

But before they could make their flight to Nagus to steal the cure Hap so desperately needed, the remaining three crewmembers aboard the soon-to-be stolen ship had to first be removed from the equation. And it needed to be done in a way that would leave them unharmed and unclear as to what exactly had happened to them.

It would be a bit of a task, but if they could pull it off, the crew would all wake in a few days, perfectly healthy and unharmed, though perhaps a bit confused at where the time had gone.

Shimmer cloaks would be the order of the day for this aspect of the operation. Fortunately, there were no heavily powered users anywhere near, so the odds of detection were incredibly slim. Even so, the Wampeh had to be quick. Speed could often overcome what fortune might not.

"Rotza, what the hell is up with the door ward?" the woman currently in command asked as a shrill warning rang out in the command chamber. "It's triggering, then resetting over and over."

"No idea," her burly associate replied. "You think Fawnti screwed up the casting?"

"It's not like her, but maybe. Take a look, will you? Before this noise drives us both insane."

The man chuckled and rose from his seat. "Back in a minute," he said, then trotted off to see about the faulty door wards.

The door looked perfectly normal, and the wards did appear to be in place. More importantly, the annoying noise had finally stopped. The Council crewman heaved a sigh of relief. This was going to be easier than he'd originally worried. Whatever had been the fault seemed to have resolved itself, though spells rarely did so.

"Well, that wasn't too hard," he said with a chuckle.

He didn't see the Wampeh coming.

Even if Hozark had not been hidden beneath his shimmer cloak, he moved and cast his spell with such speed that the poor fellow would never have stood a chance.

The spell flew true, stunning the man to the deck, a quick follow-up spell locking in a firm state of stasis, ensuring he would remain unconscious for the next week.

Hozark studied the fallen man slumbering at his feet. A bit stocky, but similar height. And fortunately not one of the more difficult races to mimic. If he possessed tentacles rather than arms and legs, the next step would be quite a bit more challenging.

Mind you, he was a master Ghalian, and it could be done, but with so little time to adopt the man's appearance, it was guaranteed to be somewhat flawed, even with his considerable skills.

"Well, that wasn't too hard," Hozark said, repeating the one sample of the man's voice he had heard before taking his place. "Well, that wasn't too hard."

It wasn't perfect, but it would have to work.

His disguise firmly affixed, Hozark strode to the command center and stepped through the door. The acting captain swiveled in her seat.

"So, what was it?"

"Well, that wasn't too hard," he replied as he stepped clear of the doorway.

She cocked her head slightly. "What's up? You seem a little bit off."

Hozark shrugged and flopped down into the nearest seat.

"Why are you in Fawnti's seat?" she asked. Hozark could feel her pulling on her konus ever so slightly.

Whether to cast a spell or just check her crewmate for possible illness, he did not know. Nor did he care. The spell he whispered wasn't the strongest available to him, but Hozark dropped the woman before she could complete whatever it was she had in mind.

This bit was far easier than anticipated. The third was not in the command center at the moment, and that had left him a bit of freedom to remove this one from the equation in a gentler manner than would otherwise have been required. But that still left one more to deal with.

He hurried through the ship, casually looking into every compartment as he did, stun spell at the ready. Hozark then opened the ship's external door and gave the slightest of nods to the empty space beside it, where Demelza was waiting to make her entry.

The disguised Wampeh and his cloaked friend strode to the command center.

"Ah, she's a bit *small*," the sturdily built woman noted. "How about the other one?"

"Not aboard the ship," Hozark replied.

"Well then, I guess there's nothing for it," Demelza replied, applying an extra bit of somewhat uncomfortable, but quite efficient, Ghalian disguise spells to help mask her larger frame and make her appear smaller, like the woman at her feet. "So, the remaining crewmember?"

"Unknown. But their absence is something of a problem. We cannot depart until he or she returns, lest we have the ship's theft reported. This changing of their security plan is clever, and may force us to alter our own plans accordingly."

He activated the ship's forward observation spell, an image appearing on the solid hull where the magic allowed in the outside view. The two Wampeh scanned the area, watching the milling people.

"It seems we are going to have to call in the others to help us locate this remaining––" Hozark paused. "Oh, my. You cannot be serious."

There, plain to see, was the missing crewmember, walking right back to the ship, happily munching from a large container of food in her hand.

"He stepped out to get a snack?" Demelza said, joining Hozark's disbelief. "Security was disregarded in this manner when the craft is clearly well-stocked and a valuable target?"

Hozark shook his head. "I take back what I said about their discipline. This is just sloppy."

"Extremely," Demelza agreed, affixing her disguise more firmly in place. "But it does save us a prolonged search."

"True," Hozark replied as he slapped a big smile on his face. "Now, let us greet our *crewmate*."

The man cleared the wards on the door and stepped aboard,

then made his way to the command center, crunching loudly as he walked.

"I hope you brought some for us," Hozark called out while he was still in the corridor.

The man looked up from his treats with a guilty expression on his face. "Uh, I thought you said you didn't want anything."

Hozark folded his arms across his chest with a disapproving stare. The man was so busy trying to think of something to say that he didn't even notice Demelza's slightly off disguise, nor the stun spell she was casting.

He hit the deck in a heap, an excuse still forming on his lips.

"Well, that was a pleasant surprise. We could have spent a great deal of time hunting down a lone crewmember in this place," Demelza said as she hoisted the man up over her shoulder with ease. "I shall get this one stowed with the others."

"Excellent. I shall retrieve the others in preparation for our departure," Hozark replied.

The woman nodded once, then carried the slumbering crewman to the cargo storage area, where the other two were already safely tucked away in large containers, carefully padded to ensure their safety should the flight get rough.

She sealed the man in, like the others, and double-checked their stasis spells. All was properly in place, and the trio would slumber soundly until the wake-up spell was applied. That would be done when they returned the ship after it had served their purposes.

Normally, they would allow them to wake at their own leisure. But as this was a crew of seven, it would be imperative they all came to at the same time. With the four in the city and the three aboard the ship rousing at once, and all unsure what had happened, they would all jump back to work as if nothing had happened.

Embarrassment was funny like that, and fear of it could make people do a great many things not in their best interests.

And that could be manipulated. Something the Wampeh Ghalian were experts at.

Demelza tidied up and put everything in place. Should anyone board the ship, for whatever reason, there would be nothing to suggest a hostile takeover of the craft. All that remained was bringing the others aboard. After that, they would begin their run for Nagus. And *that* would almost certainly be a great deal more challenging than this.

# CHAPTER TWENTY-TWO

Happizano was pale and sweating, yet was also cool to the touch. He drifted in and out of consciousness as the magical compound attacked his system from within.

At least his cries of pain had ceased, though not for good reasons.

"We have acquired the vessel," Hozark notified his friends. "The crew is safely tucked away, and Demelza is prepping the craft for liftoff as soon as we transfer young Happizano aboard."

"So let's get to it," Bud said. "No time to waste; the kid's not doing well."

"I still think we should just get him to the Council people with the cure," Laskar said. "I mean, yeah, I know they'll take him, but how do we know we'll be successful on Nagus? He's looking really bad, and this might take too long."

Hozark had to give the man a bit of credit. For a callous bastard, he did seem to have a genuine concern for the boy's health. But it was still simply not an option. The Council would cure him, certainly, but they would never get him back once he'd been secreted away.

And given what his father was doing in the interest of

sparing his son, the boy's life did not outweigh those of the thousands who would fall if Visla Jinnik were to continue his terrible work.

"I admire your concern, Laskar. However, that is simply not an option. The damage that could be unleashed would be far greater than any we have seen so far. Our best chance is to cure the boy at Nagus. But you are correct that time is of the essence. And therefore, we must move him to the Council ship we have commandeered immediately. We leave as soon as he is aboard."

Henni, Bud, and Laskar all glanced between themselves. Apparently, the talk about bringing Hap back to the Council outreach ship had been going on for a little while. But they respected Hozark's strategic mind, and as distasteful as it might be, they knew he was right about what they had to do.

"We'll box him up and head out at once," Bud said. "Henni, you want to give me a hand?"

"Sure," she said, uncharacteristically restrained in her demeanor. It seemed even she was taken down a notch with her concern.

Happizano was carefully tucked away in a cargo container, well padded for his comfort, and with adequate openings to allow for proper air flow. That was then loaded onto a floating conveyance and moved to Bud's loading bay door.

Bud, Henni, and Laskar had put worker tunics over their usual attire, adopting the semblance of the many porters who were delivering goods to the ships across town in a constant stream.

"Okay. Let's do this," Bud said. "Lead the way."

Hozark stepped out in front and walked the most direct path to the waiting vessel. It was far enough from Bud's mothership that by the time they arrived, there would be no risk of anyone noting anything unusual about the cargo.

For all they'd know, it was being delivered from within town, just like all of the other loads being brought aboard the adjacent craft.

It took longer than they would have liked, but it was essential to make their progress seem as normal as possible, and thus, they were forced to move at the same pace as the other porters. Soon enough, the precious cargo was loaded into the Council ship, and Hap was transferred to one of the bunks and carefully tucked in.

Bud and Laskar were ready to make their way back to their ship, but Henni opted to stay at Hap's side, dabbing his sweating brow with a cloth and watching over him as he fell in and out of a fitful sleep.

"We'll meet you at the moon location," Bud said as he and Lasker stepped off the Council craft.

The plan was for them to park the mothership a safe distance from Nagus, out at a moon orbiting one of the worlds farthest away from the planet. It was a fair bit of distance, but it was imperative that their getaway ride was nowhere near the incursion, just in case things went wrong.

It shouldn't have been an issue, and there was no reason to believe Bud's ship would be needed to provide an emergency rescue, but they'd learned long ago that it was far better to anticipate the worst outcome and prepare for it, just in case.

"Very well. We shall see you there," Hozark replied, then closed the doors behind them. He and Demelza then prepared for their flight to the red sun system and lifted off.

Things were about to become very interesting. An incursion on a Council world, in a stolen Council ship, no less. It was sure to be a challenge, and one with very high stakes. Hozark was confident in their odds, but he could not help but worry if the boy could hold on long enough for their success.

Uzabud tucked away his ship in a quiet crater on a moon

orbiting one of the farthest planets from Nagus. The system's red sun's rays still made it this far, but it was a frigid, dead orb incapable of sustaining life.

That made it a perfect place to set down and hide the ship.

Normally, Hozark and Demelza would have utilized their shimmer-cloaked craft to make a silent approach and landing, followed by a rapid and stealthy incursion under their own personal shimmers.

But this was a Council stronghold. A world quite likely containing one or more powerful magic users. It was simply too risky flying any shimmer craft into the atmosphere. The scrutiny was already high, and only Council ships were allowed to land in the first place.

But flying a shimmer ship in this instance contained more risks, as their adversary knew what to expect. If they even had the slightest suspicion the Ghalian assassins would make an attempt for the cure on Nagus, then they would be specifically looking for Ghalian shimmer magic.

That left just one option. The stolen ship.

After a quick liaison on the moon, the crews consolidated aboard the Council craft and prepared for the attempt on the greenhouses of Nagus. Bud loaded up his gear aboard Hozark and Demelza's ride and settled in for the approach.

Laskar, however, drew the short straw and was selected to stay aboard the mothership to keep it primed and ready to go in case they needed to make a hasty escape.

"I don't even have a long-range skree," he lamented. "What if you need me?"

"If we need you, we'll be flying back at you at high speeds," Bud said. "Trust me, you'll hear us coming when we get within range. Let's just hope that doesn't happen."

"You suck. You know that?" Laskar griped.

"You know you love me," his pilot joked. "Anyway, stay alert. Hopefully, we'll be back sooner than later."

And with that, they went their separate ways.

The flight to Nagus was short, Hozark executing a small jump to the planet's orbit to make their arrival appear just like any of the other Council craft arriving at the world. They began their descent through the exosphere, where the magical wards in place around the planet automatically recognized them as an approved Council ship.

So far, their plan was working as they had hoped it would. But they knew how quickly things could go sideways, even on the most straightforward of missions.

Hozark spotted the multiple, massive greenhouses of the region most likely to contain the Ungall shrubs. They weren't a major crop, so they took up a very small footprint within the structures, but they were also a very, very highly valued asset, and as such they were undoubtedly grown in the most secure of the buildings.

Hozark, Demelza, and Bud were all wearing the Council uniforms they had acquired for the occasion. It was far better than attempting to use any magic to disguise themselves, as the same problem as with shimmer cloaks could present itself with disguises as well.

A sufficiently strong power user could potentially see through the disguises if they were focused on detecting intrusions of that nature. And given what they'd seen recently, there was every reason to believe that could be a possibility.

Henni was the lone member of the group who remained in her own attire. As they had flown to their rendezvous, she'd become increasingly concerned about Happizano. He could have been left with Laskar, but his condition was degrading rapidly.

They just hoped the Ungall shrub would have already been compounded in the facility, as Hap would need the cure the moment they had it.

When Hozark had asked Henni to remain aboard the ship

and keep an eye on the boy, for once, she didn't bitch about being left behind. That spoke volumes, as to how serious things were.

They set the ship down in the small landing area near a trio of large greenhouse facilities.

"We need to get to the storehouses," Hozark said as he and his two friends exited their ship. "It will be far easier to acquire the Ungall there. If we enter the grow operations directly, our likelihood of discovery will only increase."

"Accessing the storehouses may be a bit of a task," Demelza noted. "I fear our entry may be somewhat delayed."

"I've got an idea," Bud said, eyeing the less-secured cluster of distribution buildings nearby. "Come on. Let's do this."

# CHAPTER TWENTY-THREE

One would have expected a pair of assassins and a former pirate to make a brazen attempt on the facility they believed contained the Ungall plant they were so desperately seeking. After all, with a combination like that, what better way to claim their prize than by stunning force?

Of course, they didn't actually know which of the buildings had what they needed, nor did they have a clue as to the interior schematics and security situation. To go charging in could work, no doubt, but it would be ugly at best.

Fortunately, Bud had a different idea. One that wouldn't get them directly on the Council's radar from the first minutes on the ground. One that would not mark them as a threat in need of squashing. While they could break in and break out, with bloodshed and mayhem galore, their odds of success would greatly diminish.

Instead, they stopped off at the low-security resupply depot before heading for the heavily protected buildings nearby. Bud took the lead, while his friends, posing as laborers, fell in behind him.

"Watch it with those!" the disguised pirate said to the two

Wampeh maneuvering the floating conveyances loaded with basic produce and supplies.

"Sorry, sir," Hozark said as he followed Bud into the secured storehouse.

Demelza was right behind him, carefully steering her load in his wake. Bud, however, was unburdened with supplies, and made a straight line to the requisitions counter in front of the heavily warded door to the storehouse vaults.

"What do you want?" the woman at the desk asked, eyeing the two loads that had come to a stop behind her new visitor.

"We're on a resupply run," he replied. "Apparently, the captain got a skree message with quite a list of items we need to take out to the fleet."

"Which fleet?"

"Several of them, actually," Bud said, covering as best he could. "We've been jumping all over the place trying to meet the demands of the warships. I tell ya, those guys go through a *lot* of supplies, and they've got us running all over the place today. But for the moment, I think the only things we need from *your* depot is a container of Issmus powder, some Fangol root, and, hang on..." He turned to Demelza. "Did the captain say it was Omantus tea he wanted, or Primantus tea?"

"It was Omantus," she replied. "I'm sure of it. His stomach's been acting up something fierce."

"Okay," Bud said, turning back to the woman at the desk. "And Omantus tea, please."

The woman was used to handling requests for some of the most dangerous and magical compounds in the system, but this was a paltry collection of the lowest-tier herbs and compounds in the entire building.

"That's all he wants?" she asked, her defenses already lowering at the middling request.

"For now, yeah," Bud said with a grin. "Of course, you know how it goes. I wouldn't be surprised if he changes his mind or gets another long-range skree and has us turn right around and come back here. But that should do it for the time being."

At that moment, part of Hozark's load began to slip, just as planned, and Bud and the two Wampeh had to jump forward to stop it from falling. In the process, a carefully placed little box of sweet pastries fell to the ground, partly smooshed from the near miss.

"Oh, damn," Bud grumbled. "We can't bring these back. Not like this," he said, opening the box and examining the mildly damaged contents. He looked at the woman at the counter a moment. "So, I really shouldn't do this, but it would be a shame to let these go to waste. Do you want to take 'em? Totally off the record, of course. We'll have to go get a new box anyway, so the captain will never know."

Bud and Hozark had judged the woman correctly when they first stepped inside. There were other treats strategically placed in the load, any one of which could have been made to fall and provide a tempting offer to a variety of tastes.

This woman, however, had the look of someone with a sweet tooth. And it was a good thing, because unlike alcohols or other pricier and more restricted goods, pastries were not generally seen as contraband.

"Well," she said, pondering the offer, "I suppose if you'd just be throwing them out, there's no harm in it."

"I couldn't agree more," Bud said, placing the partially crushed container on her desk. "Too much waste in our business as it is, right?"

"You've got a point about that," she said, a smile growing on her face as she surveyed her lucky score. "Now, you just wait here a few minutes. I need to run in the back to get your items."

"Thanks a lot. We'll be here," Bud replied as she stepped through the heavily warded door.

It was clear she was in possession of some sort of pass spell, though whether it was worn on her person in the form of a pendant or charm, or had been bonded to her body itself, they could not tell.

Whatever the case, judging by even this preliminary probing of the storehouses defenses, it was clear it would be near impossible to get past those magical protections without one. Or, at least, not in the limited time the group had.

Several minutes passed before the woman returned from the depths of the secured area carrying a small container with the requested materials in it.

"Here you are," she said, handing over the goods. "I threw in a little Primantus tea as well, just in case."

Bud took them and passed them to Hozark, who carefully stowed them on his already large pile of goods.

"You're fantastic," Bud said. "Thank you so much for that."

"My pleasure," she replied.

It really was amazing how the smallest of bribes, and a request for the most innocuous of items were able to smooth what could have been a difficult interaction into an entirely pleasant affair.

"Well, we'd better get this stuff back. No telling what the captain's going to have waiting for us next," Bud said with a pained chuckle. "Thanks again for all your help."

Hozark and Demelza were already halfway out the door, and Bud fell in behind them as they made the slow trek back to their ship. No one looked at them twice. The stack of supplies, as well as Council uniforms, made them appear just as anyone else on the surface of the restricted world.

They belonged, and no one would question their presence or actions. Not so long as they appeared to be just another cog in the Council's machinery.

"We know the basic layout now," Hozark said quietly as they took their load to the ship. "And it seems that an infiltration and theft would require a fair bit of doing on our part."

"Yeah, that place is locked up tighter than a drum," Bud

agreed. "But I think we can leverage our new friend's goodwill if we play our cards right."

"I was thinking the same thing," the Wampeh said with a grin. "Let us deposit our load, then head back to acquire what we *really* came for."

They offloaded the conveyances of roughly eighty percent of their cargo, retaining that last twenty percent to maintain the appearance that they were picking up even more supplies at their captain's request. They then headed back to the secured storehouse.

"Back so soon?" the woman asked when she saw who her visitors were.

"Yeah, wouldn't you know it?" Bud said with a lamenting laugh. "We'd just finished unloading when the captain came rushing in with a whole new list of stuff to get. Apparently, we're supposed to leave at once, so he really lit a fire under the supply teams to make this quick."

"Well, let me see what I can do for you. What do you need this time?"

"He said to tell you the teams on Lortzal skreed that they need more Ungall at once."

The woman's smile faltered.

"Is that a problem?" Bud asked. "I don't even know what that stuff is."

"It's a highly restricted substance," she replied.

"Oh, I didn't know. Do I need to get the captain to—?"

"It's not that," she interrupted. "It's just they already cleaned us out just the other day. All of the prepared compound was gathered up. Are you sure they need more?"

"Just following orders," Bud said. "But you said there's none left?"

He flashed a concerned look at Hozark. This could be a very, very bad turn of events.

"Compounded Ungall, yes," she replied. "All I've got back

there is some of the unprocessed Ungall. But it still needs to be converted if it's to be any use."

Bud scratched his chin. "Well, I guess it'll have to do. Better that than coming back empty-handed," he said.

"Understandable," she replied. "I'll fetch you what I have handy. More should be harvested within the week, but the emmik who does the compounding won't be back for at least a few weeks."

"That's okay. I'm sure the captain will know what to do with it," Bud said.

The woman once more stepped though the heavily warded door, returning several minutes later with a large sack of fresh leaves.

"I hope this will work," she said, handing over the bundle.

"It'll have to do," Bud said with his warmest grin. "Thanks again for your help. You're a real life saver, you know that?"

"I do what I can."

"Well, it's not unnoted," he replied, then turned to the Wampeh porters. "Okay, you two. Let's grab the rest of this list and hurry back. Captain won't want to be kept waiting."

They waved their farewells and headed for the doors once again, the Ungall leaves in hand, but not in the form they had expected. They were on an incredibly tight timeline, and things had just gotten even more difficult. They now had their work cut out for them once again, and with an entirely unexpected task.

## CHAPTER TWENTY-FOUR

"That was fast," Henni said when the away team returned to the ship with their booty. "You were able to get the Ungall without a fight? Thank the gods. Hap is really not doing well."

The grim look on the others' faces spoke louder than any words.

"What's the matter? You said you got the Ungall."

"We did, yes," Hozark replied. "But we were only able to procure raw leaves."

"So?"

"So, they require a particular bit of magical processing to compound them in a manner suitable for administration. I am afraid the raw leaves themselves are quite useless."

Demelza was already stowing and strapping in the supplies they had gathered as part of their diversionary tactic while Bud rushed to power up the craft for immediate departure. They'd transfer most of the haul to his mothership when they rejoined Laskar, but for the moment, time was of the essence.

"How soon can we be in the air?" Hozark asked.

"Three minutes," Bud replied. "But where are we going? There can't be many people capable of compounding Ungall leaves. It's such a rarity, I doubt most herbalists have ever even seen any."

Demelza mulled over the issue. "I would think Bud is correct. However, this close to Nagus, there will almost certainly be at least one in either this or an adjacent system."

"You think so?"

"She is likely right," Hozark interjected. "The Council would almost certainly wish to outsource some of that labor if they could. All the better to not only spread their influence to other worlds, but also free up their own specialists for local work."

"So, you think we should try the main city on Dargus?" Bud asked. "It's the only other habitable planet in this system."

Hozark thought about their options a moment. The Council was always trying to expand their reach, and this system was already firmly under their control. More likely, they would have procured the services of an herbalist in the nearest system. All the better to exert a bit of control there.

"We should fly to the next system. If my hunch is correct, the premiere herbalist there should be well versed enough in these obscure and rare compounds to provide us with what we need."

"Okay, then. I'll set us a course once we join up with Laskar."

"Your ship will need to stay out of sight, though," Hozark said. "The area may very well be under watchful eyes, and if they noted your craft in our prior engagements, its presence might draw their attention."

"Yeah, good point. I'll have him hang back in deep orbit while we take this Council ship in," Bud replied.

A moment later, they were airborne, making a painfully slow exit through the exosphere on their way to rendezvous with their hidden comrade. It was difficult to fly so slowly when time was ticking by, but maintaining the appearance of a normal Council craft on a normal Council run was crucial to their plans.

Anything else, and they might very well draw some very unwanted attention. Something they simply could not afford.

"Wait a minute, you want to do what?" Laskar asked when they drew close enough to utilize their short-range skrees.

"We have to fly to the neighboring system. The fourth planet from the sun has a pretty robust commerce hub, and that's the most likely place where we'll be able to source an herbalist who can do what we require of them."

"Bud, you're telling me we're flying to another system entirely, and we don't even know if whoever it is you are looking for there will be able to help."

"Trust me, Laskar. We don't have a choice."

"He's getting worse, then?"

"Yeah, he is."

Laskar sighed over his skree. "I told you, man. We should have given him to the mercy ship. It's a shitty option, but at least we'd know he was safe."

Hozark took the skree from the pilot. "Laskar, I appreciate your concern, but there is simply no time, and no other option available to us now. We must depart at once. Follow Bud's directions and await us in orbit. If all goes according to plan, we shall join you shortly, and with the boy recovering."

Bud and Laskar synced up their jumps, and moments later both had flashed from the quiet moon, arriving just outside orbit of the bright blue planet.

It was a single jump to this system, and that concerned Hozark more than he was letting on. The ease with which the Council could deploy reinforcements to this location was a very real threat. One they would have to be ever vigilant for.

But for the moment, there was only one pressing thing on their plate. They had to get the Ungall leaves to the herbalist, and fast.

"He's not waking up," Henni said, panic in her eyes as they set the ship down as close to the city as they were able.

"It will be all right, Henni. We shall have the cure prepared shortly," Hozark said. "All we need to do is locate the herbalist.

Once that is accomplished, we shall merely have to wait for the compound to be finalized."

"And you're sure this person can do it?"

"I am confident, yes. But sure? None can ever be sure in this life." Hozark turned his attention to Bud. "We must go. Henni will keep an eye on the boy. The rest of us shall split up and approach the herbalists working within the city. Hopefully, we can narrow the search and find the one capable of this task quickly."

"Right. Let's do this, then," Bud said. "Time for us men and women of adventure to go do some adventuring."

"If by adventuring, you mean saving the boy's life, then yes," Hozark said as the three of them stepped out of the ship. "Spread out, and good luck."

The assassins and their pirate friend separated and quickly made their way through the crowds toward different parts of the city. There were undoubtedly a good many herbalists in the region.

Compounding magical substances was a good business, and even one with just a modicum of talent could make a good living if they possessed the right kind of power. The challenge was finding the one that could handle their very specific requirements.

Hozark quickly moved from location to location, his skill in subterfuge and intelligence-gathering helping him efficiently identify the most likely candidates in his part of the search grid.

Demelza and Bud were likewise speedy in their efforts, moving through the names given to them by locals with an urgent efficiency. Soon, they had canvassed the majority of the area and it was time for them to meet up to discuss their findings.

Hozark and Demelza had reached the rendezvous point first and were discussing their next steps. Hozark had met with no success, but Demelza, it seemed, had located the one man on this world who was able to do what they had requested of him.

"We need to bring him the Ungall leaves at once," Hozark said. "How long will it take him to compound them?"

"As it is a small quantity he will be making for our needs, it should only take him a relatively short time. Perhaps a half hour at most."

"This is fortuitous."

"Indeed. But there are Council spies lurking. I noted no fewer than five of them when I entered his establishment. I had to apply a disguise, and even then it required quite a show to appear as though I was merely interested in topical moisture compounds."

"So, they will be expecting an attempt to bring the Ungall to him," Hozark said. "This complicates matters. We are up against a tight timeline, and yet we lack flexibility."

"There's Bud," Demelza said, nodding slightly across the plaza to where their friend and pilot was emerging from a small street. "Perhaps he will have another novel idea. He performed quite admirably on Nagus, after all."

"True, his plan worked wonderfully. Mayhap he will come up with--"

Hozark stopped mid-sentence.

A throng of security forces swarmed their friend, surrounding him with weapons drawn.

Demelza was about to move when Hozark gently placed his hand on her forearm, holding her back.

"Give it a moment," he said. "Note their uniforms. These are locals. Not Council forces."

"But what could it mean?"

"I believe we shall find out momentarily."

Bud slowly raised his hands in the air, catching Hozark and Demelza's eye for a split second as he glanced at the men on all sides.

"Hey, fellas. What's the problem?" he asked with a warm smile. "Surely there's been some kind of mistake. I'm just a visitor here, out on a little shopping excursion."

"You are the pirate known as Uzabud the Wicked," the captain of the guard said matter-of-factly.

"*That*?" Bud said. "That's not me."

"It is," the man said, showing him an image disc with his face and a list of crimes on it.

"Oh, I mean, that *was* me. But I'm a reformed man. I've changed my ways. I haven't done anything illegal in ages. Straight and narrow, that's my life these days."

"You can tell it to the magistrate. Take him," the captain ordered.

The men roughly grabbed Bud by the arms and hauled him off to the city's vast jails. As an up-and-coming world under the Council's watch, any unsavory types were immediately rounded up and removed from public view. It seemed that Bud was now one of them.

"We cannot just kill the guards and take him. To do so would raise the alarm, and we would never be able to get the compound for Hap in time," Demelza said.

"No, we would not," Hozark agreed, watching the men and women in the general area as they observed the arrest.

A few poorly disguised Council guards seemed to note the goings-on, but then soon returned to their work, scanning the crowds for signs of their true quarry. This gave Hozark an idea. They needed a diversion to acquire the cure for Hap, and now he might kill two Barzingi with one stone.

## CHAPTER TWENTY-FIVE

Time was quickly ticking away, and yet there was only so much the ailing boy's caregivers could do about it. Their increasing frustration was palpable because of it. The herbalist, however, was being monitored, and it seemed clear that the Council's presence on this world was more than coincidental.

It had already been a difficult situation when they landed. One that had only been made worse by Bud's unexpected incarceration. But where there was inconvenience, opportunity also lurked, and Hozark was one known to adapt and overcome. In this case, that meant he would have to utilize the resources at hand in novel ways.

"We shall have no difficulty passing the first string of guards," he noted as they discussed the expansive jail cell structure Bud had been marched off to. "All of their efforts are concentrated on keeping the inmates inside, not deterring a forced entry."

"You're going to break in?" Henni asked.

Hozark nodded as he strapped on his vespus blade. "Yes. We shall break in, in order to break Bud out."

"Count me in."

"You will serve a far more vital purpose from outside this particular conflict. Happizano needs you looking after him."

Henni nodded her understanding. "Of course. You're right. But once he's safe, someone needs a serious ass kicking."

"On that we are in agreement. For now, stay with the boy. I shall set the plan in motion. If all goes as we hope, Demelza will have the cure fabricated amidst all of the chaos. We shall then depart with it in the ensuing confusion."

The two women nodded.

"I shall be ready with the Ungall leaves," Demelza said. "As soon as the opportunity is clear, I shall get them to the herbalist. He is prepared for my arrival."

"Excellent," Hozark said. "Then it is my turn to act. I shall set out at once."

Henni watched him rise. "Good luck, Hozark."

"Thank you, Henni. But today, luck shall only play the smallest part in this," he said as he headed for the door. "I shall see you both shortly. Be ready."

"Okay," Henni said. "But what exactly are we getting ready for?"

Hozark grinned. "Oh, you will know it when you see it."

The Wampeh made his way from the landing area toward the nearby jail facility. It was situated quite near the space port, as a great many unsavory types most often originated from one of the newly arrived ships.

The strict rules of the up-and-coming world under the Council's watchful eye meant full cells and empty streets when it came to even a hint of questionable behavior. And Uzabud was now locked in there with the rest of the rabble.

The master Ghalian moved quickly. There was simply no time for a proper infiltration and rescue. This would have to be something far cruder than his normally elegant work, and yet, that would hopefully be what served his purposes even better in this particular situation.

A number of guards nearest the outer doors all fell ill within a short time of one another. Nothing serious, but enough gastric distress to allow a seemingly innocuous Council lackey to pass easily into the building.

That man was a disguised Wampeh, however, and the illness was magical in origin. Just enough to cause a lapse in security, but not enough to draw unnecessary attention.

Hozark was inside the facility, yes, but that little trick was only enough to help him gain entrance, and there was much yet to accomplish.

He reached out with his konus's power and gently tested the wards and locking spells layered throughout the facility. It seemed the cells were robustly protected from any attempts to break out, as would be expected. But he also noted they were woefully lacking defenses against *external* attacks.

It was beginning to look like he stood a very good chance of success. With the utmost care, he silently cast his most powerful disabling spells, slowly weakening the wards placed atop the row upon row of cells.

There were hundreds of men and women imprisoned there. Maybe more. And all of them were eager to be released. Hozark was about to grant that wish.

"Prepare yourself, Bud. Head for the ship," the disguised Wampeh said to the caged pirate as he walked past.

Bud didn't say a word as what was seemingly a Council man passed him by. But his sharp eyes scanned the facility as he made ready for his escape. Soon, Hozark would open his cell, and he would have to move fast to clear the building without recapture.

"Sound the alarm!" a frantic guard shouted out as not just Bud's cell, but *all* of them abruptly swung open.

Bud grinned broadly. He had to hand it to his friend. It was no small feat to unlock a guarded cell, but to open all of them? It was a story he'd tell for years to come.

If they survived, that is.

The masses of prisoners didn't waste any time with their newfound freedom, quickly overpowering the guards and taking their weapons before turning them on the group rushing to stop them. But the reinforcements were far too little and far too late.

The rioting prisoners burst through the doors into the streets, which devolved into an all-out melee of dangerous, angry people hell-bent on revenge. All available guards, and even the Council's men lurking around the city, rushed to contain the mayhem.

This was the sign.

Demelza sprinted through the throngs of rioters, then swerved into an alleyway where she shifted her appearance slightly and emerged at no more than a fast walk. She then carefully slipped into the herbalist's shop amid the confusion.

As she did, Bud was spat out onto the streets with the other prisoners, but unlike that group of conflict seekers, he raced as far from the fighting as he could, making a beeline for their commandeered Council ship.

"Okay, now that was impressive," he said to Hozark as he entered the craft. "Even for you, that was something."

"We required a distraction to give Demelza a clear path to the herbalist," Hozark replied. "It seemed like a logical option."

"You can say that again," he said, grabbing a pair of blades and a konus and strapping them on, replacing his confiscated weapons. "How's the kid?"

"I only returned a moment before you," Hozark said. "Demelza is having the cure compounded, so we should have it shortly."

Henni rushed into the command center. "You've gotta come quick. He's not breathing!"

Hozark and Bud moved in a flash, racing to the boy's side. It was as Henni had said. Happizano had succumbed to the late stages of the toxic magic, and his respiratory system had failed under the stress.

"Stand clear," Hozark ordered, summoning power from not his konus, but deep within his own body, as well as his vespus blade.

The weapon was still sheathed, but it began to glow brightly, tiny cracks of light seeping out through the thin seams of the sheath. Hozark directed the power into the boy, countering the toxin's effects, freeing Hap's lungs enough to draw breath.

"You did it! He's breathing!" Henni exclaimed.

Hozark leaned in, scooping the boy up in his arms. "Bud, Henni, we cannot wait for Demelza's return. We go to the herbalist. *Now.*"

The two looked at one another a moment. The master assassin would have his arms full. It was up to them to defend him.

"We've got you, Hozark," Bud said.

A thin sheen of sweat had already formed on the Wampeh's forehead as he continuously cast his spells, channeling the power into the unconscious boy. The amount of focus and power drain this sort of spell required was huge, even for a master Ghalian.

"We must hurry," Hozark said through gritted teeth.

The trio rushed from the ship to find themselves in the middle of a citywide riot. The diversion had worked perfectly for getting Bud out of his cell and providing Demelza cover as she snuck into the herbalist's shop, but now it was as much a hindrance as a help.

They pushed through the crowd, Bud and Henni doing what they could to clear a path. Fortunately, the majority of the heaviest fighting seemed to be taking place at the far end of the landing area. Hozark glanced up and saw the reason why.

A pale woman with a glowing blue sword was laying waste to

the swarm of ruffians who had thought the slender Wampeh an easy target. They were sorely mistaken.

Samara was surrounded, clearly taken off-guard by the hundreds of escaped prisoners, a great many of them wanting a piece of whomever they might encounter on the outside. For a moment, Hozark's former lover just happened to be in their eyeline.

Two ochre-skinned beasts of men with leathery hides and massive fists were bearing down on her as a trio of fast-moving, pale-blue sprites attempted to pepper her with flurries of blows. None lay so much as a finger on her.

At least, not a finger that was still attached to their body. Her vespus blade was carving a deadly arc through the attackers, laying waste to them even as more piled on from behind, unaware what had befallen those who had come before them.

Samara spun, her elbow smashing the jaw of a stocky Tslavar woman who managed to get a hand on her shoulder. As her teeth shattered in her mouth and she fell to the ground unconscious, the error of her actions was very clearly illustrated.

But the former Ghalian assassin did not let up one bit. She swung her blade to her right, even as her left foot simultaneously arced high, her heel cracking the nose of a particularly tall attacker. He went down at once, clutching his face as blood poured out of his ruined nose.

Samara didn't stop. She didn't even slow down. She was a dervish of violence, dropping attackers on all sides. And from the look on her face, she was rather enjoying the release. And her poor adversaries obviously had no idea who they were dealing with.

Hozark spotted her immediately, even through the chaotic riot. Though he'd thought her dead until quite recently, he would know her movements anywhere. They'd trained together nearly their whole lives, after all, and knew one another's techniques as well as their own.

Samara locked eyes with his. A brief glimmer as her attention shifted to her ex-lover.

It was clear the Council had been not only waiting here in hopes they might show up to acquire the cure for the boy. They had been confident of it. That Samara was here was proof of that. But how did she know they would come to *this* world? How was she so certain?

Hozark simply didn't have time to divert his attention to that question, and with the hundreds of rioting convicts between them, Samara would not be able to reach him even if she wanted to.

With one last look, he broke their connection and hurried off through the crowd, the critically ill boy in his arms.

Samara fought on auto-pilot a moment as she watched her former lover carrying the youth. He was taking hits, though nothing serious, as he protected the child. He was also apparently pouring his power into the youth, keeping him safe with both physical and magical efforts.

It was unlike Hozark, and a side of him she'd never seen. In fact, she never would have thought she would ever see him risk his own life to protect a child, and it gave her pause.

The swarming combatants all around her quickly drew her focus back to the battle at hand. She dispatched another handful of goons with great prejudice, their bodies separating as her vespus blade sliced with effortless grace.

The Council representative in charge of the operation made his way beside her. He was an emmik, but one of a fair amount of power. His spells flew fast and true as he lay waste to a good many aggressors.

"Do you see anything?" he asked as he drew near.

"I see a riot," she replied, then turned back to fighting off the mob, not saying a word about Hozark and the ill child in his arms.

## CHAPTER TWENTY-SIX

"Out of the fucking way!" Bud bellowed as he bulldozed through the rioters in his path.

Amazingly, the combatants parted, at least somewhat. The authoritative command from one of their own somehow registered in the part of their minds that was not currently engulfed in murder and mayhem.

"Hozark, come on!" he called to his friend as he shoved a pair of brawling women aside and swung the herbalist's doors open.

Demelza was there, a vision of calm patience, though they all knew she was counting the seconds on the inside. When she saw Hozark carry in the boy rather than meet them at the ship, she was alarmed. When she noted the power he was dumping into him to keep his lungs functioning, she immediately leapt into action.

"You must work faster," she said to the man making the compound.

"Rushed experts makes for bad results," he replied, not looking up from his labors.

He had been preparing a small batch of the leaves,

processing them with the special spells and additives that would ultimately result in their transformation from raw materials to a life-saving compound.

"Do whatever it takes. Make this happen," she said.

The man looked up at her, pausing in his work as he sensed an opportunity knocking. "You know, there's more Ungall here than you possibly need," he said, glancing to unconscious boy. "I can hurry the process, but it will cost me a lot of power to do so."

"Then do it."

"On one condition. You leave me the extra Ungall leaves when we're done. They're incredibly rare, and having them would be a boon to my practice."

"And they are also quite valuable," she added.

"That too," he said with a grin. "So, do we have a deal?"

She glanced at Hozark. The sweat was beading on his forehead as he focused his efforts on the unconscious boy.

"So long as the boy lives, and you keep our visit secret, then yes, you may keep the additional Ungall leaves," she said.

"Oh, he'll live," the herbalist said. "These are quite fresh, so this is going to be a particularly potent batch. Now, leave me in peace a moment so I can complete my work."

Demelza stepped back and waited. There was simply nothing else she could do. The man had upped his game and was pouring additional magic into the works to speed the process, but it still required a bit of time to complete.

Bud and Henni paced by the door, ready to take down any who might venture into the establishment while they were so near completion of this task. Fortunately, none entered, and in less than ten minutes, the compound was finally complete.

"Here. The boy needs to ingest this," the herbalist said. "Not too much, though. You need to be careful."

"Yes, you said it was a strong batch," Demelza said.

"Oh, it is, but that's not the reason. It's your friend's magic.

That's going to make the big difference in how the kid absorbs the compound."

"What do you mean?"

"The way he's dumping power into him? It's going to latch onto the kid's own powers for a bit. He must care for him a great deal to be willing to do that."

Demelza looked at her focused comrade. "Yes, he does," she said. "Now, what do I do with this?"

"Put a pinch between his cheek and gums," the man said. "The paste will immediately dissolve and make its way into his system without choking him. Once it latches onto the toxin, the reaction should set in fairly quickly."

Demelza did as the man directed, carefully placing a small dollop of the compound in the unconscious boy's mouth. She didn't know how much longer Hozark could keep up his efforts. It was clearly an immense drain, but she didn't dare interrupt him at this crucial juncture.

"How will we know if it––?"

Hap lurched up, promptly vomiting a stream of bile as he purged his body of the deadly poison. With confused, bleary eyes, he looked around the room. He seemed to be having a bit of difficulty focusing at the moment, but that was to be expected.

Hozark relaxed, letting his grip on his magic slide away, the steady stream of power finally cut off as the boy began his recovery. Hap looked up at the assassin with a groggy look.

"Dad?"

"No, young Jinnik. I am afraid your father is not here at the moment."

Hap's eyes began to focus better. He turned and glanced about the strange herbalist's shop.

"What... What's going on?"

"You fell ill. We have obtained treatment for you."

From outside the shop, the sounds of fighting were growing louder. The riot, it seemed, was spreading.

"What's all of that noise? It makes my head hurt."

"Ah, that. There is a bit of a disturbance in this city. I am afraid there is no time to discuss it further at the moment. We must depart for our ship at once. Uzabud, Henni, are you ready?"

"Good to go," Bud said.

"All set," Henni added.

"Good," Hozark said. "We need to get aboard and off this planet as quickly as possible. Can you stand, Happizano?"

"I think I––"

He fell over as he attempted to put weight on his unsteady legs.

"Well, I guess that's not an option," Bud said. "Ya want me to carry him?"

"No, I shall take care of our young friend," the Wampeh said. "Demelza, help Bud reach the ship. We shall require a quick liftoff. Samara is here, and that means trouble."

"Samara? Here? How did she possibly find us?"

"It is a Council-affiliated world, and one of the only places possessing an herbalist with this particular skill. It was a logical place for them to await our arrival."

"Then there is an additional urgency to our departure," she said.

"Indeed. Now, let us hurry. We––"

"Wait," Demelza interrupted.

She walked to the herbalist. "I need something from you."

"Oh, another barter. How excellent."

"Not a barter. You've been paid most handsomely for your work, and what I require is a simple matter."

The man pondered her statement a moment. He had just scored a significant amount of Ungall leaves. If what she wanted was indeed commonplace, he could likely accommodate her request.

"Very well. What is it you need?"

"Nasturian," she said.

"That's all?"

"It is. But it is something I need."

He chuckled as he pulled a vial of the incredibly potent spice from a drawer. Nasturian was a magical herb occasionally used as a food additive to increase the heat of a dish. But pure Nasturian would cause almost unbearable pain should one be foolish enough to ingest it.

What the Wampeh wanted it for, he didn't know. But for that matter, he didn't much care either.

"Use it in good health," he said, handing over the vial.

"I intend to," Demelza said as she tucked it away in a secure pocket. She turned to Hozark. "Okay. Let us go."

## CHAPTER TWENTY-SEVEN

The fighting in the streets had spread like magic fire, jumping from mere prisoners to the populace in general. There was apparently a lot of pent-up rage within the confines of the city, likely due to the overt presence of the Council in everyone's daily life.

Having a powerful entity like that shaping your destiny, regardless of what you might want, was quite the impetus for an uprising when the occasion presented itself. It was not a full-fledged rebellion, of course. But the excuse to riot, courtesy of the escaped prisoners, was all the disenfranchised citizens needed.

Just beneath the surface of the seemingly calm world, there was a churning anger just waiting to be released. And that was what they now had to swim through to get back to their ship.

"People are looting," Bud said, peeking out the herbalist's door. "It's way more than just the prisoners now. Things have really gone to shit out there."

"So what do we do?" Henni asked.

"Do? We push on," Hozark said. "Samara is here, and that

means Visla Ravik may be near. Or perhaps even Visla Maktan. We cannot afford to dally any longer than absolutely necessary."

Hozark picked up the wobbly boy and moved to the door. Now that he did not have to pour his power into the youth to keep him breathing, Hozark's energy seemed to have returned, but Demelza knew full well he had weakened himself during the process.

Hozark had tapped his internal power helping Happizano, and that was not good. He would need to feed and take someone's magic, and the sooner the better. To continue in this endeavor minus his emergency backup magic would be a very risky proposition.

"Try to stay close," Hozark said. "We possess strength in our numbers. It is an advantage we should leverage to our best possible benefit."

Bud opened the door and stepped out, the others close behind him. "Okay, let's get a move––"

Henni was already in motion, a violet-haired blur of aggression, the twin blades in her hands whirring like the deadly teeth of an angry, and very, very hungry beast. She charged ahead into the lead, laying out rioters and looters left and right.

This was not a fight calling for restraint. Not for her, though she did aim to injure rather than kill. At least most of the time. But some of the people rioting in the streets had ill intentions, and those were most certainly fair game.

"The path to the Council ship is looking pretty damn hairy," Bud yelled to his friends over the din of battle. "We've gotta get out of here before it all goes to hell."

He was right. This wasn't just a bar brawl spilled into the streets. This had the beginnings of becoming something far worse. And if that happened, the Council would wade into the conflict and quash it with great malice.

Hozark cast a breaking spell, pulling the power from what

was left in his konus as he rushed ahead with the boy in his arms. The men before him were smashed aside like twigs before a giant. He was taking no chances. Not now. Not with the boy on the mend.

But despite his drive and enthusiasm, neither Hozark nor Demelza felt much confidence they could make it to their ship unharmed. There were simply too many people between them and the craft, and those people were armed and dangerous.

It was looking like they would have to find some alternative transport when a large shadow flashed overhead.

"Hey, that's my ship!" Bud said as the mothership swooped down into a tight landing spot in the spaceport ahead.

"What is Laskar doing?" Demelza wondered.

"Saving our asses, by the looks of it," Henni said, pulling her daggers from her opponent's chest as he dropped to the ground. "See, there he is."

Laskar had rushed from the ship and into the fray the moment he'd set down. He had a sword in hand and was racing toward his friends, avoiding the crazed throng as best he could. But one man broke from the pack and charged him, quite unexpectedly.

Laskar spun, his sword woefully unprepared for the attack. But his internal magic kicked in as he cast a stun spell, dropping the man in an instant.

"How the hell did he do that?" Bud asked. "He doesn't have that kind of control."

"It is amazing what panic can do for you," Demelza said. "Call it *motivation*."

Bud was about to agree when he saw a small band of scrappers make a run at his craft, eager to strip what salvage they could from it in all of the confusion.

"Oh, hell no. No you don't!" he said, slinging spells from his konus as he raced toward the craft. "That's my ship!"

Bud rushed the men and made quick work of them, thanks

not only to his pirating skills, but also the deadly blades of his diminutive companion.

"Thanks, Henni," he said as they reached the ship.

But there was a problem. In their rush, Hozark had been left a little bit behind them. And it seemed some Council forces had taken notice. Samara wasn't with them, though, so he supposed he could thank the universe for small miracles.

"Can you stand?" Hozark asked the boy.

"Yeah, I think so," Happizano replied.

Gently, Hozark put him down on the ground. Hap wobbled a moment, but he was able to keep to his feet. Hozark didn't have a moment more to lose, launching into a fierce defense that left the Council goons shattered on the ground.

The master Ghalian didn't hesitate, immediately scooping up the unsteady boy and rushing him to Bud's waiting ship.

"All aboard?" Bud called out.

"We are," Hozark shouted back. "Get us out of here, Bud."

"But what about the Council ship?" Henni asked.

"It is too late to bother returning it. Our subterfuge has been discovered, and it is just a matter of time before the Council figures out what we did."

"So we just leave it? All of those supplies?"

"I know, but yes, we leave it. The Council figured out our trick, and it would be more dangerous flying with it than without it." Hozark turned to his pilot friend. "Go, Bud. Get us out of here."

"Don't have to tell me twice," he said, jumping them away in a desperate flight for any system but this one.

## CHAPTER TWENTY-EIGHT

In the quiet dark far between the systems, a lone ship floated tranquilly in the inky black. For a moment, at least, the crew was breathing easy, a rare bit of decompression in an otherwise frantic existence these past weeks and months.

People were still trying to track them, capture them, kill them, or worse, but for this briefest of moments, they were as safe as they could be, short of holing up in some reinforced stronghold.

Their young guest was recovering quickly from his ordeal, his spirits returned with the same gusto as his appetite. And if Happizano had been a good eater before, he was now giving Henni a run for her money.

"Wow, slow down and chew, kid," Bud said with an amused little laugh. "You're gonna choke at that pace."

Despite his chiding, Bud was quite glad to see the boy in improving health. They all were. Watching him fading before their eyes had been a terrible, helpless feeling, and having the youngster back on his feet, despite his occasionally trying ways, was a relief for them all.

"Don't listen to him, Hap," Henni said with a grin. "Go nuts. You earned it."

"Henni, it's not about earning it, it's about actually choking on his food."

"Yeah, yeah. He's made it this many years, right? I think he'll survive an enthusiastic meal or two."

Bud stared at the spunky woman a long moment, then just sighed and let it go. She was maddening, but she was right. And even if she wasn't, sometimes it was just easier to walk away from the discussion before she got heated.

"Well, I guess we might as well put all of the perishable supplies we picked up to use. We've got the spells to preserve most of it, but a lot of that produce will go bad if we don't use it up."

"You went a little nuts," Laskar said. "Like, way more than we could ever hope to use."

"Hey, we were trying to come off as a resupply ship. We had to make it look good. It's just too bad we had to leave so much aboard the stolen ship we abandoned. We could have traded that stuff for more useful supplies," the former pirate lamented.

"Do not fret, Uzabud. Your plan was a sound one, and we likely would not have been so successful in acquiring the Ungall leaves if not for it. You did a good job, and Happizano is recovered for it," Hozark said.

"Yeah, thanks, Bud," Hap said between mouthfuls.

Bud wasn't really a kid kind of guy, but he had to admit, the often-annoying youngster was growing on him.

"I'm just glad to see you feeling all right," he replied as he pulled out some produce.

Bud, for all of his rough-and-tough pirate posturing, was actually a somewhat cultured man. In all of his years galaxy hopping, he had picked up a thing or two beyond simple looting and pillaging.

Of course, he would never let on. Not in public, anyway. But here, surrounded by friends, he let one of those skills shine. His blades made quick work of the small pile of vegetables, a mise en place for his pending creative burst of energy.

It was one of the surprising things about him. This love of culinary experimentation. A meditation in motion, of sorts. And the end result was delicious, more often than not.

Hozark had been the fortunate recipient of more than a few of Uzabud's impromptu creations in the past, and he could attest to the man's skills where the kitchen was concerned.

"Is that the best you can do?" Henni asked, moving close and eyeing the chopped produce.

"I'm sorry, what was that, oh, eater-of-all-the-foods?"

"It's just, your knife skills are kinda weak. Especially for a pirate. Look at those. I mean, there's no size consistency."

"You think you could do better? I mean, I've seen you with a knife. You're all about stabbing. What the hell do you know about proper knife use?"

"Move aside, plebe," she said, bumping him out of the way with her hip.

Henni picked up the larger knife on the table and proceeded to chop and dice in a flurry, quickly reducing large things into smaller things, as chefs were so fond of doing. And, unlike Bud's somewhat messy piles, she had produced nearly uniform-sized bits, and in a fraction of the time.

"Daaaaaaamn," Laskar said.

The others looked on in a way that echoed that sentiment. Bud had no option but to admit the violet-haired young woman did indeed have some skills.

"Okay, fine," he relented. "So maybe you *do* know your way around a knife. But can you actually cook? Or are you all about chopping stuff up?"

"Oh, just you watch me."

Laskar watched the two with great amusement. "A challenge? Oh man, it is *on*."

"Apparently so," Demelza agreed, eyeing the makings of an impressive spread. "And it appears we shall be the lucky beneficiaries."

Even Happizano seemed engaged by the snarky banter the pilot and their odd, and occasionally violent, friend were engaging in. And if it meant more food for his belly, all the better.

"Watch it with that," Henni said as Bud began seasoning a pan of sizzling, protein-rich fungus that had a distinctly meaty texture.

"What? You don't like flavor?"

"No, I think flavor is great. But if you keep dumping that on it before it browns, it's just gonna taste like burnt shit."

"And I assume you have an actual frame of reference for that statement," Bud shot back. "I'm sure you've had plenty of, um, *interesting* things in your mouth if the state you were in when we found you was any indicator."

Henni shot him a particularly dirty look, and even Laskar reacted to his words. "Hey, man. That's a low blow."

Hozark and Demelza were also looking on disapprovingly. Bud, for all of his bluster, realized he'd gotten carried away in their sniping and had crossed the line. Laskar was right. It wasn't cool.

"Shit, I'm sorry, Henni. That was over the line," he said.

She was still throwing an angry stare his way, but the immediacy and sincerity of his apology seemed to sit well with her. It was a start, in any case.

"Just shut up and cook," she finally said, turning her attention back to the steaming pan in front of her.

After that, Bud was still giving her grief, and Henni was still a little shit, as he constantly reminded her, but the two seemed to reach a silent agreement of sorts, and their insults, while colorful to say the least, were all in good fun. And at the end of their unusual endeavor, an impressive spread of dishes was laid out for the entire crew's benefit.

"Holy crap, this is really good!" Hap said, merrily digging in with gusto.

Laskar was already stuffing his face. "Yeah," he said with a full mouth. "You guys need to do this more often."

Hozark and Demelza, while a great deal more restrained, were also clearly impressed with the collaborative results of the pair's efforts.

"I have to say, this is one of the better home-cooked meals I have partaken of in quite some time," Hozark said.

"I would have to agree," Demelza added. "Very well done. Both of you."

"It was all my doing," Henni said. "You just needed a real chef in the kitchen to make all of this palatable. Someone who knows how to use seasoning as an enhancement, not a cudgel."

"Oh, ha-ha," Bud said. "As if. You know full well you were just the assistant to my culinary mastery."

"You think so?" Henni shot back with a dare in her sparkling eyes.

"I know so."

"Oh, will you two just shut up and eat?" Laskar griped. "I mean, dinner and a show is fine and all, but this shit's getting old, and your plates will be getting cold. Heh, see what I did there?"

"Yes, Laskar. Very clever," Henni grumbled as she piled food on her plate.

She took a bite of one of the dishes Bud had been the primary contributor to. It was surprisingly good. "Okay," she said. "I've gotta admit, this doesn't entirely suck."

"And I suppose this isn't all that bad either," Bud said, likewise trying a bite of one of her main concoctions.

The others watched with amusement.

"Great. You're both amazing chefs. Well done. Can we all just eat in peace now?" Laskar asked.

"I would have to agree with Laskar's sentiment," Hozark said with a little chuckle. "The food is quite exceptional, though your banter, while somewhat amusing, could perhaps use a bit of refinement."

Bud flashed a little grin. "All right, I get the hint. But what now? I mean, much as I enjoy this downtime, I know you well enough to know this isn't going to last. So spill. What's the plan?"

Hozark chewed his food slowly, then washed it down in an equally languorous manner. He dabbed his lips with his napkin and finally spoke.

"The plan, my dear Uzabud, is to go and see Corann. And then we shall discuss what to do about these disturbing goings on."

"And what about the guys behind it?" Laskar asked.

Hozark considered his words a moment. "How best to deal with this troublesome Visla Maktan will undoubtedly be a part of that conversation as well," he added. "For the moment, however, let us enjoy this respite and the pleasant meal our friends have graced us with. I fear it may be some time before we relax like this again."

# CHAPTER TWENTY-NINE

Uzabud took a circuitous route on his way to the quiet world of Inskip. It was likely an unnecessary additional precaution to protect the leader of the Five, but where the Wampeh Ghalian were concerned, Bud had learned it was better not to risk unintentionally upsetting them.

And seeing as she could easily kill without breaking a sweat, visiting Corann's personal residence warranted precisely that sort of caution.

He was special among civilians, though. As a close ally of Hozark's, he had been one of the very, very few non-Ghalian ever allowed into one of the order's training facilities. And even then, his foolish, unannounced arrival would have cost him his life, had Hozark not been there to smooth things over.

The Wampeh Ghalian had survived this long for a reason, and sloppy security protocols was not one of them. The leader of the master assassins knew Uzabud's ship had arrived in her solar system long before he had even breached the atmosphere and begun his descent.

By the time Bud had landed, Corann had already baked a fresh batch of sweets, as well as set the water boiling for a refreshing pot of restorative tea. After that, she made her way outside and took up a seat in her comfortable chair.

Of course, that chair was positioned just right, its angle allowing her to survey all who approached her home from a very wide angle of view. But to anyone other than a trained killer, it merely seemed like a comfy seat on a welcoming porch.

She was quietly knitting as she waited for their arrival, smiling warmly at her neighbors as they passed by and waved their greetings.

Little did they know, the kindly, motherly woman was one of the deadliest killers the galaxy had ever seen. In fact, she had more deaths by her hands than any of them had friends. *Combined*, most likely.

Hozark and Demelza greeted Corann with little bows of respect as they ascended the few steps to her porch, the others following right behind them.

"You look well, Master Corann," Demelza said quietly, a warm smile pasted on her face for the benefit of any who might be passing by. She was supposedly the older woman's niece, and her visits, as such, would be inherently pleasant experiences.

"And I feel well," Corann replied. "And your little group? All is in order once more, I see," she said, noting Happizano's chipper appearance.

"Yes," Hozark replied. "We had a little issue with some Marbus vine pollen, but it has been addressed."

"I heard from our network that there had been a mass poisoning on Lortzal and had wondered if perhaps you had been present there as well. It is such an unusual compound, after all."

"Yes, it is. And that one would be willing to go to such measures to recapture young Happizano was indeed most disconcerting. Not only for the means, but also that they had managed to plant a false lead as to the whereabouts of his father, luring us to that world in the first place."

"Yet another trap, it would seem," Corann said. "They are becoming a rather troublesome group, the Council of Twenty."

"Indeed. But I have to wonder if this is the work of the Council itself, or if it is the plotting of a small handful of its members."

"Ah, you refer to Visla Zinna Maktan. Yes, he is quite the picture of harmlessness. Or, as harmless as a Council member can be. In fact, he seems the epitome of normalcy."

"The dangerous ones often do," Laskar interjected.

"Oh, but not the infamous Imania Tokin. That one was clearly crazy. And deadly."

"Well, yeah, *she* had some serious issues," Laskar agreed. "But she was an exception. As a general rule, it tends to hold true is all I'm saying."

"A valid observation," Corann noted. "This is something we Ghalian have noted for many, many years. But he is rather exceptional in how normal he appears. Yet his name keeps popping up in the most unexpected places."

"That it does. I fear we may have to deal with this threat sooner than later, given his latest escapades. But we shall need to determine his whereabouts and routines, first."

Corann smiled at her friend and fellow Ghalian master. "Oh, but my dear Hozark, we have been stalking him for some time now while you have been away."

"Oh? Our network has been hard at work, I see."

"Yes. Gathering information, observing his movements. The usual sort of thing. But in this instance, there is also a personal element involved. A particularly angry one."

"Master Prombatz?" Demelza asked.

"Yes. He is fully healed from the injuries he sustained at the hands of Maktan's men and has returned to work."

"That is excellent news."

"It is. And as he completes his tasks, he is slowly replenishing his powers from the careful acceptance of contracts that just so happen to be linked to Visla Ravik, or Visla Maktan."

"The guy's draining his kills? And he's specifically going for the ones that have something to do with the guys who caught him?" Laskar said.

"Oh, yes," Corann replied.

Laskar nodded. "Well, I mean, it's kinda gross, but it's gotta be pretty damn cathartic."

"One could say that," she agreed. "What he suffered was a risk of our profession. But what was done to poor Aargun was horrific. And for that, he is experiencing an unusual reaction for our kind. He is finding himself desirous of revenge."

It was true. The poor Ghalian aspirant under Prombatz's wing had not only been captured and tortured, he was also experimented upon, his eyes and tongue removed. The mistreatment of the young student had left his teacher in something of a state for some time as he healed from his own injuries.

But now, a master Ghalian was on the hunt, and it was personal. Bud knew what that meant, and heaven help those who drew his ire.

"Has he had much success in hindering Ravik and Maktan's plans?" Bud asked.

"It appears so. But in the course of his activities, he has uncovered a few *interesting* developments."

"Such as?" Hozark asked.

Corann turned to face her friend. "Such as rumors of another experimentation facility, with the bodies of power users found in a state much like you reported from your prior experience."

"This is a significant development, if true," he said. "We should look into this further."

"And we shall. But first, I feel we must all wait for Master Prombatz's return. He is due back any day now, and given his most recent contract, I think he may be returning to us with information that may prove most interesting, indeed."

Laskar cocked his head slightly. "Exactly what kind of contract is he out on?"

Corann shone her kindly, motherly smile upon him, the expression not betraying an ounce of her deadly demeanor.

"The kind that will result in much bloodshed," she replied with a grin.

# CHAPTER THIRTY

No one ever paid much attention to servants as they came and went with a visiting emmik's or visla's staff. After all, any who were a part of those households had been thoroughly vetted long before arriving at Emmik Partsuval's estate.

Or so they thought.

But a master assassin in deep cover and under the protection of a very well-cast disguise spell would be virtually undetectable to all but the most powerful casters. And Emmik Partsuval was not so powerful.

Nor was Emmik Jarmisch. And Prombatz had successfully removed and replaced one of his newer servants several weeks prior with no one being any the wiser.

Of course, selecting a new face helped. There was only so much back story research he could do on a person before assuming their identity, and the newer hires would not have as extensive a history with the other staff. That meant less inside jokes and references the impostor would simply have no way to know about.

Prombatz had taken on the guise of a relatively young member of the emmik's entourage. A general servant named

Togga. He was not tasked with food service, nor was he trusted with any of the emmik's more important matters. He was the new kid, doing all of the grunt work the more senior staff wanted no part of.

"Of course. I'll get right on it," was his typical refrain when asked to do something distasteful.

It worked wonders, doing the unpleasant tasks for the others, and Prombatz soon found himself very comfortably embedded within Emmik Jarmisch's core staff, and not a single person had noted the real Togga had been replaced.

All that mattered was they had a new peon to do their bidding. A role he was happy to play, and one that would keep him close to the emmik when he traveled off world.

Prombatz had known through the spy network that Jarmisch would be one of the peripheral Council-affiliated casters visiting his actual target in coming weeks. It was for that reason that he subjected himself to mind-numbing boredom of grunt work, all in preparation for the big day. The day he was told to come with on their flight to see Emmik Partsuval.

And in just a few short weeks, as he had already learned the trip had been scheduled, that opportunity finally presented itself.

"Bring the baggage. And don't forget to load up additional food for the galley. The emmik sometimes likes to take unplanned detours on the way home," one of the senior staff commanded.

"Immediately," the disguised Wampeh replied, hurrying off to gather all of the things he'd been asked to collect.

Normally he'd have used a floating conveyance to load the ship, but as he was cheap labor and magic was valuable, the other staff had taken to having him carry things the old way. By hand.

It was a form of hazing, really, but so long as it reinforced his position, Prombatz did not mind one bit. And besides, a little bit of extra exercise was always a welcome perk for the Wampeh Ghalian. Fitness was one of their edicts, and even the least assuming of their order possessed strength and stamina greatly exceeding their appearances.

When the contract had come in on Emmik Partsuval, Prombatz had jumped on the opportunity. More than the other low-level Council goons he had been picking off as their contracts came up, this was a great opportunity to not only claim a fair amount of power for himself, but also to learn more about the machinations of the mysterious Visla Maktan.

It seemed that this emmik was a close associate of the visla, and if Prombatz was able to play his cards right, there was a good possibility he might ascertain some new information about the mystery man's nefarious dealings.

From what the spy network had picked up in the whisper channels between the systems, Maktan's name had come up more frequently of late. And from what they could tell, the man was quietly worried about rising levels of discord within the Council.

The Twenty were not always known to play well with one another, and when drama flared among them, there was bloodshed more often than not. And with their guards down in a supposedly secure estate, the odds of the two emmiks discussing Council affairs candidly were greatly increased.

Servants did not count as actual people to them. They were moving, breathing furniture, there to serve their needs and nothing more. It was amazing just how much was openly discussed in the presence of staff and slaves, and Prombatz was taking full advantage of that laziness.

The two emmiks dined and chatted well into the evening, enjoying the shared griping about common issues within the Council, as well as other, more personal grievances.

It seemed both had mistresses who were becoming a bit too

demanding of them, making their formerly relaxing love lives far more difficult than need be.

"I really think I might sell her off," Jarmisch said of his longtime paramour. "It was supposed to be fun, and it was, for a time. But now she has become almost work in her incessant nagging. The sense of entitlement is galling."

"I relate," Partsuval said with a knowing look. "Two of mine are getting a bit lippy as well."

"I don't know how you manage that stable."

"With much rest, good food, and enthusiasm," Partsuval said with a laugh.

"Sure. And also a healthy dose of Vigora root, I'd wager."

"Once in a while. But only when their nagging brings me to distraction."

"It seems they take their position for granted, eh, my friend?"

"Yes, that is for certain. They need to remember how they arrived at their station, and by whose grace. I may sell one of them to the pleasure houses just to make a point."

"A bit harsh, perhaps."

"But the remaining ones will learn," Partsuval said.

Jarmisch nodded his agreement. "A valid point."

The two men then shifted their conversation to all manner of things, but neither touched on Maktan for more than an instant. From what the silent, observing servant patiently waiting for orders could tell, there were plenty of other things weighing on their minds besides the rogue visla.

Then Emmik Partsuval finally said something that the disguised assassin found most interesting.

"You know, when the turnover occurs, there's a very good possibility you and I might make our way into the Council itself."

Jarmisch looked unimpressed. "I've heard that before, but it never pans out."

"But this time there is talk of a cleaning of house. At least part of it. And if we are productive in our efforts to assist our friend, there is a very real chance it could happen."

"If Maktan can pull it off, that is."

"You must admit, he's nothing if not motivated."

"That's for certain," Partsuval said. "No one can say he isn't willing to do whatever it takes to achieve his goals. And with impressive amounts of subterfuge and backstabbing in the process."

"So long as it is not *our* backs in which he decides to sheath his blades, I think we will be okay."

"With his power, hidden as it is, there is nothing we could do if he wanted to," Partsuval said.

"So we stay on his good side. The winning side, we hope. Now, what of your trip to Omplata?"

The two men's conversation then devolved into a discussion of the wine and women available at the recreation spa on the playground planet of the wealthy and powerful.

It wasn't a lot of information, and it wasn't any specific, actionable news, but what Prombatz heard did reinforce the general trickle of information that had been slowly making its way to the ears of the Ghalian spies.

Maktan was amassing power, preparing to overthrow Council leadership, it seemed. Corann and the others would find this most interesting, no doubt. But Prombatz had a job to finish, and one he was looking forward to bringing to completion.

The pair of power users chatted for a fair while longer before finally turning in for the night. In the safety of Emmik Partsuval's secure walls, the men quickly dropped off into a deep slumber, confident in their safety. It was near impossible to get into these grounds without setting off alarms, tripping wards, or drawing the attention of the guards. Once inside, they were safe.

Prombatz, however, did not get that memo, and he had bloody work on his agenda.

The Wampeh assassin silently slinked into Emmik Partsuval's chambers, the visiting power user's unwitting assistance in this endeavor saving him a great deal of hard work that would have otherwise been spent gaining access.

If there was more information to be gained through torture, he might have kidnapped the emmik and extracted what he could in a more comfortable setting. But as it stood, the emmik, while certainly involved in Maktan's ploys, was still no more than a pawn in the machinations at play.

The sleeping emmik did not even stir as the Wampeh's fangs slid into his neck, the Ghalian magic rendering him unconscious as his blood was drained along with his power.

Prombatz drank slowly, savoring the rush of emmik magic flooding his system. As he did every time he killed one of the Council's faithful, he felt a little smile tickle the corners of his mouth. Aargun was being avenged one contract at a time.

It was a cathartic bit of revenge for a man normally impassive to surges of emotion. But after what he had been through, perhaps it was not entirely a surprise that he might have some deep-seated feelings bubbling to the surface.

Soon enough, the sensation of power flowing to his lips faded as the emmik's life force flickered out. Prombatz pulled his lips free and looked at the dead man a moment, then quietly left the chamber and the estate altogether, never to be seen on this world again.

# CHAPTER THIRTY-ONE

Corann and Hozark had spent a great deal of time discussing the unusual affairs of a certain Visla Zinna Maktan over the course of the days spent waiting for Master Prombatz's return.

It had been a pleasant enough time. The hospitality of Corann and her neighbors was near legendary. But eventually, even the tranquil Wampeh was beginning to get a bit impatient.

They'd been through a number of ordeals of late, and Prombatz was to return with vital information about their adversary. Or so they hoped. And the more they learned about the impressively deceptive Maktan, the better their odds of stymieing his plans.

It was somewhat odd, waiting for a third member of the Five to show up at Corann's home. A rarity, really. There were only five of them, after all, as their name suggested, and the regular process of the order was to ensure no more than two were ever at a location less robustly defended than a training house at the same time.

It was a rule put in place to prevent potential catastrophic loss to their leadership from a lone incident.

But these were unusual times, and given the nature of the

threat that Visla Maktan was posing to not only the Council and the systems it controlled, but the order of the Wampeh Ghalian as well, an exception was deemed well in order in this instance.

But there was a young boy present, as well as a somewhat unhinged and rather stabby young woman, both of whom appeared to need a bit of a stable break from the recent events.

Hap had recovered from his ordeal well, especially for one so young, but he had other things on his mind besides being nearly killed by someone who wanted to control his father's power. Namely, finding him and reuniting, a task that was proving far more difficult than originally anticipated.

Henni, however, was a different story. She was actually quite acclimated after being rescued from her difficult circumstances living on the streets. But despite that positive shift of lifestyle, a somewhat aggressive undertone had been increasingly shaping her interactions.

Then there was the matter of her unusual eyes, and the strange power that seemed to be lurking within her. Corann had been actively researching tales of similar individuals, but they were so few and far between, it was difficult to get anything resembling an accurate representation of just what she might be capable of.

For the meantime, regardless of all of their varied concerns, they were guests in Corann's home, and she was putting on her best mama hen act for them, keeping them fed, cozy, and comfortable while she and the other master assassin awaited their colleague. It was a carefully performed dance, and one that served its function perfectly.

So perfectly, in fact, that when Master Prombatz finally arrived, it was an almost anticlimactic event.

"Lovely to see you, Corann," the older Wampeh said as he greeted the head of their order. "And Hozark, it has been too long."

"Prombatz, it is good to see you in such good form," Hozark replied, noting the man's highly energetic power signature.

He had indeed been feeding, as Corann had noted, and the addition of all of that power was doing him much good.

"Thank you, brother. It was a long road for a stretch."

"Yes, I can imagine. But you've come out the other side," Hozark said.

"Yes, he has," Corann agreed. "Now, come. I have some fresh-baked pastry inside for the occasion. We really do have much to catch up on."

The three Ghalian masters seemed to be having a perfectly benign and casual conversation, but to them, the undertone was obvious. They had much to discuss, and the sooner they could step away from not only public scrutiny, but their non-Ghalian company, the better.

"I suppose you could convince me to have one or two," Prombatz said with a grin. "Lead the way, Corann."

"Did you say pastry?" Hap asked, running up to them from where he'd been playing with a local boy.

"Yes, there is a fresh batch," Corann said. "Why don't you be a dear and come with us and get a tray to bring out to the others. Can you do that for me?"

"Sure!" the boy said enthusiastically.

It was a pleasant interaction, but one of the group watched the goings-on without the joy the young boy possessed.

Henni, though comfortable with Corann now, still had a somewhat wary look in her eye as the woman led the boy inside. Her intuition was on point when it came to the Ghalian leader, and she knew the full measure of the violent deeds she had committed over the years.

Just another unusual, hit-and-miss aspect of her strange powers. Sometimes it would work, but other times it was completely silent. Like with Hozark. For whatever reason, he did not set off her Spidey sense one bit.

But Corann, for all of her sweet, motherly charm, radiated an aura of death that the violet-haired girl could not possibly miss.

"I'll be back in a minute," Hap called out to the others.

He followed Corann into the kitchen and returned a few minutes later with a tray of steaming-hot pastry, just as was promised. And as he passed them out to his friends, the three Ghalian masters seized the window of freedom to talk privately amongst themselves.

"I assume you learned more about Visla Maktan's plans?" Corann asked.

"He is a confusing man," Prombatz said. "There have been several conflicting tales of Maktan's motives and attempts at influence. Some say he fears the discord growing within the Council."

"That seems to fit his normal demeanor," Corann said. "From what we've heard in the past, he has always been quite calm, and dare I say, normal."

"It does fit, and that is his usual public persona. But then there is also talk of Maktan seeking to *disrupt* the Council and seize power for himself. The positions are in conflict with one another. It is quite confusing."

"It almost sounds as if he is on the periphery, attempting damage control," Hozark noted.

"And yet, the deeper one digs, the more frequently his name is uncovered. Maktan is most certainly the one pulling the strings," Prombatz said.

Hozark mused this a moment. "Has there been any word on Visla Jinnik's location? The boy needs his father, and from what we've all heard, the visla has been wielded as a powerful, blunt weapon to bring many under the Council's control."

"Sadly, of late, all has gone silent. There has been no whisper of Visla Jinnik's location," Prombatz said. "He is amazingly well hidden, especially for a power user of his magnitude. Someone has gone to great lengths to keep him from notice."

"It appears our entire network is coming up short on that front," Corann noted.

"Then we keep looking," Hozark said. "We owe it to the boy."

Corann and Prombatz shared a look.

"Hozark," Corann said, "are you concerned about the him beyond your professional responsibilities?"

The Wampeh nearly flinched as he realized that perhaps he actually was.

"If I am honest about it, then yes, I suppose I am," he replied. "We all joined the order having been taken from our normal worlds. I imagine the experience for the boy is likely much the same in terms of initial trauma."

"Only, he will not be a Ghalian assassin at the end of his time with us," Prombatz said.

"No, he will not. But enough about the boy. What of Visla Maktan? Do we finally end this, once and for all? His meddling in Ghalian affairs has gone far beyond that of mere nuisance, as I'm certain Master Prombatz would agree."

"We cannot simply assassinate a high-ranking member of the Council of Twenty," Corann said. "Not without a contract, no matter how deserving he may be. Word could get out, and if that happened, the order would be compromised. Perhaps fatally."

"Of course, you are correct," Hozark said after a long pause. "So, for now, we must have our resources gather all of the information they can about his routines, his habits, his weaknesses. We may not be utilizing that at the moment, but eventually we will strike, and when we do, we must be prepared."

## CHAPTER THIRTY-TWO

"A non-Ghalian?" Prombatz mused at the news that Demelza had taken it upon herself to train the young boy in basic combative techniques. "It is unheard of, Corann."

The head of the Five was in agreement, but she'd had a bit more time to come to terms with one of their own sharing knowledge with outsiders. That, and the two Demelza had taken under her wing were proving to be somewhat valuable members of Master Hozark's team.

Henni had demonstrated not only her rather violent proclivities on more than one occasion now, but also a hint at the potential magic stored within her. It was by no means a sure thing, but if she did in fact possess power, as Corann believed, she might become a powerful asset one day.

And the way things were shaping up in recent months, they could likely use an ace in the hole like that.

As for Happizano, he created value in a different way. The young son of the powerful visla was providing an unusually grounding energy for the assassin charged with looking out for him. And, interestingly enough, it seemed to be doing the solitary man some good.

Not that Hozark was anti-social or anything of the sort. But having to care for the boy and deal with his ups and downs had made the man who was notoriously not a fan of children far more receptive to helping the younger aspirants in the order.

Of course, Demelza had no such qualms, and she had seemed to be quite glad to instruct such enthusiastic pupils.

"The boy is doing quite well in training, Prombatz," Corann said. "And it seems to be having a rather positive effect on his overall well-being. He is more confident in himself, and though he still misses his father, he harps on it far less."

"And the angry one?"

"Henni is unusual, I admit. But her loyalty to Hozark and Demelza is unquestionable. And her potential, it is... well, you have seen her eyes."

Prombatz pondered a moment. "I have. And if she turns out to just be a woman with interesting eyes and nothing more? She is learning Ghalian skills."

"If she is just a normal woman, then she is still a well-armed addition to Hozark's little team. Really, Prombatz, I do not think we need worry about Demelza revealing any actual Ghalian secrets to the pair. But the basic combative training she is imparting is useful for *everyone*. Come, let us observe her lesson and put your mind at ease."

Corann led the way to the area Demelza was using as a small practice space. She and Prombatz quietly took up positions along the far wall, making sure not to disturb the sweating trio in the center of the chamber.

Hap and Henni were running through an empty-hand sparring sequence that combined a series of punches with blocks, wrist locks, and leverage moves designed to throw the opposing party off balance.

Henni was faster than Happizano, but the boy was actually holding his own against the woman.

"Good," Demelza said. "Now, feel it in your hips. Relax your shoulders and let your body sense the direction of your opponent's attack. Soft is strong. Hard is vulnerable in this exercise. Flex and move with it while seeking your opportunity."

Both combatants did their best to heed her words. Henni, while better at this sort of thing, given her tough life on the streets, was nevertheless not outpacing Happizano by much. The visla's son, once he had gotten over his sense of entitlement, was proving to be a quick study.

The two Ghalian masters watched a while longer, impressed with the calm, clear manner Demelza imparted knowledge to her pupils.

"I admit, she is quite good," Prombatz said. "Really, she is better than many of our official teachers."

"I agree," Corann said with an amused little smile. "Prombatz, I have an idea."

"Oh?"

"Let us contribute to the lesson. Give them something else to consider. What do you say?"

He pondered it a moment. "I suppose I am not opposed to sharing non-Ghalian skills with our allies," he finally replied.

"Excellent. I think this could prove a most enlightening experience," she said. "Demelza, might I have a word?"

"Continue," Demelza instructed Henni and the boy. "Yes, Master Corann?" she said as she walked over.

"Master Prombatz and I would like to contribute to your instruction. With your consent, of course."

"It would be an honor!" Demelza said. "I am no teacher, and to learn from the likes of you would be a wonderful experience for them."

"Oh, do not sell yourself short," Corann replied. "I've watched you teach, and you are quite a proficient instructor."

"Thank you for the kind words. I am merely doing the best I can."

"Which is quite good," Corann said. "Now, Prombatz, what do you say we change things up for these two?"

Demelza called over Henni and Happizano and explained that the two masters would be taking over for a time.

"Oh, cool!" Hap said of the prospect.

Henni, her heightened senses of the woman's deadliness still making her a bit wary of Corann, was slightly less enthused, but she went along with it anyway.

Corann went first, seeing as the pair was already a bit sweaty from physical exertion. A momentary respite to cool down a bit before Prombatz's casting tutorial.

"I shall instruct you in the basic elements of subterfuge and misdirection," she said. "One need not always work harder to achieve one's goals. Sometimes, a little bit of creative pressure can achieve impressive results."

Corann proceeded to break down both physical and psychological misdirects often used in the spy trade. She covered altering one's appearance to take someone off guard, and even adopting a different, more familiar accent to make someone feel at ease.

Of course, she also delved into the myriad tricks that could be employed to sway a person's opinion or convince them to do something not actually in their best interest.

It was by no means a master class in spycraft, but it was an eye-opener for the young woman and the boy.

Laskar and Hozark strolled in toward the end of Corann's lesson and quietly began to watch just as it was Prombatz's turn. Admittedly, his was the more visually interesting lesson of the two.

He began with simple spells, teaching the pair how to focus on the intent behind their spell rather than just the words. All practiced without a konus, though it was quite likely that both pupils possessed power of their own in one degree or another.

He then moved on to actual casting, giving each of them a

very minorly powered konus. Where Henni was the quick study of martial styles, Hap was proving quite proficient at casting. Being a visla's son had afforded him many years watching skilled power users wield their magic.

"You will never otherwise see this," Hozark quietly told Laskar. "Demelza, perhaps, but Ghalian masters do not teach outsiders. Not ever."

"So why are they okay with it now?" Laskar wondered.

"Because of what we are dealing with. What lies ahead. This speaks to the seriousness of the situation before us."

The men stood silently a long while watching the lesson. Finally, Laskar spoke.

"You gonna take out Maktan?" he asked.

Hozark paused. "Eventually, yes. But we require a contract for all but the most extreme situations. And for one as powerful, connected, and wealthy as he, it would require not only a significant amount of coin, but also a well-respected employer. One we can verify and trust. We do not kill just anyone, Laskar, nor do we do so for just any reason."

"Even after all he's done?"

Hozark chose his words carefully. "There are rules we live by. We are not an order based on revenge," he finally said.

"Well, with all he's been up to, maybe it's time you guys think about it. Eventually, you can't just let things go and hope someone takes out a contract, ya know?"

"Your point is well taken, Laskar. But it would require a most heinous act for the Wampeh Ghalian to forego our established system."

"The mutilated student wasn't bad enough?" Laskar asked, a bit too loud.

Prombatz turned from his students, a little flashback of the torment inflicted on his former pupil welling up within him.

"I think that is enough for today," the master Ghalian said. "I need to visit Aargun shortly. He is mending, but it is still a long road ahead."

Corann looked at Hozark and his friends, then at Prombatz. An idea was growing in her head.

"Perhaps you could take our new friends with you. It would do them well to see the other side of our profession."

Prombatz thought on it a long moment. "Perhaps I shall," he finally said. "Perhaps, indeed."

# CHAPTER THIRTY-THREE

"No eyes?" Henni asked again, looking a little squeamish, which for her was saying something.

"That is correct, young Henni," Prombatz said. "Nor a tongue. Injuries inflicted upon Aargun by the Council."

"That's fucked up," the violet-haired girl said, clearly disturbed.

"Indeed," the older Ghalian agreed.

"So, where exactly are we going?" Laskar asked uneasily.

Sitting in the center of the Ghalian ship carrying them the several jumps to their secret destination was odd for him. He was used to being the one flying, not being a passenger, and having no idea where they were was an incredibly disconcerting sensation for the man typically in charge of plotting their course.

"The world is never named, nor is the system," Hozark said from his nearby seat. "And no matter how trusted a party may be, only a select group of Ghalian pilots know the actual location."

"It is an easy thing keeping a hidden facility hidden when one does not know where it is. Even the Five do not know its location, though we have immediate access if needed," Prombatz said.

"Why? You guys run everything," Happizano asked.

"Because, young Jinnik, sometimes even the most powerful of us might find themselves in a difficult situation. One where they might be pressured to reveal things. Things such as the whereabouts of the most secret Ghalian healing facility."

"You mean there are people who could catch you?" he asked with a bit of disbelief.

"None are infallible," Hozark replied.

"Infall..."

"Infallible. It means incapable of making a mistake."

"A word for the careless and weak-willed," Laskar said with a self-satisfied chuckle.

Hozark stared at the cocky copilot a moment, then turned back to the boy. "And trust me, Happizano, no matter one's confidence and skill, *everyone* makes mistakes."

Laskar snort-chuckled. He obviously knew that to be the case, but one such as he didn't make many mistakes. At least, so he believed.

Had Bud been with them, he'd have certainly given his copilot a hearty ration of shit for his overconfidence, but he and Demelza were working with Corann to install upgraded defensive spells to his mothership while prepping for whatever potential fight would undoubtedly come their way.

Demelza had initially planned on joining the trip to the Ghalian healer as well. Aargun had trained with her shortly before his injuries, after all, but Corann had personally asked her to stay behind and work with Uzabud in his labors.

Having one such as her helping the former pirate would make certain the somewhat novel Ghalian spells were properly locked in place. Bud was talented, no doubt, but given the nature of their most recent conflicts, the leader of the Five wanted to take absolutely no chances.

Demelza knew her point was entirely valid, and she would undoubtedly visit Aargun soon, as she had a few times since his initial injury. Master Prombatz would understand her absence, and she knew the injured Ghalian would as well.

Sometimes, duty took priority, and this was one such time. And so it was that only Hozark, Laskar, Happizano, Henni, and Prombatz were aboard the craft as it flew to its secret destination.

Additional spells were layered over the ship's hull, ensuring no form of tracking magic could attach to the craft and reveal its course. But even so, the pilots took multiple additional jumps to random systems and the places between.

It may have seemed excessive, but they were heading to the location of the most vulnerable of their brothers and sisters. The seriously injured.

Minor wounds could be healed just about anywhere, and a great many healers were on the Ghalian payroll for just such emergencies. But for truly severe cases, only one place would do. A facility hidden in plain sight on an innocuous world, holding the most severely injured assassins. Those who might not survive their hurt, regardless of the skills of those treating them.

Aargun had been one such patient, but despite the severity of his wounds, the young man possessed a strength uncommon even among his older peers. His eyes and tongue would never grow back, and he could not continue on his lifelong path toward being a Ghalian assassin, but he would live.

And that was more than many could say.

The ship touched down within the compound at its relatively small landing facility. The passengers would unload, then the craft would relocate to the larger landing field at the outskirts of the city until it was needed once more.

"Now, while I am sure you are cognizant of the situation within these walls, I would nevertheless remind you three that this is a place of healing," Prombatz said as they walked into the building from their shielded arrival site. "As such, please act accordingly. Some of the patients here are suffering more than just physical injuries, so, please, be respectful of their circumstances."

The three non-Ghalian nodded their understanding and followed the master assassin into the belly of the building. Hozark came behind, taking up the rear of the procession.

It was a well-lit place of healing energy, and the many open and airy rooms were populated with pale killers in varying state of recovery, their mending improved by the magically charged air of the location as well as the skills of the staff.

From within those walls, even the most basic information about the city, the world, and even the system they were in, was blocked by the spells locked in place above. Not even the color of the sun could be discerned.

"They're all so young," Henni noticed, pointing this out in a hushed voice.

"Yes, a great many are," Prombatz replied. "But not all. While the benefit of age and experience often confers a bit of protection from some injuries simply by muscle memory, we are all vulnerable, nonetheless."

Henni and the others nodded their understanding, but the age and skill differential of those at this facility compared to the assassins they had been traveling with was a stark reminder that not all Wampeh Ghalian were as seemingly invincible as the top-tier killers they had been spending so much time with.

Prombatz led the way down the corridors to the room he had visited so many times in the months since his young aspiring student's injuries. The staff nodded to him as he passed, giving the master Ghalian and his guests a respectful bit of space as they made their way to Aargun's room.

The wounded aspirant Ghalian was seated in a large chair, basking in the warmth of the sun's rays filtering through the spell-shielded window. The magic was carefully placed to alter the color and heat to ensure no burning of patients no matter how long they rested in its comforting light.

Across the room, a table held a few weapons, and a wooden block rested against the wall. The assassin's favored weapons, never to be used on a contract again.

The wounded man turned his head slightly as the visitors approached. He may have lost his eyes and tongue, but his remaining senses had sharpened even further for the lack of them.

"Aargun, I have brought friends today. Those who travel with Hozark and Demelza. She sends her regards, by the way, but another task required her presence today."

Aargun nodded his understanding.

"Hello. I'm Happizano," Hap said, unsure exactly how to greet the man. Should he shake hands? Or give a little bow? Ultimately, he opted for just a simple verbal greeting.

Aargun's eyes were covered with small bandages, but he turned and gave a little nod directly to the boy. Laskar watched with fascination, and he wondered exactly what the blind man could still do despite lacking vision.

He'd seen some amazing feats by the assassins he traveled with, and the odds of Aargun still being quite lethal was undoubtedly high. He would not be carrying out any contracts, but so long as he could hear clearly, he could most likely handle himself should any wish to cause him harm.

"I'm Laskar," the copilot said, shifting silently to his left as he spoke.

Aargun tracked his movement despite lacking eyes and nodded a small greeting, confirming Laskar's assumption about his senses.

"He seems to have an amazing sense of what's around him," Laskar said. "I wonder if he's still got his Ghalian tricks up his sleeve."

"He is blind and mute, not deaf," Prombatz said. "And a Ghalian never loses his nature."

"Oh, right. Sorry, I didn't mean to speak about you in the third person," he apologized.

Aargun nodded, an eyebrow slightly arched with mild amusement.

"I'm Henni," the violet-haired woman said, walking up to him and putting her hands on his shoulders.

It was an unexpectedly personal greeting, especially from so standoffish a woman, but she and Aargun seemed to connect on some level, and her comforting touch was greeted with a little smile as he gently rested his hands on her waist. Henni smiled, squeezed once, then stepped back.

Laskar watched with a confused look on his face. "So, I guess you must be taking up some new hobbies," he said, turning to Prombatz. "What sort of things do they have to help keep him busy in here? I'd imagine it must get a bit——"

A small knife flashed through the air and thudded smack-dab in the center of the wooden block across the room.

Laskar spun back to the blind assassin. Aargun turned his sightless face to the startled man and grinned.

"What the hell?"

Henni walked to the wooden block and pulled the knife free, sliding it back into the sheath hidden within her coat from where he had stealthily taken it.

"What?" she asked innocently.

"That was so cool!" Hap gushed. "Can you teach me that?"

"Aargun is not a teacher," Prombatz said, "but I am sure he would be glad to demonstrate the technique for you further. However, I think you might be more interested in something else he has been working on." He turned to Hozark. "I think you may find this quite interesting as well, brother."

Aargun did not wait for a go-ahead, sliding on a konus then holding out his hands gently, furrowing his brow ever so slightly.

"What's he doing?" Laskar asked.

"Wait and see," Prombatz replied.

They all stood silently observing the blind, mute man, and it took nearly a minute for anything to happen, but when it did, all were shocked.

"How is he doing that?" Laskar asked, staring with true shock at the faint illumination glow hovering above Aargun's hands. "He's not saying anything. He shouldn't be able to cast without saying the words."

Aargun smiled as he relaxed, allowing the glow to fade. It was the most basic, beginner level of casting. A simple illumination spell taught to all children at a young age to help them cope with their fear of the dark.

And he was casting it without words.

It should have been impossible. The sounds, discovered and refined over millennia, were what made the spell, though it was the intent behind them that ultimately made the spell function or fail.

And, yet, here was a man with no tongue somehow casting. Sure, it was a beginner's spell, but that was utterly beside the point.

Hozark and Prombatz shared a look. *This* was exceptional. Extraordinary, in fact. And it made the two masters wonder just what else might be possible that they did not yet know.

"We have long known that certain older magic could be cast silently. The ancient Zomoki could do so, for instance," Hozark mused.

"But they've been extinct for centuries," Laskar said.

"Yes, ever since the incident with Visla Balamar," Prombatz agreed. "However, perhaps some aspect of their ability exists in other species."

"And as Aargun was already an accomplished caster when this injury befell him, that may have given him the advantage that those attempting this from scratch might never have had,"

Hozark noted. "A fascinating turn of events, Prombatz. And *very* well done, Aargun. You continue to do the order proud."

The blind Wampeh could not answer, but the little smile that graced his lips spoke far more than words ever could.

"Now, would you be up to perhaps guiding a lesson for our young guests?"

## CHAPTER THIRTY-FOUR

Aargun may have been blind, but that did not hinder the muscle memory of years upon years of training. He had always been proficient with blades, and as soon as one was in his hands, eyes or no, he felt at ease.

There was a certain comforting meditation that came with moving through familiar motions ingrained since his youth. And now he was teaching a pair of newcomers the art of the blade.

Technically, Aargun was not a Ghalian teacher and should not have been giving instruction, but, with Master Prombatz and Master Hozark's encouragement, he was glad to show the basics to Henni and Happizano.

"Every blade has a center of balance," Master Prombatz said, providing a voice for the mute assassin as he demonstrated the principle, balancing a knife on his index finger at the flat spot where the blade met the grip. "Some are more forward weighted, others more to the rear. Others still are perfectly central in their weight. All of this makes a difference in how you shall wield the weapon. Henni, what do you make of this?" he asked as Aargun held out the knife for the young woman to examine.

She took it and turned it in her hands. This one was not one of her own daggers, but a longer variety with a sturdy blade. The grip was not particularly rough, though, and she thought it might be a poor choice for so-called wet work.

She felt the balance of the knife, carefully noting how it rested in her hand.

"I think it's probably more of a throwing knife than a stabbing one," she said. "The blade's not over weighted, but it's still pretty substantial, and the point seems like it was designed to take a bit more abuse than some of the more delicate dagger styles."

Aargun smiled and nodded his approval.

"Yes, that is correct," Prombatz said for him. "Your instincts serve you well."

Aargun drew a different knife from a sheath hidden somewhere on his body, as Ghalian assassins were wont to do. Typically, none saw them draw one, though, and those few who did, did not live long enough to tell of it.

That one recently bedridden, blind, and mute would still be hiding weapons on his person, despite being in as safe an environment as possible, might have struck an outsider as a bit odd, but Hozark and Prombatz would have expected nothing less.

"Happizano, what do you think of this one?" Prombatz asked as Aargun extended the knife, handle first, to the boy. Again, he moved with unerring accuracy.

Hap took it from his hand and studied it a moment. Unlike Henni, he didn't possess the natural proclivity for violence and general stabby behavior, but he had been learning a thing or two from his new friends.

"I don't really know," the boy said. "But this one looks a lot smaller, so maybe it's meant to be carried around?"

Aargun nodded, then gestured for him to go on.

"And? What else?" Prombatz urged.

"Uh, well, it seems to be balanced right at the middle," Hap said, resting the knife on his finger as he'd just been taught. "And the tip is still pretty solid. So, maybe it's for throwing too?"

Aargun smiled and nodded, then gestured toward the wooden block.

"Throw it?" the youth asked.

Aargun nodded.

"But I've never thrown a knife before."

"Aargun has shown you the basics of the technique," Prombatz said. "Now all you need to do is practice and develop a feel for it."

"Go on, Hap. You've got this," Henni said, eagerly watching.

"Yes, young Jinnik. Do not fear. We all required a bit of time to learn––"

The knife flew across the room and stuck in the wooden block. Not in the center, and skewed off at an angle, barely penetrating the wood, but it had stuck nonetheless.

Hap grinned brightly.

"Or in your case, perhaps a bit less time. Most impressive," Hozark said, patting Hap on the shoulder.

Laskar let out an exaggerated sigh. "This is boring. Let's see how that magic stuff works."

"I am afraid that is not possible," Prombatz said. "But improving your knife skills is."

"I don't see the big deal," Laskar said, casually throwing the knife carried on his belt. It flew true, landing in the center of the target.

"You used magic," Prombatz noted, a tad surprised.

"Well, of course."

"He possesses a small bit of internal power," Hozark explained. "Not much by any standards, but it seems to help him on occasion with certain things. Apparently, knife-throwing is one of them."

Laskar seemed a bit put out by not being able to learn to use the strange power Aargun had tapped into, but he let it go. For now, at least.

"My turn!" Henni said, pulling the twin daggers from her sheaths and throwing them in quick succession.

The first flew true, sticking in the wood with a satisfying thunk. The second went a bit askew, bouncing off the wall to the side.

"Oops. Sorry."

"It is of no concern," Prombatz said.

Aargun reached out, and Henni placed her hands in his. He moved them one after the other, demonstrating the rhythm required for dual wielding. It took a moment, but Henni nodded her understanding.

"The key to successive throws is to––" Prombatz began.

"Yeah, I got it," she said, retrieving her knives, as well as the one Hap had thrown.

Prombatz looked at Hozark with a raised brow.

Henni's ability to read others seemed to function quite well with Aargun. Despite his lacking a tongue, she could discern what he was trying to impart to her without much difficulty at all.

It was a striking demonstration of the potential Corann had told him about. The possibilities of the odd, violet-haired girl's powers. But for now, her talents still seemed limited.

"Henni, would you mind helping Happizano and Laskar with Aargun's instructions?" Hozark asked. "Master Prombatz and I have things we need to discuss."

"Sure thing, Hozark," the young woman said.

The two masters stepped from the room, leaving them to continue their lesson with the unlikely instructor.

"This has been a good thing, Hozark," Prombatz said. "It is

therapeutic for Aargun to engage with people like this. He was always one of the more social of our students, and this is doing him much good."

"Yes, I can see," Hozark replied. "And it has also been a good lesson for our guests, beyond the martial skills they are learning. Seeing the other side of Ghalian life is important. Understanding that, no matter how skilled one may be, it is always possible to be on the losing end of a conflict."

"Indeed."

"Aargun seems to be recovering quite well. But have the healers ever figured out what exactly was done to him?"

Prombatz furrowed his brow slightly at the thought of what had been done to his young student.

"The details of his torture and the experimentation that was performed upon him are, unfortunately, lost. His eyes were the first thing taken from him, and shortly thereafter, his tongue. That much he relayed in writing when asked, but after that, he does not recall a thing."

"Trauma has that effect."

"Indeed. And from what the healers said, Aargun lost a great deal of blood at the earliest stages of his torture."

"How can they be so sure?" Hozark asked.

"The healing abilities our kind possess were hindered, resulting in a pattern of scar tissue that highlighted the sequence of injuries inflicted upon him."

"They would have had to drain quite a lot for that to have happened," Hozark noted.

"And it seems they did."

"To what end, is the real question in play."

"Indeed, it is. But we do not know what they were attempting with his, or any of the other victims' experiments. For now, it remains a mystery."

"Yes, and quite a mystery at that," Hozark said. "But at least he is recovering."

"And, as we have seen today, he seems to be progressing far better than one might have expected. I believe having these new visitors to interact with has given him a renewed sense of purpose."

"I agree. And I am pleased to see that his abilities appear as sharp as ever," Hozark said.

"Yes, they certainly are. And his casting? Well, you have now seen firsthand what he is capable of. It is remarkable, to say the least."

"Quite surprising indeed. Not to mention the way he and Henni communicate," Hozark said. "It is something special we have witnessed, and most fascinating, though I think it is also an ability unique to him that he happens to have developed. Others have lost the ability to speak in the past, but they could not cast as he does."

Prombatz nodded his agreement. "It is quite possibly something to do with the experimentation he underwent that caused his body to react in this way. But as we are in the dark as to what was done to him, I think it unlikely we shall ever truly know why."

"In any case, I think you and I are of the same mindset that his unusual casting ability should be nurtured and encouraged. Only the Old Ones have ever been able to perform spells without speech, but perhaps he will be able to develop the skill. Or some semblance of it."

"Perhaps," Prombatz said. "But the Old Ones were Zomoki of exceptional power and intellect. And after the fall of Visla Balamar at the hands of the Council of Twenty, they are all long dead."

"In any case, he should be encouraged."

"Yes. And if your friends are willing, I think further visits could be of great benefit to that end. Especially the violet-haired woman. Her ability to communicate with Aargun appears to have given him a much-needed boost in morale."

"I am confident they would both be glad for further instruction," Hozark replied. "For now, however, we should be returning to the others. If our network has been successful, we will need to be ready to move quickly to find Happizano's father."

"The boy is holding up surprisingly well. You have done a good job cushioning the blow, Hozark."

"Thank you, brother. But a boy needs his father, and I hope to reunite them sooner than later."

# CHAPTER THIRTY-FIVE

Hozark and Prombatz quietly stood at the door to Aargun's comfortable room. They were both pleased to find that there was actually a little smile on the blinded assassin's face as he listened to the satisfying thunk of blades sinking into wood as his unexpected students gained proficiency with their throwing skills.

Hozark watched with pleasure as Happizano threw the small knife he had been given to work with. The boy had refined his technique in just the short time working with Aargun, and though he lacked the proficiency and technique to bury the tip deep in the target, his release had already improved by leaps and bounds.

The blade flew true, sticking in the target, though far from center.

"Nice one, Hap!" Henni said, pulling the boy's knife from the wood. "You're really getting the hang of it."

It was odd, seeing the typically abrasive young woman treating the equally difficult boy almost like a kid brother. Odd, and refreshing. It was a dynamic Hozark would very much like to see continue upon their return to the mothership.

Laskar, meanwhile, just watched with that odd aloofness he sometimes projected.

"Hey, guys," Henni said to the two masters as she picked up a piece of firm fruit from the dish on the table.

She gave them a wink, then threw it across the room to Aargun. The blind man snatched it out of the air effortlessly, a knife already appearing in his other hand, slicing off a piece in an instant.

He offered the slice to Hap, who gratefully accepted with a grin as the Wampeh sliced off another piece for Henni.

"Thanks, Aargun," she said, walking over and taking the treat, then handing Hap his knife.

Hozark and Prombatz shared a look, each raising a brow slightly. It seemed that Aargun and Henni were working *quite* well together, and the man's senses were as sharp as ever despite his lack of eyesight.

"You are both greatly improved in your knife skills, I see," Hozark said. "Good work. Aargun, you have my compliments. You are quite a skilled teacher, it would seem."

The blind man smiled. It seemed the extreme stoicism of the Wampeh Ghalian had given way to a bit more of an emotional response to things since his injury. He was healing, but part of that coping mechanism involved a re-emergence of emotions kept in check throughout his years of training.

Hozark had watched Aargun and Demelza practice together just before the incident, and while he was not a particularly special aspirant, Aargun had nevertheless impressed him with his general skill level.

The young man had been undeniably ready for the final trial to become a full-fledged Ghalian, and at the time, Hozark had no doubts that he was up to the challenge. If not for what befell him and Prombatz, he would likely be roaming the galaxy completing contracts with the utmost professionalism and skill.

But that was not meant to be.

"Is it really time to go?" Hap asked.

"I am afraid so, young Jinnik. We must return now, but if Aargun is willing to continue with these lessons, I think, perhaps, we could arrange additional visits. What do you say, Aargun?" Hozark asked.

"Can we?" Hap asked, excitedly.

Aargun's face lit up ever so slightly as he nodded.

"He's game," Henni said.

"Excellent," Prombatz said. "I think we have an arrangement, Master Hozark, wouldn't you agree?"

"I would," he said. "It is decided. We shall return your two students to you in as short an order as possible, Aargun. And I once more thank you for your service. Now, if you are all ready, we have a craft to board."

"Oh, thank the gods," Laskar grumbled, his boredom clear.

Hap held out the sheathed knife. "Thanks, Aargun. That was really fun."

The Wampeh held up his hand and smiled at the boy he couldn't see.

"He wants you to keep it," Henni said.

"Really?" Hap turned to Hozark. "Can I, Hozark?"

"Of course, Happizano. Every man should carry a blade, and this is a fine piece of Ghalian craftmanship to start you down that path. A very fine gift indeed. Thank you, Aargun, you are most generous. Laskar, would you escort Hap back to the ship? We will be right behind you."

"Already moving," the copilot said. "Come on, Hap, let's get a move on."

"Okay. Thanks, Aargun!" Hap chirped.

Aargun nodded once as Hap strapped the knife to his hip and trotted off toward the waiting ship. The contented glow around the Ghalian was clear to all present, though it was not visible, and was not magical in origin.

Henni leaned in and wrapped her arms around her new friend.

"Thanks, Aargun," she said, releasing her grip. "That was a lot of fun. I can't wait to pick up where we left off."

He smiled and patted her on the shoulder, then cocked his head slightly in a questioning posture.

"Yeah, I'll keep practicing," she said. "Don't worry."

Aargun seemed pleased with her reply. It was clear that a new friendship had been formed today, and both the troubled young woman and the wounded Ghalian seemed better for it.

"Come, Henni. It is time to go," Hozark said, turning to Aargun. "Rest up and heal well, brother. We shall return soon."

Aargun nodded his farewell, and his visitors took their leave.

Comfortably aboard their ship, prepped for the return trip in the windowless central chamber, Hozark and his friends settled in for the flight from the secret facility.

It was an unusual trip, and not exactly what was planned. What had been intended to be a rather sobering lesson in the flip side of the Ghalian life, had turned into a quite positive adventure for the unexpecting visitors.

Yes, they had seen the downside of the assassin's lifestyle. Disfigurement and worse were quite likely in the pursuit of a target. But so too was glory, though of a quiet and unassuming variety. But now, with Aargun's strange new ability, and his silent, brotherly connection with Henni, things were a bit different, and Hozark wondered what exactly that might mean moving forward.

As for Happizano, the boy was merrily playing with the small knife he had been gifted. It seemed the days of his toys might have finally ended. Or, at least, they might have been replaced with playthings of a new variety.

"The blade fits your hand well," Hozark said. "And I saw that you had gained in proficiency in that short time."

"Yeah, it's a lot of fun," the boy replied.

"We shall continue your practice until you are able to visit Aargun next. I think you may have the makings of a fine blademaster in you yet, and I am quite interested to see what else you might show skill at."

"You'll teach me more?"

"Of course," Hozark replied. "As will Demelza, naturally. Both you and Henni have shown quite a great deal of potential in the short time she has been working with you, and I, for one, am looking forward to seeing where your training takes you."

The boy was beaming for the entire flight back to Corann's, and Henni, likewise, was in fine spirits, though hers seemed to also stem from having connected with Aargun as she had.

It was an utterly non-romantic thing she felt between them, but a unique and powerful one regardless. And with it, it seemed her inner powers had come alive, at least a little bit.

All it took was that first spark to ignite the kindling. And for whatever reason, that wounded Ghalian had been tainted with just the right kind of strange magic from his torture and experimentation to trigger the reaction.

Laskar, on the other hand, just seemed a bit mopey. He found the knife training boring, and was unimpressed by the stories of how Aargun came to be the way he was.

The Ghalian's unusual ability to cast without words, however, had definitely caught his attention. But with no one able to explain to him how it worked, Laskar found himself both enthralled yet stymied, all at the same time.

It was understandable, Hozark thought, why he was frustrated. But aside from that little hiccup, the two Ghalian masters agreed, it had been a very productive trip.

"Corann! Look what I got!" Hap shouted out as he ran to the sweet woman as soon as they'd landed.

"Oh, that's a nice knife you've got there," she said, clocking Aargun's gift.

"Yeah, and look what I learned how to do."

Hap took aim and threw the knife at a nearby fruit tree. The blade stuck into the trunk at an odd angle but stayed embedded.

"That's very nice, Happizano. But you just threw a knife into my Goramus tree."

The boy hesitated, realizing what he'd done. Corann's lips softened into a faint smile.

"Oh, don't fret. I'll be able to heal the damage. But promise me, from now on, you'll only use a target we set up for you. Is that a deal?"

"Deal!"

"Good. Now, why don't you head on into the kitchen. Something tells me there might be a tray of warm cookies on the counter that just came out of the oven."

Hap didn't need to be told twice. His blur of chatter abruptly ceased, and he took off to find the others to show them his new knife––while gathering up a handful of cookies, of course.

Henni watched with wary eyes, but she felt the ice thawing a bit. Corann was still a cold-blooded killer, and always would be, but Henni felt something else about her now. That despite her murderous ways, she was actually a very principled and kind person.

Until she needed to not be.

Corann noticed the violet-haired woman eyeing her. "How did you find the trip, Henni? I hope you were not too disturbed by Aargun's disfigurement."

"Nah, I didn't even really notice it once we got chatting."

Corann's brow lifted slightly. "Chatting?"

"Henni and Aargun seemed to have shared something of a connection," Prombatz said.

"Ah, you *read* him, then?" Corann asked.

"No. I mean, yes. But not really. I didn't mean to. He was just... *there*. But once we got started, it was all fine."

Corann assessed the woman with a curious gaze. "You know, you could be quite a force to be reckoned with if you were able to control this gift."

"Yeah, well, it's just a thing that happens sometimes," Henni said.

"If you are open to the prospect, I would be honored to assist you in your efforts to learn your power," the master Ghalian said.

Henni looked unsure, but Corann didn't set off the warning bells in her head like she used to.

"Maybe," she finally replied, then headed inside to join Hap.

Corann nodded. It wasn't perfect, but it was good enough for now.

# CHAPTER THIRTY-SIX

The spread laid out by Corann for her guests was nothing if not impressive. The woman had long ago mastered the art of entertaining, and had she ever decided to give up her life heading the order of the deadliest assassins in the galaxy, she could have done quite well in the bed and breakfast hospitality industry.

Henni and Hap were eating with gusto the moment the first course arrived. Apparently, training in Ghalian knife techniques was some hungry business, and they were more than eager to replenish their energy stores.

The others were likewise ravenous, though more due to the quality of the meal presented to them. The head of the Five did not hold back when it came to feeding those of her order and their friends.

"The installation was a bit tricky, but we got it done," Bud said. "I wish we could have come with you guys. It sounds like it was a real eye-opening experience." He turned to Prombatz with an apologetic blush. "Sorry. No offense."

Prombatz let out a low chuckle. "None taken, Uzabud. Aargun may have lost his sight, but his sense of humor has remained quite intact, and I assure you, he would not take it personally."

"Good. Sometimes I really need to watch what I say."

"Ain't that the truth," Henni agreed through her full mouth.

"You're one to talk. And, hey, manners much?" he shot back.

Henni swallowed her food and stuck out her tongue.

"Like freakin' children," Laskar lamented, shaking his head.

"Hey, I have better manners than that," Hap interjected.

"Your father taught you well, then," Corann said.

"Bud, what was it you were saying about the ship?" Laskar asked. "The installation of the modified konuses to the hull, and those new defensive spells?"

Bud took a swig of wine and wiped his lips. "Yeah, Corann's upgrades took some doing, but if those Council goons try any funny business, we've got a nice surprise in store."

"New offensive spells?"

"Nah, we've already got those aplenty. But the ship can now defend against multiple spectrums of attacks, both magic and physical at once. Like, if we have some potent spells being hurled at us at the same time as some magically lobbed projectiles, we can stop both without having to switch from one mode of defense to the other."

"We can do that? I thought it was impossible," Laskar mused.

"It should be, and really, it still is, for the most part. But as we talked about ways to better protect the ship, Corann, Demelza, and I came up with a really novel way to help the ship cast on multiple levels."

Laskar, being the copilot, and having had the Council craft attempt to blow him from the sky along with his friends, was eager for anything that might give them even a slight edge. But this? This could be a game changer.

"So? Come on, Bud, you're killing me here."

"Right. So, what we wound up doing was using the ships to our advantage."

"Ship, you mean."

"No. *Ships*."

Laskar furrowed his brow as he wondered precisely what Bud was talking about.

"Think about it," Bud said, urging him on.

"I am. We've got one ship, Bud."

"Ah, but do we?"

Suddenly, the crazy realization dawned on the confused man. "Holy shit. Are you serious? You somehow tied in the spares and junkers we've been lugging around to the main ship's defenses?"

Bud grinned wide. "Yep. And since we have 'em docked to the hull, that means when we overcharge their konus defenses, the protection spills over to the main ship."

"That can't be stable," Laskar said.

"It's not the best, admittedly. But Corann and Demelza managed to work some of their Ghalian wonders with the konuses, though they won't tell me exactly how. Trade secrets and all that. Anyway, now that they're all intercommunicating and connecting their spells, it's made a network of defenses out of the group, rather than the individual."

"Mind you, the right type of attack would negate this advantage," Corann noted as a plain-looking woman from town calmly entered the room and walked close. Corann noted her, then finished her thought. "But in a very general sense, this will provide a considerable improvement in defenses. If you'll excuse me a moment," she said, stepping out to speak with the visitor.

Laskar sat there, floored. The implications were enormous. Their clever use of a system never before attempted had managed to do the impossible. And if they could keep the links in that chain intact, there was no telling how many attacks they could fend off without too much trouble.

The magic-saving benefits were exponential as well. Rather than draining one konus to keep them safe, fractional magic draws would occur, leaving the overall power of the individual konuses barely touched.

"Okay, I've *got* to see this in action," Laskar said.

"After dinner," Bud replied, shoveling another bite into his mouth. "Gotta have priorities, man."

"Food takes precedence over the most badass defensive system in the galaxy?"

Bud flashed a grin. "Hey, I'm hungry."

"I believe you may have to postpone both your demonstration, as well as the rest of your meal," Corann said, hurrying back into the room. "I have just been informed that the spy network has word of some most unusual activity."

"Unusual? How unusual we talkin' here?" Laskar asked.

"A rather stealthy group of Council goons appear to be strong-arming a settlement not too many systems from here," she replied.

"I hate to say it, but that's kinda what they do," Bud noted.

"True, but these are not only imposing their will. They are also taking the main planet's power users under subjugation. And from the description of the attacking force, it seems to be very likely these are the same ships that previously brought Visla Jinnik to strike down uprisings, though he has not been seen in action yet."

"*Yet*, is the key word," Bud said. "I bet they're just keeping their most powerful asset on standby until they need him."

"My father is there?" Hap asked, a hopeful glow shining in his eyes.

"We do not know for certain, Happizano," Corann said. "But there is a likelihood of his presence, yes."

"We've gotta go, then!"

"On this we are in agreement," Hozark said. "But do not allow your hopes to rise too high. I would not wish for you to be disappointed should this prove to be a false alarm."

Bud was already on his feet and moving. "Laskar, come on. We've gotta get prepped to launch, like, yesterday."

"Right on your tail," the copilot said, following him in a quick exit.

"Demelza, will you please assist me in gathering the last few additional supplies? We might find them of use in this potential conflict," Hozark said.

"I shall. Henni, please go with Hap and board the ship. We shall join you both momentarily."

"You got it," the young woman replied. "Come on, Hap. Time to boogie on outta here."

The pair rushed off to their ship, eager to see what might unfold when they reached their destination. Hap tried as best he could to keep his anticipation to a minimum, but the prospect of actually seeing his father had given him that spark of hope that could easily flare into a flame if not carefully managed.

"Corann, we thank you for your hospitality, as always, and for the upgraded defenses to our transport. I hope we will not need to employ them, but if we do, I am sure they will come in very handy," Hozark said.

"Best of luck to you all," Corann said. "And good hunting. We shall have a few of our network observing from a distance. Summon them should you require assistance."

"I shall, Corann. Thank you."

"Fly safe, brother," Prombatz said. "Keep an eye on him, sister Demelza."

"I will do my best," she replied, suppressing a tiny grin. To have not one, but three of the Five treating her as almost an equal was a heady experience, even for a stoic Wampeh Ghalian.

She and Hozark quickly gathered the last of their supplies, as well as a few additional slaaps and konuses of particular strength that might prove to be of particular use should they indeed encounter the Council forces the spies described.

Even if they could get Visla Jinnik to stand down, there was no way he would be traveling without a substantial force of Council muscle to bolster and secure the results of his efforts. The visla might be able to be removed from the equation, but not the mercenary and Council troops, and it was far better safe than sorry when it came to dealing with them.

"You guys ready to roll?" Bud asked after they boarded the ship and stowed their gear.

"We are," Hozark replied as he and Demelza slid into their seats.

"All right, then. Laskar, you have our jumps dialed in?"

"I do."

"The shorter path, right?"

"Yes, Bud. The shorter path. But it'll put a bit of strain on the Drookonus making fewer, but longer, jumps."

"I know. But time is of the essence here," Bud replied. "Okay, let's do this."

He launched the craft and made a casual ascent, all for the benefit of the locals around Corann's abode. But once in space and free from prying eyes, Uzabud engaged the powerful travel spells and set the ship in motion, jumping from the skies in a blink of an eye.

# CHAPTER THIRTY-SEVEN

The jumps Laskar had plotted actually didn't strain the Drookonus terribly much. The device did get a bit heated from the shortened cool-down period between jumps, but otherwise, it fared quite well as its stored Drook magic rushed Bud's ship to their destination.

"This doesn't look all that intimidating," Bud said as they approached the planet in question from the darkness of space, making sure to draw near while the world's shadow protected them from being illuminated by the system's sun.

"Get us closer, Bud," Hozark directed.

"You got it."

They adjusted their angle of approach and slipped into a high orbit that allowed them to observe the surface as well as whatever ships might be circling below them in a lower path, but there were no lurking Council ships in the skies, only on the surface.

"Nothing," Laskar said. "We're alone up here."

"At least so far as Council ships go," Bud said, noting a handful of small, civilian craft exiting the atmosphere.

"This does not seem right for what we were led to believe was the situation," Demelza said. "Might this be a trap?"

Hozark looked at the goings-on down below with cautious eyes. It seemed that all of the magical hostilities were taking place on the surface, while none of the Council ships remained in orbit.

It was highly irregular, to say the least. And not what he expected to find.

"We find ourselves in an unusual situation," he finally said. "There are some of Visla Ravik's forces down below, and I can sense traces of Visla Jinnik's magic. He is present, but I do not sense Ravik anywhere near. If we can overwhelm Ravik's men and distract them, we might be able to pull close enough to Visla Jinnik to prove his son's safety."

"And then he will cease complying with the Council's will," Demelza noted. "With the visla on our side, we should be able to drive back Ravik's forces with ease, even if Visla Ravik should make an appearance."

"Yes. But first we must separate the main body of ground forces from the support of their ships. Bud, can you and Laskar draw them away?"

"Does a Bundabist shit in the woods?"

"I shall take that as a yes, then. Good." Hozark turned to Laskar. "We have a long-range skree aboard now. Should we require assistance, you are to summon the Ghalian ships both within this system and beyond. They will provide support."

"What ships?" the copilot asked. "I didn't see any ships, did you, Bud?"

"Nope," the pilot said with a grin. "But they're Wampeh Ghalian. You know they won't be seen if they don't want to be."

Hozark ignored the comment and continued on. "The force on the ground appears to be relatively small. Judging by the use of power, it is highly likely that Visla Jinnik is with the forwardmost of their party, though I have sensed his power at the rear as well. It is entirely possible he is being employed to deal with the insurgents on all fronts."

"That's gotta be a bit draining, even for a visla," Bud said.

"Potentially. But it gives us a better chance of avoiding direct conflict with the visla before we can make Happizano's presence known."

"You're taking the kid with?" Bud asked.

"Yes. He shall descend with Henni and remain within my ship, shimmer-cloaked and standing by until such time as his father's position is acquired. While the visla might detect the cloaked craft, none of the Council lackeys seem to possess the power to sense it."

"You sure about that?" Laskar asked.

"So far as I can discern," Hozark replied. "In any case, this is our best option. Demelza and I will make our way through their ranks while you two draw away their support ships. Splitting their forces like that will give us a far greater likelihood of being able to separate the visla from the others."

"And if you don't?"

"Then we run," Hozark said.

"Run? A Ghalian?"

"There is no shame in retreat, Laskar. Especially when said retreat is strategically sound."

"I know, it's just not exactly something I'd expect to hear from one of you guys, is all."

"Well, now you have. Bud, prepare to open your proverbial can of whoop-ass, if you would. Demelza and I shall launch our shimmer ships shortly."

"We'll be ready, Hozark."

With that, the master assassin hurried off to gather Henni and the boy to inform them of the plan and load them onto his craft. Their approach would be stealthy and silent, as would Demelza's.

Once the two assassins had landed, they would make their

way into the Council troops' ranks in their shimmer cloaks and lay silent waste to as many as they could, while seeking the exact location of Visla Jinnik.

At that point, once he was found, they would focus all of their skills on reuniting the boy with his father and turning the tide of the conflict. Having the visla freed of the threat against his boy would provide them a valuable ally, and one who could definitely shift things to their advantage.

Henni and Happizano were both unusually quiet as the little shimmer ship bumped and jarred as it descended to the surface. The air turbulence on this world was a bit harsh in the upper atmosphere, and that led to an uncomfortable ride.

Hozark was a skilled pilot, and they knew no harm would befall them––at least not on the descent––but this was it. This was what they'd been waiting for. Finally, Hap would see his father. But it wouldn't be easy, and there was no telling what nasty surprises the Council might have waiting for them down below.

Demelza flew a fair distance away, planning to set down at a position that would allow her to cut through the ranks on her way to join Hozark. By splitting up like that, they hoped to find the visla all the faster, for the longer they delayed, the more likely was their discovery.

"Stay here until I summon you," Hozark said once they had set the ship down at the outskirts of the skirmish. "When I have located your father, only then should you exit the safety of this vessel. Until that time, the shimmer cloaking will protect you from discovery."

Hap shifted in his seat but remained silent.

He stared hard at the boy. "Happizano, it is imperative you follow this direction. Are we clear?"

"Yeah," he replied.

"Don't worry," Henni said, resting her hands on the pommels of her knives. "I'll look after him."

Hozark nodded once, then donned his shimmer cloak and stepped from the craft.

The fighting was close, but not so close that he emerged right into it. And camouflaged as he was, Hozark was able to move a fair distance through the battling men and women before he was forced to engage by sheer proximity.

The men he slayed dropped silently to the ground without so much as slowing his progress, and in the chaos of battle, no one noticed they had fallen by an invisible hand.

As Hozark made his way through the fighting masses, it became clear to him that this was no more than a rather small rebellion being squashed by the Council's mighty fist. It was no wonder Ravik hadn't bothered to come himself when he could deploy others to do his dirty work.

But despite his power hanging in the air, Visla Jinnik was still nowhere to be seen.

"Demelza, what news?" the cloaked assassin asked the empty air nearby where a Council goon suddenly fell for no apparent reason, a bloody hole sprouting from his back.

"No sign of Jinnik," she replied. "And something about this feels wrong."

"I agree," Hozark said as he pulled a konus from the wrist of a dead Council goon. "We must make quick work here. I believe this whole endeavor has not been as it seemed. And on top of that, we have no idea what Bud and Laskar may actually be up against."

He could not have been more prescient in that comment, as far above, the former pirate and his copilot were engaged in a dogfight with the dozen or so Council ships they had drawn from their positions on the ground.

Strafing them with a vicious magical attack from above had taken the craft by surprise, and more than a few sustained significant damage from it. But now, as a group, they were coming back, and doing so with force.

"They're moving to block us from jumping," Laskar noted.

"Yeah? Well, we're not trying to jump," Bud growled as he spun them out of the line of fire of a pair of closing ships while simultaneously casting a trio of stun spells in hopes of disabling their pursuers' Drooks and knocking the ships out of the equation.

One of them seemed to fall victim to his ploy, abruptly drifting off at an angle, leaving the fight. The other, however, avoided the attack and stayed on their tail.

Fortunately, the modified defensive spells of the remaining ships mounted to the hull provided a robust shield against the barrage of magical attacks flying their way.

"This is getting to be too much," Laskar said. "I don't know how much longer we can hold them off."

"We just need to distract them until—"

"Laskar," Hozark's voice crackled over their close-range skree. "Summon the others. They will handle the Council ships."

Laskar snatched up both skrees and spoke into the smaller one. "But what about—?"

"Visla Jinnik is not here," Hozark cut him off.

"Wait, he's not?" Laskar said.

"No, he is not."

"Shit, so we're out of luck."

"No, we are not. I know where he is."

"You do?" Laskar asked with surprise.

"Yes. Plot a course to Gravalis, and tell Bud to meet us at the rendezvous point."

"On it," he replied, then switched to the larger, long-range skree to call in their backup.

They hadn't seen the other Ghalian ships, but that's how shimmer cloaking was meant to work. When the Council craft around them suddenly began bucking and shaking from invisible attacks a few minutes later, however, they knew the message had been received loud and clear.

The ship shook from impacts as Bud peeled away from the skirmish.

"What are you doing?" he asked as Laskar still had the long-range skree clutched in his hand. "Use both hands, idiot!"

"What? Oh, shit, I didn't notice," he said, quickly stowing the device. "I'm not used to using two of them at once. Look out!"

Bud reacted and narrowly avoided a rapidly approaching Council ship. One of the cloaked Ghalian craft lay into it with a flurry of spells, knocking it from his path.

"Damn, that was close," Bud said as he banked sharply out of the way, pulling from the danger zone as quickly as he could, then headed to the far side of the battlefield.

It was not too far away, but not close enough to be readily engaged by the hostile forces. It was a choice location to meet should they need to do so while still within the atmosphere.

He set down fast, the tone of Hozark's message having relayed the urgency of it clear enough.

The sensation of the two cloaked Ghalian ships docking on the larger craft's hull was slight, but on the surface, and in full gravity, the pilot and copilot noticed. In space, however, the Ghalian often came and went without a trace.

Happizano stormed through the ship straight to his room. He was clearly distressed by the turn of events.

"Shit, the poor kid," Bud said, watching him pass.

"Don't worry. I've got him," Henni said, following in his wake.

"So, what happened?" Laskar asked as Hozark and Demelza joined them.

Hozark turned the konus in his hand over and over, studying the bright metal. "Come. I shall show you."

# CHAPTER THIRTY-EIGHT

With Hap and Henni safely aboard their mothership, Hozark led Bud and Laskar onto the battlefield while Demelza stood guard in her shimmer cloak at the ship's entrance, just in case.

They didn't expect any to come looking for a fight. Not this far from the main engagement. Not where so many lay dead or dying. There was nothing to gain here, only death and misery.

"What's this you were saying about Visla Jinnik not being here?" Bud asked. "You said you felt his magic. And I know you, Hozark. You're not wrong about that sort of thing. Not ever."

Hozark gave his friend a pained little smile. "And I was not mistaken this time, either," he replied.

"I'm sorry, I don't follow," Laskar interjected. "You said he was here, but he wasn't."

"That is correct, in a sense."

Hozark walked among the corpses feeling for traces of the magic he sought as he walked. After a long moment he paused and bent over one of the Council soldiers littering the ground.

Far more of the rebel forces lay dead or dying. They had been overwhelmed by a magical barrage the likes of which they simply could not withstand. But, nevertheless, they fought on, and some of their attackers fell.

The Council soldiers wore the insignia of Visla Ravik, but many of those nearby were lacking any identification whatsoever. And most were Tslavars. Given the Council's relations with the Tslavars, they were almost certainly Mercenaries in Council garb.

Hozark pulled the man's arm up, showing his blood-covered konus, still shining on his wrist. The weapon must have been quite powerful given the damage before them.

"Lucky shot must've taken him down," Bud noted. "Looks like a conventional weapon. Maybe a spear."

"Who uses spears?" Laskar asked. "That's so primitive."

"Most of these rebel groups are limited in resources. And a sharpened piece of wood will end you just as much as a wealthy man's sword will."

Laskar cocked his head slightly as he mulled over that detail. "So, this clan of the pointed stick, they somehow overcame Council troops? That's unexpected."

The man at Hozark's feet stirred. In a flash, a hidden dagger appeared in the assassin's hand and buried itself into the man's head, piercing his skull like a piece of fruit.

None could ever say Ghalian blades were not kept in a condition of peak sharpness.

The man twitched a few times, then fell silent. This time for good. Hozark pulled the konus from his wrist, wiped it on the fallen man's tunic, then tossed it to Bud.

"So, it's a konus. We see these all the time."

"Look closer, Bud. Look at the others on the battlefield."

The former pirate scrutinized the metal. There did seem to be a slight design to it, though nothing terribly ornate as one might see in some elite units. Those were typically decorative and did not enhance function at all, but it did give the men a sense of cohesion as they fought alongside one another.

"It's got a different bit of marking to it," Bud said. "But what does that have to do with—"

"It is powered by Visla Jinnik's magic," Hozark said. "All across this battlefield, traces of his power can be found."

"Wait, you're saying Jinnik *made* these?"

"No, of course not. The Visla, powerful as he is, does not possess the metallurgical skill to craft a konus. But he *can* imbue one with its power. And it seems he has done so. Done so to a great many konuses and slaaps, in fact."

Bud and Laskar looked at the fallen men around them. Could it be that all of this damage had been done with Jinnik's magic, but without him actually being there himself? The answer seemed quite clear.

"So, there are a bunch of Jinnik-powered weapons here? That's what you sensed?" Laskar asked.

"Indeed," Hozark replied, walking through the corpses to the next dead man with a similar band on his wrist.

Hozark pulled it free and continued on his way.

"What are you doing?"

"Gathering as many of these as is reasonable, given our constraints," Hozark replied. "Possessing a collection of Jinnik-powered konuses and slaaps, even the mostly drained ones, may prove useful in coming days. Now, if you two would please assist me, we should gather what we can and return to the ship. Time is of the essence, but this delay may well be worth it."

Bud and Laskar began quickly scouring the bodies nearest them for any sign of the slightly different weapons on them. Each managed to find a few, but after a good five minutes they only possessed a dozen between them.

"It will have to suffice," Hozark said. "We should not dally here any longer."

The trio turned and headed back to the waiting ship, the ongoing battle still raging in the distance, though the Ghalian forces were now providing a bit of stealthy air support, not only helping those on the ground, but giving Hozark and his friends the clear path they required to make their escape from this system.

Bud turned one of the konuses over in his hands as he walked, considering what this must mean.

"The Council is having him power weapons for them now?" Bud finally asked.

"Yes."

"I know I'm stating the obvious, but he has to be doing it under duress, right?"

"You would be correct."

"I figured as much. But even so, that sort of thing draws attention. All of the Council's facilities are either under surveillance or have leakers inside of them. I mean, I'm no Ghalian, but when I was actively pirating, even we knew what was going on and where to steer clear of."

"And where to raid," Hozark added.

"Well, yeah. That too," Bud admitted. "So with that in mind, what I'm saying is, there's no way they could keep this thing so quiet. We'd have heard something."

Hozark stepped aboard the ship, the others close behind.

"Unless it was a secret facility," he said as the doors sealed.

He took the konuses and placed them in a storage container, which he tucked away for the time being. They would need to be properly cleaned at a later time. But for now, the blood and gore could stay.

"A secret facility?" Bud asked. "Nice thought, but that would make it, oh, I don't know. *Secret*. Doesn't help us much now, does it?"

"I know the place where these konuses were produced," Hozark said. "I have been there before. Inside the very facility where the smelting took place."

"Wait, you what?"

"It was a Council facility," the assassin replied. "And that, dear Laskar, is why I asked you to plot a course. We are going to Gravalis."

## CHAPTER THIRTY-NINE

"You said you were on some Ghalian errand," Bud said, a bit of an edge to his tone.

"Yes, Bud, I did," Hozark replied.

"You were gone for weeks taking care of some official business. That's what you said."

"And, again, that was correct, for the most part."

"But you were actually on Gravalis, under deep cover, infiltrating a Council facility, and breaking into a super top-secret weapons manufacturing facility."

"As I have explained. Yes."

"And you were trapped."

"Briefly, yes," Hozark replied calmly.

Bud stared at him a long moment, then looked at the others who were staring at the assassin with a similar gaze. All but Demelza, that is. As a Wampeh Ghalian, she was in on this little piece of information he had withheld from the rest of them all this time.

"You lied to me, Hozark."

"I did. And I am sorry to have had to deceive you, Bud, but it was necessary that you remained in the dark as to my outing to Gravalis. The Ghalian network was set to task investigating what this might mean. Too much was at stake."

"What, you don't trust us? You don't trust *me*?"

"That is not the case at all. But if, by some unfortunate turn of events, you were to be captured and tortured, well, you know the understanding we have always had."

"Yeah, I do," Bud said, grudgingly accepting the explanation, though he didn't like it. But he and Hozark had a long history, and in this case, he could see why that seldom-used clause had been invoked.

"What are you talking about? What understanding?" Henni asked.

Bud turned to the violet-haired woman. "Basically, it goes a little something like this: 'You cannot spill information you do not possess.' Isn't that about right, Hozark?"

"I could not have said it better myself," the master assassin replied.

Henni fixed her gaze on Hozark. "So, you actually went and lived with them? For weeks? Oh, man, that must have been horrible."

"Surprisingly, it was actually not unpleasant. The regular Council workforce were a bit rough around the edges, but they seemed to be decent folk eking out a living however they could."

"But you killed them anyway? That's harsh."

"Oh, Henni. I did not kill anyone. It was a stealthy infiltration operation, and to leave corpses would have alerted the Council of my presence as an intruder. So, no, there was no killing."

"But you were trapped," Laskar said. "How did you escape?"

"The power user who set the trap has a bit of a theatrical, sadistic streak," Hozark said. "His cockiness left me the means of my escape."

He then went on to describe how the bones strewn about the

bottom of the pit he had fallen into were meant to unsettle whoever fell into the deadfall before they perished. It was the work of a cruel mind, and would be the last thing seen upon impact as the victim slowly bled out.

But Hozark's magic had saved him from being impaled upon the spikes at the bottom of the long fall, and those prop bones, when broken into sharp shards, had proven to be quite sturdy climbing tools.

"So, it was a full-fledged weapons factory?" Bud asked.

"Not exactly. The work being done was quite skillful, as these konuses and slaaps will attest, but they were lacking adequate power to charge the devices upon their forging, and thus were moving at a slow pace. A number of Ootaki had been shorn, that I could see. It was mostly that limited bit of power they were using when I was last there."

"But now they have a full-fledged visla doing their dirty work for them."

"Indeed. And, as we have seen from these weapons, he apparently completed a sizable number of them for the Council. Though more and more, I am of the belief that this might not have been an official Council endeavor."

"Ravik?" Bud asked.

"Yes. And possibly another."

"Visla Maktan?" Laskar asked.

Hozark nodded. "I am fairly certain he is the one behind this operation."

"Then you should take him out. Enough pussyfooting around. This guy is a menace and a threat."

"That he is. But the time is not yet right for such an action."

"If not now, then when?"

"Soon enough, dear Laskar. I appreciate your sense of urgency, but these things must be done properly. Especially where a visla in the Council of Twenty is concerned."

Laskar grumbled to himself but let it go at that.

"So, what now, then?" Bud asked.

"Now? Now we jump the rest of the way to Gravalis, where we shall storm the facility holding Happizano's father and reunite the two of them once and for all."

"You make it sound like it's gonna be easy," Henni said. "And what if his dad attacks us?"

"We will be bringing Happizano with us," Hozark said.

"*With*? Into a full-on fight? That doesn't seem like a great idea," she said. "I mean, yeah, he's getting decent with a knife, but a battle?"

"We need Happizano with us to present to his father. Only then can we be assured any attacks by him will cease."

"It's too risky," Henni said. "What if something goes wrong? What if he gets hurt?"

"I'm with Henni on this one," Bud said. "The kid's just too vulnerable."

Hozark pulled a konus from his pocket. It still had a little bit of dried blood on it, but was clearly one of the devices taken from the fallen on the battlefield.

"We have several more jumps before Gravalis. And I intend to use that time to train young Happizano in key defensive spells, as well as a few combatives, should he require them."

"But he's just a kid. And it takes time to learn to pull power from a konus like that," Laskar noted.

"Yes and no," Hozark replied. "Yes, he is just a boy. But in this unusual circumstance, these konuses were charged by his father. That is bloodline magic flowing through them. It's his father's familial magic. *His* magic. And as such, there is a high likelihood that he will instinctively have a far greater grasp on it than a regular user would."

"But enough to actually use them?" Laskar asked. "Can the kid really do that?"

"We shall find out soon enough," Hozark replied. "But first, a bit of assistance cleaning the other konuses would be appreciated. There is a fair bit of blood dried onto them, and I would rather not begin the boy's tutelage utilizing konuses soiled so."

## CHAPTER FORTY

"Again," the pale man directed his young pupil. "*Feel* the power in the konus and let it blend with your own. Then direct it with the *intention* of the spell, not just the words."

Happizano furrowed his brow but did as the Wampeh instructed him. It was a relatively simple force spell, one that would push an empty container but not be any risk to the ship.

Casting any powerful spells in space was a big no-no as the possibility of something going wrong and an accidental breach to the hull was very real. If that happened, death was all but certain because, no matter how powerful you might be, no one can cast if they have no air with which to speak the spell's words.

But this was a far lesser bit of magic. More than Happizano had used to date, for as the son of a visla, he had never had need to move items from place to place as a common laborer might. But despite his unfamiliarity with the spell, the boy was getting the hang of it.

Unfortunately, the slow nature of the process was frustrating him no end.

"*Ifran horakus*," the boy said, focusing his will on the container before him. The box did not move.

"*Ifran horakus*," he said again, this time with even more force. Once again, it remained in place.

"Why won't it work?" Hap griped, clearly agitated.

"It was difficult for me as well when I first started. All must endure the hardships of the process. Now, try again. You can do this."

"I can't do it. It won't work!"

"Yes, you can. And yes, it will. You merely need to practice. To focus your attention on what is going on within as well as the words you are speaking. Remember what I taught you?"

"It's the intent more than the words that make a spell work," the boy grumbled.

"Exactly. Now, you have the words learned perfectly. The sounds are crucial for channeling the energy from yourself and your konus. But it is the internal focus. The *intent* from within powering those words that truly drives the spell and makes the casting succeed."

"But I suck at this."

"Just give it another try. I know you can do this if you but focus."

The boy stifled a snarky comment. Hozark was helping him, after all, and he was a master Ghalian. The man knew his stuff, and even though he wasn't a natural power user, he did have a significant amount of stolen magic flowing through him. It would be smart to listen to him, no matter how frustrating it was.

Hozark watched calmly. Hap was clearly getting worked up from the ordeal, but the boy took a deep breath and forced himself to focus on the spell once more. He wrapped his mind around the words, but also the *intent* behind them.

The syllables connected to the power from his konus, blending with his own internal magic, aligning in purpose to make them do what he wanted them to do. To push the container away from himself.

"*Ifran horakus*," he said, straining what power he possessed to force it to do his bidding.

The container remained in place.

"Dammit! This is stupid!" he shouted, kicking a smaller box.

The box, however, was heavily loaded, and his foot bounced from it with a painful crack.

"Ow!" Hap yelped, hopping on his good foot. "Stupid, damned box!"

A slight crackle flickered across his skin.

"Happizano, get a hold of yourself," Hozark said, trying to calm the boy.

"I *am* calm," he shot back, turning to the container once more. "*Ifran horakus!*"

The container did not slide on the ship's deck. No, it flew through the air with speed, smashing through the compartment wall before tumbling to the ground in the adjacent chamber.

The magic on Happizano's skin faded as the look of shock on his face grew. Hozark watched the boy regain control of himself with both amazement as well as concern. Apparently, he possessed his father's unpredictable power leaks as well.

Hozark gently took the konus from Hap's wrist. He had pulled the power from it far more than from his own internal supply, the assassin noted. It was a wasteful use of it, though. A skilled caster could have accomplished the same with a tenth of the magic used.

But, regardless, Hap had succeeded in tapping into the konus's magic, and that was what truly mattered.

"What the hell was that?" Bud shouted as he ran into the chamber, his sword in hand, ready to fight whatever unexpected attacker had somehow made it into his ship.

He looked at the rough, gaping hole in the wall, then at the ruined cargo container in the other room. He turned his gaze to Hozark.

"We appear to have had a little accident," the Wampeh said with an apologetic grin. "But the upside is, our young friend here appears to have quite the knack for magic after all."

Despite his churning emotions, Hap blushed at the praise.

"I'm not in trouble?"

"No, of course not," Hozark replied. "It was entirely my fault for not giving you a better area to practice in. No, young Jinnik, you did nothing wrong, and quite a lot right." Hozark looked at Bud. "I think we will need to make a little stopover at the next habitable planet."

"But, my dad?"

"This won't delay our progress, *will it*, Bud?"

Bud caught his meaning immediately. "Of course not. The Drookonus will need to cool down a bit after the next jump anyway, so we'll need to pause for a bit regardless. It won't be slowing us down any at all."

Hap seemed satisfied with the answer.

"So, what do you say, young Jinnik? Shall we continue your lessons in a less restrictive environment?" Hozark asked. "I would be very interested to see what you are capable of in such a setting."

The boy slowly shifted from agitation to excitement. He had used power. Not just some stupid little thing like making a piece of ice or casting an illumination spell. This was *real* magic. The good stuff.

"Yeah," he finally said. "That'd be cool."

"All right, then. Why don't you get something to eat? You've done good work thus far, and you will need your energy for what I have in mind once we make landfall."

"Okay. Thanks, Hozark!" Hap said, his mood flipped one-eighty back to one of chipper excitement.

"That kid's gonna be a handful one day," Bud said as he watched the boy trot off down the corridor.

"Indeed, he may be," Hozark agreed.

"So," Bud said as he examined the hole in the wall. "Who's gonna fix my ship?"

## CHAPTER FORTY-ONE

"You know, the kid actually seems to have a knack for it," Bud said as he, Laskar, and Henni watched the two Wampeh Ghalian working with the boy in the open field beside their parked ship.

"He's not bad, I guess," Laskar said dismissively.

"For his age? That's pretty damn good."

"Meh. I was better."

Bud chuckled. "I've seen you cast. Believe me, your skills are nothing to brag about."

Laskar bristled ever so slightly at the dig, though anyone who had seen him attempt to use his own minimal magic would have to agree. The man simply couldn't do all that much with his power. And that was fine.

To be fair, most people didn't even possess the limited magic that Laskar had. But Happizano? He came from a bloodline of exceedingly powerful magic users, and it was looking as though he might just grow into that power sooner than expected.

Necessity, it seemed, was forcing the youngster to grow up.

"He's got shit for aim," Henni noted as Hap used his force spell to propel a medium-sized rock along the ground. "I mean, good for him, being able to cast and all, but it won't do much good if it's all over the place like that."

"Give the kid a break," Bud said. "This is, like, his *first* time really casting."

"What, you're on the kid's side, now?" Laskar joked. "I thought he got on your nerves."

"He does. But that doesn't mean I can't appreciate what he's accomplishing. Why are you being such an ass about his casting, anyway? Feeling threatened?"

"By a child? As if," Laskar scoffed.

A loud crash echoed across the field as the rock the young student was moving unexpectedly flew through the air and shattered against a nearby tree, nearly toppling it in the act.

"Sorry!" Hap said.

"You are very much *not* sorry," Demelza said with a friendly smile. "And with good reason. That was an excellent use of power. Here, let me see your konus," she said, taking his wrist in her hand.

She placed her fingers on the device around his wrist and sensed its power. Yes, it was still well charged with Visla Jinnik's magic, which was now intertwined with that of his son, but it seemed Happizano had not drawn an excessive amount from the device. In fact, he'd barely used it at all.

Demelza let his arm go and gave Hozark a slight nod. "It seems you are getting stronger than you realize, Happizano," she said.

"Not really. I'm just using my dad's power. It's cheating, kind of."

"Nonsense."

"You don't think using someone else's magic is cheating?"

"No, I don't mean that at all. What I mean is, you are barely using your father's power, Hap. What you just did was almost entirely your own doing."

Hap's mouth fell slightly open in shock at her words. Hozark chuckled and patted him on the back.

"Well done, young Jinnik. It would seem you possess your father's gifts after all. But this has been offense. However, one must also learn to defend oneself. Are you ready to learn the basics of shielding?"

"Yeah, I think so."

"Good. Then come with me."

Hozark led Hap a little distance away from the ship to ensure that any deflected magic would not potentially go astray and risk hitting the craft. It was very well shielded, but it would be a waste of good magic to defend against themselves.

The master assassin sat with Hap for a short while, instructing him in the words and meaning of the most basic of defensive spells. It was a simple spell, used to deflect a fairly wide array of offensive magic.

It would not stand up to a forceful attack from a skilled caster, but against your run-of-the-mill grunt, it might just suffice, provided their konus was not overly powerful.

And if they happened to be using one of the units charged by his father, there was a distinct possibility that Hap's spell might actually absorb the familiar magic and use it to bolster itself, rather than expend his own energy. A fluke of magic, often protecting a member of the bloodline from familial harm.

But for now, the purpose was to teach the boy the basics, and as the Drookonus would be nearly cooled and ready for their next jump, there was not terribly much time to do so.

"You have the words," Hozark finally said after several long minutes. "And you seem to possess an understanding of what it means to cast with intent. Now, let us see how well you put the two together, shall we?"

He stepped back several paces from the boy and cast a modest protective spell around himself, just in case of any misfire.

"Cast your defense," he instructed his student. "Draw the power from the konus and use it to supply the magic you require. Your own magic should be reserved as a last resort whenever you have such a device at your disposal."

"Okay," Hap said, then began reciting the words to the spell.

Demelza was standing ten paces from him, ready to cast. She wouldn't use any substantial magic, of course. Just a very mild stun spell. But if Hap didn't properly defend himself, he would definitely feel its sting. And that was how he would learn, just as had all Ghalian youth through the ages.

Hozark reached out with his senses and felt the magic beginning to coalesce around Happizano. When it seemed the spell would hold, he nodded once to Demelza.

"*Dispanus*," she quietly said, casting with only modest intent.

Hap was immediately knocked to the ground, and hard, his spell failing tremendously at first contact.

"Are you all right, young Jinnik?" Hozark asked, moving to help the boy to his feet.

"I'm fine," Hap grumbled. "But that stupid spell didn't work."

"It *was* working," Hozark noted. "I was probing your defenses while you prepared for Demelza's attack. You lost focus when she spoke the words to the spell, and that shift in attention allowed her to overcome your defenses. Does that make sense to you?"

Hap thought on it a moment. "Yeah, I guess so."

"Are you ready to try again?"

"Yeah," the boy replied.

"Very well, then. This time, keep your focus. Let nothing distract you from your intent, and you will feel the difference. When her spell contacts yours, do not flinch from it, but lean into it, pushing back with your magic. You can do this, young Jinnik. I have confidence in you."

Hap puffed up a little from the pep talk and took his position once more. Hozark stepped back again as Demelza sighted in on the boy.

"Are you ready?" she asked.

Hap nodded.

Demelza did not hesitate. To do so would be a disservice to the boy. He needed to learn, and fast, and going easy on him would not accomplish that end.

Her stun spell flew true, connecting with Hap's defensive spell, but this time it stalled for a long moment before overpowering it. Hap fell on his rear once again, but this time he quickly hopped back to his feet, dusting himself off with an excited look in his eye.

He was getting the hang of it.

"Try it again," he said, his confidence building.

Demelza smiled and nodded. The whining of recent weeks was not making an appearance today. This was a reassuring sign.

They practiced a little while longer, though the Drookonus was quite ready for their next jump. But Hozark didn't rush it as he instead watched the boy get better and better as his comfort with this novel type of casting grew.

"Enough for now," Hozark finally said, interrupting their practice. "It is time for our next jump. But know that you have progressed more in this short bit of practice than many do with weeks of training. You should feel proud of your accomplishments."

"Thanks, Hozark," Hap said. "And thank you, Demelza. That was really cool."

"I am glad you enjoyed the lesson," she replied as they walked back to the ship.

Safely aboard, Bud lifted them up into the air, then cleared the atmosphere for the comfort of space. And then, with their final destination locked in, he jumped.

## CHAPTER FORTY-TWO

It was a tense final jump taking them to Gravalis. What awaited them on the other end was unknown, but given the lengths that had Maktan and Ravik had gone to in order to force Visla Jinnik into their service it was almost certain to be a difficult endeavor.

And quite likely a deadly one.

The mood in the command chamber was somber and quiet. Joking was put on hold for this flight, and the normally chatty crew was focused intently on the displays the moment they exited the jump.

Whether or not they were flying into a trap would become clear very quickly.

Hozark and Demelza immediately separated from the mothership, engaging their shimmer cloaks and spinning away from the much larger craft. If there was an enemy lying in wait, they would be better able to handle them and even the odds if they were flying free.

For the approach to the planet, however, a visla of Jinnik's strength would see them coming if he focused his energies. Yes, he had hired this pair of Ghalian to retrieve his son, but there would be no way for him to know it was them approaching until it was too late.

In any case, the two Wampeh had a plan for whatever their circumstances wound up being. If Jinnik attacked them, they would peel away and come from multiple directions. If the Council was waiting for them in orbit, they would again split up and engage while Bud got the visla's son to the ground.

But if they were truly fortunate, and their arrival was a surprise, then they would dock with Bud's mothership and come in gently for an unremarkable landing before infiltrating the grounds.

"You see anything?" Bud asked his copilot as he scanned the dark skies. "It's awfully quiet out there."

"That's a good thing, Bud," Laskar replied.

"Yeah, but it makes me a bit nervous. Too easy always does."

"I hear you on that. But I think I'll take easy today, if that's an option."

"What's that over there?" Bud asked, looking intently.

"I don't see anything," Laskar said.

Bud squinted hard. "I guess you're right. Could we really have gotten this lucky?"

They had jumped relatively close to Gravalis, assuming the guise of a trader ship coming in just like any other vessel. That meant no sneaking in from afar. Not if they were to land at the site of a secret Council facility and not raise suspicion. They had to look just like any other ship coming in to land.

But that also meant their options for escape were very limited from the moment they exited their jump. Hozark and Demelza had slipped away unseen, at least for a moment, but the larger ship would be a sitting duck.

"Nothing," Laskar said, letting out the breath he didn't realize he'd been holding for the minutes after they exited the jump and closed in on the atmosphere. "I think we're in the clear."

Bud felt the rock-hard tension in his shoulders begin to lessen, just a little bit. "Okay, I'm going to line us up for entry."

"What about the others?" Henni asked, craning her neck to see what was going on.

"Don't worry about them," Bud replied.

"But how are they going to meet up with us if—"

"Do not concern yourself with our rendezvous, dear Henni," Hozark said as he walked into the command chamber.

Demelza joined him a moment later.

"How did you two—" Henni marveled.

"I've learned not to ask," Laskar said. "These two come and go like geists. Most of the time, I can't even tell that they've docked. At least, not in space."

"And now we make our descent as one," Hozark said. "But do not let this fortunate bit of grace lull you into a sense of complacency. This will still be a difficult task ahead of us yet. We are to break into a secret Council facility and rescue their prize prisoner. Hopefully, before they turn his power against us."

"My dad wouldn't do that," Hap interjected. "He's a good man. Everyone says so."

Hozark looked at the boy with kind eyes. "Young Jinnik, sometimes adults are put in situations that requires they do things contrary to their normal desires and beliefs. It does not change who they are inside, but it can lead to some difficult moments, regardless of their true intentions or desires."

"That's why you are coming with us," Demelza noted. "When your father sees you are safe, he will no longer be forced to do these terrible things for the vislas he believes are holding you."

Hap didn't say anything, but the slight crackling on his skin belied his agitation. Hozark would have to work with him on controlling his emotions, lest his magic get out of hand as he grew in strength. But, then, if everything went as he hoped, the boy's father would soon be the one teaching him these things.

Bud landed the ship at the site on the outskirts of town, setting down among the few other civilian craft present. There were some Council ships present as well, but nothing striking in either size or firepower.

It had been the same when they descended through the atmosphere. Nothing out of the ordinary. Just a small flotilla of Council craft, as would be expected above a secret base, but nothing overtly hostile.

For all intents and purposes, this was just another Council outpost on a perfectly normal world.

But Hozark knew better.

His prior encounter with the secret smelting operation had very nearly cost him his life, though through no fault of his own. An extremely clever trap had been set, and he had found himself caught in it.

This time, however, the master assassin was entering the danger zone forewarned, and, thus, forearmed.

"Follow me," he said, leading his crew into the Council-run town.

When he had last been there, it was under the disguise of Alasnib, a jovial trader. He had spent several weeks embedded with a Council work group, drinking, eating, and carousing with them after a good day's labor. He had inserted himself into the workforce, and had gained a level of access that comes with familiarity.

This time, however, he had arrived without the disguise, and in the company of a group of visitors, no less.

"The town seems kinda quiet," Henni noted. "Is it always like this?"

"Not always, no. But the work teams are still on shift," Hozark replied. "When they come back this evening it will be a livelier sight. But we shall not be here for that. We must take full advantage of the end of the day shift to approach the secret facility."

"So, what do we do until then?" Laskar asked. "Maybe get a drink or three?"

Henni flashed him a look, but it was Hozark who replied.

"We shall make our way to an observation point not far from the facility into which we must gain access," the Ghalian said. "We shall then await the lull and make our move for the ingress."

"A stealth approach and silent ingress?" Demelza asked.

"Indeed. We cannot afford to allow them to note our presence if we hope to avoid any possible hostilities by our young friend's father before he realizes his son is with us and safe."

"So, we go it hard and fast," Bud said. "Just like the good old pirate days."

"Ideally not," Hozark replied. "But we shall be prepared for whatever comes our way. And remember this important directive. There is to be absolutely no magic whatsoever used once we are inside the smelting operation. The risk of catastrophic melding of magic in that unstable environment is quite real, and quite serious."

"How serious are we talking?" Bud asked.

"Serious enough that none of us would stand a chance of ever telling Corann or anyone else what went wrong if we misstep," Hozark replied. "So, conventional weaponry only once inside. Are we all clear?"

All nodded their understanding. For Hozark to make such a pronouncement was unusual, and thus its impact was all the greater.

The group stopped into the local provisions shop and purchased a small assortment of foods, talking casually amongst themselves as they did. It was all part of the plan, of course. A diversion to allow them to go where they would without raising suspicion.

"I saw a really pretty field just outside of town when we flew in," Demelza said, her demeanor suddenly that of a girly-girl, rather than a deadly killer. "We should picnic over that way."

"That sounds delightful," Bud said. "You all good with that?"

The rest of the team agreed.

"Excellent. Then let's pick up the rest of our goodies and make our way out there. We've still got a fair amount of daylight, and the weather is quite pleasant." He turned to the shopkeeper. "Does it get terribly cold at night? We're going to be coming back after dark, most likely."

The man behind the counter was about to make a fairly good-sized sale, but if he could add to it, he most certainly would, and these newcomers seemed ill-informed as to the nature of the planet's mild weather.

"Well," he began, with a somewhat serious look in his eyes, "it can get a bit chilly once the sun sets. And if there's wind, you can get downright cold."

"That doesn't sound fun," Henni said.

"Maybe we should just skip the picnic entirely," Hozark said, knowing full well the man was lying.

"Oh, there's no need for that, friend. Just add a few of these blankets here to your order and I'm sure you'll be warm as can be."

"That seems a lot to carry, though."

"Oh, these are light and compact, and guaranteed to keep you warm and comfortable," the shopkeeper replied. "And I'll tell you what, since you nice folks are new to the area, I'll even knock twenty percent off the price."

"Wow, twenty percent?" Hozark asked, knowing full-well the man was gouging them on already overpriced merchandise. He just smiled wide, playing the part. "That would be great. We'll take 'em."

"Great. I'll package things right up for you," the shopkeeper said.

A few minutes later, the group was marching through town,

a picnic's worth of supplies in their possession and not an eye turned their way.

Hozark led them across the main thoroughfare to a lesser-used path he had come to rely upon when making surreptitious outings. It skirted the major routes but still brought him to the large Council facility outside of town, allowing him to surveil it from a safe distance.

"Follow me," he said quietly, then stepped off the beaten path and onto the one less traveled, his loyal team close behind.

## CHAPTER FORTY-THREE

"I don't see why we don't just take them out," Laskar said quietly from his position hiding in the bushes.

A group of men and women were working nearby, blocking their access to the far side of the Council facility. And it was only from around the corner of that far side that the entrance to the secret facility through the rear of the building could be accessed.

The armed guard was pacing at his usual assigned location, just as Hozark had remembered from his previous visit to this place. It seemed his original intrusion had still not been detected, and the security patterns had not shifted as a result.

"We do not kill innocents if it can be avoided," Hozark said quietly as he watched the people who had been his ersatz friends during his infiltration toil under their heavy workloads.

"And if we have to?" Laskar asked. "I mean, this is slowing us down, here. A full-frontal takedown would be the way to—"

"It would be the way to warn the entirety of the Council forces on this planet that their top-secret facility is being breached," Hozark said. "No, we shall do this quietly. *After* they depart the area."

Laskar looked like he was about to say something, but a

sharp glare from Bud silenced him like a hot slap from an irritated hand.

"But my dad's in there," Happizano said, doing his best to stay calm. "How much longer do we have to wait around?"

Despite his efforts, a faint crackling emitted from his skin for an instant.

"Control yourself, young Jinnik," Hozark gently urged the boy. "You can do this."

Hap did his best to calm his emotions, and he was actually able to get his power back under control. It seemed the stress of the situation, along with the proximity of his father's power via the Jinnik-powered konus he was wearing on his wrist, was ramping up Hap's nascent magic, and with it, the same unpredictable surges his father often suffered.

"Well done, Happizano," Demelza said from their hiding spot deep in the treeline. "Your control is improving."

They waited a while longer. The sun was getting lower, and dusk threatened to engulf them, but still a few of Hozark's former co-workers still lingered.

"I'm with the others on this. We've gotta move, Hozark. And I mean now," Bud said. "If a new shift comes on, we're screwed."

The evening crew was lesser-staffed, but he knew his friend's point was accurate.

"Very well. But I shall take care of them. Demelza," he said, turning to his fellow assassin, "remove the guard from the equation. There will be a small tripwire spell near the rear corner of the path he walks. That should be sufficient to draw his attention without alerting the rest of the guards. I shall handle the others."

She nodded silently and was gone in a flash.

"What are you gonna do to them, Hozark?" Laskar asked, a blade appearing in his hand. "You need help taking them out?"

"As I said, I shall handle them."

"But——"

"Leave them to me."

Laskar looked as if he was about to protest, but Hozark was already in motion. The assassin quickly skirted the area through the treeline, making his approach from the far end of the path, opposite where Demelza would be striking down the guard.

If he played it right, he could remove the few workers who were still lingering in the area from the equation without alerting anyone. And that would let his cohort make their move. But first he would have to approach the men and women out in the open. And to do that, he'd need to adopt the persona they all knew.

Alasnib the trader would be making an appearance, and the familiar face's unexpected return would put them all at ease. And that should give him ample opportunity to strike.

Hozark was, unfortunately, not wearing his usual trader's garb that went with this persona, and his vespus blade was strapped to his back. It was *not* Alasnib's style to carry any weapons, but as a trader, he could play it off as just another of his wares for sale.

Of course, it was a most rare and powerful weapon, but they wouldn't know that, and swords and knives were quite commonplace, especially with traders. So long as he did not unsheathe his, the glowing magical blade would go unnoticed.

But he intended to take care of them long before that could happen. Even so, he adopted the characteristic easygoing smile and casual stride of the jovial man they knew and liked.

"Alasnib? Is that you?" the nearest of the workers said.

"Good to see you again!" Hozark called out, a big smile plastered on his face.

He counted five of them. The others must have already started the trek back toward town, leaving these stragglers to finish up and meet them afterward.

"Hey, it's Alasnib," the man called to the others. "After you took off without even saying goodbye, we all figured the job finally got to you and you'd gone back to trading."

"And you'd be correct," Hozark said in his jovial character's chuckling voice. "I mean, it was a good time, have no doubt, but it's a different kind of labor than I've been used to."

"I guess trader life actually *isn't* so bad after all, then."

"You've got that right, my friend," Hozark replied, his grin still beaming wide.

The others came over to see their newly returned friend, patting him on the back and wishing him well. It had been a relatively short time he'd spent in their company, but they had all found him a most agreeable companion.

Of course, that was part of his Ghalian training. In addition to being assassins of the greatest skill, they were all also actors whose talents could put most professional thespians to shame.

Hozark stole a glance toward the rear corner of the building, where Demelza was headed. He didn't see the guard anywhere. Knowing the man had been making his rounds just a few minutes before, Hozark was confident she had already taken him out of the equation.

"What's with the sword?" one of his work friends asked.

"Ah, yeah, that," he replied with a shrug. "I picked it up last week. Pretty nice blade, actually. It's a little pricey, but I was thinking one of the guards might maybe want to buy it."

"You came all the way back here just to sell a sword?"

"And other stuff, of course. But you should see this thing. It's a beauty."

Hozark make a clumsy show of removing the sword from his back with all the lack of skill one might expect of a trader, and not a killer. The five workers gathered close to see this allegedly impressive blade. Hozark smiled.

That meant it would only take one stun spell to drop them all.

He cast quickly and quietly, the magic striking them down in a flash before any could even realize what was happening. Hozark then piled the unconscious workers on the lone floating conveyance they had been using and quickly relocated them to the woods.

They would wake in several hours, wondering what had happened. By that point, it would all be over, and Hozark and his friends would either be victorious, or dead.

The assassin quickly returned to his waiting teammates.

"We make our attempt now. Follow me."

He headed out, not waiting for a reply. The others fell in line behind him as he moved quickly for the rear of the large building where it butted up against the hillside.

"All of them dead?" Henni asked.

"Stunned," Hozark replied. "They shall recover in a few hours."

She seemed a bit surprised but let it go. Laskar, on the other hand, was not so quick to move on from that little twist.

"Mercy?" the copilot asked as they rushed to meet Demelza. "Doesn't seem like much of a Ghalian thing."

"They are innocents," Hozark replied. "And rather amusing company, at times."

"Still, they work for the Council," Laskar persisted.

"They do, but there is no advantage, nor honor, in taking their lives. They are merely men and women doing their jobs. Not all who work for the Council of Twenty are bad, Laskar. In fact, I have found the vast majority are simply living their lives. To them, employment is employment, and the Council is just another source of coin."

"But if they tell anyone we're here?"

"If we are still inside by the time they awaken, we have far greater problems than that."

The group arrived at the rear of the building. There was no sign of the guard, though a small patch of dirt had been shifted to cover what appeared to be a small spatter of blood.

Demelza un-shimmered, appearing before them out of nowhere.

"Shit, that's spooky how you do that," Laskar said.

"A tool of the Ghalian. Nothing more," she replied.

Hozark nodded slightly. She had done good, clean work here, though he expected no less from her. He moved to the doorway and began releasing the magical locks and wards sealing it.

To most, it would be a rather daunting task, but for a talented caster such as he, it was almost child's play, albeit time-consuming child's play. Unlike his prior entry into the building, this time Hozark had the advantage and pleasure of being able to take his time, for the most part, at least.

He didn't need much time, though, and he had the wards and locks disarmed in moments. But it did allow him just that extra moment to double-check his work as he went. He didn't expect anything to have changed from the last time he'd broken in, but it was always possible, and you didn't get to his age as an assassin by being careless.

"You need a hand?" Henni asked.

"No. But thank you for the offer," he replied as the door quietly slid open.

Henni and Hap both moved to step inside, ready to get this show on the road, but Hozark held them back.

"Not yet," he said, stopping the impulsive pair from making an ill-advised entry. "There is yet more to do."

"Like what? I don't see anything," Hap said.

"Watch and learn."

## CHAPTER FORTY-FOUR

The open doorway seemed innocuous enough. An entrance into an illuminated hallway leading to a doorway at the far end. An easy enough way in, now that they had bypassed the guard and magically warded entryway.

Or so most would think.

But the reality of the situation was far different. And it was something Hozark had already encountered once before.

"Stay outside of the threshold, and note the lights above," he instructed the others.

They gazed up at the magical illumination. It didn't seem all that interesting, if they were to be honest.

"Uh, Hozark? What's so special about the lights?" Henni asked, her eyes adjusting.

"Do you sense anything about them?"

"What do you mean?"

"Those lighting spells. Can you feel how they are tied to the wards inside the doorway?"

Henni strained a bit.

"Hey, wait a minute. I actually do feel something. That's weird."

"Why is it weird?" Bud asked.

"Because I never feel magic. Why now?"

"Because you have gifts," Hozark said. "And you have slowly been coming to use them, though in limited amounts."

"Huh," the violet-haired woman said. "But I don't get it. What does the lighting being tied to the warding mean?"

"Demelza, would you care to explain?" he asked his associate.

The pale assassin reached out with her power and felt the web of spells and wards in the hallway. It was all a little bit too easy, she thought. If they had gone to this much trouble to keep the entry protected, why would it be a cake walk once inside?

"It would appear to be designed to entice one to disarm the wards in order, the corresponding illumination spell above giving a visual reinforcement of that misdirection."

"Very good," Hozark said. "This hallway is indeed a trap. You would all do well to learn this lesson. Our adversaries are clever. Far more clever than one would expect from Council types."

"But they're so powerful," Henni said.

"Yes, but they rely on that power rather than subterfuge more often than not. To encounter a deception such as this shows a higher degree of non-conventional thinking than typically found in Council affairs. But we do not have the time to discuss this in depth at the moment. Stay close, and watch carefully."

Hozark then reached out and triggered the secret trigger that he had previously discovered near the threshold. The seemingly solid wall released and swung open to their left, revealing a wide entrance––the *true* entrance––to the hidden facility within the building.

Hap nearly jumped when the wall abruptly became not-a-wall, his magic crackling on his skin again as he unintentionally drew from the konus on his wrist.

"Happizano," Demelza said quietly.

The boy realized what he'd done and forced the magic down once more. Like a pubescent boy's erections, it was looking more and more as if he had little control over when and how they would make an appearance. And that could be dangerous.

"The lighting is dim, but sound carries in this place. Walk quietly, and with great care," Hozark said, drawing a pair of wicked-looking blades, then disappeared through the threshold.

The others followed close behind, with Demelza taking up the rear, guarding against any sneak attacks as they made their move for Hap's father.

Deeper into the facility they moved, the group staying quite silent despite their lack of practice, compared to the assassins. The acrid smell of hot metal smoke was lingering in the air, and the overall heat of the place told the story of a great deal of labor taking place.

But something was amiss. For all of the signs of fabrication, there was one thing conspicuous in its absence.

"It's too quiet in here," Bud whispered.

Hozark knew he was right. He'd known it as soon as they had stepped inside. The telltale sounds of the labors of the Council's smelting minions was notably absent.

No ringing out of metal on metal. No muttered spells cast to stoke the magical fires providing the molten ore into which the visla's magic would be directed, charging the devices into deadly weapons rather than inert metal bands.

Hozark put up his hand, gesturing for the others to stay back. He slowly rounded the corner to the smelting area, his magical vespus blade firmly sheathed, but carrying a deadly blade in each hand, ready to dispatch any who might cross his path. But, as he feared, none rose to greet him.

In fact, the handful of men and women present were all either Ootaki or Drook, and they were clearly long dead.

"It is safe to come out," Hozark called to his friends. "Henni, Happizano. Be warned, there are bodies present."

The group rounded the corner and took in the sight.

The crucible was still hot from the molten metal it had contained a short while ago, and the floor showed scuff marks that abruptly disappeared, marking where crates of konuses and slaaps had been dragged before being loaded onto floating conveyances.

The remainder of the tools and molds had been cleared out of the facility. In fact, everything of value had been stripped, and in quite a rush, it seemed. The bodies of the drained magic users, however, held no further value.

They might have been sold off for Zomoki food, but they were clearly not worth the effort in this instance.

"They cleared out of here in a hurry," Bud said, looking at the signs of a hasty departure all around them.

"Yes. And Visla Jinnik with them, I am afraid," Hozark replied. "I can sense his magic clearly now. He was in this place, and not long ago at all." He bent down to Hap's level. "I am sorry, young Jinnik, but your father is not here."

Happizano, to his credit, held his emotions together admirably for a boy his age. He'd had the carrot of reuniting with his father dangled in front of him and then snatched away several times in recent weeks, but he was almost becoming accustomed to the disappointment.

"Hey, what's this?" Henni asked, picking up a partially melted knife laying on the floor.

Hozark took it from her hand and carefully examined the ruined metal.

"This is most unusual," he said. "They were attempting to craft an enchanted blade, forcing Jinnik's magic into a weapon never designed for such a purpose." He paused, straining his senses even more. "It is a bastardization of the vespus spell. But not for Wampeh. And not cast by a master of the arts."

"Can you even do that?" Bud asked. "I thought a very specific kind of bladesmith had to craft one from scratch with very specific spells for it to work."

"And you would be correct," Hozark replied. "But it seems our friend Visla Maktan is branching out into other forms of weaponry. Or, at least, he would like to be. This is most disconcerting, indeed."

"Yet, it is a clue that may help us discern more about our enemy than they realize," Demelza said. "And of the items left behind, it would seem far more remains that is of use to us than they would have anticipated."

"What do you mean?" Laskar asked.

"The items utilized for weapons manufacturing are gone, yes, but the origin of many of those items, as well as other tools they had been putting to use, may possibly be discerned from their hasty and somewhat careless egress."

"How so?"

"Most power users are unfamiliar with the daily work of their minions, but lesser beings would know about this," she said. "You see, a great many items possess small markings of origin. And, if we can piece together enough of them, we may very well determine where Visla Maktan and Visla Ravik have been sourcing them from. And with that information, we might backtrack and learn the location of Visla Jinnik's current confines."

"You can find my dad with this junk?" Hap asked, allowing himself a tiny bit of hope.

"There are no guarantees, young Jinnik. But we shall do our best," Hozark said.

"We should fan out and see what's here, then," Laskar said, striding over to where the largest pile of abandoned gear lay. "There's bound to be some good stuff lying around."

"Wait!" Hozark called out as the copilot began tossing aside the bits that seemed to have the least importance.

"What? I'm just doing what you—"

A rumbling filled the room.

"Everyone out!" Hozark bellowed.

The tone of his voice made it abundantly clear that there was no time to lose. Wampeh Ghalian did not spook easily. In fact, they did not spook at all. And for him to react so strongly meant only one thing. They were in deep, deep shit.

"What the hell is that?" Laskar asked as they sprinted through the building toward the secret door.

"It was a fucking booby trap, you idiot!" Bud shouted back.

"How was I supposed to know?"

To that, Bud didn't have a good reply. And even if he did, he was using every bit of his breath as he ran full bore while the rumbling around them grew in intensity.

The walls ahead of them seemed about to collapse, while the area behind them filled with a deadly, swarming black magic. It was the final trap left for any who might find this place, and it was looking as if it might kill them all.

Hozark and Demelza both cast as quickly as they could, supporting the crumbling walls with force spells. They wouldn't last long, but long enough for them to make their egress. That is, if the rapidly approaching death magic didn't catch them first.

The two Ghalian were entirely focused on keeping them all from being crushed. To split focus might cost them all. But it was looking like there was no choice, when Laskar desperately blurted out a blocking spell.

It was nothing terribly special. Just something Hozark and Demelza had been teaching Happizano, and that the boy had been practicing recently. But shouted from Laskar's lips in this time of panic, his middling power somehow rose to the occasion, and the spell actually pushed back on the rolling tide of death.

"Outside!" Hozark yelled, ushering them all to the relative safety out of the building.

Like bees swarming from an angry nest, they all burst forth, running for the trees as fast as they were able. Behind them, the deadly magic spewed out of the door, then dissipated as it contacted the last rays of the planet's setting sun.

Apparently, a safety mechanism had been left in place to ensure the damage would be limited in nature. And from outside the building, there appeared to be no trace or sign that anything unusual was going on inside at all. But it was quite likely an alarm had been sounded, and that meant it was time to leave. Immediately.

"Back to the ship at once," Hozark commanded once he had ensured all of his people had made it out intact.

"What the hell was that?" Bud asked as he picked himself up from the ground.

"Laskar appears to have tripped a booby trap left by the facility's former occupants."

"Nice going, dumbass," Henni griped.

"It is not his fault, and we do not have time to play the blame game," Hozark said. "There is a very real likelihood that the Council ships above will have been alerted, and we do not wish to be anywhere near here when they arrive."

"Oh, shit," she said.

"Yes. Oh, shit is a valid assessment. Now move!"

Hozark did not wait for any further discussion, instead taking off at a quick pace through the trees down a small game path he'd sussed out on his last stint on the Council-run world.

It would take them close to their ship, after which they would have to step out into public view and act as though nothing had happened as they made their way to their craft.

That would be the hardest part. The casual strolling when every cell in their bodies screamed at them to run. But running would draw attention, and they could not afford that. Not now.

"Act normal. Act relaxed and happy," Hozark instructed them all as they reached the treeline and prepared to re-enter the populated area.

It was difficult, keeping in character as they walked, but they managed to make it to their ship in relatively good time, and Bud took off and got them out of the atmosphere and away from the planet without trouble.

"How the hell could they have known we were coming?" he asked once they were safely clear. "Someone had to have tipped them off."

"Yeah, but who?" Laskar asked. "Who'd have known we even found out about Visla Jinnik charging those konuses?"

Henni furrowed her brow a moment. "It must've happened on the battlefield. Even if we weren't in the thick of the fighting, if they saw us gathering up konuses, they could have put two and two together."

"Unlikely," Hozark said, "but still possible. And given what has occurred, there does not appear to be a better explanation. At least not yet."

"I would tend to agree," Demelza said. "But this leaves us one question that remains the same regardless."

"Which is?" Bud asked.

"Where is Happizano's father now? Where is Visla Jinnik?"

## CHAPTER FORTY-FIVE

The thick chains were more than adequate to restrain any normal man. Any above average man, for that matter. But Visla Jinnik was even more than that. He was a power user of rare strength, and anything less would likely not have been able to hold him. Not for long, anyway.

But these chains were enchanted, having been fed a steady stream of magic over a lengthy period of time, the spells within refined and reinforced into a formidable tool of bondage.

On top of that, the visla was wearing a hefty control collar, the gleaming golden band imbued with an utterly massive amount of magic to keep the man under its sway.

When he had first started working for the mysterious Council goons who had stormed his home and taken his boy, Jinnik had been at full strength, and despite the efforts of those directing his powers as he lay waste to rebellions and innocents alike, he could have broken free had he really tried.

But they had his son, and putting the boy at risk was simply not an option.

Now, however, the outings to quell uprisings and subjugate worlds had come to an abrupt end, and the visla found himself locked down tight in a dungeon-like smelting facility on some backwater world in a distant system.

He had been captive in a relatively spacious, albeit dark and smoky facility for a few weeks, helping the Tslavar overseer with his task, filling konuses and slaaps with their initial magical charge. But as time went on, he grew resistant to the task absent proof his son was safe. Visla Jinnik began to refuse to work.

And that was when the forcible draining commenced.

Had he not already weakened himself in the preceding weeks, there would have been a very real possibility of his pushback leading to an actual escape. But he was depleted just enough to be unable to break free.

And, worse yet, the draining devices put in place by Visla Maktan were most powerful indeed. Wielded in the right hands, the weapons makers would most certainly be able to forcefully draw his magic from him. All they required was time.

Now, forced to abruptly flee their former operation, they were holed up in a new location. A far cleaner one, actually, but that was mostly because the smelting had not yet tainted the air and very walls of the place with their acrid stink. In any case, they had put up the visla in a far nicer cell than he'd previously inhabited.

Not that it made much of a difference, though. A prison was a prison, regardless of the gilding of the bars. They had been forced to stun the visla in order to move him. But once he came to, shaking off the stun spell a bit too easily for their comfort, it was clear that he was undamaged from the process.

Jinnik's power was great, but once they overcame his initial resistance, it was simply a matter of overpowering him with Maktan's magical leverage. Of course, they had to be careful in the process.

It was far less efficient taking power from the man rather than having him give it freely. He was somewhat like an Ootaki in that regard, though his power resided in his body, not merely his hair, and his would replenish in short order.

An Ootaki, on the other hand, could take years to have their golden, magic-storing locks filled with power. And the metalsmiths who ran this place had knowledge of that firsthand, having shorn, and also killed, quite a few Ootaki in their quest for more power for their weapons.

But they had broken through Visla Jinnik's resistance and were now pulling power from him, straining to claim their prize like weary fishermen finally hauling their exhausted prize from the sea.

But they had to be careful. This method of imbuing power into the hot metal of newly smelted konuses was a tricky bit of business, and it was far more dangerous to the man's life than when he gave it of his own free will. In fact, despite the impressive amount of raw power he possessed, it was entirely possible they might even kill him in the process if they were not careful.

And *that* would anger their employer to a degree none had any desire to witness, for if they did observe his reaction in such an instance, it might very well be the last thing they saw.

So, they did what they could, working slowly, powering up the konuses and slaaps whenever the visla had recovered enough energy to be of use to them.

"It doesn't have to be like this," the Tslavar overseer said as he unchained and hauled the exhausted Visla Jinnik from his cell. "Just cooperate, and it can all be so much easier for you. For all of us."

Jinnik looked at the man with bloodshot eyes. Eyes full of wrath, even if he lacked the power to enact it. He was weakened, no doubt, but while his natural defenses might have been broken, his spirit most definitely remained intact.

"My son," he said, not needing to say any more.

He'd made the demand, and had given his captors more

than ample time to prove his boy's safety. But when they had failed to even do so on a most basic of levels, he had come to face the horrible realization that Happizano might very well be dead. There was really no other reason for them to keep him secreted away like this otherwise.

"You know what the visla said. If you cooperate and do as you're told, he'll let you see your boy once you've finished powering the konuses for him."

Jinnik let out a grim laugh even as he was pushed down into the sturdy metal seat beside the magical weapons' cooling table.

"This Maktan you work for. If he is truly keeping my son safe, then have him speak to me in person. Or is he a coward?"

"You'd be wise not to call him that," the Tslavar said as he affixed the chains in place.

Visla Jinnik was now firmly fastened to the magically imbued chair. The freshly minted devices would be carefully placed before him, orange-hot and ready to accept his magic. A simple focusing of will and a man of his skill could divert power to them with ease.

Only, now he would have that power forcibly taken from him, courtesy of the spells powering the chair he was fastened to. The chair itself was a massively powerful device, having a steady stream of lesser casters recharging its spells one after another while their victim recovered from his last session.

Most of the men and women doing so were emmiks, though, occasionally, a visla would join the mix, contributing to the magic forcing the captive to do their bidding.

The original spell had been put in place by their leader, named Maktan, Jinnik had learned, and it was impressively powerful magic. The man was obviously a visla, and a very powerful one at that. Not powerful enough to have overpowered Jinnik at his best, but a formidable foe nonetheless.

But at this point, Jinnik could hardly have bested an emmik, let alone a skilled visla.

"Begin," the Tslavar commanded.

For the next several hours, konuses and slaaps were carefully forged from the molten metal, the devices cast then placed in front of the captive visla while the next batch of metal melted in the orange-hot crucible.

His power was pulled from his body in a most painful manner. Yes, it could have been designed to spare him at least some of the discomfort, but he had angered the Visla Maktan with his reticence and was now paying the price for it.

Finally, after what seemed like an eternity, the Tslavar overseer held up his hand.

"Enough. He's done for now. Bring in the casters to power up the chair," he said as he unfastened the chains holding the nearly unconscious man in place. "You two, help me get him back to his cell."

Two of the green-and-black-skinned weapon makers helped heft the visla up, then dragged him back to his cell, where he was unceremoniously dumped on his small cot. His chains were fastened once more, and the men exited the chamber.

"Rest. We shall continue again shortly," the Tslavar said to the exhausted man, then sealed the door behind him.

# CHAPTER FORTY-SIX

Uzabud felt odd flying his friends at such a leisurely pace, but after what had happened, they simply had no reason to rush *anywhere*. Their last lead, their *best* lead had turned out to be worse than a bust.

Visla Jinnik had actually been in the facility that had so nearly taken their lives. At long last, they had the opportunity to reunite Hap with his father. Unfortunately, they had missed him.

With that disappointing failure, they were left with little to do but wait. Seek out whatever information they could find as they did so, but wait, all the same. And waiting was a bitch.

"Ormitzal? Are you sure?" Laskar asked when Hozark gave him the final destination to plot their next series of jumps. "That's a black sun system if I'm not mistaken."

"You are not."

"Sooo, that's not really a pleasant kind of environment to hang back and chill, is all I'm saying."

Hozark nodded slowly. "I understand your concern, but it is a safe planet."

"As safe as any in that kind of system, you mean."

"No. Safe, as in frequented by Ghalian on a regular basis. The planet seems quite normal, and it is to all who visit. But should the need arise, our network may be tapped into readily, and a great amount of resources brought to bear in short order."

"Really?"

"Really. But we are not going there for that reason. We are merely selecting a safe location where unpleasant surprises are unlikely to pay us a visit," Hozark replied. "Given the number of unexpected problems that have sprung up in our path, I felt it was a much-needed bit of respite while we replenish our supplies and spirits before resuming our quest."

"So, we're still looking for my father?" Hap asked, a hint of hope in his otherwise dejected eyes.

"Yes, young Jinnik. We shall never give up on your father. What occurred back on Gravalis was an unfortunate setback, but we were close. And we know your father is embedded with Visla Ravik and Visla Maktan's forces. It is only a matter of time before we ascertain his location."

The boy had all but given up on ever seeing his father at this point, but the assassin's words put his mind ever so slightly at ease nonetheless.

"Thanks, Hozark."

"Of course. Now, we still have a bit of a flight, so I suggest using this time to rest and unwind."

"I thought that was what we were going to Ormitzal for," Bud said.

Hozark nodded. "And it is. But I have found some people can react oddly to darker systems, and Ormitzal's black sun does emit a low level of a rather unusual energy. We Wampeh actually find it quite pleasant, but there is no telling how you each might react. And, thus, going in with your bodies well-rested would be the wisest course of action."

"Just in case?" Bud asked.

"Just in case."

"All right. I guess everyone should get some sleep in while the Drookonus cools down for the next few jumps. I'll keep an eye on things."

"I've got it," Laskar said. "You go catch some rest."

"I appreciate it, but it's my job. Go relax for a bit. You've already dialed in the next jumps. I can handle it from here."

Reluctantly, Laskar joined the others in heading off for their rooms. Soon, only Hozark and Uzabud remained.

"Quite a wild ride, eh?" Bud chuckled.

"A wild ride, indeed."

Ormitzal's system was precisely as Bud had imagined it. Down to the odd feeling the pulsing black sun gave off as it spewed its strange magic throughout the space around it.

The others seemed to notice it too, and Hap and Laskar were equally uneasy with it. Henni, on the other hand, seemed to feel energized when they entered the system. Her mood improved greatly, and her eyes even seemed to sparkle more than usual.

Someone, it seemed, reacted *very* well to this unusual power.

"We should be setting down in five. You all ready?" Bud asked the others.

"As ready as we're going to be," Laskar said.

Demelza looked at their approach. "I believe that landing area over there, beside the arena, would be the best place."

"You're the boss. But it's gonna cost ya."

"Cost me?" the Wampeh asked.

"Yeah. My price for dragging us all to this dark and depressing place is a sizable dinner and endless drinks. You think the Wampeh Ghalian might be able to foot the bill?"

Demelza looked at Hozark, and the two shared a chuckle. "Not a problem, friend," she replied.

Laskar sighed. "You've seen him drink, right?"

"Yes, just as I have seen those two eat," Demelza said,

nodding toward Henni and Hap. "In any case, we are well-funded for this outing, so it shall not be an issue."

Bud grinned wide. "Now *that's* music to my ears."

The magical lighting cast across the permanently dark city lent an almost eerie shade to everyone and everything. While the casters here were plentiful and skilled, magical illumination, however good it might be, could not compare to a sun's natural light.

Most on this world were of paler complexions. It was an effect particular to this type of system. The many races represented amongst the native populations would see their pigments lessen from birth in the low-light environment. But there were plenty of off-world visitors to the system as well, all of them readily apparent by their darker tones, not yet faded by the lack of light.

Hozark and Demelza, however, blended right in, as pale-skinned Wampeh were sure to do in such a place. It was no wonder the Ghalian had selected it as a safe world. They could preserve their energy and not focus on disguises here, while their naturally light skin would be better camouflage than any spell.

"Come, I know a particularly good tavern just up ahead," Hozark said, leading the way through the milling throngs of men, women, and those whose morphology made it utterly impossible to tell which they were.

Of course, some were both genders, and still others were more than the most common two. But with arms, legs, tentacles, and whatnot, it was best to be polite and not question. Just let everyone be who they were and go about your own business.

And in this case, the business was eating. And in the dining hall to which Hozark was taking his friends, business would be good.

## CHAPTER FORTY-SEVEN

"Now *this* is what I'm talking about," Bud said as he reclined in his comfortable seat, his belly already happily full, and a seemingly bottomless drink in his hand. "Oh, yeah. I heartily approve."

"I am glad it is to your liking," Hozark said, noting the similarly satisfied demeanors of the rest of his companions.

They had been fed well. Extremely well, in fact. The establishment was one of the go-to places Ghalian assassins often frequented when they visited Ormitzal, and the proprietors knew how to take care of their deadly, good-tipping guests.

But this? *This* was Hozark. One of the Five. To have him in their tavern, undisguised, no less, was a boon. Word would get out––quietly, of course––and when it did, people would flock to their doors to eat where so illustrious a Ghalian had dined.

But they were quite aware that privacy was of the utmost importance to the wary assassins, and it would be some time before they confirmed any such rumors. To do otherwise might do more harm to their establishment than good.

The table at which they had placed their special guest and

his friends was located at the back of the tavern, adjacent an easily accessed door in case the need for rapid egress arose. It also provided a clear view of the entire dining hall with a solid wall at their back.

In addition to those simple, yet effective safety precautions, there were layer upon layer of muting spells cast upon the private table, making the conversation of those seated there entirely unheard by any, no matter how close they might be lurking.

But, in this case, no one was remotely foolish enough to even think of having ideas of attempting to eavesdrop on the master assassin and his friends, let alone making any sort of move on them.

"So, are you all feeling well fed? Adequately decompressed from our incident on Gravalis?" Hozark asked.

The others nodded and voiced their approval of the current setting compared to their recent flight for their lives.

"Beats having a building trying to fall on our heads, that's for sure," Henni said. "And the food's pretty damn good too!"

While Bud might have been relatively full, the young woman with the sparkling eyes seemed to have actually grown her appetite since their arrival, if that was even possible.

Hozark and Demelza both wondered if it might have something to do with her own mysterious power suddenly getting a kick-start from the sun's unusual rays. But there was simply no way to tell for sure. Henni was an enigma, and quite possibly a powerful one. Or so they presumed.

"I could go for a refill," Laskar said, holding up his cup, only to find it being topped off a few moments later by a particularly attentive staff member. "Wow, these guys do *not* mess around."

"One of the many reasons the Ghalian continue to frequent this establishment," Hozark said. "Now, if we are all feeling our equilibriums evened out, let us discuss what happened on Gravalis. What we saw."

"We were all there, Hozark. We all saw the same thing," Hap said.

"Ah, but there is where you are mistaken, young Jinnik. There are always multiple interpretations to any event, and even eyes observing them at the same time, and in the same place, will have different takeaways."

"He is correct," Demelza said. "For example, what can you tell me of the entryway traps?"

"I don't know. Maybe that they were set up to catch you when you stepped inside?"

"A correct observation, but I saw it differently. What was apparent to me, at first glance, was that the floor was too clean for the foot traffic a facility like that would normally have."

"Very true, sister," Hozark said with a pleased grin. "And I noted the slight discoloration to the side, near the secret doorway. A doorway that had to be large enough to accommodate the oversize crates and materials that would be passing into and out of the building."

"So, you see, Hap, we each perceive different elements of the same thing. Does that make sense?" Demelza asked.

The boy nodded his understanding. It was this sort of real-world lesson that really stuck with him. Far more than any of the book learning his tutors tried to drive into his head. But his tutors were dead, killed when he was kidnapped. And that memory brought his mind back to his still-missing father.

"He was there, though, wasn't he? My father?"

"Yes, he was. His power was still lingering in the facility," Hozark replied.

Hap's face grew dark. "We shouldn't have stopped for me to practice casting. We wouldn't have been late otherwise. We would have gotten there in time to find my father. This is my fault."

"I understand where this emotion is coming from, Happizano, but rest assured, though we just missed Visla Jinnik, something very important was clear the moment we set foot inside."

"Yeah, that he wasn't there."

"No. That the entire location had been cleared out of all valuable materials," Hozark said. "Even if Uzabud had run the Drookonus until it was white-hot, even if we had burned it out racing to get to Gravalis, the simple fact is the timeline was not in our favor. The facility was emptied before we could have ever reached it, no matter how fast we flew. Our little stopover played no part in missing them before they left. It was simply not meant to be, young Jinnik. Not this time."

Hap, to his credit, took the assessment somewhat in stride, at least compared to his prior tantrums and sulking. He was saddened about his father, no doubt, but he was becoming stronger in the course of his tribulations.

He was still a boy, but the ordeal was making him a man, though a good deal before his time. But he was not the first such victim of circumstance forced to grow up too fast, nor would he be the last.

"You know they were experimenting on power users, right?" Bud said. "I mean, you guys saw the bodies."

"Clearly," Hozark replied. "Ootaki and even Drooks."

"Seems like a senseless waste, killing them like that. Ootaki can regrow their hair, and Drooks? Those guys are constantly replenishing their power."

"Yes, but when attempting to charge new weaponry, a large initial amount of power is required."

"But Drooks can't power konuses," Bud said. "Their power is only good for one thing. Flying ships. Everyone knows that."

"But what if someone actually *had* managed to find a way? Someone in quite a rush to amass a sizable quantity of weaponry in as short a period as possible? *Then* they would be a force to reckon with, indeed."

"I understand what you're saying, Hozark. But it was Jinnik's magic that was being used the other day, not some weird Drook bastardization."

"Yes, Bud, I know. But that does not mean our dear Visla Maktan is not making the attempt."

"Makes you wonder what the hell the guy is up to."

"It truly does. More concerning, however, is that when I was last on Gravalis, there was another body present. A deceased Wampeh."

"They killed a Ghalian?"

"No, it was not a member of the order. But their slaughter gives me pause nonetheless."

He looked at Demelza, and it was clear the same thought had flashed through her head. What if someone was trying to harness their unique power? The power only a tiny fraction of their kind possessed? It could be catastrophic, to say the least, if a visla, or anyone for that matter, could steal the power of another.

Fortunately, that was a nearly impossible feat. In fact, it had never occurred. But impossible and *nearly* impossible were not the same thing, and they had both learned long ago not to discount the possibility of any such instances, no matter how far-fetched.

"Ya know, there was another interesting bit of magic in play," Henni said. "Laskar here actually managed to keep us all from getting crushed by that wave of trap magic."

"Yeah, nice job, that," Bud agreed. "But, your magic has always been pretty damn weak, no offense."

"None taken," his copilot replied with a wry grin.

"So, how exactly did you manage that?"

"I really don't know," Laskar replied. "It was all happening so fast, and I just threw whatever spell came to mind. Somehow, it seemed to work."

"Panic casting," Hozark said. "He did the same during the riot with a stun spell."

"What?"

"Panic casting. Sometimes, albeit rarely, a desperation surge can be drawn upon that is much more substantial than the magic a user is normally able to control. In your case, that was an impressive amount of power, indeed."

Laskar blushed slightly. "Really, it was nothing."

"It was. You saved us, even if you did not do so intentionally," Hozark said.

Despite his rather obnoxious ways and endless cockiness, the assassin was beginning to wonder if, perhaps, Laskar might have some potential yet.

This was just one instance of significant power use, but if he could learn to tap into it on a regular basis, he could become quite an asset to their team. But for now, he was content to have the man on their team, whatever his gifts might prove to be.

# CHAPTER FORTY-EIGHT

Dinner had been followed up with a leisurely dessert, which for Bud and Laskar had consisted of more than a few drinks at a little dive bar near the lodgings Hozark had procured for them. Fortunately, the former pirate and his right-hand man, while happily buzzed, refrained from any excessively drunken shenanigans for a change.

Happizano had been thoroughly wiped out, both physically and emotionally, and turned in almost immediately. He'd held up quite well through the whole ordeal, but a solid night's sleep was going to do him wonders, and, hopefully, help reset his stress levels.

Henni, however, was a bundle of energy, and after joining Bud and Laskar for a few drinks, she headed off into the night to see what interesting things she might find in this fascinating place.

She had never been to a system like this, and the unusual nature of the world, combined with the constant high she'd been on since the sun it orbited began feeding her its strange power, was like an open book of wonders, and she was an eager reader.

By morning, however, she had returned to her room for at least a little bit of sleep. When she roused, she was once again full of pep and ready to go.

"Ooh, some more of those biscuits," the violet-haired girl said, snatching another still-hot pastry from the plate on their table.

She promptly split it in half and smeared Dizmus jam on it, then proceeded to stuff her face.

"Good Lord, woman. Do you *ever* stop eating?" Bud joked.

"Not when there's food like this around," she shot back.

The others were also in particularly good spirits. Spirits that were abruptly dimmed with the arrival of a pale young messenger. Her name was Dohria, and she was part of the order, but not like the others.

The Wampeh had trained with them but had not graduated to the level of a full-fledged Ghalian assassin.

But as a particularly skilled trainee––though one who did not excel at the killing arts––she was put to work in a different role within the family. Rather than acting as a killer, she was an elite messenger of the highest order. With a memory of astounding accuracy, and the infiltration and stealth skills of the Ghalian, she could bring detailed messages to just about anyone, just about anywhere.

Time, secrecy, and lack of extraordinary need, however, kept her from being put into constant use. But something of particular importance had arisen, and the young Ghalian had heeded the call.

"Master Hozark," she said, rather than asked.

Of course he knew the elusive messenger. All of the Five did.

"Dohria," he said with a respectful nod.

"News from Corann and Prombatz," she said, double-checking that the muting spells were in place around them while adding another of her own.

Hozark noted her attention to detail with approval. "Urgent,

I see," he said. "And what have we learned that warrants your visit?"

"Not just a visit, but my validation of the event in person as well."

"Oh?"

"There has been a slaughter on a somewhat desolate world. Bitzam is its name."

"Never heard of it," Laskar said.

"Nor would you have. It is sparsely populated, though habitable. In the Maskus system."

"Not much out there," the copilot noted. "How was there a slaughter?"

Hozark nodded once. "Yes, Dohria. Please, enlighten us as to the nature of this incident."

"There was a brutal killing on that world," she began. "Council craft, under Visla Ravik's command. But mercenaries, believed to work for Visla Maktan, were present as well."

"Unpleasant business, no doubt, but unlikely the only reason you have come," Hozark noted.

"Indeed. There was more. A contingent of pirates engaged those forces. A terrible battle ensued, adding new carnage to the already bloody event."

"Pirates?" Bud asked. "We need to go there."

"Agreed," Hozark replied.

Dohria looked at him with a puzzled glance. "There is no need. The battle is over, and only the dead remain."

"And dead men tell no tales," Laskar added, grimly.

Hozark pushed back from the table and rose to his feet. "We shall go immediately, nonetheless," he said, turning to Laskar. "And you might be surprised to know, the dead often *can* and *do* tell tales. To the right eyes, that is."

It was a relatively short series of jumps to Bitzam, and the blood had yet to fully coagulate by the time Hozark and his friends set foot on the site of the bloody scene. Happizano remained aboard the ship. There was simply no need for the boy to bear witness to such carnage.

Dohria had described things with perfect recall, as was her talent. It was, indeed, a wasteland of the dead, with no sign of any survivors. And, just as she had informed them, there was still trace magic lingering in the air. That of Visla Ravik, they now knew, having dealt with him and his goons on more than one occasion.

And there were also remnants of that strange, masked magic that had to be Visla Maktan's. It was powerful, yet oddly subdued, much as the traces of another visla's power.

That of Visla Jinnik.

"They have utilized weapons powered by Happizano's father," Demelza quietly said to Hozark.

"Yes, I can sense it," he replied. "And that same fading of the energy is present with Maktan's power. The man sent his lackeys to do his dirty work, using konuses he filled with power. But he himself kept his hands clean of whatever dirty work went on here."

"It is the only way he can maintain his semblance of normalcy," Demelza said. "Corann said the spy network still had found no overt sign of him skirting the Council to carry out his dark plans."

"And if he had charged weapons prior to setting things in motion, he could very well pretend to have nothing to do with this while actually directing things from afar," Hozark mused. "A most clever adversary, I admit."

The others were picking through the corpses, trying to piece together what had happened. There were no Council forces left. Only their spilled blood remained, their injured and killed taken from this place when the fighting had ceased.

Or so it seemed.

"This can't be right," Bud said as he turned over the body of a dead pirate.

"It's what the messenger said. Pirates were part of this too," Laskar replied.

"No, that's not what I mean. This isn't normal ground assault gear," Bud said. "Look at his kit."

Laskar leaned in and examined the man more closely. His body was a wreck, but his friend was clearly right. This was space-fighting equipment.

"What does it mean?" he asked.

Bud looked up at the sky a long moment, straining his senses. But there was nothing.

"It means, this fight took place in the air," he finally said. "Whatever happened here on the ground, it was civilians versus Maktan's goons. But it looks like they were interrupted."

"By pirates," Henni said. "*Flying* pirates."

"Exactly. Probably trying to steal whatever it was the Council goons had taken from these people."

"But this is a remote world of no value. What could they possibly have possessed that would be of that much interest?" she asked.

"Let us find out," Hozark interjected. "I sense something else. Something that way, over the horizon line."

"You can sense that far?" Laskar asked, clearly impressed.

"Ordinarily, no. But there was simply so much of this magic in play, the remnants actually remain tangible, though fading."

"So, it was an overuse of power that left a trail?" the copilot asked. "That seems like a pretty serious oversight by these guys, if you ask me."

"And it was. Another few hours and the traces, regardless of their strength, would likely be gone, even to one as practiced as I am."

"Then what are we waiting for?" Henni asked, turning back to their ship. "Let's go see what's over there!"

"For once, I agree with the bottomless stomach," Bud said.

"Bite me, creeper. I'm just hungry a lot, is all."

"Oh, I know. We *all* know," he shot back with a grin. "Our poor galley will never be the same."

"Hey, I'm pulling my weight around here."

"Never said you weren't. But if you keep eating like that, you'll need to increase that number by a fair amount," Bud replied.

Hozark sighed, shook his head, and began walking. "Come, you two. You may bicker to your hearts' content once we are aboard the ship."

"Yeah, what he said," Henni added.

"Guys, it's *my* ship. Are we forgetting that?" Bud asked.

"Of course not, *Captain*," Hozark said. "So, Captain Uzabud, what are your wishes, then?"

"Uh, let's load up and go see where this trail leads us," he replied.

"Excellent. I look forward to seeing what awaits us," the assassin said with a curious look in his eye.

They'd be airborne in minutes, and would have their answer soon enough.

# CHAPTER FORTY-NINE

It was a relatively short flight, but it was easy to see how Dohria had missed the signs of the additional combatants in all the chaos of the killing grounds. It was pure carnage, but on top of that, she, and most others, for that matter, lacked the sensitivity of the Ghalian masters.

Some power users would be able to pick up traces of magic used, of course, but aside from those vislas and handful of emmiks, only the most skilled of Ghalian had the training and practice to sniff out their prey in this manner.

Thin tendrils of smoke could be seen wafting up from the other side of a small hill, but they were faint and dissipated in the air as soon as they reached the crosswind atop the rise.

"We're almost there," Bud noted as he slowed his approach and swerved wide just above the treetops.

He made sure to stay low as he circled the terrain, an old pirating trick utilized to afford them the angle of approach while maintaining the best cover. Had their objective been airborne, however, the tactics would have been far different.

"What do you think that is?" Henni asked. "Cooking fires? Smelting operations?"

"Something far worse, I'm afraid," Bud replied as they crested the hill. "Look."

The source of the smoke was clear now. Sources, plural, to be precise. Smoldering plumes from the wreckage of a pair of crashed ships wafted into the air. One of them was a rather sizable Council ship, lying smashed and ruined on the rocky terrain.

Nearby, the remains of the smaller pirate ship that had gone down with it were scattered about, the craft having broken into multiple pieces after receiving its fatal blow.

The holes in its hull provided an explanation for the few dead pirates at the battlefield. They had been blown out of the ship at altitude. Combat may not have killed them, but the fall certainly had.

Judging by the state of the Council vessel's own violated skin, it seemed pretty clear what had happened.

"They were boarding," Bud said, reading the scene with the eyes of a former pirate. "Looks like they already had good penetration in multiple areas when the Council ship landed a few fatal blows."

"Why did *both* ships go down, then?" Henni asked.

"Likely, the attackers had applied strong grappling spells to anchor themselves to the other ship. If they thought they'd be exiting into space, it would have kept their prey from jumping away without them."

"Seems like a pretty logical step, actually," Laskar noted.

"Yeah, it is. But only in space. These morons did it *in atmosphere*, and that's a big no-no, for obvious reasons."

"When one ship fails, both fail," Hozark said.

"Precisely."

"And if that Council ship was part of a larger group, they will likely be sending forces back here," the Wampeh said. "It appears as though our timeline has been a bit truncated by these circumstances. We must hurry."

"On it," Bud said, spinning in fast for a quick landing beside the largest intact portion of the pirate ship.

"Why the pirates first?" Henni asked.

"Because, say what you will about us pirates, this is our livelihood. We always go for the important stuff first, so if these poor bastards managed to get anything of value off that Council ship, it may still be aboard," Bud said, grabbing his weapons and rushing for the door.

Henni secured her daggers and raced after him, with Laskar, Hozark, and Demelza right behind them.

There were body parts strewn about the wreckage, though the impact left them unidentifiable as to race, age, or gender. All present were glad Happizano had not balked at being left behind this time. The boy had seen enough death already and wanted nothing more to do with it if possible.

"Anyone you know?" Laskar asked as Bud strode into the intact section of the pirate craft, pushing corpses out of the way as he did.

"No. I've never seen this ship before, but it looks like a new outfit. And from what I can tell, these guys had plenty of gusto but not too much sense. See those blast marks over there?"

"Yeah."

"Someone used magic *inside* the ship. For all we know, they might damn well have taken themselves out of the equation if the Council hadn't landed those shots on them. No one *I* know would fly with a crew that careless."

"You guys do have a reputation, though."

"Sure, but we earned that reputation by *surviving*. Feats of derring-do don't really count for much if you're not alive to brag about them."

Hozark and Demelza quickly moved past the two men, silent in their rapid progress.

"Damn, it's spooky how quiet they are sometimes," Henni marveled.

"They're the best for a reason," Bud replied. "Come on, let's catch up."

The group made quick time surveying the downed ship but realized it was a pointless exercise in short order.

"To the Council ship," Hozark said. "There is nothing for us here."

They turned their backs on the ruins of the craft and wove through the wreckage to the far less ruined vessel not too far away. It was still hopelessly destroyed and would never fly again, but at least much of the hull was intact, and its occupants had not been flung far and wide.

"Stay attentive," Hozark said as they stepped in through a large tear in the ship's side. "This craft is in far better structural condition. Be ready for a fight."

"You think there are survivors?" Laskar asked, shifting his grip on the blade in his hand. "Dangerous ones?"

"There is a possibility, yes. And if they did survive, the Council's troops will undoubtedly attack first and ask questions later if we stumble upon them after they were engaged in such a heated battle."

"Shit. Gotcha. Staying sharp, then," the copilot said, his gaze flicking from side to side.

Henni had left her daggers sheathed until that moment. She was quick enough to draw them in a flash anyway, after all. But if Hozark was concerned about something, then she was damn sure going to take it seriously.

Both knives quickly found their way into her waiting hands, ready and primed to be put to deadly use. Bud couldn't help but grin. Whatever her many annoying faults were, the young woman was undeniably something of a fearless badass when the chips were down. And this was precisely such a moment.

"This way," Hozark said. "There is a series of intact bunk and barracks units ahead, if this ship is true to design."

"How do you know that?" Laskar asked in a hushed voice.

"It is wise for a Ghalian to familiarize him or herself with all manner of craft they might encounter on a contract," Demelza answered, then fell silent as they approached the warped material of the next chamber's walls.

"Stand ready," Hozark said, then drew power from his konus and forced the buckled wall open.

The team raced in, weapons primed and searching for a target. But what they saw was not even remotely what they'd expected.

"Holy shit," Henni said, her clenched daggers slowly lowering to her sides.

"What the hell is this, Hozark? What were they doing here?" Bud asked as he stared at the broken and cold Ootaki and Drook bodies all around them. "These aren't troops. These are civilians."

Bud moved closer, forcing himself to see the scene with objective eyes. It was what Hozark would do, and if the Wampeh could do it, then he was damn sure not going to let his emotions get the better of him.

But that said, the scene was horrific, even for a hardened pirate. The Ootaki in the chamber were all dead. Several had been shorn, their magic-storing hair safely tucked in containers tossed around the room.

Others still possessed their lengthy locks. But once robbed of their lives, those golden tresses had faded to pale yellow, all of their magic dissipated at once upon their owner's demise.

A pair of Council workers lay crumpled on the deck, their necks and backs broken from the impact.

"It would seem they were trying to harvest as much as they could before the crash," Demelza noted. "A sound, albeit futile, plan of action, given the circumstances."

"Why would they have all of these Ootaki out here?" Bud asked. "It makes no sense. The Drooks I can understand. Using their magic to power the fleet seems pretty straightforward. But the Ootaki? It's just weird."

He lifted the head of one of the dead prisoners. She had been perhaps twenty years old, if that. And now she was robbed of all she would ever have. It made an angry heat rise in his belly. Bud may have been a pirate, and he'd done some pretty terrible things in his day, but murdering innocents was never one of them.

Then something unusual caught his eye.

"Oh, shit."

"What is it?" Hozark asked.

"She doesn't have a collar," Bud replied, quickly checking the other bodies. "Most of them don't."

"You mean, these were *free* Ootaki?" Demelza marveled. "One of the secret enclaves?"

"It would appear that way," Hozark said, checking the bodies near him. "And one of the uncharted ones, as well. That would explain the slaughter at the battle site. These innocents had likely been part of the local society."

"But why would locals fight for a slave race?" Laskar asked.

"Because they were not slaves," the master assassin replied as he examined the rest of the bodies around him. "And with their magical hair to barter for goods and services, and freely given, no less, they were undoubtedly a valued part of this community."

"Friends to be protected," Henni said quietly.

"Exactly."

"Freely given hair?" Laskar marveled. "The power must have been enormous. They say Ootaki hair loses a huge amount of power when it's taken, but not if it is given of their own free will."

"It is true," Hozark confirmed. "Though rare, this gifted Ootaki hair is many orders of magnitude more powerful than what is typically harvested. But it is almost never seen."

"No wonder the locals fought so hard for them. They were worth a fortune," Laskar said.

"They were their friends," Henni grumbled. "Of course they fought. That's what friends do."

"Whatever you say," Laskar chuckled.

"What's that supposed to mean?"

"It means you've got a very, 'do-it-my-own-way' attitude for someone who believes in that whole friendship bond."

"Leave her alone, man. We've still got a lot of ship to cover, and not much time," Bud interjected.

Henni was about to say something snarky, but held her tongue. This was not the time. She stepped around the fallen slaves and made her way to one of the tears in the bulkhead leading into another chamber.

"Oh my Gods! You guys! Come here, quick!"

The others raced to her side. What they saw startled them all.

## CHAPTER FIFTY

"Oh my Gods," Henni exclaimed as she quickly sheathed her daggers and rushed into the compartment.

"There are so many," Laskar marveled, standing stock-still while the others jumped into action right behind the violet-haired young woman.

The compartment was similar to the one they had just been in. A holding area for prisoners. New slaves. Ootaki and Drooks. But unlike the other, where the captives had been held in a loose corral-type setting, this was apparently a different sort of workspace.

Rows of sturdy tables rose from the floor, and secured to them were dozens of the newly captured Ootaki. Most still had their hair, and as they had been restrained when the ship crashed, a good many were still alive. Nevertheless, some would clearly not survive the day.

"Help me," Henni called out as she struggled to release the nearest injured Ootaki.

Bud rushed to her aid and jammed a small enchanted blade he kept concealed on his person for *true* emergencies into the fastening apparatus. The spells holding the Ootaki were reasonably strong, but they were no match for the magical tool.

"I didn't know you had one of those," Henni said as she watched Bud work.

"Secret backup weapons are not really something you broadcast," he replied as he broke the final spell, releasing the Ootaki.

Henni helped the dazed young man to his feet. He immediately slumped to the floor, however, the trauma and exhaustion of the ordeal leaving him too weak for the moment.

"Help the others," Henni said as she propped the Ootaki against the table's base. "Rest. We'll be back for you in a minute." She then rushed off to help free the other survivors.

"There are dozens," Demelza noted as she and Hozark quickly broke the bonds holding the prisoners down. "And not only Ootaki. There are Drooks as well."

Hozark had already been scanning the room, taking count of the rough numbers of captives, as well as the unusual apparatus strewn about the floor. This was not a mere holding area. This was an experimentation chamber.

Despite the restraints sparing them, the majority of the victims had still perished in the crash. But at least, some still lived.

"We must get the survivors to our ship at once," Hozark said. "If the Council was harvesting a source of magic this great, it is an inevitability they will send additional vessels to this world. And far more quickly than we had anticipated. We must be gone before they arrive."

"Laskar," Bud said. "Laskar! Come on, man, help out here. We're on a clock."

"What?" the stunned man said, still gazing at the room full of powered individuals. "Uh, right." He snapped out of it and quickly set to work helping free the remaining survivors.

Most of the Drooks had perished, but it was far harder to tell with them as, unlike the Ootaki, they did not have golden hair that faded when its owner's life was extinguished.

It was a grim form of triage, but the readily available signs of life, death, and pending demise readily visible on the Ootaki did rather streamline the rescue process.

The group was making quick work of freeing and reviving the handful of survivors when Henni abruptly shrieked and jumped back from the table she had approached.

"What is it?" Bud asked as he rushed over, knife in hand.

The prisoner was still firmly secured to the table, but this one was wide awake. A boy, barely a teenager by the looks of him. Pale, with jet-black hair and a wild look in his eyes. A Wampeh.

"It's just a kid, Henni," Bud said, lowering his guard. "Why did you——"

The boy snarled at him, snapping with fierce jaws even though restrained.

"Oh, shit!" Bud exclaimed. "Hozark! Demelza! You need to get over here. Right now!"

The two assassins rushed to their friend's side in a flash.

"Uh, guys? Is that normal?" Henni asked, standing slightly behind Bud, not concerned about taking a razzing for it later in the slightest.

The boy's eyes were wide with panic, rage, and confusion. More than that, he was snarling like a caged animal. And he was sporting extended fangs.

"Oh, my," Hozark said.

"Oh, my? That's all you have to say?" Henni said.

"He is a Wampeh, Henni. One of my kind."

"Obviously. But he's got fangs. That's not normal."

"No, it is not. The boy possesses the *gift*."

"Gift?"

"What makes the Wampeh Ghalian unique from our regular Wampeh brethren. But only a fraction of a fraction of our kind possesses it. And of those, the smallest number have it in the strength needed to become one of the order."

The boy thrashed in his restraints. Apparently, the sight of other Wampeh did nothing to calm him.

"Where could they have found him?" Demelza marveled.

"Seems pretty obvious," Laskar said as he looked down on the restrained youth. "Hard to miss those fangs, ya know."

"Indeed," Demelza said. "But the Ghalian network identifies those with the gift from a very early age, monitoring them as they mature. If one had gone missing, it would have been noted."

"Unless he was found outside of the Wampeh colonies," Hozark noted. "The odds are incredibly small. Minuscule, in fact. But it appears as though this boy is feral."

"Feral? As in, an animal?" Henni asked.

"As in, raised outside of culture and society. At least that which we are accustomed to. He likely has no idea what he is capable of and is acting out of instinct."

"But why so aggressive?" she wondered.

"You weren't terribly docile when they found you either," Bud noted.

"It's not the same thing, ass."

"I know. But I'm just saying, it doesn't take much for someone to snap. And if he had an entire youth of that, it might be all he's ever known."

Henni pondered that thought. A young boy fighting for survival his whole life, never living anything remotely resembling a normal childhood. Hers had been a tough time. Very tough. But now she wondered if this strange young boy might have had it far worse.

"So, is that why he was held with the power users?" she asked. "Were they trying to tap into his Ghalian gift?"

"I told you, Henni, just because one possesses the gift does not make them a Ghalian. A lifetime of training is required to even dream of achieving that."

"So, they were just trying to steal it, then? To take his ability and use it for themselves? I mean, I know you two can drain magic from power users. Seems like it'd be a pretty valuable tool for Maktan to get."

"Wait a minute," Bud said. "I thought you said no one could do that. That it was bound to you by your blood."

Hozark cocked his head slightly. "I did say that," he replied. "And that is the belief of how our power works. No one should be able to take it."

"But what if they found a way?" Laskar asked.

The master assassin paused a moment. "*Then*, dear Laskar, we would be in a world of trouble. But I think it would take a great deal of time for one's biology to shift enough to allow the melding of Wampeh Ghalian blood with that of another race. Possibly generations. And even then, they would have to be tremendously powerful to do so."

"But you think it is actually possible?"

"Honestly, Laskar, I do not know. But we do not have the time to ponder these things right now. We must get these survivors to the ship and depart at once."

"What about the rest of this wreck?" Bud asked.

"You get these victims to the ship. Demelza and I shall make a fast pass through the remains of this vessel."

"Whoa, hang on. I'm not getting bitten by that kid," Laskar said. "I'm a power user. He'll smell it on me."

Hozark chuckled. "One, you are a minor power user, barely worthy of a snack for even the most power-starved Wampeh. And two," he added as he hit the boy with a small stun spell from his konus, "the boy is unconscious and will pose you no threat for the next hour or so. Now, please, do hurry."

He and Demelza did not waste a moment longer. They raced

off to survey the rest of the wreck like only assassins of their skill could.

"You heard the man," Bud said, unfastening the stunned boy's restraints. "We've gotta round up all of these people and get 'em aboard. Come on, let's move!"

Bud and Henni quickly organized the survivors by level of injury and strength. The stronger ones were tasked with helping the weaker ones as best they could. The walking wounded tending those worse off, in essence.

It was a slow trek back to the mothership, but the small caravan of Ootaki and Drooks finally arrived, exhausted, traumatized, but safe.

"I've only got a few rooms available for you guys," Bud said. "But they're all yours. Get some rest. We'll lift off shortly."

The survivors filed into the open doors of the offered chambers in a daze. They weren't really set up for a lot of passengers, but there were some bunks, and some chairs, and more importantly, there were no restraints. At least, for all but one.

The young Wampeh was bound securely and placed in his own compartment. A struggling, thrashing, pointy-toothed Wampeh was bound to unsettle the others, no matter if he'd also been in captivity with them.

"Who's that?" Hap asked, walking into the room as Bud secured the Wampeh's bonds. "Why are you tying him up?"

"Ah. That. Yeah, well, you see—"

"He is of my people," Hozark said, appearing suddenly behind them.

"Jeez, I wish you wouldn't do that!" Bud said, using all of his self-control to not jump out of his skin.

"Yes, I sometimes forget. My apologies, Uzabud," Hozark replied, handing a large sack to the pirate. "Would you mind putting this aside somewhere secure? I will be delivering it to the order shortly."

Bud looked inside, but he kept his expression neutral. A full bag of Ootaki hair. All that had been shorn before its owners perished, by the look of it. Hozark had gathered it all as he and Demelza made their race through the ship.

It made sense, of course. Though it was well known the Ghalian despised slavery, the hair had already been taken, and to leave it behind would ensure it fell into the wrong hands. And at least this way it would be in the possession of those who might use it for better ends. Or simply store it away in their vaults. The pirate really didn't know, nor did he want to ask.

"Sure thing, Hozark," he said. "Okay, I'm gonna get us airborne. No telling when the Council will show up."

"Thank you, Bud," Hozark said, then turned his attention back to Hap. "Now, as I was saying. The boy is a Wampeh, but he has been poorly treated and is a threat not only to himself, but others as well. For that reason, he must be restrained for the moment. For both his own and everyone else's good."

Hap thought on it a moment, then seemed to accept the rationale. "And what about my father? Was he there? You said his magic was here."

Hozark's gaze softened slightly. "I am so sorry, young Jinnik, but your father was not present. The magic we sensed was his, but only that imbued into the konuses being used."

Hap deflated slightly, but seemed almost used to the disappointment.

"I promise you, Happizano, we shall not stop trying to find him. On this you have my word."

The boy shrugged. "Okay. I know you're trying. But what about him? And the others? I saw a whole bunch of people come on board just now."

"We have places for the Ootaki and Drooks. Secret, free colonies established by the order."

"Those are real?" Laskar asked. "I thought they were just rumors."

"The Wampeh Ghalian abhor slavery, dear Laskar. Most are just victims of circumstance, but Ootaki and Drooks are particularly sought out for their power. Thus, anytime we free one, they are offered safe passage to a colony of their own kind."

"Wow. The sheer value of that power—"

"Will never be known. Only a few know the location of any of the colonies, Laskar, and all would die before revealing them. Once relocated, the survivors shall be quite safe."

"And what about the kid? He's not like them."

The copilot was correct. The feral Wampeh youth was certainly a unique problem, and one they would have to deal with in other ways.

"Corann and the others shall do what they can for him. Rehabilitate him if possible."

"They can do that?"

"Unknown. But that discussion is premature at this juncture," Hozark said. "Now, please assist Bud in command. We must get these poor souls to Corann."

"And then?"

The assassin paused a moment. "Then we shall plan our next steps. Whatever they may be."

## CHAPTER FIFTY-ONE

The young Wampeh was free of restraints, his wounds tended, and his body healed by the best hands available. The room in which he was pacing anxiously was clean, warm, and inviting, though sparsely furnished.

Given his agitation, there was just no telling what the unpredictable, and rather unstable, youth might do with anything that was not fastened securely or was not too heavy to lift.

The window was wide and allowed in a full spectrum of comforting natural light. A nice trick of magic allowed the soothing breeze to flow in, while the spells locked in place prevented anything larger than a gnat to pass the windowsill. It also kept the agitated boy from leaping out in a fit of pique.

An additional little bit of magic had been installed as well, in case his appearance, or the angry utterances he made, might draw unwanted attention. A cleverly cast obfuscation spell had been set firmly in place on the outside of the window, along with a substantial muting spell.

The former gave the appearance of a normal, empty window, while the latter stopped all sounds in their tracks. One wouldn't want the neighbors to come rushing in out of concern if they heard something unsettling, after all.

"What's he doing?" Henni asked Corann and Hozark, having tagged along with the two Ghalian masters while they checked in on their new guest.

"He appears to be pacing," Corann replied.

"Well, duh. But why?" Henni asked, clearly more comfortable around the woman whose bloody past she could sense clearly.

"Like a caged animal, he is upset by his confinement, even in a rather spacious and comfortable room, I would note."

The boy raced at the open door, his fangs bared with rage, then bounced back, Corann's force spell keeping the opening quite sealed to his attempts. The young Wampeh let out a low growl, then abruptly turned and ran for the window, leaping high and hard.

Normally, such an effort would have seen him landing on the ground outside, making a quick escape. But the spell on the window simply redirected his efforts, knocking him back to the floor, though without injury. In an instant, he was back on his feet, pacing once more like a caged animal, which, in essence, he was, in a way.

"He has been at it for the past three hours," Corann said. "Ever since the moment his stun spell wore off, in fact."

"Isn't he going to hurt himself?" Henni asked.

"The boy appears to be quite strong, and the gift flowing through him conveys certain additional benefits. Such as a rather rapid healing process," Hozark noted. "He will be fine."

Corann cocked her head slightly as she watched the amped-up boy's agitated state a moment longer. She then crouched and slid a tray of freshly cooked food and still-warm bread through the small gap between the force spell and the floor.

It was just large enough to accommodate the tray––by design––and there was no chance of the boy making an escape via that tiny opening, though he would undoubtedly try if given the opportunity.

For the moment, however, the mouth-watering smell of Corann's finest work was more than enough to distract him from thoughts of escape. He grabbed the tray and began rapidly shoveling the warm food into his mouth with his hands, eschewing utensils entirely.

Henni saw the look on Corann's face and grinned. "Bread's as good a spoon as anything," she said. "And besides, it's edible."

"And we do know how you enjoy anything edible," Hozark said with a little grin. "Though it looks as though you may now have some competition."

The three of them watched the young Wampeh devour his food without so much as pausing to taste it.

"Poor kid's gotta be starving," Henni said. "I mean, I eat fast, sure, but at least I enjoy it."

Corann's lips creased with a faint grin. "Oh, I think he will be slowing down momentarily," she said.

Sure enough, just as the tray was cleared of its contents, the boy seemed to lose steam, falling quickly into a languorous stupor. A few moments later, he was snoring contentedly.

"You drugged him?" Henni asked.

"Yes," Corann replied matter-of-factly. "If we wish to help him, we must first calm him."

"Indeed. And quite a specimen he appears to be," Hozark added. "Strong with the gift, but I fear that he may not be able to be fully integrated and rehabilitated, given his age and what he has endured."

"But if not, then what can you do?" Henni asked. "You can't just throw him out on the streets."

Corann smiled her kindest, warmest smile. The one that all of the children in the neighborhood knew. The one belonging to the kindly older woman who lived on her own and loved to bake for her neighbors.

"He will be sent to the finest healers, dear," she said. "Kept under close watch, of course, but the boy will be rehabilitated as best we can. However, Master Hozark is correct in his worry. Despite having the gift, the boy appears to have not only been through much since his capture, but given his feral nature, he also seems likely to have been raised in relative isolation."

"I guess that would explain the outbursts," Henni said.

"And the lack of social skills. Yes," Corann noted. "But if, after all avenues have been exhausted, he is still unable to achieve a level of normalcy, then he shall be set free. Somewhere far, far away where none will find him, and he can live out his life in peace."

Henni liked the sound of that far more than dumping him like a piece of unwanted refuse if he did not meet the Ghalian's high standards. But she was nevertheless concerned.

"And if he drains someone? What then?" she asked.

"We shall still have our people keeping an eye on the boy," Hozark replied. "Not Ghalian, per se, but those who work closely with us will keep tabs and report in."

"Observing is fine, but what if he can't be rehabbed? What if he still goes after people? I mean, you saw how he was."

"That we did," he said quietly.

"Well, isn't there some way to make sure you fix him enough to at least prevent that?"

"That is up to the boy. Obviously, we hope he is able to control himself and overcome the horrible circumstances that have befallen him. But if he cannot, if we are forced to intervene, lest he use his gift against the innocent, then, and only then, will we resort to the far less desirable option."

Henni knew what that meant. No matter how nice they were, no matter how normal they might seem, these were the deadliest assassins in the galaxy, and there was no mistaking what would be done.

She knew it would be a highly distasteful act on their part, and one they would do with great reluctance. But if it was ultimately called for, the Wampeh youth with the gift, but no control, would have to be put down. He would be far too dangerous a thing not to.

She wished with all her heart that would not be the case. But only time would tell. For now, she just hoped for the best, knowing the Wampeh Ghalian would do all they could for the boy.

# CHAPTER FIFTY-TWO

"Four sacks of Azmus flour?" Bud asked. "Are you sure?"

"Yes, Uzabud, I am sure," Corann replied.

"The big ones?"

"Yes, the big ones."

"That's an awful lot of flour. Especially for a specialty item like that."

"It may seem like a substantial amount, but you are not the only ones I bake for," the motherly killer replied. "I regularly give treats to the neighborhood children and their parents."

"All the better to blend in and avoid suspicion, eh?"

"Indeed. A little goodwill goes a very long way, you know. And I have generated a *lot* of goodwill over the years."

Bud chuckled. There was no denying the efficacy of Corann's methods, and as a result, her false identity as the sweet, caring older woman in the neighborhood was as firmly fixed in the residents' minds as if placed there with a powerful adhesive. No one suspected her of a thing, let alone of being one of the deadliest women in the galaxy.

"Hey, whatcha all doing?" Henni asked, strolling into the kitchen. "Ooh, cookies!" She began to reach for one, then stopped herself short, turning her attention to the amused Wampeh watching her. "Do you mind?"

"Of course not, dear," Corann said. "Those are for all of your enjoyment. Please, help yourself."

Henni didn't need any further goading. The first cookie disappeared into the black hole that was her mouth in an instant, but she did slow down for numbers two and three.

"Okay," Bud said. "I see what you mean about going through the stuff pretty quickly. I'll take one of the away craft and fly out to your supplier. Boram's the name, right?"

"Yes, that is correct."

"And you said he was over in Makkus, right?"

"Yes. It is a relatively short flight, all things considered. Makkus is the main industrial and commerce hub across the water," Corann replied. "There are distributors closer, but their product is not nearly as fresh, and dear old Boram and I have a longstanding relationship."

"Always nurture those," Bud said, nodding his approval.

"Indeed. I shall skree ahead and let him know you are coming. All you shall need to do is present yourself at his establishment and he will provide you with my order."

"All right, then. I'll fly out straightaway."

"Thank you, Uzabud. And for your troubles, I think I shall bake you up a little something special upon your return."

"Treats?" Henni asked, her interest piqued at the thought of Corann going above and beyond her already considerably delicious comestibles. "Hey, lemme come with. I can help."

"I don't need your help, pest."

"Shut it, creeper. You know extra hands are always a good thing. Especially when you're loading up on stuff. Isn't that right, Corann?"

The Wampeh couldn't help but be amused at the two's bickering. "Of course, the girl is correct," she replied. "Take her with, Uzabud. It will do her good to see more of my world."

Bud wasn't about to argue with the Ghalian master. He could have, without fear of repercussions, but Corann had taken him and the others in without hesitation, and her hospitality was damn near legendary at this point.

"Okay, Corann. You've got it," Bud said. "Come on, Henni, let's load up and get moving. Might as well get this show on the road."

Henni flashed a quick grin and trotted off to the mothership. Bud would be along momentarily.

"Anything else you can think of you might need?" he asked.

"No, that is all," Corann replied. "I think you will enjoy Makkus. It can be a bit of a rougher town than here, but that provides it a certain feeling that our kind finds comforting, wouldn't you agree?"

"In a strange way, yeah, I do," the former pirate said with a chuckle. "Well, I'll see you in a bit, then."

"There is no rush, Uzabud. And thank you for running this errand for me."

"It's the least I can do."

"Do not downplay your efforts. While, yes, this is not a large or inconvenient request, your providing me with this assistance is nevertheless appreciated."

"Well, okay, then. I'll be back soon."

With that he headed off to join Henni at his mothership. Of course, the large vessel would remain parked where it was. There was no need to take the main craft on such an insignificant little run. Instead, they would utilize one of the smaller craft Bud kept docked to the mothership's exterior.

Not the Ghalian shimmer ships, though. Those were Hozark and Demelza's personal craft. They were off limits for joyrides and little tasks such as this. And the banged-up transport that had been largely stripped when Happizano had stolen it––only to lose the craft when he was captured by pirates––was still in need of a great deal of repairs from that incident before it would once more be flight worthy. But there were still several options available to them.

"Which do you think?" he asked. "The Panassian cargo shuttle? Or maybe the Delvian transit craft?"

"That one," Henni said, pointing to a sleek, fast-looking little vessel positioned toward the front of the mothership.

"*That* one? Oh, I haven't used that since I, uh, *acquired* it," Bud said.

"I like its lines," Henni said. "Come on, let's take it for a spin."

Bud thought on it a moment. "I guess we might as well," he finally said. "Probably do it some good. Work out the cobwebs and whatnot."

"Cool!" Henni said, trotting off to board the ship.

A few minutes later, Bud had slid a small Drookonus into the long-empty receptacle and powered up the craft. All was in order, it appeared, and the craft was ready for the flight. In any case, they weren't going to even be leaving the atmosphere, so even if there were a few bugs to work out, they wouldn't prove life-threatening.

He uttered the small spell he knew like the back of his hand, and the ship's docking spells were released.

"Everything seems to be checking out," he said as he rested the propulsion spells and basic navigational commands. "Well, then. Okay, here we go."

## CHAPTER FIFTY-THREE

"Wow. This place is a dump," Henni said as she hopped out of the sleek ship Bud had just brought in for a landing.

"I wouldn't go *that* far," the former pirate said. "Besides, didn't they find you in a *real* dump? I've smelled those old rags of yours, and I can't imagine that place could have been remotely as nice as this."

"That was different," she protested. "And besides, this is a *nice* world. *All* of the cities should be nice."

"If only it were so simple," Bud said with a chuckle.

The thing was, Henni was right, to a point. But while Makkus was indeed a great deal dingier and more rundown than Corann's idyllic little town, it really wasn't all *that* bad. At least, not for a bustling commerce hub.

In fact, compared to some that Bud had visited in his day, this place was downright luxurious.

"Come on," he said, casting the sealing spell on the ship behind him. "We should go track down this Boram character while it's still early. If we get Corann's Azmus flour straightaway, we should have time for a little exploring. That is, if you're up for it."

"Up for exploring?" Henni said with a little smirk. "I'm *always* up for exploring."

Bud chuckled. "All right, then. But first the flour. Once that's done we can partake in a bit of meandering about."

The two headed off from the landing area and made their way into the belly of the bustling city to seek out the flour vendor. Unfortunately, even with directions, the area possessed a bit of a confusing layout for newcomers, and these two were no exception.

"Excuse me, do you know where we might find Boram?" Bud asked a woman selling hot buns from a street cart.

"Boram? Who's that?"

"He sells baking supplies. Artisanal flours, that sort of thing."

The woman pondered a moment. "I don't know any Boram. But you might wanna try Vindoga's shop. She's got excellent quality goods."

"Oh, really? Where exactly is that?"

The woman pointed out the smaller side street up ahead. "Just turn left. You can't miss it."

"Thank you, we'll give it a look," Bud said, moving along.

"Why didn't you just tell her that's not what we're looking for?" Henni asked as they followed the course the woman had laid out for them.

"Because another supply shop might know where to find the one we're looking for. They all likely know one another."

"But we could have just asked someone else and not wasted time with that woman."

Bud gave her a judgmental look as they turned into the side street. "You know, being pleasant goes a lot farther than being a pain, and you never know whom you might want on your side if things go tits up."

"Why would things go wrong? Seems a pretty pessimistic assumption."

"Trust me, they always do."

"Not always."

"Look, just assume they will and you won't be unpleasantly surprised, okay?" Bud said. "Anyway, it's a good habit to get into. You should try it."

"What? Ass kissing?"

"Being less abrasive. Who knows? It might suit you. Though knowing you, I kinda doubt it."

"Oh, ha-ha," she replied. "You're soooo funny. Absolutely hysterical."

Rough hands grabbed them both and threw them inside a building, the door slamming shut behind them before they could even draw their weapons.

"What was that you were saying about not being unpleasantly surprised?" Henni asked just as a pair of stun spells dropped them both to the floor.

"Ow, my head," the violet-haired girl said, cracking her neck in a slow circle.

"Glad you're finally back with us," Bud said.

"Shut it. You know, you're a real––" Henni stopped herself. "What the hell?"

She yanked on her restraints, but her arms and legs were firmly tied to the chair in which she found herself bound. Her eyes quickly adjusted to the dim light, and she saw that Bud was likewise trussed up in an identical way.

Pacing the room, staring at them with a disturbing grin, was a thick-necked man with deep gray skin. His arms and legs looked like tree limbs compared to normal people's proportions, and his powerful hands seemed as if they might crush rocks into gravel without much effort at all.

On the small table nearby, Henni's twin daggers sat in a pile along with the other weapons and possessions the pair had on them when they set out for this little outing.

The konus Bud had been wearing was just a standard one of no significant power. They were on Corann's world, after all, and doing an errand for her. The likelihood of needing their fighting tools were slim to none. And yet, here they were, prisoners of this hulking man.

"Look, we don't have any coin," Bud said. "But take what we have, please."

"Already done that, haven't we?" the man growled in a low, rumbling voice.

"Those are *my* knives. You can't give him my stuff!" Henni blurted.

"Please forgive her," Bud said, shooting the angry woman a look that practically screamed *shut up!* "Of course you have them, and you're welcome to them. But we don't have any more valuables on us."

"Already know that, too, don't we?" the man said with a menacing laugh.

Bud shifted in his seat a bit and felt that even his hidden knife had been taken. These captors, whoever they were, had been thorough to say the least. And that was particularly disconcerting.

"I'm not putting up with this," Henni said. "Who the hell do you think you are?"

"Henni, please," Bud hissed. "Don't make things worse."

"Worse? What good are you? Just sitting there all tied up like that. Not even trying to get us out of this."

Bud smiled meekly at the large man looming over him. "Sorry, she gets carried away sometimes. Please forgive her."

The man snorted and walked to the table to pick through their belongings.

"Anyway, you can clearly see that we are not rich people.

And you already have our possessions, so you might as well let us go. We wouldn't want to take up your time, and--"

"You're not going anywhere," the man said, dropping Bud's sheathed knife back on the table.

Had he pulled it free, he'd have noticed the enchanted blade. Only by this tiny fluke had he not bothered to more thoroughly examine his and his accomplices' haul, though thus far, Bud hadn't seen the others who made up this "we" he spoke of.

"But we don't have any coin," Bud replied. "And surely you don't keep your mugging victims locked away when you--"

"You're not mugging victims," the man said. "You're hostages."

"Hostages?" Henni asked, voicing Bud's confusion as well.

"Yeah, you heard me. We saw you land earlier. Took you both for the ransom, we did. Easy, it was. Both of you too busy bickering, didn't even see us coming."

Bud hated to admit it, but he had a point. Nevertheless, their captors also appeared to have made a rather sizable miscalculation.

"Uh, sir. I'm sorry, but we have no coin to pay a ransom with," Bud said.

"Oh, you'll pay," he replied.

Finally, Bud had enough. "Okay, listen, fucko. We *seriously* have no coin. You've already taken all we have, so you know we're telling the truth. And if you think our--"

"Recognized your ship, I did," the man interrupted. "One of Emmik Vargus's craft. Going to send a message, we will. He pays the ransom for his underlings, or we off you both and keep the ship. Just need your names. And now that you're awake..."

Henni looked at Bud with a confused expression. Bud ignored her, focusing on their lone visible captor.

"So, you know who we are, then," the pirate said. "Damn, you found us out. Well done. Really, good work, that. But listen, we've had a long, hard day, and we really do want to cooperate, but couldn't we have a little something to drink first? I know I'm parched, and that one has a medical condition. If she doesn't have a glass of Boramus milk ever eight hours, her organs start to fail."

"You're bluffing."

"Why would I bluff about that? And besides, it's just a glass of milk. Such a little thing to keep your valuable prize from dying before you can claim your ransom. So, what do you say?"

The man studied them both a long moment, then shrugged.

*Ah, he's not the actual boss*, Bud realized.

"I guess," the man said. "But don't try anything while I'm gone."

"We're tied to chairs. I don't think there's much we could do, even if we wanted to, am I right?"

The large man shrugged again, then stepped outside, leaving the pair alone.

"Boramus milk? Gross!" Henni blurted. "I am *not* drinking Boramus milk."

"Shut it, will you? I just needed to buy us a little time, and that stuff's really hard to come by."

"This is all your fault in the first place!" she grumbled. "And what's this about Emmik Vargus?"

Bud sighed. "Shit, I stole that thing a while back from a trader I was haggling with."

"You stole a ship? And you kept it?"

"Hey, the bastard tried to triple-cross me on the sale. Of course, now it looks like he stole it too, only before I did. Funny world, ain't it?"

"Yeah, real funny," Henni grumbled. "So what do we do?"

"Do? We figure out how to get out of this, that's what we do."

"But won't Corann and the others come looking for us?"

"Eventually. But we can't risk blowing Corann's cover. Not for something as dumb as this. And besides, it might be days before they find us, and by then they will have notified the emmik, and once that happens, there'll be too much scrutiny on this whole planet. We need to put a stop to this ourselves before that happens."

"Fine. But how?" Henni asked.

"Leave that to me," Bud said, his casual bravado hiding the fact that he didn't have the faintest idea.

## CHAPTER FIFTY-FOUR

"Does she ever shut up?" asked the short, deep-red-skinned man with the bright blue eyes and horn-like protrusions along his brow line.

"If you think this is bad, you should try spending a few weeks with her," Bud replied with a knowing chuckle. "I'm telling you, it'll be a lot less hassle if you just let us go. I tried telling your buddy, but he just didn't want to listen."

"He got your friend her Boramus milk, didn't he?" the red man said, pointing to the empty glass he had poured into Henni's mouth.

"Yeah, that's true. And thanks for that. She obviously feels a lot better now."

"I do not feel better! You damn near drowned me with that crap. What were you thinking?"

"Oh, don't mind her," Bud said, shooting her a look. "She gets this way after she eats. But trust me, she *loves* Boramus milk. It keeps her healthy."

"I don't see how anyone can enjoy it," their captor said. "Nasty stuff."

It was true, Boramus milk was more than just an acquired

taste. The rather strong flavor was bad enough, but when combined with its almost syrupy viscosity, it was something few but a baby Boramus would ever consider tasty.

Of course, cheese was made from the protein-dense liquid, and a lot of suckling animals were fed with the nutritious milk if their own mother was not properly lactating, but *people* pretty much never drank it. And yet Henni, firmly bound to her chair, had just had a tall glass poured down her gullet.

Bud almost regretted the little joke he'd played on the girl while buying them some time to plan an escape. But given the epic level of pain in the ass she had been, he figured she kind of deserved it.

At least a little bit. Plus, he hadn't expected them to actually find any.

"Well, we thank you for it. But, seriously, you should just let us go. This is all going to be more hassle than it's worth."

"Not a chance. The boss already sent out word to Emmik Vargus to get that ransom paid. Shouldn't be long now until we're all rich!"

Bud sighed. This really wasn't going as he'd hoped. The false names he'd given would definitely not hold up to scrutiny.

"That's great, but can you do me a favor?"

"What do you want? We already fed your friend."

"Yeah, and it's appreciated. But I've gotta take a leak something fierce. You think you could let me take care of business?"

"No way I'm untying you."

"Oh, just one hand and one foot will suffice. I can hop over to the bathroom, and while two hands would be preferable––"

"You know you're not that big," Henni snarked.

"As if you'll ever know," he shot back. "Anyway, that's all I need."

"I don't think so."

"But if the emmik's people show up and I'm covered in piss,

they'll be angry. Why, I bet they might not even pay the full ransom, seeing as how we've been mistreated."

The red-skinned man was clearly at odds with his orders. Their boss, whoever that was, had obviously given him instructions, but now something that required a bit of actual thought had arisen, and he had to make a judgment call. Not exactly his strong suit.

"Uh, well," he said.

"Just for a minute. And you can tie me up again right afterward. No one will ever know. Please."

"Well, okay. But no funny stuff."

"I wouldn't dream of it. I just have to piss something fierce."

The guard unbound Bud's right leg first, then his left hand.

"Bathroom's right through that door," he said, gesturing across the room.

"Thanks," Bud replied, shaking out his wrist to restore blood flow. "I'm a rightie, but this'll work. Back in a jiff."

He stood on his one unbound leg and got his balance, then hopped to the doorway, dragging the chair with him, and banged his way through it.

"Leave the door open!"

"Will do," he replied. A few moments later, the sound of a stream of urine hitting the bowl faintly reached the ears of Henni and their captor. Bud then hopped back to his place and sat again with a thud.

"Now, hold still," the guard said.

"No problem. Sitting still," Bud replied as the man bound his foot once more.

When he moved to his wrist, however, he jerked back suddenly.

"You pissed on your hand!"

"Well, jeez, I'm sorry. But I told you I'm right-handed. It was the best I could do."

Grumbling, the red man gingerly re-tied the restraints around Bud's urine-soaked hand.

"Okay, now you two sit quietly. I'll be right back. The emmik's men should be here shortly."

"We're not going anywhere," Bud said as he watched the man step through the front door.

"What the hell? Your daddy didn't teach you not to piss on yourself?" Henni asked in a snarky tone.

"Says the girl who lived in filth-stained rags up until recently."

"I never pissed on my clothes."

"Oh? So whose piss was it then?"

"Shut up. You're a real shit, you know that?"

"Yeah, so you keep saying. But you know what else I am?"

"What?"

Bud pulled his hand loose from the restraints. "I'm free."

"How the hell did you do that?"

"Pissed on my hand," he replied with a wink. "That made him less enthusiastic in tying the knots. I kept just enough pressure on the rope as he worked that when I relaxed, there was some slack. Combine that with a half-assed knot and voila."

"Then get us out of here!"

"In a minute. The other ropes are still tight," he said, hop-scooting his chair toward the table with all of their weapons.

"Hurry!"

"I'm trying. This isn't easy, you know."

"Well, do you still have that enchanted blade tucked away?"

"Nope. They took it all. I've gotta get to that table if we want out. Now shut up and let me work."

"What, you can't scoot a chair when I'm talking? It distracts you too much?"

"No. When you're talking, I can't hear if the bad guys are coming back."

Henni paused. "Oh."

"Yeah. *Oh.*"

Bud hop-scooted the chair as quickly as he was able until he bumped into the table.

"Come here, my pretty," he said, lunging straight for his enchanted blade.

He hadn't even had a chance to unsheathe it when the sound of voices could be heard down the hallway outside the door.

"They're coming!" Henni hissed.

"I know," he replied, biting his sheathed blade in his teeth then grabbing one of Henni's. He then hopped his chair back to its original place.

Bud quickly tucked Henni's dagger under her forearm on the chair. It was just slender enough to be concealed. More importantly, the tip reached her restraints. He then hid his own knife underneath his leg and slipped his hand back into the ropes, giving it the appearance of being properly tied as best he could.

The door opened, and the large gray man stepped through the opening, followed by the smaller red-skinned man, both striding into the room and glaring at the two captives with clearly upset looks. Bud wondered what had upset them so. He'd soon find out.

A moment later, a tall, lithe, green-hued woman entered, walking straight up to the pair of captives and eyeing them with a contemptuous gaze.

She stared a long moment, saying nothing. Her annoyance was as clear as crystal.

"Uh, hi," Bud said. "I was just telling my friend here that it sure is great Emmik Vargus will be getting us out of here soon. Yep, that's gonna be great, all right. Isn't that right?"

Henni did a quick double-take. "Oh, yeah. Right. That's going to be fantastic. Can't wait, really."

"You two may cease your prattling," the woman growled. "The emmik's representative has replied to our demands."

"Oh? He has?" Bud asked, doing his best to hide his surprise.

"Yes, he has. And Emmik Vargus's envoy says that he knows the ship you two arrived on quite well."

"Well, there are a lot of ships in the fleet, and––"

"He says it was *stolen* from the emmik not so long ago."

Bud paused just a split second, then promptly shifted course. "Look, I can explain. You see, there was this trader out on the moon off of Gorkus who had a ship for sale. Well, wouldn't you know, we were negotiating, when that sonofabitch tried to––"

"Silence!" she bellowed. Her look made it quite clear she was not playing around. "We will make our money one way or another. If they will not pay a ransom for you, then at least they will pay a small salvage fee for the return of the ship."

"Then we're of no use to you," Bud said.

"Yeah, you should let us go," Henni added. "It's just stupid keeping us around if you can't––"

"Henni, please. Shut. Up," Bud said, exasperated.

"Oh, like you have a better plan."

"It beats calling our captors names. Jeez, are you serious? You really think that's a good idea?"

"You have a better one?" Henni shot back.

"Shut up, you two," the gray man warned.

"Oh, my ideas make yours look like Bundabist droppings," Bud continued. "You're so dense."

"Oh, yeah? You're denser than a black hole, and there's nothing denser than that!"

"You're going to go there?"

The green woman glared, and her underlings reacted immediately.

"I mean it. Shut up, both of you!" the large man said again, quite a bit louder.

"Why? We're of no worth to you. Just let us go and we'll call it even," Henni said.

The ringleader laughed, and it was not a happy sound. "No

worth? Oh, my dear little thing. I will get every last coin out of your hide. Whether I sell you for Zomoki chum or for some emmik's new play-slave, you *will* line my pocket before we're finished with you."

Bud's mood shifted abruptly, his anger focused squarely on the green-hued woman. "You'll do no such thing."

"Oh?" she said, amused.

"Yes. No one puts a control collar on her ever again. No one."

"As if you are in a position to do anything about it, little man," she replied, utterly unimpressed. "And you have little value beyond Zomoki food. Enjoy breathing, while you are still able," she added with a malicious grin.

The little red man picked up a konus and knife from the table. "Hey, boss. We can always sell all of this stuff. I'm sure there's some decent value to it."

She nodded her approval of the idea, but the gray man's attention seemed to sharpen in focus.

"Hey. Why's that sheath empty? Where'd you drop the dagger? They were a matched pair."

"No, there's only one here," the smaller man replied.

"I'm telling you, there were two."

"Idiots. Find the other one. I swear, if you can't manage to keep track of––"

"You looking for this?" Henni asked, holding the blade up high.

"How did she––"

"Oh, sorry. That was this no-value idiot's doing. Oops. My bad," Bud said as he rose from his chair and stretched casually, his faintly-glowing blade firmly in hand.

"They're free! Idiots! You had one job!"

"But we––"

"Grab them, quickly! Before they get away!"

Henni flashed Bud a little smile then turned her gaze on the woman. "Oh, we're not trying to get away," she said.

The look of understanding that registered on the green-tinted woman's face was quickly replaced by one of abject fear as the small, but surprisingly fast and violent little woman lunged at her, burying her dagger deep in the woman's shoulder just shy of her chest.

Their captor cried out in pain, the stun spell she was attempting to cast cut off by the blurted exclamation.

Bud, meanwhile, was already at work on the other two, dropping the larger of his two opponents quickly with a solid kick to the groin––the ensuing gasps preventing him from casting so much as the tiniest of spells. The stronger of the pair temporarily out of commission, he then turned his attention to the red-skinned man.

"*Invarius hor––*"

The thrown knife buried itself in the man's throat all the way to the hilt, cutting off not only his spell, but also severing major blood vessels and his spine in the process. The man dropped to the ground, his lifeless eyes staring at his struggling comrades as they faced their demise.

The gray man had managed to lay a hand on Henni, pulling her off of the green woman and throwing her across the room into the wall before she could finish her off. The bleeding woman did not hesitate, bolting for the door.

Bud yanked the gore-covered knife from the dead man's throat, but the green woman was already gone. The gray man, however, was still there, and upon him in an instant.

Bud drove the knife hard into his torso, but even with an enchanted blade, the man's sheer bulk prevented the pirate from landing a killing blow.

"I'm gonna make you pay, you little––"

The large man suddenly went limp, his eyes rolling up into his head. He keeled over to the side, allowing Bud to scramble free.

"Hey, get this guy off me," Henni's muffled voice called from beneath the dead goon.

"Shit, hang on," Bud said, quickly pulling the dead man's body from atop her.

Henni yanked her dagger from the back of the man's head and scrambled to her feet, ready for a fight, but their final captor had already fled.

"Well, shit. The bitch got away," she said, reclaiming her other dagger from the spilled pile of their possessions and securing it on her person.

"Yeah, but we can worry about that later. Right now, we've gotta get out of here before she comes back with help."

"You think she will?"

"You want to wait around and find out?"

Henni pondered a moment, then sheathed her blade. "Nah, you've got a point," she said, moving for the door.

They stepped outside and raced several blocks before getting their bearings. It seemed their captors hadn't moved them far at all from where they'd taken them.

"Hey, where are you going?" Henni asked. "The ship's this way."

"Yeah, but we still have to get Corann's Azmus flour."

"Seriously?"

"Hey, do you want to tell the deadliest woman in the system that we let a couple of half-rate goons prevent us from getting her flour?"

"Well…"

"And do you want her to be prevented from baking us her wonderful creations because of it?"

Henni paused a second. "Well, when you put it that way, lead on!"

"That's the spirit," Bud said, assessing the girl with fresh eyes. "By the way, nice job back there."

Henni, for once, put the snark on hold. "You too. Thanks."

"Don't mention it," Bud said, his smile far warmer than normal, at least where Henni was concerned. But time was short, and he quickly put his game face back on. "Okay, come on. We're behind schedule," he said, leading the way into the marketplace.

# CHAPTER FIFTY-FIVE

"Everything you requested," Bud said as he hefted the four enormous sacks of Azmus flour from his ship onto the floating conveyance waiting for him at the landing site.

"I am glad to see you were able to acquire what I asked of you," Corann said, smiling warmly as he transferred the load.

Corann had sent the conveyance ahead to the landing area earlier in the day. A little something to ease the process for the pair when they returned. But it had taken them a bit longer than anticipated to return, and when she heard Bud had finally docked his smaller ship, she stepped out and made her way over to the landing area to greet Bud and Henni.

"Sorry we're late, Corann," Bud said. "We were, uh, *delayed*."

The older woman arched an eyebrow slightly at his word choice and tone. "Oh? Not a problem, I hope."

"Nothing we couldn't handle," he replied as Henni stepped out of the ship.

Corann had particularly sharp observational skills, and the tiny blood spatter still clinging to the young woman's shoes spoke volumes about the actual cause of their delay.

But this was a public place, and hardly the location to

discuss whatever it was that had happened. So, she smiled broadly, and welcomed them with great cheer, chattering on about all manner of bright and happy subjects. Precisely what any passersby would expect of the kindly woman who lived down the road.

"What happened, and whom do I need to end?" she asked, her smile disappearing immediately as soon as they were safely within the muting spell-silenced walls of her home.

"We got kidnapped," Henni blurted, though she and Bud had previously agreed he would do the talking.

"Kidnapped? A *pirate*? On *my* world?"

Bud sighed. "Yeah, Corann. It's embarrassing, but they hit us with a stun spell while we were distracted looking for your friend Boram. Nice guy, by the way. He sends his regards, along with a little sample bag of some whole grain Azmus flour variant for you."

"Ah, yes. A lovely man, Boram, and quite generous. But tell me, what of this attack. How many were there? What did they look like?"

"Just three that we saw. A stocky, gray-skinned fellow, and a shorter red one were our main guards, but eventually a pale-green woman came to see us."

Corann's jaw muscle flexed ever so slightly. "Was she particularly lean? Tall?"

"Yeah, she was," Henni said. "I put a dagger in her chest, but she moved at the last second, so it only got her up by the shoulder instead of her heart."

"And the others?"

"Not so lucky," Bud replied. "But yeah, their boss lady got away. She had a mercenary feel to her. Far more competent than her underlings."

Corann hefted the flour into its storage compartment with ease, moving the massive sacks as though it were nothing but child's play. Quite the difference from the airs she put on in public, reinforcing for Henni the impression of the woman's hidden deadliness.

"Moratza," she said as she tossed the last of the flour into its place.

"Moratza?" Bud asked.

"She's a local ruffian I am quite familiar with. Not much of a problem normally, though she has been warned in the past by my associates to keep her criminal activities to a small and acceptable level."

"So, everyone just tolerates that sort of thing?" Henni asked. "That's messed up. We were tied to chairs! They made me drink Boramus milk!"

"No, Henni. *This* is not tolerated. Petty crimes? Those are common on all worlds and are nearly always overlooked. But nothing like this. *This* is overstepping the generously long leash we've given her and the others. Uzabud knows as well as any, there will always be a criminal element in a commerce town. But one that can be controlled is far preferable to one that runs amok."

"So, this kidnapping thing?" Henni asked.

"*Not* acceptable. But do not dwell on it further. I shall see to it."

"See to it?" Bud asked. "Should we come with?"

"Do not worry yourselves," the assassin replied. "It shall be handled discreetly and with great care. But she will not bother you, or anyone, again."

Neither needed the deadly woman to go into detail as to what would happen, nor would they have asked if they did. Corann was keeping her home in order, and that meant Moratza would pay the fiddler.

But the Ghalian master's presence had to remain quiet. A secret. This place was a quiet respite, and her true identity could not be leaked. Not on this world.

"Well, there's nothing to do for it at this very moment, and I baked while you two were away. Would you care to assist me in delivering some care packages to my neighbors? I could use the assistance."

Bud and Henni knew full well she had no such need of help, but to keep up appearances with the locals, kindly old Corann couldn't very well be seen hefting armloads of baked goods as if they were nothing. And an excessive show of magic floating them down the pathways would likewise draw attention.

"Of course," Bud said. "We'd be happy to help."

"Help with what?" Laskar asked as he walked into the kitchen. "Help eating? Because I smelled something wonderful as I was passing by."

"You want to eat?" Bud asked. "You can eat. But you've gotta earn it."

"How many more?" Laskar asked. "My arms are getting tired."

"Just four more," Corann replied cheerfully as she walked burden-free down the pathway.

The others, however, hadn't been quite so lucky.

Corann was known for her generosity and baking acumen across town, and there was not a single person who had ill to speak of her. Though not the only reason by a long shot, the periodic edible gifts she would drop at people's homes might have helped cement her reputation, and Laskar was now the primary beast of burden in their delivery.

Bud and Henni had handed over their loads first, and their copilot friend was carrying the last few packages, though not without complaint.

"Oh, fine. I'll take one," Bud said, easing his friend's load. "But don't say I never do anything for you."

Laskar let out an exaggerated sigh of relief when Bud took the parcel from him.

"It's not that heavy, man. Jeez, overact much?"

"Hey, no fair," Laskar protested. "You guys delivered yours first. I've been carrying these the whole way."

"Fine. Whatever."

"You two are ridiculous," Henni chuckled.

"Oh, you are *so* not one to talk," Bud shot back with a good-natured grin.

"Where are we going with this one, anyway?" Laskar asked. "This is kind of out of the way."

He was right. They'd made a rather long trek outside the main town to a quiet little residence up on a hill. It wasn't much more than a hut, really, but the grounds around it were lush and verdant.

An exceptionally healthy vegetable garden spoke to the fecundity of the land as well as the gardener's skill, and Henni recognized some of the more unusual produce from Corann's kitchen.

"Arina is a very dear friend," Corann said as they approached the door. "She doesn't get to town very often these days, though."

"Why does she live all the way up here?" Laskar asked. "Seems like a boring place to spend all of your time."

"Boring? It's beautiful," Henni said. "You've got messed up taste."

"Seriously. It's gorgeous," Bud agreed.

"You all are nuts. But, whatever. If it lightens this load, it's good enough for me," their copilot grumbled.

Corann chuckled. "Arina lives away from others because she is a sensitive woman. She has seen and experienced a great deal in her long life, and now, in her old age, she wishes to merely be left alone to her garden and her thoughts."

"Except for the occasional baking swap, I take it?" Bud asked.

"Exactly."

"Corann! What a treat!" a hunched old woman said, rising

from her garden. She had been almost invisible, as camouflaged as a hunter as she crouched among her plants.

"Arina, it is lovely to see you," Corann said, her smile bright and wide.

For some reason, Bud thought that *this* time, her reaction was less acting than usual.

"And what have we here?" Arina asked. "You brought friends?"

"Yes. This is Uzabud, Laskar, and Henni."

"A pleasure," the old woman said.

"And you know I brought you a few things, of course," Corann added, squeezing her friend warmly on the shoulder, then taking the largest package from Laskar's arms and placing it on her friend's small gardening conveyance.

"Oh, you. You're too kind, Corann. But here, have some fresh produce to take back with you. As always, I seem to have grown far more than I can use myself."

"Thank you, Arina. I would be thrilled," Corann said. "Bud, Henni, would you two please gather those up for me? An old woman has to mind her back, you know."

"You're half my age, Corann, and I'm still working in my garden."

"Yes, but I find a kitchen is more to my liking. Less stooping and kneeling is easier on the body, after all."

"Just wait until you're my age," Arina said. "But in any case, I'll gladly accept your baking any time." She turned to Bud and Henni. "Come, let me load you up with some produce."

Bud and Henni walked over to the woman as she gathered up bundles of vegetables.

"A pleasure to meet you," Bud said.

"Oh, such a strong young man. I can see why Corann has you around," Arina said with a wink.

Bud chuckled as she loaded him with greens. "I try to be of help," he replied, pretending the comment flew over his head.

"Hi," Henni said. "Nice to meet ya."

Arina shifted her attention to the girl and froze.

"What? Do I have something on my face?" Henni asked, uncomfortably shifting under the intensity of the old woman's gaze.

"Your eyes," Arina gasped.

"Yep. I've got two of 'em."

"By the gods, I've not seen one of your kind since I was a girl. I thought you were all extinct."

"Uh... not extinct. Just a girl picking up some veggies for Corann."

Arina ignored her. "Corann, how did you come across her?"

"She flies with some distant family of mine who have come for a visit. But why, Arina? You seem unsettled. What is it?"

"It's just, I never thought I'd see another in all my days. They were so rare to begin with."

"Uh, what exactly are we talking about, here?" Henni asked.

"Yeah. Extinct?" Bud said. "I mean, sure, she's unusual, but––"

"Unusual? She is a being of immense power," Arina said. "Those with galaxies in their eyes. The Faraway Kind. Power users of massive potential."

Corann turned and assessed the young woman once more. "I have heard some old tales of those with similar eyes having some skills. A bit of unusual magic."

"Those old wives' tales? I've heard them all," Arina said, cupping Henni's face and staring deep into her eyes. "But there are many stories, and nearly all are utterly wrong."

"So, what's up with her, then?" Laskar asked, his interest piqued. "I mean, she's a reader, that much we know, but other than that, she really hasn't done much."

"Oh, my dear boy––"

"I'm a man, thank you very much," he replied defensively.

"I meant no disrespect. But my dear *man*, this young

woman's kind are anomalies. A rarest of bloodline from millennia ago. Their magic is something akin to what is found in Zomoki. Or *was* found in them. The Old Ones possessed similar abilities."

"You're saying she's a super-powered Zomoki creature?"

"No, nothing like that."

"Okay, because you had me worried that––"

"She is potentially far more powerful than a mere, average Zomoki."

"Potentially?" Laskar asked.

"Their kind was wildly varying in their degree of both power as well as their control of it. Once, a long, long time ago, those who were discovered were enslaved. Drained of their power. The remaining few were scattered to the stars, their bloodline thought lost forever. It was only a fluke that when I was but a young girl, I happened to meet an ancient being with those eyes. She took a liking to me and shared her story. I thought it was just a tale, but over my life, I have never seen another like her. Not until now."

"So, she's some super rare kind of magic user?" Laskar asked.

"Oh, the rarest," Arina replied, her excitement growing. "What can she do?"

"Eat. Sleep. Curse. Eat some more. Be annoying," Bud said.

"And stab things," Laskar added.

"Yeah. And stab things," Bud agreed.

"No magic?"

"Not really, no," Bud said. "Though she is a reader."

Arina's eyebrows furrowed slightly. "Most unusual. No other power of note, you say?"

"Just her ability to eat," Laskar joked. "Though Hap is giving her a run for her money."

"Hap?"

"A boy we're, uh, babysitting," Bud said. "And hey, where is he, anyway? I didn't see him when we got back, and he's always lurking around the kitchen."

Corann chuckled. "Hozark felt the boy needed some respite from the boredom of home life. He gave him some coin to go buy sweets. I am sure he will be there when we return."

"Yeah, with an open mouth and hungry belly, no doubt," Bud said.

"But for now, Arina, if you don't mind," Corann said. "Please, do tell us more of what you know about Henni's kind. This is most fascinating, indeed."

## CHAPTER FIFTY-SIX

If the commerce city of Makkus was a bit of a rough-and-tumble place, Corann's hometown was anything but, though no one who resided there ever wondered how it remained so tranquil and crime-free.

Had they, the answer would surely have surprised them.

Any thugs and hooligans were either summarily run out of town, leaving without so much as a word, or they simply went missing straightaway, though in such instances, the omnivorous Bundabist kept in pens on the outskirts might appear a bit better fed than usual.

It was in this zone of safety that Hozark had turned young Happizano free with a fistful of coin and a rather serious sweet tooth.

"You have been through a lot, young Jinnik, and you have trained hard regardless. I think you are more than deserving of a little reward for all you have endured," he said as he handed the boy a small pouch containing a modest amount of coins. "Go ahead. Head into the town center and get yourself a few treats."

A broad smile spread across Hap's face. "Really?"

"Yes, really."

"Thanks, Hozark!" he said before tearing off out of Corann's house with glee, running all the way to the marketplace.

He had been there several times, but always with Corann, Hozark, or Demelza when they picked up supplies for their stay. But this time he was on his own. The master of his own destiny, even if that destiny encompassed not much more than figuring out which sweets he wanted.

Pastry or candy? Or, perhaps, a little of both? There were so many options for the boy to choose from.

Hap looked in the little pouch and smiled. There definitely enough for at least a few goodies, and he would be sure to make very good use of the coin. Not far away, a pair of youths, not much older than himself, watched from a doorway as he walked between the stalls and made his purchases.

He was smaller than they were. Younger. Weaker. Vulnerable. Precisely the kind they were used to preying on. But as the boys were not actual criminals––at least, not yet––their youthful hijinks were allowed to pass by the watchful eyes of the town's invisible overseer. They operated in an unwitting state of grace. At least until they reached maturity.

Oblivious to the lurking bullies, Happizano made his way to the last vendor on his quest for goodies and acquired his final treat. He handed over the coin and received a large roll with a dusting of flavorful spice on top. With an enormous grin, he took a big bite and headed back the way he came.

He turned down a little alleyway––a shortcut he knew from his outings with Corann––but just around the bend a pair of hands grabbed him and pushed him up against the wall. It was a horribly familiar sensation.

"Whatcha got there?" the smaller of the boys asked while his larger companion held Hap immobile.

"Nothing. Just a couple of sweets, is all," Hap replied.

"Give 'em here," the boy ordered.

"No."

"Did you just say no?"

"Yeah," Hap said, assessing the two boys. "I'll tell you what. I won't give you *all* of my snacks, but I will share them with you if you let go of me. I'm Hap, by the way."

"I don't care what you're called. Just hand 'em over."

"Like I said. No," Hap said, a cooling look in his eyes.

"Take them," the smaller boy instructed his larger friend.

The bigger boy swiped at the bag, but Hap was too quick, moving it out of his reach in a flash.

"Hey, gimme that!"

"Nope."

A little game of cat and mouse ensued. It would almost have been comical, the larger boy futilely grabbing the empty air where his target had just been, but the smaller youth stepped in and delivered a quick punch to Happizano's lip.

"Ow!"

"Now, hand 'em over or I'll beat the ever-loving hell out of you," the boy snarled.

Happizano touched the trickling blood on his lip with his tongue, and in that instant, something snapped within him.

"Hand 'em over!"

Hap did no such thing. Rather, he carefully put the bag on the ground behind him, not once taking his eyes off of his attackers, then stood tall.

"Come and take them," he said, coolly.

"Oh, you're going to regret this. Get him!"

The two boys rushed him at once, but Happizano shifted his feet quickly, throwing punches as he moved, the force coming from his hips, just as he'd been taught. Though his fists were relatively small, the force with which he struck the larger boys was significant, and blood quickly welled from the larger of the two's nose.

"You broke my nose!" he shrieked. "You little shit, you broke my nose!"

The smaller of the pair used the brief distraction to kick Hap in the leg. It didn't cause any real damage, but it did cause it to spasm, allowing his attacker enough of a gap to get his hands on him.

He quickly pulled Hap into a modified headlock, holding him tight while his bloody-nosed friend began pummeling him without mercy. Hap took several substantial blows, but rather than going fetal and popping in a thumb, he reacted with a violence he didn't know he possessed.

Hap stomped on the smaller boy's foot, loosening his grip as he cried out in pain. But he didn't stop there. He followed up with a quick kick to the groin, then punched the other, larger attacker in the solar plexus, driving the wind out of him.

Both of the boys were surprised by the fight in this one, but they weren't about to swallow their pride and admit defeat at the hands of some little kid. They came at him harder than ever, the smaller one grabbing a piece of broken debris from a small refuse pile and striking Hap with it.

The blow only glanced off his shoulder, but had it made contact with his head, it would have done severe damage. Hap kicked out hard, shattering the larger boy's knee, then punched him hard in the throat, leaving him gasping for air.

The smaller, more aggressive of the two swung the improvised weapon again, but Hap moved aside, tripping him as he passed, shoving him into the wall. The boy spun to attack again just as Hap reached under his tunic and pulled a small dagger. There was no play in his eyes as he dove forward, the point of the blade poised to do deadly damage.

"That will be enough," a familiar voice said out of thin air, an invisible hand stopping the boy's fatal attack. "You two. Become scarce, lest I allow the boy to finish what you started," the voice said.

The two youths paled in terror and ran as fast as they could, given their injuries.

"I could have handled them myself," Hap said as Hozark shed his shimmer cloak.

"I am aware, young Jinnik," he replied. "I bore witness to your trial by combat, and you asserted yourself well, and with not only great skill, but also cunning and wisdom."

Hap looked at the knife in his hand and realized what he had been about to do. Not in training, with a false blade, but for real. He quickly sheathed the weapon, ears red with shame.

"I'm sorry, Hozark."

"There is no need to apologize. You not only overcame two larger, stronger opponents, but you showed great restraint before hostilities began."

"I was going to kill him."

"Perhaps. But first you offered to share your bounty with them. A compromise that might well have defused any tension, and perhaps even have made you a pair of new allies had things gone differently. No, there is no need to apologize. You did well. Better than that, in fact. You showed the poise and wisdom of a man twice your age."

Hap blushed slightly from the compliment. He knew Hozark did not throw around words of praise lightly.

"Corann's gonna be pissed," Hap said, feeling the discoloring bruises already forming on his face and shoulder.

"There is no need to concern her with this," Hozark said, donning a small konus from his pocket and casting a series of healing spells.

It was a fair expenditure of magic, fixing his wounds so quickly, but Hozark felt the boy deserved it. Of course, he would tell Corann what had happened. Word would get to her regardless, and it would be far better if she heard it from the mouth of a Ghalian. But the others would be kept in the dark. Happizano did not need the additional worry of fearing Corann's displeasure on his plate.

"There, that's better," the master assassin said. "Now, what do you say we head back?"

"Okay," Hap replied as he picked up his small sack of treats, though he'd quite lost the appetite for them.

"And once we've settled back in, I think a little training session might be in order. If you feel up to it, that is," Hozark added.

Happizano smiled, his mood shifting once more.

"Sounds great," the boy said.

"Excellent. Then, shall we?" the deadliest man on the planet asked.

The two walked the short distance back to Corann's at a relaxed pace, Hap's head held high. And to any watching him since his arrival, it might even have seemed as if the boy had grown an inch or two.

## CHAPTER FIFTY-SEVEN

"There you are," Corann said when Hozark and his young ward stepped into her steaming-warm kitchen. She and Demelza were cleaning up from another baking session. "Everything is all right, I hope?"

"Yes, Corann. Happizano was just out stretching his legs for a bit. He appears to have been quite successful in his acquisition of treats in the marketplace."

Hap held up his bag. "I picked up a whole bunch of things," he said.

Corann had immediately spotted the scuffs on his clothing and the telltale speckling of blood invisible to all but the most highly trained eyes, as had Demelza, but neither said a word. Hozark would fill them in later, but for now, the boy seemed fine. Corann shifted her attention to his overloaded bag.

"You seem to have learned the fine art of haggling to make your coin stretch," the older woman said, noting the quantity of sweets he had acquired. "I just hope you will still have enough of an appetite for some hot biscuits. I put a batch in the oven just before you returned."

"Oh, yeah!" Hap said.

Of course he would have room. The boy was like Henni in that regard. Always eating, or ready to eat. He was growing rapidly, after all, and a growing boy needs nourishment.

"Why don't you go see what the others are doing? Corann, Demelza, and I have a few things to discuss."

"Okay," the boy said, then trotted off to see what Henni and the gang were up to.

"Rough time?" Corann asked when the kitchen was finally empty.

"Nothing he could not handle. Just a few boys being delinquents. But Happizano's training seems to have taken hold better than we had imagined. He bested two larger opponents with relative ease."

"He does have his father's gifts," Demelza noted.

"Yes, but he did so without any of his magic."

"Likely a good thing, seeing as he lacks control," Corann mused.

"Indeed. Though I did have to prevent him from driving his knife into the heart of one of the boys."

"Oh?" Corann asked.

"Yes. He has the instincts and reflexes. But I would spare him that path. At least until he is older. If his father wishes to take him down it, *then* I will gladly instruct the boy in the basics."

"You seem to have taken a shine to him, Hozark. I thought you were not fond of children."

"I am not. However, this one is a good boy, for the most part, and he has great potential."

"Indeed, he does."

"But what of your efforts? Something is obviously afoot," Hozark said.

"Yes, and more than one. Impressive things at that."

"News of Maktan?" he asked.

"Yes. But also surprising new facts about your friend. Such power."

"Most astonishing," Demelza added. "And right under our noses all this time. Tell him, Corann."

"Laskar?"

"No," Corann said. "Henni. The girl is descended from a rare race, Hozark. A powerful race. One with capabilities that might even have matched those of the Old Ones."

Hozark blanched, which for an already pale man was saying something. "You are saying that our violent little friend could be more powerful than a fully mature Zomoki?"

"Potentially, yes. Though the girl has no idea of her own abilities, let alone how to harness them."

"Henni, a power user. Admittedly, it is somewhat unsettling," Hozark mused. "She is rather impulsive for one possessing power of that magnitude."

"I would tend to agree," Corann said. "In any case, I trust my source. Arina is a dear friend of mine, and when she said that she came across one of her kind many years ago––completely unprompted, I might add––I sensed no misdirection on her part."

"So, Henni is a power user," Hozark marveled. "We shall have to address that issue at some point. Help her learn to harness and direct her power."

Corann nodded. "I agree. But that is not all on our plate at the moment. Something of great serendipity has occurred. The Wampeh Ghalian have received a contract on Visla Maktan."

Hozark was surprised by that bit of news. If there was a new contract, it would have had to have been made incredibly recently for word to only now have reached Corann.

"Are we confident this is not another trap?" Demelza asked.

"It was made through several intermediaries, but that in and of itself is not terribly unusual for individuals keeping their hands clean," Corann noted.

"Especially when it involves one of the Council of Twenty,"

Hozark noted. "Taking out a contract on one of the Twenty is not the sort of thing you wish people to know about."

"Most importantly, all of those involved have checked out," Corann noted. "And this is a very well-paying contract."

Hozark and Demelza were both a bit surprised that despite all of his care to remain behind the scenes, Visla Zinna Maktan had somehow managed to piss off the wrong people. Whatever he had done, it had set some very powerful individuals against him indeed. More than just the usual back-stabbing machinations within the Council.

"Of course, there is more to the story," Corann continued. "In his quest for additional power, Visla Maktan has stepped over the line on this occasion. Enough so that we Ghalian would have done this job for free, had the contract not been taken out."

Hozark and Demelza's interest piqued.

"What did he do, Corann? I've heard nothing from our spy network," Hozark said.

"That is because in seeking out a weapon maker, he carried out a particular treachery in a distant place. One very few dare venture. But those who do, have taken this offense *very* personally."

"Where was it?" Demelza asked. "What could possibly have elicited this response?"

Corann hesitated, and they could both see it was not for effect. "I am sorry to be the one to inform you both, but the entire world of Xymotz has been destroyed. Crushed when its magical protections were broken down. It seems Maktan was attempting to harness the gifts of a certain resident who had taken refuge there, and things went a bit sideways on them all. The result was the complete collapse of the protections leading to and maintaining the habitable areas within the gas giant itself."

Demelza felt her stomach flip. And even Hozark's

unflappable demeanor betrayed him as the vein in his temple began thundering with rage.

"The *entire* planet?" Demelza asked. "All of the people? They're——"

"Yes. I am afraid *all* inhabitants perished in the attack."

"So Master Orkut? He is——"

"Dead. Yes. I am sorry, Demelza, but he will not be fashioning a blade for you after all."

Hozark had convinced the master swordsmith to craft him one of the finest vespus blades ever created not too long ago, and Demelza had begun working alongside Hozark as a direct result of Orkut's curious machinations.

And now the man who had set them on this path was gone. Killed by the man who had been a constant thorn in their side.

"He must be eliminated," Hozark said in a frighteningly quiet voice. "Sooner than later. What do we know, Corann?"

"He is both easy, yet hard to trace. But our spies believe they have reliable intel on a vessel linked to Maktan. A secret one, kept from all but a handful's knowledge."

"And we know about it how?" Demelza asked.

Corann smiled coolly. "The vessel's path and coordinate details came up under some particularly *enhanced* questioning of the crew of the one mercenary craft we could definitively confirm was party to the destruction of Xymotz. I can say with some degree of certainty, they were not lying."

"Then I shall handle this without delay," Hozark said. "I leave at once."

"I'm coming with you," Demelza said.

"There is no need. You know that we normally——"

"This is *personal*," she said.

Hozark could see the rage in her eyes matched his own. Orkut meant as much to her as he had to Hozark. More, in fact.

"Very well. We shall inform the others then leave at once."

## CHAPTER FIFTY-EIGHT

The Drookonuses aboard Hozark and Demelza's shimmer ships were both growing hot from the use they were being subjected to as the pair of assassins raced across the galaxy, linking jumps far longer and far more frequently than would otherwise be prudent.

But they had but a small window of opportunity, and they had to strike before it closed. Visla Zinna Maktan had killed the great swordsmith Orkut, and he would pay. Sure, Maktan had killed countless others at the same time, but this was different.

Orkut's loss was *personal*. And Wampeh Ghalian never took things personally. It was a rare instance, indeed, that saw them react with anything like this sort of emotion. The others understood as soon as they heard what had happened, of course, and wished them the best of luck on their quest.

Bud and Laskar had simply nodded their farewell, both men harboring no illusions that they would be asked along on this particular mission. The contract would be carried out by the Ghalian duo alone, and it would be done with extreme prejudice.

"Kick his ass," Henni said when she heard what the

mysterious visla had done to an entire planet. "And make it hurt."

"We are professionals, Henni," Hozark replied. But then he paused a moment. "But if it should happen to hurt in the process, so be it."

"Come back soon," Happizano said.

"Of course, young Jinnik. Now, you watch out for the others while we are gone, okay?"

"I will."

"Good. We shall return as soon as we are able."

Hozark and Demelza then departed without another word, both of their shimmer ships undocking from Bud's mothership, then silently lifting off into the sky.

As soon as they cleared the atmosphere, they began their series of long jumps. In short order, Visla Maktan would pay the ultimate price for what he had done.

Hozark gave the go signal to Demelza as soon as they arrived in the system their intel had directed them to.

Rather than risk a potentially tapped skree conversation, he simply spun his craft one time. It was easy enough in space, and as there was no up or down, a simple spin in whichever direction would serve the purpose just fine.

Demelza immediately engaged her shimmer cloak and began the cautious approach on the area the target ship would be orbiting. Normally, a talented and powerful visla like Maktan would be able to sense their cloaked craft, but the sheer volume of traffic in the sky, and the amount of magic propelling it all, would likely provide them with adequate background noise to make a stealthy approach.

It was a relatively busy world down below, with a wide variety of vessels coming, going, and circling the planet. But they were looking for one in particular. It would take a bit of doing, but they at least had an idea where to start. The craft they were seeking would be in a particular quadrant at a particular height as it drifted above the globe.

"That can't be right," Hozark said to himself as he zeroed in on the craft in question. He checked the coordinates again. This was the right ship––it had to be.

He knew that at that same time, Demelza was undoubtedly thinking the same thing as she approached the unusually small craft from the other side.

The thing was, it was clearly a Council ship, though of a model neither was terribly familiar with. It appeared to be a mid-sized cargo craft, but it had been modified with a new external shell and sported an array of casting armaments the likes of which neither assassin had ever seen.

It was also far too small for a visla of Zinna Maktan's rank. But if he was skulking around in secret, keeping his movements hidden, this was precisely the type of vessel no one would dream of finding him utilizing.

The whole thing was confusing and unusual, but rolling with the unexpected was just part of the job, and the Wampeh Ghalian were well known for their ability to adapt and overcome just about any obstacle in their way. This was no different.

As they had planned, Hozark made his approach from the rear of the craft, skimming the hull as he moved to the forward starboard flank. Demelza performed a similar maneuver, but she soft-docked on the port side. Both would make a rapid ingress and seal the breaches behind them, leaving a pair of visual cloaks over the rifts, making the hull seem undamaged to all but the closest inspection.

By the time anyone might think to do such a thing, the visla should be long dead.

Hozark pierced the hull and dropped into the corridor without a sound, his vespus blade, fully charged with as much magic as he'd been able to come by since its last use, was strapped to his back, and all manner of other weapons were secreted on his person. His clothing was that of a Council officer. An additional diversion that could buy him valuable seconds when the confusion and bloodshed began.

Any fight with a visla would be deadly dangerous, and there was always the possibility Hozark would be the one to fall on this day. But one could always stack the deck in one's favor as much as possible, and that was precisely what the assassin had done.

Demelza, likewise, made her entry to the opposite side of the ship, as well armed as he was. She quickly disguised her entry point and drew her sword and dagger as she rushed to meet up with her deadly partner.

At a middle crossing of corridors, the two joined forces.

"This is strange. I did not encounter any resistance upon my entry, nor since I have been aboard," Demelza said.

"Nor I," Hozark replied.

"I was expecting a fierce fight."

"Indeed. Or at least a bit of resistance. For a visla's ship, the security arrangements are most unusual."

"Could it be the visla has them all with him in the command center?" Demelza wondered.

"We shall find out soon enough," Hozark said, shifting his focus to the long corridor ahead of them. "Come. We have work to do. Be at the ready."

The two of them moved quickly to the command center entryway and paused. It was silent, and they had still not encountered a single soul. Hozark nodded once, and they quietly slipped through the doorway, utilizing a cloaking spell to briefly maintain the image of a closed door.

It wasn't much, a cheap parlor trick, really, but it was often enough to buy the needed seconds to land a killing stroke. But as they rushed the command center, senses on high alert, one thing was abundantly clear.

There was no power user here. In fact, it seemed there was no power user aboard at all.

The crew of four seemed utterly shocked at the sudden appearance of a pair of pale, armed killers in their midst. None of the crew were armed. They didn't even have weapons anywhere within arm's reach. It was a joke of a defense, if that.

"Who are you? How did you get aboard my ship?" the captain blurted, his pale blue skin going several shades lighter with shock. His eyes quickly scanned the intruder and registered the Council uniform. "Uh, apologies, sir. But who are you?"

Hozark immediately sheathed his sword and adopted quite the opposite of the killing visage he had put in place when they stormed the ship. Now, it was one of a stern but friendly ally.

"We were sent to check on the status of your craft. You fell silent, and the concern was that perhaps you had been boarded by pirates."

"Pirates? But we're a Council ship. Pirates know better than to--"

"You would be surprised," Hozark cut the man off. "But where is the rest of your crew? Our preliminary security check showed no one else."

"We're it," the captain replied. "Just the four of us. Honestly, I still don't know why they even sent us out here."

"The visla works in unusual ways," Hozark said. "But tell me, where is Maktan now?"

"Maktan? We were deployed from Visla Ravik's fleet," the man replied. "Uh, who was it you said you were again?"

"Council security detail. Ravik and Maktan are currently working together, though you are *not* to mention that to anyone outside of this chamber, is that clear?"

"Uh, yes, sir."

"Good. Now, I must return to make my report. You carry on,

but tell no one of our visit. You have done well, and it will be recorded in my assessment, Captain."

Hozark did not wait for a reply but turned and strode out of the chamber. Demelza gave a curt nod and followed.

"This was never Maktan's ship," Hozark said when they were out of earshot.

"No," Demelza replied. "Someone was feeding our people misinformation."

"Yes. Someone who knew we would be with Corann," Hozark said, increasing his pace. "This whole contract was merely a decoy meant to draw us away. And it succeeded."

"That means the others are in danger."

"It does. They are coming for our friends," Hozark said, breaking into a run for his ship. "We must get back at once."

# CHAPTER FIFTY-NINE

The attack on Corann's quiet little world came out of the blue. Or out of the black, to be more accurate, as the attackers arrived from space in a rapid series of jumps.

No sooner had the three large Council base ships popped into a low orbit than they disgorged several assault landing craft that immediately began making their rapid descent to the surface.

No one on the surface was concerned at first. There was no reason to be. This was an uncontested and rather unremarkable planet, after all. And watching their approach, it just seemed to be another group of ships coming down to trade or make a pit stop on their way to some other destination.

But soon enough the true nature of the craft became readily apparent.

"Protect Hap!" Bud called out to his friends as a pair of Council ships touched down in town perilously close to their host's home.

The pirate and his copilot armed themselves to the teeth, and Henni and Happizano likewise strapped on their blades.

Someone had come for the boy, but they were damned if they'd let him be taken without one hell of a fight.

Corann had already vanished the moment the first craft showed any signs of hostility. But she was not gone. Rather, she had shed her kindly older woman persona in the mere instant it took to arm herself with all manner of weapons, magical and conventional, before she took to the streets.

Before she stepped out, however, she affixed a strong disguise spell, hiding her identity from any of her neighbors who might happen to see the mysterious person slaying Council forces by the dozen. Seeing friendly old Corann covered in gore with a sanguine grin on her blood-dripping, long fangs might tarnish her image, after all.

But they weren't alone in raising the alarm. The rest of the citizens realized violence was coming their way soon enough, and a rag-tag group of armed locals as well as visitors to the planet began streaming into the streets to confront the threat.

"Shit! Another one just dropped down on the other side of those buildings!" Bud shouted in alarm. "They're going for my ship!"

Laskar drew his sword. "I'm on it. Stay here and protect the kid!" he said, then took off running as fast as he could.

Corann was already hard at work, mowing down approaching Council goons from the shadows. Unfortunately, the crazed nature of the melee did not lend itself to the use of a shimmer cloak. It would be too easy for a friendly to accidentally hit the strange figure fighting off the invaders.

Regardless, she did what she could as quickly as she was able, thinning the ranks to the best of her ability without inadvertently harming the locals with overly powerful magic.

Had she known this sort of thing would be happening, the deadly claithe held in the Ghalian vault would have been readied for the attack. As it stood, she was forced to rely on her more conventional skills, which were nevertheless myriad and unmatched.

"On your left!" Bud shouted out to Henni, the duo keeping Happizano as safe as they could between them.

Henni spun left and turned into a violent stabbing machine, peppering her assailant with dozens of direct hits from her daggers. Even had the man been wearing stronger armor, the enraged young woman's blades would have eventually found a weak spot at that rate.

He fell to the ground, and Henni spun back to face the others approaching, once again protecting their young friend with great violence of action. Far across the fray, a flash of blue struck down a pair of locals as they raced into the fight.

"Oh, shit," Bud said, blanching as he glanced over and realized exactly what that weapon was, and who was wielding it.

"What is it?" Henni asked as she yanked a dagger from a dead man's grip and hurled it at the nearest Council goon.

"That's a vespus blade," Bud said. "And only one other person I know of has one. It's Samara."

"Corann can take her," Henni said, for once glad of the woman's secret, violent past.

"Yeah, but it looked like they lured her toward that other landing site. I think she's too far away to sense her."

"Then fuck it," Henni growled. "*We'll* deal with her. Together."

Bud ducked as a woman flew through the air over his head and landed between the two of them.

"Protect Hap!" he started to yell, when the woman dropped dead on the ground.

Happizano bent and pulled his little knife from her forehead and returned to his state of alert readiness. Bud and Henni shared a quick glance and a smile. It seemed that Aargun's lessons had truly sunk in.

But they couldn't stop to admire the boy's progress. Samara

was dropping all who advanced on her while the emmik overseer beside her was both casting spells as well as directing more troops their way.

A wave of mercenaries crashed down on the defenders, and many from both sides fell in the onslaught.

Bud was fighting for his life, using every last one of his pirate tricks to stave off a killing blow against superior numbers. Henni was doing the same, but the sheer quantity of assailants was just too great.

"Aaah!" the violet-haired girl cried out as a sword sliced into her side.

Bud spun and saw the rapidly spreading stain on her shirt. Rage and concern flooded his body, and despite being outnumbered, he began tearing through the men blocking the path between him and Henni with gusto.

It was a ballet of death and dismemberment, Bud using a sword in each hand as well as casting from his konus as he moved. He would be utterly drained and exhausted tomorrow. If they survived, that is. But for the moment, he was a whirlwind of ferocity on a rampage.

As Henni clamped her hand over her wound and struggled to fight off her attackers, a strange crackling of magic flashed in her eyes. That power unique to her and her alone. But she could not control it. Hell, she didn't even know what it could do.

Struggling with the odd sensation, she caught a glimpse of Bud and the concern in his eyes. But then she had her hair snatched from behind, yanking her off her feet. Before she could react, a brutal stun spell followed immediately, slamming her to unconsciousness.

"Bring her!" the Council overseer instructed his men over his skree, safe in his vantage point beside Samara.

"No. Not the girl," Samara said as she slew another foolish native trying to stop them. "This was to be an assault to disable that troublesome smuggler's ship, nothing else."

The emmik laughed. "So far as you were told, perhaps. But I have my orders."

"I said *no*," Samara replied, her gaze icy. "We are not kidnappers. We are not *slavers*."

"We are today," the emmik said, returning her hard stare. "You know who issued those orders."

The angry tension hung crackling in the air between them a long moment, but Samara reluctantly relented, watching silently as the young violet-haired woman was rushed from the battlefield.

"Know your place, woman," the man said as he cast several violent spells, clearing the path for his mercenary goons carrying their captive.

A roar rose up from the streets behind them.

"It would seem we have more company," the emmik mused. "And they are between us and our ship. It would seem it is finally time for you to earn your keep, assassin. Get to work."

Samara sighed, then shifted her grip on her blade, ready to take on the next wave of defenders. For a great many of them, it would be the final, albeit heroic, thing they would ever do.

## CHAPTER SIXTY

The fighting in the streets was at a fever pitch not far from Corann's home, and the ground was slick with blood. Much of it had been spilled at the hands of the mysterious figure none of the locals recognized.

Disguised, Corann was in her element, mowing down scores of Council troops and their mercenary support goons. It had been such a long time since her early, bloody years, and she'd only performed precise, limited executions for longer than she cared to admit. But this? This felt like coming home in a way.

Abruptly, a signal went out to the skrees of the attackers, and as a unit, all seemed to begin falling back at once. But that was not so easy as it might have sounded. With the battle in full-tilt, simply turning and walking away was simply not an option. Especially as more reinforcements from neighboring towns began flooding into the streets to help their friends defend against the intruders.

Corann flowed through the crowd, careful to avoid the blows of not only the enemy, but also those of her own people who did not recognize her in her disguise. Her blades and spells made quick work of those foolish enough to cross her path, but she was attempting to do more than merely slaughter the enemy. She was looking for answers.

Someone had come to her world. Attacked her city. But now they were suddenly leaving, and without a prize in hand. It made no sense.

"The boy," she realized.

Happizano had already been taken by the Council once, and they had attempted to re-take him a second time. It seemed impossible, but somehow, they had tracked him down to her world and were trying to capture him once more. To force his father to do their dirty work. And, she feared, to steal his nascent power, if they could.

She spun on her heel and raced back toward her house, hoping the others had held strong.

Bud was furiously mowing his way through the retreating Council forces, keeping Hap close at his back as he charged ahead toward the men carrying Henni's unconscious form.

But the kidnappers had the advantage of not only numbers, but also the ease of passage granted by having the ranks of their fellow combatants part to let them pass while Bud had to fight his way through like a fish swimming upstream against a vicious current, his young ward close in his shadow.

"They're taking Henni!" Hap cried out as he wildly slashed at a passing Tslavar mercenary with his knife.

The man stumbled as the blade dug into his leg, allowing Bud a clear shot to finish the man with his sword. The boy and the pirate had fallen into an unlikely rhythm, working together as a single unit. Happizano, it seemed, had stepped up to the challenge and then some.

A roar echoed out across the clashing ranks as a cluster of what appeared to be more elite fighters charged from the invading mass right toward Bud and Hap. It seemed they *had* come for Hap as well. Or, at least, they saw an opportunity when it presented itself.

"Stay close," Bud said, steeling himself for a fight he knew he could not win.

He counted over a dozen armored men and women racing toward them. His options were limited, and there was simply no chance of escape. This was his last stand. And if it was to be, he was damn sure going to make one hell of a show of it.

Bud gritted his teeth and tightened his grip on his weapons while drawing upon his most violent spells. There wasn't much magic left in his konus, but it would be enough to take at least a few of the attackers with him.

A blast of violent magic ripped into the charging horde, tearing the outermost three to shreds while tossing the others aside as though they were rag dolls. Moments later, a pale duo raced through the survivors, ensuring that particular status was short-lived.

The glowing blue blade in Hozark's hand cleaved heads from necks and limbs from bodies with laughable ease as the master assassin unleashed hell on the woefully outmatched mercenary force.

Demelza, likewise, was making quick work of those in her immediate vicinity as she and Hozark provided their friends with a little breathing room.

"They've taken Henni!" Bud shouted out, pointing to where the unconscious girl was being carried into the waiting ship.

Hozark reacted at once, tearing into the hapless fighters who happened to be in his way as he ran toward the ship. Standing in the open hatch watching the violet-haired young woman being loaded aboard, stood a familiar face. One with her own glowing blue sword in hand.

Samara sensed his presence before she even saw him, looking out across the battlefield until she finally locked eyes with her former lover.

"Why am I not surprised?" Hozark growled as he charged forward with all of his might.

Samara, however, did not move to engage. The emmik directing the attack whispered in her ear then disappeared into the ship. The former Ghalian sheathed her vespus blade and cracked a tiny, pained smile, then turned and followed.

The hatch sealed behind them, and the ship lifted off into the air without further ado. The other forces were clearly retreating to their own ships as well. Whatever their intent, they were done. But why Henni?

Hozark rushed back to the others, the fight thinned to a trickle as the attackers now wanted nothing to do with anyone on this world. He saw Demelza crouching next to Happizano, checking him for injuries. She flashed a quick thumbs-up to him, then shifted her attentions to Bud.

He sported a fair share of small injuries, but nothing life threatening. But his eyes spoke of a deeper harm. Henni had been snatched from his protection, and that cut as deep as any blade ever could.

"They took Henni," Bud said, his voice quivering with angry emotion. "They took her, but they didn't even try for Hap. Why would they do that?"

"I do not know, my friend. But we will find out," Hozark replied.

A blood-streaked figure burst from the nearby side street and raced right toward them. Hap's eyes went wide, and he began to wind up to throw his knife, but Hozark stayed his hand.

"Steady, young Jinnik. She is with us."

Corann knelt by the boy and briefly revealed herself through her disguise spell. "Are you okay, Hap?" she asked before slipping her disguise back in place.

"Yeah, I guess. But how did you do that?"

"A Ghalian trick," she replied, once more looking nothing like herself.

"Can you teach me?"

The disguised face didn't show it, but Hozark could almost

sense the smile beneath it. "That might be able to be arranged," she replied, then turned to Hozark. "It was Maktan who orchestrated this."

"Are you certain?"

"I extracted that bit of information from a captured Council fighter."

"You did that in the heat of battle?" Bud asked incredulously.

"Let us say that I was quite motivated to find some answers. They attacked my world, Uzabud. And that cannot be allowed to pass."

"The contract on Maktan was a decoy, Corann. Meant to draw us away. I assume they thought you would accompany us as well, leaving this place entirely unprotected."

"Hey!"

"I am sorry, Bud. But you know what I mean."

"Yeah, I know."

Hozark turned back to Corann. "He knew of your homeworld, Corann. This goes beyond a mere contract now."

"I agree," she replied. "It is time to end him. *At once.*"

Across the rapidly emptying battlefield, Laskar came running at a rapid clip, his blade still drawn and blood smeared on his face. Blood that did not appear to be his own.

"The ship's okay," he gasped, winded. "They were trying to disable it. I managed to get close enough to engage the layered defensive shielding. But it still took a pounding. They sent some pretty serious casters." He noted his friend's off demeanor. "Hey, what's wrong?"

"They took Henni," Bud said.

"Henni? Why would they take Henni?"

"I don't know. But you said the ship is safe?"

"Yeah. It's a little beat-up, but it's intact."

"Then we need to go after her."

"We must remove the threat Maktan poses," Corann said.

"Who's that?" the copilot asked.

"Corann. She's in disguise," Bud replied.

"Really? That's Corann? Wow, impressive casting," he said, squinting at the camouflaged woman.

"Thank you," the Ghalian master replied. "Now, we must move, and quickly at that if we hope to strike Maktan while things are still in disarray."

"But Henni––" Bud said.

"We will retrieve her while we move to end this rogue visla's threat." She turned to the other assassins. "Notify the order. We shall strike at *all* of Maktan's likely locations at once. We do not know where he truly is, but if the fates favor us, one of us will succeed."

"But that might take some time to get in motion, and Henni needs us *now*," Bud said.

"Yes, we know," Hozark replied. "And that is why we shall pursue at once."

## CHAPTER SIXTY-ONE

Gearing up to chase after the kidnapped girl should have been a difficult endeavor. She could be anywhere, after all, but Corann immediately reached out to all of her eyes and ears on and around the planet and learned something surprising.

The surface assault ship that had taken Henni had ascended to join up with the larger craft that had remained in orbit during the assault. And it seemed that it had encountered more than a few angry locals in its flight, thoroughly delaying its docking and delaying their jump away.

It was interesting that the overseeing ships had opted to remain in orbit. Apparently, the big wigs had decided to steer clear of the actual fighting but wanted to be present for the show. And that little mistake could very well be their undoing.

"We haven't much time," Corann said as she joined the others rushing into Bud's mothership. "If the base ships retrieve their away craft, they will jump."

"How many?" the pilot asked as he fired up his Drookonus and prepped the ship for launch.

"Three larger ships," the Ghalian master replied.

"You get that, Hozark?" Bud asked over his open skree, not

caring one bit if anyone was listening in. An ass kicking was coming their way, and he had no problem at all telegraphing it.

"I did. We shall make our own way as soon as we reach our vessels. It should not take us more than a few minutes to launch," the assassin replied.

It was broadcast in the clear.

It was also a cleverly played misdirection.

Hozark and Demelza had actually already exited the atmosphere and were streaking toward the trio of Council craft. The Ghalian were using their shimmer cloaks to hide their approach, even though they tended to be less effective in space.

But with the chaos of the many smaller ships badgering the departing Council attack groups, it would provide them enough cover to draw close unseen. Or so they hoped.

Each would latch onto one of the larger vessels and make a silent ingress. It was a crapshoot which ship Henni would be taken to. They just had to hope their random selection was the right one.

Hozark dodged a few small craft that were in hot pursuit of one of the Council attack ships. They appeared to be pirate ships, though small in nature. But it was entirely possible they had been at the trading and commerce centers when this all broke out and decided to jump into the fray.

After all, where there was fighting, there was quite often profit to be had. But Hozark paid them no further mind. He had a far more specific task at hand, and it would require all of his attention.

He spun into a quick dive and approached the back of the Council ship nearest him, just as he knew Demelza would be doing on one of the other two base craft. He applied a trio of clamping spells strong enough to hold his ship in place should the larger craft unexpectedly jump while he was still aboard, then engaged the umbilical spell providing him an airway as he breached the hull.

He paused a moment, using a tiny rent in the hull to sense for crew or magical wards beneath him. None seemed to be present, so he cast the full force spell and parted the material enough to enter, then quickly sealed it back up and applied a camouflaging spell to the small breach.

He could have sealed it to the point where it would have been good as new, but when it was time for a rapid escape, the extra casting to force the repaired hull open again might wind up taking too much time. A weakened seam was far preferable in this instance.

Hozark paused and surveyed his entry point. It seemed he had boarded the ship within someone's quarters. Someone with rank, from what it appeared, given the lack of bunks. This was good. This meant the odds of being spotted were far less than had he dropped into the crew showers or some such.

Hozark examined the uniform in the closet and quickly cast a disguise spell to alter his own appearance to mimic that of the crew. He also darkened his pale-white skin to a copperish tone, further helping him blend in.

There would be a full complement of crew from a wide range of worlds and races aboard a ship of this nature. He just needed to be like them enough to walk freely. A ship this size, the odds were he could go unnoticed for some time before his presence was questioned.

As for his vespus blade, however, that would draw attention. A non-standard weapon was most unusual. But in a combat situation, the crew *would* be armed. He simply had to alter his carrying style from the secure spot on his back, to the less secure position on his hip.

A minor glamour he cast on the blade would make it seem like just another sword, barring close inspection. With that final piece in place, Hozark stepped out into the corridor and began making his way through the ship.

The layout was a bit unusual, but familiar nonetheless. It

was clearly a visla's craft, judging by the degree of opulence built into the normally utilitarian structure. That meant that Maktan had to be close. He smiled at his good fortune. If all went to plan, he could rescue Henni and kill Maktan in one run. Two birds with one stone, as it were.

But first, he had to find the girl, and that meant the landing hangar where the assault craft would be returning.

Hozark walked quickly––but not *too* quickly––in that direction, moving with the urgency of someone on a task. Someone following orders.

He had given himself a low-ranking uniform, thus making him seem more like a peon doing as he was told. He was all the less likely to be questioned that way, and better able to talk his way out of any queries if he was stopped.

"Hey, you can't go in there," a guard said as Hozark reached the hangar door.

"But I was told to deliver a message in person," the assassin said, even managing to make his voice waver in fear as he told the lie.

"That doesn't matter. No one passes but the visla."

"The visla is down here?" Hozark gasped.

"No, idiot. He's in command." The man's eyes narrowed slightly. "What unit are you wit––"

The blade dove into his heart before he could finish the question, and his body was stashed in the nearest compartment before his blood could even stain the deck. Hozark was not wasting time. Not today. Not with Henni's life on the line and Visla Maktan nearby.

He rapidly shifted his disguise, adopting the face of the man he had just killed. He then stepped through the door into the landing bay.

It was a fair-sized space, and one of the returning assault craft had already landed. A group from that ship had already disembarked at the far end of the hangar and were just hurrying from the craft into a corridor, but Hozark could not make out if Henni was among them.

The assassin shifted gears, moving along the perimeter at a fair clip as he strode toward the corridor the others had disappeared into. If Henni was with them, that was where he would find her.

It was iffy, but as of yet, no other ships had landed, so this was his best bet. He just hoped Demelza was having better luck.

## CHAPTER SIXTY-TWO

Stalking through one of the other Council base ships, Demelza was making quick time getting her bearings as she infiltrated the crew, hunting down those who took her violet-haired friend.

There had been a total of four assault craft on the surface, so far as she could tell, and two of them had just landed aboard the base ship she had made her way into. Odds were, Henni was in one of them. But which one?

As with the ship Hozark had boarded, the landing bay was a guarded area, but Demelza had less of a difficult time entering it than her associate had. And she had managed to avoid killing the guard at the entrance with a simple ploy. Namely, she started a small fire nearby when one of the swarming pirate craft bombarding the larger vessel landed a shot.

Normally, magical impacts wouldn't cause fires to break out. These ships were powered by magic, after all, and thus there was not fuel or electricity to spark a blaze. But strange things happened in battle, and it was precisely that fact she took advantage of.

"There's a fire! All hands are needed to get it under control!" she shouted to the guard from a fair distance down the hall.

The man hesitated, unsure if he should leave his post.

"Did you hear me? There's a fire. If it grows, the whole ship could be lost! Now, move your ass!"

Demelza spun and ran toward the blaze without waiting for a reply. She then tucked into a small room and waited. Sure enough, the man came thundering down the corridor moments later. If they were all dead, there would be no one to be upset at him for straying from his post. And if they survived, he might even get a commendation for his quick actions.

The assassin slipped out of her hidey-hole the moment he passed, silently running back to the doorway he had left unattended. She was through in an instant, quickly making her way to the landing deck. No one questioned her presence. If she was there, she obviously had the clearance to be.

The pair of assault ships that had returned to their base craft were more or less identical, and neither one had any overt means of discerning their contents. Henni could be in either, so it seemed Demelza would have to make a quick recon of each of them in turn. Hopefully before their precious cargo was unloaded and moved somewhere more secure within the ship.

She strode across the deck with the purpose of one who knew damn well she would not be questioned. A tactic that more often than not worked. Act as if you belong, and you will be treated as such.

The assassin then stepped aboard the nearest of the two ships and made her way to the interior of the craft. What she saw was not what one would call a well-oiled machine. In fact, it seemed that in the panic of their hasty retreat, the majority of those aboard had no idea what their orders were aside from, "Get back to the ships. We're leaving."

On top of that, with the swell of battle on the ground below——and the unexpected ferocity of the defenders——a good many Council troops and mercenaries alike had apparently boarded the ship nearest to them, whether it was the correct vessel or not.

The result was a hodgepodge of injured and dying lying about the craft in far greater numbers than one would normally expect. Obviously, this one had been closest to the fighting, given the numbers aboard. It was also not the ship Demelza was looking for.

That much was clear. Samara was not on this ship. Say what you might about her shifted loyalties, she would never have allowed a crew on a craft she was aboard to fall to such disarray. That meant it had to be the *other* ship.

Demelza pivoted to exit, but a gasping man pointed at her and let out a gurgling cry, and a few eyes turned their way. Her Ghalian-trained memory recognized him immediately as one of the many she had encountered on the battlefield below. Apparently, the blade through the chest had not finished him immediately, as she had believed.

It would have been considered sloppy under any other circumstances, but given the overwhelming numbers she and the others had been facing, even with the help of the inexperienced locals, a little leeway was to be expected.

"Oh, you poor man," she said aloud as she crouched beside the injured mercenary and quietly slid her dagger into his heart. "You hang on. We'll get you some help." She looked to the men and women around her as she stealthily sheathed her blade. "Can you help me? This man is gravely injured."

One of the Tslavar crew came to her side and squatted down beside her. A quick check of the man told him all he needed to know.

"Sorry, he's gone," the man said.

"Damn it. He was hanging on."

"But by a thread. We can't save 'em all," the Tslavar said, patting her shoulder, then heading back to tending other injured troops.

Demelza rose to her feet, but shifted her complexion slightly darker before she did. A tiny extra bit of disguise before she continued on her way. And it was a good thing, for as she walked, she recognized several others she had encountered in combat.

And she dealt with them all in a similar manner, though she forewent calling others for help any more. She merely ended them all with stealth, finishing her original work in this new setting.

It may have seemed cold to some, but for a Ghalian, it was just part of the job. And more than that, in circumstances like these, it meant there would be less of them coming back to the fight for her and her friends to deal with later.

No one seemed to notice the increased number who succumbed to their injuries around the time the rather unremarkable woman had walked through their ship. Given the number of wounded, a few extra dying wasn't surprising at all.

The whole affair had only slowed Demelza by a few minutes, and she was clear of the craft in no time. She stood tall, her back military-rigid, and strode to the other ship and made her way aboard. As before, her confidence parted those before her easily, and she gained access to the deepest reaches of the craft.

It was far less of a chaotic mess than the other had been. This vessel was clearly not only one that had been a bit farther from the hottest spot of the battle, but it was also commanded by more efficient leadership.

That said, she quickly discerned that Henni was *not* on this ship either. It was both disconcerting, as well as a great disappointment.

"Say, there's a tall, pale woman I've seen around. Not part of the regular crew. Any idea where she is?" Demelza asked one of the logistics crew who was tallying up the resources used and lives lost in this little endeavor.

"The Wampeh?" the woman replied. "Yeah, I've seen her. But

she's been flying with the visla. And I think he landed on Captain Gorlik's ship."

"Ah, gotcha. I was wondering what she had to do with all of this mess. Seemed an unusual sort to be hanging out on the battlefield."

"Who knows what's up with her? I just know she's pretty much always around the visla these days."

"Odd, but I guess these are odd times," Demelza said.

"They are at that. All the way out here for a snatch and grab? I don't know why we didn't just send the Tslavars."

"Your guess is as good as mine. Well, good luck with all of this mess," Demelza said, gesturing to the myriad people and supplies the poor woman had to account for.

"Thanks. Be safe."

Demelza quickly made her way off of the assault ship and out of the landing bay. This was the wrong base ship, and there was simply no reason to stay a moment longer. She didn't know which ship Hozark had landed on, but *this* one was a bust.

She would reboard her shimmer ship and make a fast run to one of the other base ships as quickly as she could. Hopefully it would be the one with Henni aboard.

## CHAPTER SIXTY-THREE

"Master Hozark," Demelza said as she stumbled upon the disguised Ghalian.

"Demelza. I take it the base ship you landed on was non-productive?"

"It was. But I was told that Samara and the visla had flown to Captain Gorlik's ship."

"And that is this vessel," he replied. "I gleaned that much information from the crew I have interacted with. But still there is no sign of Henni, Samara, or the visla, for that matter."

"Good fortune, the latter," Demelza noted. "Visla Maktan is formidable, and his guard will be up due to this conflict."

"Yes, but aboard his own base ship, there is always a possibility he will make an error. He will not be expecting us to already be aboard."

"No, he will not."

"Nor will he be expecting Uzabud's friends to help."

"What friends?" Demelza asked.

A tiny grin spread across the Wampeh's face. "The pirates who were resupplying on the surface. They had associates in orbit, and all have agreed to consolidate forces to join the fight.

Where there is the promise of pillage, there are always those willing to take the risk."

"So, we have substantial numbers backing us."

"Yes. And they should be forcing their way aboard at any time now. And with that distraction, we will have a clear shot at the command chamber. If Maktan is truly distracted, then perhaps we will be able to end him here and now while they work on the visla's crew."

"But Samara––"

"Will go to fight them off, most likely. If not, well, we shall deal with her when that time comes."

A rumble shook the ship.

"There is a breach," Hozark said. "They have begun."

He and Demelza made their way toward the command center, but a surprising surge of armed crew came racing their way. They had a choice. Blend in with the crew and follow, or fight through all of them and lose the element of surprise.

"You two! With us. We're being boarded!"

Hozark ran the numbers. There were simply too many for this to go remotely in their favor. Not in the narrow confines of the corridor. He nodded once, then he and Demelza joined the group racing toward the invading pirates.

"Where's the visla?" Hozark asked as they spilled into the landing bay and saw the scale of the attack.

There were pirates everywhere, it seemed, and they were putting on a very impressive showing against the ship's defenders. Those who had been slowly taken from the assault landing craft to be triaged for healing were abruptly thrown back into the middle of a fight.

Most did not fare well. Not for long, anyway.

The others, along with the rest of the crew, who were not part of the landing team, were mounting a solid defense. But it seemed the pirates stood a very good chance of pushing through to the inner corridors. From there, it would be a compartment by compartment battle, and an ugly one at that.

"The visla was in command, last I saw," the man replied, then cast a stun spell.

Unlike most spacecraft, this base ship was somewhat unique in that the landing bay was both large enough, and magically shielded enough, to allow the use of magic without so great a risk of accidentally blasting the crew out into space.

It was still a possibility, of course, but the likelihood was far less with so much room to work with, and the thick layering of spells keeping the atmosphere inside while allowing ships to enter. Only a truly enormous bit of magic would pop that bubble.

The sort that a visla might cast, for instance.

A blast of magic tore through a group of pirates, shattering their combined shielding with ease.

"The visla has come to help!" one of the crew said with obvious relief.

Hozark spun, his hand on the grip of his vespus blade, ready to strike Visla Maktan before he realized his troops had been infiltrated. But what he saw was not what he expected.

"You *dare* attack *my* ship?" a voice boomed out from across the landing bay. A visla's voice. But they knew this voice. It was the voice of Visla Ravik.

Demelza glanced at Hozark. Both were using minimal magic in their disguises at the moment, so there was still a good chance he would not note their presence while he was entirely focused on the seemingly sole front of invaders. At least, not yet.

The two assassins were in a temporary bubble of grace as they had wisely refrained from engaging the ship's guards, thus not raising any alarms prior to the pirates' arrival. But now they were in the thick of it, and the *wrong* visla was here. And this one they had fought before.

He had escaped that encounter, but only when Corann had easily killed his ally, crushing him with a violent spell from her claithe. Using the incredibly dangerous weapon had nearly killed her in the process, but the show of magic greater than his own had caused the man to flee. And now, here he was, yet again.

The assassins realized they had made a classic blunder. They had assumed it was Visla *Maktan* directing the attack, and when they heard talk of the visla, they'd assumed it was *he* being referred to. But that was inconsequential at the moment. What *was* of importance was they were about to face one of the Twenty. Just not the one they had expected.

Encouraged by the presence of their leader, the men and women of the ship pressed their attack on the boarding pirates. But more ships were swarming the breach in the hull at the far end of the landing bay, and, so long as their magical conduit held, their pirate crews would storm through the breach to reinforce those already inside.

All knew that Visla Ravik could shatter the spell if he wished, but the vacuum of space would suck them all out in the process, likely so quickly even the visla himself wouldn't be able to stop his ship from tearing to bits. So it was going to have to be the old-fashioned way. And it would be ugly.

The hand-to-hand fighting was heavy as the landing bay filled with combatants, their swords and knives flashing in the magical illumination. Small spells were being cast, but all involved were so accustomed to avoiding the use of magic in shipborne conflicts that it required some effort to overcome that habit and begin casting again.

Outside, the other pirate ships were defending whoever's ship was sending their men through the breach, knowing the favor would be returned in kind when their turn arrived. It was a mutual assistance action, and one that brought disparate pirate factions together for this one, potentially *huge* score.

But none of them knew it was a visla's ship. At least, not until they got inside.

Visla Ravik strode into the fray, smashing aside all who dared stand against him. Aboard his ship, with just a small contingent of pirates to deal with? Why, this was almost fun for him. At least, it was until the sting of a vespus blade pierced his defenses and opened a small gash in his side.

Ravik jumped aside and powered up his defensive casting even harder. Had he not already been layering extra defenses on top of his usual array, Hozark's blow might have been a fatal one. But luck was with the visla this day, and he had escaped that fate.

Hozark released his hold on his disguise magic. There was no sense using up valuable power now. And in his true, pale form, he would be something of a distraction to the man, hopefully allowing Demelza a chance to step into place, using her disguise to gain proximity.

But Ravik had already heard this song. He knew this particular Wampeh Ghalian, one who quite unusually worked with others rather than alone. Immediately, he cast his sensing spells, unmasking Demelza in an instant.

"There you are," the visla growled, then cast a killing spell her way.

Demelza was ready, wearing fully charged konuses, as well as holding a large reserve of power taken from her most recent kills within. Even so, it required enormous effort to block the spell. Had she not been able to throw one of the visla's men in its path, the poor soul absorbing much of the spell, she might not have survived it.

Hozark did not wait even an instant, but was in motion the moment the visla cast, launching his own magical attacks from his konus and slaap, while moving through the mass of the visla's ranks, using them as living shields against a counter attack.

But this could only go on for so long before he would run out of power. However, with the visla being attacked by not one but *two* Wampeh Ghalian, the pirates found a shift in the tide, allowing them to begin making forward progress against the defenders once more.

In addition, the crew's resolve had shifted from utter confidence to trepidatious uncertainty. The visla was being attacked, and he was actually challenged by it. One of the Council of Twenty, under siege on his own base ship? It was unheard of. And that caused a near panic among the crew.

They still fought, of course. To do otherwise would be certain death at their leader's hands. But this was something the likes of them had never expected to see.

Ravik, for his part, had adapted to the dual attack and was making a good show against the unusual situation. He cast back and forth, attempting to stun or stagger one of the assassins long enough for him to deliver a crushing blow to the other. And while they were rapidly draining their magical devices and what power they had previously stolen for this conflict, *he* was ever-regenerating his own power.

And Visla Ravik was *strong*.

Hozark was the first to take a significant blow, a killing spell--absorbed by a hapless crewmember--followed immediately by a stun spell. The Wampeh managed to deflect much of it, but enough caught him to send him flying into the wall, dazed and hurt.

Demelza was running low on magic, but Hozark needed time to gather his wits. If not, he would be a sitting duck. She charged Visla Ravik, letting out a war cry as she did.

Of course, as an assassin, everything she did was for a reason, and this was no exception. The normally silent killer had effectively given herself a clear shot as her bellow startled those around her out of the way. Unfortunately, it also gave the visla a clear shot at her as well.

Her spell was cast first, though, and it made partial contact before Ravik's own defensive spells could diffuse it. But his follow-up volley was fierce, and the impact of the magic took the woman off her feet.

Both assassins were down, the man was clearly still groggy, while the woman was quickly attempting to scramble to her feet. Ravik, though temporarily staggered, was, however, more than ready to deliver a killing blow. He cast his deadly spell, directing it at the more immediate threat. The woman already back on her feet.

His magic flew true, and he could tell his target did not possess the power to defend against it. Demelza was as good as dead.

The spell shattered against a wall of magic. *Strong* magic, followed by a simultaneous burst of blistering intensity that tore through his defensive spells. He spun and recognized the caster immediately. The older woman who had slain his ally with her claithe.

Ravik felt his body flush with adrenaline, a shock of fear rushing through him that was unfamiliar. Unfamiliar but for the previous time he had encountered this deadly woman.

Corann smiled at him, the pirates she had arrived with fanning out around her and engaging the defenders in a new wave of magic and metal.

"Nice to see you again," she said with her warmest smile.

Ravik knew he couldn't defeat her. Not with her claithe. She had already demonstrated the power of the weapon once before. But something about her seemed different this time. He just couldn't quite place what it was.

Corann just stood there, her gaze locked with his, a little smile on her lips. But she wasn't using the claithe on him. That was when he realized what was different.

He chided himself for missing it after her first attack. All of that power had been *hers*. She possessed enormous magic within her, yes, and she wore a potent konus. But her claithe was nowhere to be seen.

It made sense. A weapon of that type would not just be hanging around, ready to be used at a moment's notice. She was strong, but far less prepared than he had initially feared.

A smile spread across his face. He had felt her magic, and though it would be a difficult fight, he knew he was stronger than she was. Visla Ravik summoned power from deep within and aimed his fiercest killing spell at her.

The startling electric shock of hot-yet-cold fangs sinking into his neck made him weak at the knees. Moments later, he was on the ground, unable to stand, let alone fight. Weakening rapidly, he saw the battlefield around him with great clarity. The older woman, the younger one. And the realization that the wounded man had not been nearly as harmed as he had first thought.

He had fallen into a trap, though a rather hastily constructed one. But the man who would be his end had fooled him, Ravik realized. And now, the visla's remaining power would become his.

## CHAPTER SIXTY-FOUR

"Corann, you made it to the same ship as us," Demelza said.

"Yes. Uzabud and Laskar gave me a ride up before rejoining the fight, and just in time to see you departing the other base ship."

"I was shimmer cloaked."

"Yes, but you do not get to my age without learning a few tricks," the older woman replied. "And we all know shimmers are notoriously imperfect in space. I saw you head toward this vessel and thought you might use the assistance."

"And you were right," Hozark said, joining them. "Thank you, sister. You arrived at the most opportune of moments."

"Fortunately, Visla Ravik remembered our last encounter. It took him quite off guard."

"Yes, he did seem to panic when you first appeared," Demelza said. "And thank you for that. I did not possess enough power to defend against his attack. But you used so much of your own in the process."

"Not to worry. With the visla dead, I am not nearly so concerned about power users who may remain," Corann said.

"Now, the fight is not over. We must take the command center before this ship jumps."

"To command!" Hozark shouted out, urging the pirates to follow.

The defending crew in the landing bay had just seen the man not only kill their visla, but drain him of blood as well. That meant he could only be one thing.

"A Ghalian!" someone shrieked.

"The visla is dead!" cried another.

The outburst set off a wave of panic, and while many stood their ground and fought, the greater majority seemed to lose confidence, and a good many turned and fled.

Hozark did not hesitate to seize the advantage and took off running down the corridor, his glowing blue vespus blade in hand, parting the sea of defenders, and often, their heads from their necks.

It seemed word of the nature of this particular attacker had spread quickly, and people were scrambling over one another to get out of his way. No one wanted a piece of the deadly Wampeh Ghalian who had killed their visla. If he was capable of that, who knew what more he might be able to do.

The last stand of guards outside of the command chamber, however, were strong of heart and steady of will, standing ready to fight whoever came their way. Even a Wampeh Ghalian.

What they hadn't expected was three of them.

The sight of the pale trio made even the stoutest of warrior's bowels loosen just a little. This was certain death they were staring down. But they had their duty, and if they failed, the visla would strike them down just as certainly as the Ghalian would.

"Out of the way," Hozark said. "You have this one opportunity."

His offer was met with a volley of small spells, but nothing of consequence. For one, they were within the narrow confines of a corridor, and in this setting, the use of magic was all but verboten. For another, Hozark was now sporting a full load of stolen visla magic. Shielding himself and his companions was child's play.

"Very well," he said, then strode into the fight.

The visla's top guards were competent fighters, he had to give them that. But they soon fell just as readily as any other men and women would. The last few finally felt their courage leave them and turned and raced into the command center itself.

Hozark, Demelza, and Corann followed directly behind them, a small throng of pirates close on their heels, finishing off the wounded and any who might have thoughts about striking from behind once they'd passed.

"You," Samara said, looking up from a display showing the battle outside of the craft. "Why am I not surprised?"

"That is my line, Sam," Hozark said, holding his vespus blade at the ready, his power standing by to counter whatever trick she might throw at him.

The command center crew was already scrambling toward the escape hatches on the far end of the chamber. They were for emergency egress only, but given that there were now *four* Wampeh Ghalian in the room, if you counted the visla's personal aide, this seemed like as much an emergency as one was likely to get.

If any had any doubts, the pirates streaming in behind them solidified that opinion immediately. That, and word that Visla Ravik had been slain, sent every man and woman for themselves.

"Why are you doing this, Samara? The Council? And kidnapping innocents? This is not like you."

"Let it go, Hozark."

"No, I will not," he said, moving slowly closer to her.

"Stop right there!" she bellowed, freezing everyone in their steps. "I have placed a ward. One more step and it blows a hole in this ship."

"Taking us all with it."

"Precisely."

"That seems a rather drastic way to avoid this conversation," Hozark said, a faint grin growing on his lips in spite of himself.

Samara, for all of her faults, including working with the Council of Twenty, was still an impressive woman. And one he had considered his closest friend for a very long time. It was something he had forgotten how much he missed. But then, a Ghalian never admitted such things, let alone showed them to others.

"Hello, Corann," Samara said as she stepped toward an escape hatch. She turned her attention to Demelza. "Nice to see you again, little one. Perhaps we shall cross blades again sometime. I would very much like to see what more you have learned from Master Orkut."

"Master Orkut is dead," Demelza said. "Or did you not hear that your beloved Maktan killed him?"

Samara faltered. "Dead?"

Her reaction was real. Hozark knew her well enough to be certain. "I believe for all of her apparent faults, Samara had nothing to do with that."

"I would never," she said. "I am sorry for the loss, truly."

"Then why all of this, Samara?" Corann asked. "It is not in your nature to betray your oath. Your loyalty."

Samara did not answer. Only the slightest of shadow falling across her countenance betrayed the sting of those words.

"Be seeing you," she said, but nothing more. Then she stepped through the hatch and was gone.

"The ship is yours," Hozark said to the pirates, all of whom had frozen in place at the mention of Samara's deadly self-destruct spell.

"But she said there's a ward," one of the pirates said.

"Oh, there is. *Was*, I should say. But it was only a relatively minor stunning spell, and I have long since disabled it."

"So, the self-destruct?"

"A lie."

"Then why didn't you take her?"

Hozark turned to the man. "I have my reasons. Now, gather your men and position them in their stations. You have just commandeered a Council base ship and all it contains. I would suggest you make the most of your exceptional bounty."

"And what are you going to do?"

"We are going to find our friend."

# CHAPTER SIXTY-FIVE

The trio of Wampeh split up and searched the visla's commandeered base ship from end to end, yet, to their dismay, there was absolutely no sign of Henni aboard. Even the few crewmembers who had not managed to escape had not seen a trace of her.

It seemed incredibly unlikely, but Henni apparently had never been aboard the base ship at all. Not even with Visla Ravik's assault ship having landed there and the visla himself taking control of his craft.

"This is disconcerting," Demelza said when the three Wampeh regrouped. "If she is not aboard this ship, then she would have been transferred mid-flight to one of the others. And not aboard a regular landing craft, such as we saw on the surface."

"I agree," Corann said. "This shows an anticipation of our actions, and a concerted effort to misdirect."

"Meaning Henni is almost certainly aboard the one base ship we did not manage to board," Hozark noted. "We must make an attempt on that vessel at once."

"You must go without me," Corann said. "With Ravik dead,

and Samara fleeing, I am of more use on the surface than here. And you now possess much of Ravik's power, Hozark," she said, stripping off her konus and slaap and handing the charged devices to him. "Take these and bolster your power. Should it come down to it, you will need them."

Hozark nodded and slipped them into his pockets, ready for deployment should the need arise.

"But what will you do, Master Corann?" Demelza asked. "The fighting is in space now, and returning to the surface will be somewhat daunting."

"I shall make do. I am sure our new pirate friends will give me a lift."

"Nonsense. Take my shimmer ship," Demelza offered. "I shall travel with Master Hozark to the other base ship. You should fly under cloak so none will see your return," she noted.

Corann only hesitated a moment. "A sound suggestion, and a kind offer. Thank you, Demelza. I shall take you up on that."

Hozark did not waste a moment. There simply wasn't one to spare.

"Demelza, this way," he said as he took off toward his own cloaked ship.

Corann headed to command before she would make her descent.

They had stormed two of the Council base ships, clearing one of the possibility of containing their friend, while actually capturing the other. That left but one option. And if Henni was already aboard the third craft, it was only a matter of time before they jumped away with their valuable prize.

The two Wampeh rushed through the corridors, the pirates pillaging the ship clearing the way for the assassins. They had heard what happened to the visla and knew better than to delay the killers when they were on a quest. And that seemed to be precisely what was happening.

Corann, however, remained, and she gathered the pirate

leaders for a quick meeting now that the ship was theirs. She applied a bit of a disguise first, though, altering her appearance, but not her coloring. She was still clearly a Wampeh Ghalian, and a fierce and deadly one at that. But definitely *not* the kindly older woman who lived on the surface below.

"You have done well today," she said. "You should all take great pride in what you have managed to accomplish. And with this victory, you have acquired an incredibly potent, and valuable piece of Council property."

"Yeah, but ain't they gonna come lookin' for this?" a stout man with ochre dreadlocks and piercing green eyes asked.

"Oh, of that there is no doubt," Corann replied. "But it will take time for that to happen. The Council will do everything in their power to keep word of this humiliating defeat quiet. And in that brief time, you must take this ship as far from here as possible."

"Why would we do that?" a heavily scarred woman asked.

Corann recognized her from prior encounters in her career, though not while she was working under this particular disguise. The woman was called Oxnatza, and she was a brutally effective killer. She was also extremely fond of coin, and would do just about anything in the acquisition of more.

"If you stay here," Corann began, "you will be at the very first place the Council will come to seek out this ship. They will assume a rowdy band of pirates would argue over which faction gets to keep the spoils of this prize, thus delaying any transit."

She paused, looking over the assembled pirate leaders. It was true, they would almost definitely quarrel over who got what. But in this brief moment of grace, the Ghalian assassin held the floor and all of their attention. And they *would* listen to her.

"However, if you all work together and put aside any petty squabbles, you will be wealthier than you could imagine from a single score. And that applies to each of you and your crews. But you must work together. If you do not, you will undoubtedly lose this ship before you can salvage even a fraction of its wealth. And, more than that, if you were to utilize this ship wisely, one might even imagine a situation where an enterprising group of pirates might join forces, using this visla's base ship to draw close to *other* Council ships, seizing them and their riches as well."

"You would have us flying around the galaxy luring in and taking out Council ships?" Oxnatza said with a laugh. "That is utter madness."

"Perhaps. But it is madness that would work," Corann replied.

Oxnatza laughed heartily. "Oh, Wampeh, I do like the way you think."

"You two serious?" the dreadlocked man asked. "It seems insane."

"Insane because no one's ever done it," Oxnatza said. "I mean, she's got a point. We've all got pretty good ships, and skilled crews. But we're small on our own. But this ship? It's got a freakin' landing bay. And one big enough to hold a few of our craft at that."

"Or big enough to lure in Council ships," another captain said, seeing where she was going with this.

"Precisely. Why, if we play our cards right, we could be set for life with a good run of scores using this base ship before the Council finally catches up to us."

"But if that happens, we're all screwed," a deep green man sporting exceptionally thick limbs said. "And they'll keep coming, you know."

Corann reinserted herself into the discussion. "Yes, of course they will. But with the kind of coin you will amass during your reign of pillage and conquest, you will be able to afford the best intelligence. And as I am asking this of you, I am willing to *personally* direct the Ghalian spy network to warn you when it seems imminent that the Council will catch up with you. At that point, you can scrap the ship, take every last item of value, and fly it into a sun, leaving them no trace and no way to find you."

"You would do that?" Oxnatza asked.

"I recognize you, Oxnatza," the disguised Wampeh said. "One of our most respected masters has spoken very highly of you in the past. And with her confidence in you, I feel certain she would uphold my promise knowing you were part of the operation."

The pirates discussed amongst themselves a moment. It *was* an impressive plan. Audacious as hell, and it would require them all joining forces and cooperating. But the real potential of the idea was just beginning to sink in. They could be a force the likes of which no one had seen. And when their time had finally run out, they could retire, wealthy and secure.

"I do not wish to pressure you," Corann said, "but I really must be going. Things to attend to, people to kill. You know how it is."

Oxnatza and the others laughed. The Ghalian were terrifying, even to battle-hardened pirates, but they were also comrades of a sort, and this one knew just the right tone to tickle each of their fancy.

"I shall be departing shortly," Corann continued. "But I will make this easy for you. If your pirate brothers join this craft and jump away in, say, the next ten hours, I shall assume you accept this offer. And from that point on, the Ghalian network will keep an eye on you. We cannot stay the eventual arrival of the Council, but we can warn you of it to the best of our ability. If you are smart in your actions, of course."

"Of course," Oxnatza said. "We'll talk among ourselves, rest assured. And thanks for the offer. It's tempting, indeed."

Corann simply nodded once, more than a mere seed planted in the pirates' heads, then left them. She had placed a near-fruiting tree there with all of the free advice, and she was all but certain they would take her up on the offer. They'd be fools not to.

Corann then rushed to Demelza's ship and departed the captured vessel, speeding quickly to the surface, where she would make many very public appearances as she helped her neighbors clean the remnants of the horrible attack.

Of course, the Council would show up and ask around. But this Wampeh would raise no suspicion. Not once every single person interviewed said the same thing about kindly old Corann. She was terrified after the attack. Shaken. But she pulled it together to help them clean up the aftermath and rebuild.

And with that, their world would be safe. Just an unfortunate location that happened to be where a troublesome group of outlaws decided to face off against Council forces.

Corann set the shimmer ship down in a copse of trees, its shimmer cloak hiding it from view. She then hurried into her home, emerging shortly to begin her performance. As she did, she couldn't help but wonder how the others were faring.

"It has traveled far," Demelza noted once Hozark managed to maneuver them clear of the ongoing space battle around the base ship they had just departed. "The one I was already aboard is close, but the other--"

"Yes, I see it," he said, adjusting course and pushing the Drookonus to get them there as quickly as they could without crashing into the other craft dotting the sky.

They knew there was always the possibility that Henni had been secreted away aboard a different craft. Perhaps a small ship that they had somehow missed. But for such a high-value prize as she apparently was, they would not have gone to such efforts to leave her so vulnerable to easy retrieval.

The distancing of the other ship from the group also

confirmed their suspicions. Yes, one of the assault craft had landed aboard it, but with all of the fighting going on with the other ships, it was highly unusual for it to be heading away from the battle rather than into it.

That seemed to add up to one thing. They wanted to stay as far from the conflict as possible. Likely to provide the smaller craft that was carrying their precious cargo as clear a route as possible to their landing bay.

Hozark wove through the thinning swarm of craft dogfighting in the sky, pushing toward the base ship with great speed.

"We are almost there," he said, locking in his final approach and bolstering their shimmer cloak. "Prepare to dock and board."

Demelza readied herself, knowing it would be a tough time of it once they reached the interior of the craft. But they were Ghalian. This was simply what they did.

Inside the base ship, a violet-haired young woman lay strapped to a floating conveyance as she was hurried from the landing bay where the small craft that carried her aboard had just landed.

"Hurry. The visla said we were to jump immediately once the prisoner was secured," the small craft's pilot said as he accompanied the captive.

"I know, I know," the receiving crew's leader said. "We'll have her stowed in just a minute. The Drooks are ready to jump as soon as the captain gives the word."

"Great. Then let's––"

The conveyance banged hard against the wall as they rounded a corner.

"Watch where you're going. You'll wake the girl."

Henni's eyes flew open, a visceral panic flooding her body, along with the same power that had been building when she'd been stunned to unconsciousness. Her eyes darted side to side, taking in her captors as she struggled against her restraints.

"By the gods, look at her eyes. They're sparkling," the small ship's pilot said.

"Shit!" the lead guard blurted in shock. "Quick, stun her again!" he shouted while fumbling for his own konus.

Henni strained hard, but her limbs were bound. Adrenaline surged as she felt the terror of helplessness flare within her, cascading into a full-fledged panic. Her eyes grew brighter, the light flashing out, temporarily blinding those around her.

Then they jumped.

The ship suddenly arrived in another part of space entirely, though no one knew precisely where. As quickly as they were able, the guard and pilot cast their stun spells, knocking Henni back to unconsciousness.

The crewmen looked at one another, clearly shaken.

"Uh, did your Drooks just do that?" the startled hopper ship pilot asked.

"I don't think that was us," the guard replied. "I don't know *what* just happened."

Outside, floating in the dark of space in their cloaked shimmer ship, Hozark and Demelza watched helplessly as the base ship jumped away just as they drew near. But this didn't seem like an ordinary jump.

The magical residue hanging in the sky was different. Different, and not entirely unlike that of a Zomoki when startled, as they'd witnessed on rare occasion when coming across the lesser relatives of the Old Ones. Like the magic Corann's friend said resided within Henni.

Whatever it was, it didn't matter. What did was that the ship was gone. And with it, their friend.

## CHAPTER SIXTY-SIX

The mood was both festive yet somber at Master Prombatz's temporary residence on the world of Galoom. Hozark and the others had gone straight there after the Council's resounding defeat, regrouping and replaying the events from each of their unique points of view.

"I tell ya, the ship just *poofed* out of there," Laskar said with barely contained excitement.

"We lost our friend," Bud said.

"I thought she bugged the hell out of you."

"She does. But still, Henni's part of our team, and she's gone."

"Well, yeah. And that sucks, sure. But did you *see* the magic? I've never seen anything like it."

Master Prombatz watched the discussion with interest. He had not been present for the battle, but Hozark had filled him in on all of the details as soon as they had arrived. Prombatz had a vested interest in the fall of Maktan and all of his lackeys.

Aargun was there as well, finally released from the healing facility, his spirits and health improving nicely under the care of Prombatz's personal staff. Unfortunately for Aargun, he had been looking forward to more lessons with Henni and Happizano. Henni more than the boy, though.

Having someone who was a reader and able to discern his thoughts and intents without the need to speak––which was impossible with his lack of a tongue––was a great joy to him.

When he heard of Henni's capture, Aargun remained quietly stoic. But it was clear the wounded assassin was shaken by it.

"We shall get her back," Hozark said. "We shall make it our priority. But for now, we must mend our hurt and prepare ourselves for what is to come. We have won this battle, but a greater struggle still remains."

Happizano had been kept safe for some of the fighting, but not all of it, and he had been present when Henni was taken. Having had the same thing happen to him not so long ago, her situation really hit home.

"Is she going to be okay, Hozark?" he asked.

"Fear not, young Jinnik. I feel that, like your father, she is too valuable for Maktan to allow any harm to come to her."

"But it's just Henni."

"You were not present for it, but it seems she possesses quite a store of power after all," Hozark informed the boy. "And as such, she will be kept safe."

Of course, Hozark knew full well Visla Maktan would be trying to find a way to harvest Henni's unusual magic. But how, exactly, he had come to know of it in the first place was a mystery.

But with the abrupt jump that took place, courtesy of what was almost undoubtedly Henni's mysterious power, Maktan had all the confirmation he would need as to her value.

She would be safe. Well cared for, even. But she would be a prisoner, no doubt. Still, it was the best they could hope for. And they *would* get her back.

Hozark turned to Bud. "So, my friend. I understand you took quite a beating out there."

"It wasn't that bad," Bud lied.

In reality, had his mothership not possessed the overlapping shielding spells Corann had arranged for him, the ferocity of the Council's defenses would almost certainly have caused catastrophic damage to his craft. Perhaps, even, beyond repair.

"Ah, yes. I am glad to hear it," Hozark said, playing along. "But please, allow the order to repair your vessel. It is the least we can do for your efforts."

Bud nodded slowly. "Well, I suppose my baby *could* use a little sprucing up," he said.

"Excellent. I shall make the arrangements. And while the work is being done, the spy network shall track down our missing friend," Hozark said. "We will get her back, my friend. And we will end Maktan once and for all."

It took almost a full week for Bud's ship to finally be returned to top space-worthy condition, and in that time a great many things happened, both at Prombatz's estate as well as back on Corann's, where Hozark and his friends had finally returned.

The leader of the Five had done as she had planned, joining her neighbors in the cleanup and rebuilding of the portions of town that were damaged in the startling attack. And a handful of Council ships did arrive to do what seemed to all who did not know better to be just a casual investigation as to the whereabouts of their missing base ship. But it was gone, and the pirates had done a fantastic job covering the true events that had led to the theft of that craft.

By the time the Council ships had arrived, the stolen vessel had not only jumped a great many times, but had done so with great speed. The Drooks aboard had their control collars cut from their necks almost immediately, and the former slaves were thrilled to be freed. And as paid crew on what was now a pirate ship, they now found joy in what had normally been a forced task.

The pirates running the ship had also formed a surprisingly cohesive alliance. There was no telling how long it would last, but for the moment, they were acting as a unified front. And with the might of the Council base ship at their disposal, they had already begun luring, capturing, and dismantling all manner of Council craft.

But Corann would not hear of those pirates who had agreed to her offer falling prey to the Council. At least not directly. She propagated the rumor that it was a group of Outlander pirates who had managed to seize the visla's ship, protecting the identities of the real culprits.

More importantly, as Outlanders were scorned and shunned across the galaxy, Oxnatza and the others were free of suspicion, each of them departing the base ship for brief times and making periodic appearances on other worlds to reinforce their innocent appearance in regards to the whole affair.

The ploy, it seemed, had worked, and not only were the pirates relatively in the clear, so too was Corann's adopted home. Nothing linked the stolen craft to the locals. Everyone told the same story. It was some troublesome pirates who had stymied the visla's plans when the Council craft showed up unexpectedly, offering a tempting prize. And that was all there was to that.

"All to your liking?" Hozark asked his friend as they walked through his restored ship.

"Not bad," Bud said. "Not bad at all."

"And there are additional defensive wards now residing within the ship's structure itself," Hozark said. "But let us keep that little upgrade to ourselves, shall we?"

"You never know when a little secret will come in handy," Bud agreed. "How's Hap doing? He seemed to be pretty torn up over still not finding his father, but that appears to be shifting."

Hozark smiled. "He had a lot to process, Bud. He killed a man in battle."

"Tough for a kid his age. But he saved my ass doing so."

"I am aware. But now he is training with Aargun again, and I believe that is greatly improving his spirits, as well as his coordination. And Demelza is running the poor boy ragged in his practice. Honestly, I believe Happizano may simply be too tired to truly dwell on his woes."

Bud chuckled. "Good thing, that. We've all got stuff on our minds."

"Indeed. Though I think Happizano will be pleased to show off what he has learned when we finally do recover his father."

A slight shadow flashed across Bud's face. "And Henni."

"Of course. She has not been forgotten. And more than that, Corann sent word that the spy network has heard whispers about a powerful caster. One they have not seen but have caught wind of. One that may very well be held against his will."

"Oh, shit. Have you told Hap yet?"

"No. Not until we confirm the rumor."

"Makes sense, I guess."

"It does. But Bud, there is more. There has also been verification as to the actual location of Visla Maktan. Confirmed by multiple sources."

"So we can take him down! Excellent!"

"Hold your enthusiasm. We will still have a hard time gaining access to the man. He is a visla in the Council of Twenty, after all."

"So was Visla Ravik," Bud reminded him.

"Yes, but he was careless. And he put himself squarely in harm's way. The puppet master behind this plot is far more cautious, it would seem. But when Laskar returns, we shall begin planning in earnest. Have you heard from him?"

"No, but that's the point of personal days. I think the strain was finally getting to him, despite the casual game face he kept glued on. A bit of rest and relaxation will do the guy some good."

"I would tend to agree," Hozark said. "And what about you? You've not taken any respite."

Bud looked at his ship, rubbing his hand along the smooth, reassuring mass of it. "I've been planning," he said. "And that's all the rest I need at the moment."

"We will find her, my friend. And we will get her back. It was not your fault she was taken. I hope you realize that."

"I do. But it still pisses me off."

"They will pay, Uzabud. And soon."

"Yeah, I sure hope so," the pirate replied, then forced his usual cheerful demeanor back onto his face. "So, anyway, now what?"

Corann walked toward them on the nearby path and called out to the pair. "If you two are interested, the others have come in for dinner. Get it while it's hot."

"Thank you, Corann. We shall be there momentarily," Hozark called back, beginning the walk to her inviting kitchen before shifting his attention back to his friend. "Now?" he said. "Now we gather ourselves. We focus our search. We refine the efforts of our people. And then we find Henni. We find Jinnik. We find Maktan. And when we do, we settle this once and for all."

# EPILOGUE

The flight to the hidden smelting facility had been a long one, and Henni found herself moved from ship to ship repeatedly, constantly kept in a stunned daze. After the little stunt she'd somehow pulled, jumping an entire Council base ship on her own, no one dared leave her to her own devices.

But finally, after what seemed like an eternity in that mental haze, but was only a week in reality, Henni was finally locked down tight in her new home. And a heavy golden collar rested around her neck.

Slowly, she began to rouse. Panic filled her as she realized she was restrained once more. A dangerous sparkle filled her eyes, but the control collar activated, slamming her to the ground.

A short time later, she woke again. This time, she was careful and measured in her reaction. She was alarmed, yes, but she also had no interest in being stunned again. And given the heft of the thick collar they had fitted on so small a woman, whoever had taken her prisoner had spared no magic in ensuring she would not escape.

"I wouldn't try that again, if I were you," a quiet voice said from the shadows of the far end of the cell block.

A magical divider separated the two prisoners, but nothing more. To the naked eye, it was just one open space.

"Thanks for the tip," Henni snapped. "Couldn't have figured that out for myself, obviously."

The man chuckled and rose from his seat, walking slowly into the light. From what Henni could tell, he had been clothed in some rather regal attire not too long ago, but whatever hell he'd been put through had left them soiled and tattered. His eyes, however. Those possessed a spark of power, though one layered with exhaustion.

"The guards who brought you in seemed to be quite scared of you, you know," he said. "I wonder, what does one so small as you do to frighten the likes of them?"

"I wish I could tell you," she replied, gently tugging on the band around her neck.

"Do not bother. None but the strongest could even hope to budge a collar of that power. I would offer my services, but I am a bit drained at the moment," he said with a grim chuckle.

"You're a weirdo," Henni grumbled as she moved to a more comfortable position seated on her low cot. The light caught her violet hair for a moment as she did.

"Perhaps I am a bit weird," the man said with a slight chuckle. "But I am not an inconsequential one. Your hair is lovely, by the way."

"Uh, there you go with the weird thing again."

"Of course. My apologies. It is just, the color reminds me of my son. He has his mother's skin."

Henni sat up straight, then rose, walking quickly to the invisible divider.

"Hang on. Who exactly are you?"

"I am Dinarius Jinnik," the man replied. "A pleasure to meet you, though this is hardly the first impression I would wish to make. And you?"

"Holy shit. You're *Visla* Jinnik."

"Yes, as I said. But you? Who are you that warrants such treatment?"

"What? Oh, me? I'm Henni. But if you're Visla Jinnik, you're Hap's father."

That got his attention, his posture straightening in an instant.

"Happizano? You've seen my boy?" he said, a brief, faint crackle of magic traveling across his skin.

"Shit, we've been looking all over for you. We have your kid. He's been traveling with us."

"Us?"

"Some Ghalian and a few others."

The visla let out a breath he hadn't known he had been holding. "Then, he is safe?"

"Yeah, he's safe. Eats like a starved Bundabist too."

Jinnik let out the first real laugh he'd had in far too long. "That he does," he said. "But if he is with your friends, that means the Council does not possess him."

"Like I said."

Jinnik thought on that a moment, then rose to his full height and wrapped his fingers around his control collar. "This changes everything."

A crackling of power began emitting from his hands as he pulled on the band, striving to separate the magical bond holding it together. He struggled for nearly a minute, then ceased, exhausted.

"It is no use. I am too weak."

Henni leaned in close to the partition. "Can I help?" she asked, her galaxy eyes sparkling in the dim light.

Visla Jinnik saw them and felt wonder. He had heard tales of a race with eyes like that as a boy but had always thought them to be just that. Tales. But what if...

"I wonder," he said.

"Wonder what?"

"If, with a little guidance, perhaps you *can* help."

"Guidance?"

"Can you follow instructions? Are you willing to learn?" he asked.

"Uh, why? Are you some kind of creeper?" Henni asked, her eyes flickering a bit with her irritation.

Jinnik's smile broadened at the sight. "Because, my little friend, with the right focus, you could very well be our ticket out of here."

Henni's irritation dimmed, as did the magical sparkle in her eyes. "You think?"

"Perhaps."

"Well, I guess I've got nothing better to do. When do we start?"

Jinnik felt giddy with anticipation. "Oh, my dear, we already have."

# PREVIEW: HOZARK'S REVENGE

## SPACE ASSASSINS 5

The wet smack of a blood-dampened fist echoed off the cool stone walls. It was not the first blow to be cast on this day, nor would it be the last. The young woman hadn't planned on being beaten today, but then, sometimes things just don't go according to plan. And her plan was to find Visla Maktan.

Visla Zinna Maktan was a difficult man to track down. Not just because he was one of the more powerful magic users in the combined systems, which afforded anyone a higher degree of security, but also because of *another* rather unique status.

Visla Maktan was a member of the Council of Twenty, a galactic, power-hungry group that had strong-armed their way into controlling most of the known systems over the centuries.

Given the sometimes truly heinous acts the Council carried out in their quest for more power and control of the inhabited systems not yet under their yoke, it was only natural that they would take security a bit more seriously than most. Scores of disgruntled people whose entire worlds had been forcibly placed under Council control, or who had witnessed their families enslaved or worse, would have great interest in causing the Twenty harm.

But getting close enough to so much as lay a finger on one of the Council's inner staff or guards was daunting enough of a challenge. To actually reach one of the Council themselves? It was only in those rarest instances of foolish overconfidence that an individual Council member had been reached. And even then, they were so powerful that the threat was neutralized with the greatest of ease.

Recently, however, one of their own had not only placed himself in a precarious position, he had actually fallen in the process, his light snuffed out by a Ghalian assassin, and in front of his own men, no less.

Word had spread like magic fire through the ranks, and the Council had reacted as one might expect of those whose braggadocio was often greater than their common sense.

They had quietly doubled, or even tripled, their personal security details, while publicly downplaying the entire incident, stating the death of Visla Ravik had been no more than a fluke, and entirely of his own doing. That it had been a Ghalian assassin at whose hands––and fangs––he had fallen, was not mentioned at all.

It was this unfortunate shift in security protocol that had snagged several infiltrators and spies, most of them actually under the employ of the other members of the Council. While they may have worked together as a unified body in public, the backstabbing and scrabbling for power behind the scenes was just as Machiavellian as found in any fiefdom or feudal world.

But one spy was unlike the others who had been unexpectedly found out. One inoffensive and utterly benign woman of robust stature and sweet demeanor had been caught during a surprise sweep of Visla Maktan's staff. She was a relatively recent hire, her orange skin and warm, yellow eyes only adding to her cheerful appearance.

She had been working in one of the kitchens on one of the

many worlds upon which Visla Maktan had a residence, helping keep things tidy, preparing staff meals, and procuring supplies from vendors.

The visla hadn't been to that world in ages, and there was no telling if or when he would be dropping in. His comings and goings had always been unannounced, but after the fall of Visla Ravik, they were even more so.

And so it was that this spy passed the time, ingratiating herself to the other staff, building trust and establishing herself as an integral cog in the estate's internal workings. This could have gone on for some time. The best of spies often spent years on assignment, worming their way into places so slowly that none ever once suspected they could be anything but what they appeared.

Now, however, the sweet kitchen worker all had known as Zanna was beaten and chained in a dungeon, a guard keeping eyes on her at all times. That is, when she wasn't being tortured by her captors.

It had been a particularly specialized bit of casting that had pierced her magic during an unannounced sweep of the property's grounds, and the Wampeh's magical disguise had fallen in the process.

"Ghalian!" the caster leading the sweep called out when Zanna's orange coloring abruptly shifted back to her natural pale skin and black hair––much to the surprise of her fellow staffers.

The guards who had been accompanying the caster quickly surrounded her, all of them training their blades and konuses on the intruder, ready to slay her if she so much as moved a muscle. Ghalian assassins were not to be trifled with, and it was only their relative distance from the target that had allowed them to survive as long as they had. Or so they believed.

Zanna, however, was not an assassin. Her skills lay in her

considerable gift for subterfuge and infiltration, not in fighting off hordes of armed guards. But escape was something spies were also trained in, and Ghalian were known to vanish into seemingly thin air from their cells when captured, leaving a great many confused guards to pay for their failure in their duties.

This was different, however. A visla had recently been killed, and any spy was treated with a great deal more concern than in previous years. And a Ghalian? None wanted to face the wrath of their employer if one such as this escaped on their watch.

"I will come quietly," Zanna said, slowly raising her empty hands over her head.

The guards led her to the estate's dungeon, keeping their distance and having called in reinforcements. Nearly two dozen now stood ready should she move to flee, though within the constricting environs of the subterranean corridor, to try would be utter folly.

The time for escape would present itself, but this was definitely not it. To make such an attempt would mean certain death, and that was not what she had in mind. Not one bit.

This particular estate was one of Visla Maktan's smaller retreats, and as such, its dungeon facilities were quite small and lacking the myriad devices often used in prying the truth from prisoners that the larger facilities possessed. But once the head of the visla's personal guard heard of this intruder, a specialist would be dispatched, and they would bring with them the full weight of the Council of Twenty.

In the meantime, however, the locals would do what they could, crude as their methods may be. To pry any information out of a Ghalian would be a massive coup in their favor.

"Who hired you, Assassin?" the captain of the guard asked.

Zanna merely spat the blood from her mouth and smiled at him and shrugged. It was about all she could manage from her position, chained to an interrogation chair.

"You can make this easy, or you can make it hard," the man continued. "We have ways––"

"Of making me talk?" the captive said with a chuckle. "I believe I have heard this speech once or twice before. I know how this works, Captain."

"Then you know I can make things very, very unpleasant for you."

"Indeed. But you should also know that I truly know nothing. I was simply hired to keep an eye on things around here, nothing more."

"Liar. Why would a Ghalian do this sort of job?"

"We are not all about killing, you know. Information is an important bit of trade, after all. Your visla knows a thing or two about that, I'm sure. In fact, all of the Council have retained our services on many occasions."

The captain's face remained impassive, but inside, he shuddered. The thought of these disguised killers silently lurking among the staff of other estates was terrifying.

"I don't believe you," he finally replied. "But we have ways of––"

"Yes, yes. Let's just get on with it then, shall we?" she said with a resigned sigh.

Zanna had been tortured before, and it was not pleasant in the least. But she had been well trained, and the Ghalian spy was more than prepared for whatever her captors had in store. And until the visla's personal guard arrived, she would be treated with kid gloves.

Or so she had thought.

The caster who had been leading the search strode into the chamber and glared at the restrained woman. She could feel the relatively substantial power he possessed. An emmik, no doubt. Not as strong as a visla, but if possible, it would be nice to feed on him before making her escape.

But that would require placing herself at a bit too much risk for her liking. Unless the opportunity presented itself, getting far away as quickly as possible would be the order of the day.

"Who hired you?" the emmik asked as he turned his back to her and unlatched a small case on the nearby low table.

"You know I cannot reveal that," she replied. "But you likely also already know it is probably one of the other Council members. Such a suspicious group, always digging into one another's affairs."

The emmik turned back around, and Zanna felt a sudden surge of fear in her body. On his wrist was a slaap, and a considerably powerful one at that. The magically charged tool was stronger than a konus, and entirely martial in function. Only a fool would attempt to use a slaap for torture spells. The results could be catastrophic.

Or they could be effective at prying out even the most stubborn of secrets, though often at the cost of limbs and permanent damage to the subject. The wicked smile on the emmik's face told her he was well aware of that fact.

"Now, we have a few days before the visla's man arrives to interrogate you. But I intend to get answers from you long before then."

The emmik flexed his power, melding it with the magic stored within the slaap, then uttered the smallest of torture spells.

"*Koxora malecti*," he said, testing out the device.

Zanna writhed in pain, unable to contain herself.

It was unlike a Ghalian. Their training typically allowed them to go to a safe place within themselves in these instances. But this emmik, greedy for recognition and advancement, was pushing the envelope, seemingly unaware of exactly how much damage he was truly doing. It was always a risk when the inexperienced did the torturing. But usually they were not in possession of a tool of this degree of power.

The captive slumped in her seat, drawing in rapid breaths as she regained her bearings. She hadn't cried out at least, of that she was proud. But this interrogation was going to be far worse than she had anticipated. And it just might kill her before she could make her escape.

## ALSO BY SCOTT BARON

### Standalone Novels

Living the Good Death

### The Clockwork Chimera Series

Daisy's Run

Pushing Daisy

Daisy's Gambit

Chasing Daisy

Daisy's War

### The Dragon Mage Series

Bad Luck Charlie

Space Pirate Charlie

Dragon King Charlie

Magic Man Charlie

Star Fighter Charlie

Portal Thief Charlie

Rebel Mage Charlie

Warp Speed Charlie

Checkmate Charlie

### The Space Assassins Series

The Interstellar Slayer

The Vespus Blade

The Ghalian Code

Death From the Shadows

Hozark's Revenge

**The Warp Riders Series**

Deep Space Boogie

Belly of the Beast

**Odd and Unusual Short Stories:**

The Best Laid Plans of Mice: An Anthology

Snow White's Walk of Shame

The Tin Foil Hat Club

Lawyers vs. Demons

The Queen of the Nutters

Lost & Found

## ABOUT THE AUTHOR

A native Californian, Scott Baron was born in Hollywood, which he claims may be the reason for his rather off-kilter sense of humor.

Before taking up residence in Venice Beach, Scott first spent a few years abroad in Florence, Italy before returning home to Los Angeles and settling into the film and television industry, where he has worked as an on-set medic for many years.

Aside from mending boo-boos and owies, and penning books and screenplays, Scott is also involved in indie film and theater scene both in the U.S. and abroad.

Made in United States
North Haven, CT
17 March 2025